When I Had Nothing

The Atholton Series, Volume 5

Erin FitzGerald

Published by Erin FitzGerald, 2022.

When I Had Nothing

Thomas & Natalie

Erin FitzGerald

Never allow someone to be your priority while allowing yourself to be their option. - Mark Twain

ONE

Natalie

It was too hot out for anyone in their right mind to be stripping shingles off a roof and I stepped outside with a cold beer in my hand, a fresh slice of lime sunk to the bottom. It was after five anyway, and I wanted a good look at the guy my new next door neighbor said was "the most deliciously troubled eligible bachelor in town." Then behind her hand she grinned and said, "And the most stand-offish asshole you'll ever meet. But you look like a girl who likes a good project." She'd gestured toward my derelict house.

As I'd been called worse things, even quite recently, I decided to get an eye full of the man who'd arrived at an ungodly hour and tipped a ladder up against my house. He was up on the roof even before I'd had coffee and from my current vantage point, all I could see was that he was shirtless and sweating, ropes of muscle twisting as he maneuvered his body to strip off another line of shingles.

Yes indeed, the view was just fine.

"You must be thirsty," I called up, craning my neck and shading my eyes with one hand. Thanks to my mother, the professional trophy wife, I knew better than to squint.

"Nah," he called back over his shoulder without looking at me. "Got a cooler of water in the truck."

"I'm surprised you don't have someone to help you–that's a big job."

"Can't afford someone to help me and besides, I'm perfectly capable." He sounded grumpy.

Well, that was that.

I waited in the shade of the sycamore on the front lawn, sipping my own beer while the cicadas put up their terrible racket. They were far louder than the sound of the shingles crashing to the ground.

Maybe if I stared at his back long enough, he'd get uncomfortable and come down. In the meantime, staring at him wasn't a hardship.

It was another fifteen minutes before I heard him grunt from the other side of the roof: "There...finally."

Since the ladder was on the back of the house, I didn't see him descend. He walked around the side of the house, tools in his hand, pitching them easily into the open bed of his truck. They clattered and skidded across the bed while he stripped off the sweaty shirt he'd clearly just pulled on, grabbed a folded towel from the cab and vigorously toweled his chest and hair, then pulled a clean t-shirt over his head.

Thankfully, I remembered to close my mouth just before he looked up, which was right around the time my brain stopped working entirely.

And that was it: I must have a head injury.

Dropped on my head at birth or something, because the *only* thing running through my overheated brain at the moment was how to get my hot little fingers all over those muscles.

Holy flexing gloriousness.

"Lady, you know you got *four* layers of shingles on that damn roof?" he growled, finally moving toward me.

"There's not much I know about this house yet," I said haltingly. Language felt entirely new and my cheeks felt hot. I'd just imagined *licking* him. "It was a foreclosure, so I had some idea of what I was getting into–I just expected the worst–and the roof is definitely the worst."

He shook his head while looking at his feet, but I got the distinct impression he was shaking his head at *me*, like I was the town idiot.

"This is the old Jacobson place, from what I've been told." He looked back up and I forgot my name when I saw his golden-brown eyes. "Everyone knew it was a tip. Probably cheaper to tear it down and start from scratch."

Shit. The last thing I needed to hear.

"Doubt I can afford *that*," I said, extending an arm to offer him the rapidly-warming beer.

"Thanks." He glanced somewhat askance at my hand, but he didn't reach for it. "I don't really drink much."

"Uh...ok. Religion, or personal problems?" I asked stupidly and he looked away for a second.

"Personal *experience*, if you don't mind." His response was short, the words clipped. There was a muscle in his jaw that ticced two or three times when he said it. It was clearly meant to make me feel like I was overstepping, and it did.

Setting both bottles on the ground, I moved a few steps closer and held out a hand. "Natalie," I said, and he looked up at me quickly, like I'd cursed at him.

"Thomas." He shook my hand like the physical contact was detestable and I wondered if he was afraid the cooties on my hand would jump over to him and infect him with my rudeness.

There was something unusual about this man, all right. I thought of the days spent trying to get him to return my call. The estimate that had shown up in my mailbox–I'd not seen a soul even though I'd been home all day long–had been astonishingly low. It occurred to me that for some reason I'd still hired the man to do the job without ever having met him. (I blamed the attractive estimate.)

Right now his body language was telling me the only thing he wanted to do was get into his truck and get away from me as quickly as possible.

"Well Thomas," I said, leaning over to retrieve both bottles, "it was nice to meet you in person. Let me know if there's anything you need while you're up there tomorrow." I pointed toward the roof. "I generally work from home, so it's no trouble."

He nodded, but he didn't respond and he was walking back toward his truck before I could even start for the front porch. I stood watching as he turned over the engine and pulled a tight three-point turn to drive away.

Not a look.

Not a wave.

Kind of an asshole, really.

I let myself back into the house, grateful the ceiling fans stirred the air. I was glad they worked at all, considering the shape the house had been in when I pulled the moving truck into the driveway and unlocked the front door. *A tip*, Thomas had said, and that was generous.

It had been three months, but I'd managed to clean the cobwebs and paint a few of the rooms. The floors were rough and battered, but I liked the distressed look of a well used hardwood floor, and after cleaning and waxing them I put down the few big rugs I'd brought with me from my previous home in Boston.

The roof, however, made it known shortly thereafter that it was in even worse repair than my home inspector had indicated, and when I borrowed several buckets from my new neighbor to deal with the downpour happening in my bedroom, she mentioned Thomas. "Bit of a case, that one," she'd laughed gently, her crisp northern accent a piece of home in my new town, where everyone had a drawl that went on for days. "But you won't find anyone who does a better job, and he's fair. That's more than I can say for most people."

She helped me haul over more five gallon pails, two at a time, and her eyes traveled quickly around the house as she followed me up the stairs. "I've always wanted to see the inside of this house. It looks like you really have your work cut out for you."

I ducked my head a little. She had no idea how much work I'd already put into the place, and I had only some idea of how much was left to do. I was used to having a team, but I'd left my design practice behind in Boston, sold to my longtime assistant. I was handy enough, but most of my DIY skills came from stubbornness, bravado and YouTube tutorials rather than actual experience. Documenting the process just happened to be a large part of my livelihood. As it turned out, people found my misadventures hilarious and I wasn't too proud to capitalize on that.

She helped me push my bed to the only corner of the room that didn't seem to be experiencing monsoon season. "I have a nightlight in my guest room; I'll bring it over after dinner. You're going to need one in here in the middle of the night with this mess."

Before she left, Gerry whipped out her phone. "Give me your number; I'll text Thomas's number to you and he'll probably be out in a couple days to look at your roof. He's the best choice, since that big racket over in Mobile will take the shirt right off your back and they won't do half as good a job." She blew out an irritated breath. "Ask me how I know."

I cocked an eyebrow at her. Her sales pitch for the guy was impressive enough. He was either a real sob story or God's gift to homeowners, and I couldn't decide which. Gerry didn't look like the type to fall for either, with her razor-sharp bob and her plain, dark clothing.

That's how I found myself, one week later, standing in my living room with a warm beer in my hand. I contemplated pouring it down the drain before I thought better of it, popping it into the freezer for a few moments.

Waste not, want not.

There was a mountain of mail sitting on the kitchen countertop. It was one I'd been neglecting for several weeks and I eyed it suspiciously. There were no overly large envelopes, though I wasn't sure whether that was a good sign or a bad one. I'd been expecting a process server or a large packet of documents to show up for weeks, but maybe Ahmad was waiting for me to file first. My lips curled up derisively at the thought.

He can go fuck himself.

I was suddenly, tremendously tired.

Living the life of a home and lifestyle blogger seemed like a sham when I looked around at the house I'd lived in for twelve weeks. There wasn't great lighting, thanks to small windows, of which there weren't nearly enough.

The rooms were small and boxy, all the electrical fixtures terrifyingly antique.

When it rained, which seemed to happen often, I walked around the house wearing heavy rubber gardening gloves, hoping they were enough to keep me from getting zapped when I flicked off a light switch. (So far, so good but I was probably, literally, playing with fire.)

Finally completing my mental tour of the house and fetching the slightly cooler beer from the freezer, I walked into the small living room and plopped down on my favorite leather sofa. I flicked on the TV, trying to lose myself in the upbeat home improvement shows that followed one after another on my favorite cable channel. Usually they were an inspiration, but tonight I felt defeated. I spent most of my days feeling like I was underwater, trying to surface just long enough to draw another breath. Just enough to keep me going a little longer.

I guess having the Aubusson ripped out from under you will do that.

Dinner was a pint of my favorite ice cream, as it had been with increasing regularity, and finally I had to admit to myself that my pants were not shrinking. My new and significantly more sedentary lifestyle, combined with shitty eating habits and a healthy topping of depression, was making me fat.

This was not where you were supposed to be at forty.

I groaned, dumping the container into the trash and slotting the spoon into the dishwasher. It joined the rest of my silverware drawer, already in the dishwasher, and I grimaced when I realized it hadn't been run in a week.

Dropping a detergent tablet into the machine, I cranked the ancient dial and prayed to the appliance gods for their mercy as I fired it up. The avocado green beast whirred and groaned and clunked, and mercifully the sound of trickling water could be heard.

It took very little to tighten up the house for the night. In fact, if you didn't notice the stack of mail on the counter, or the fact I hadn't made my bed in days, one could be forgiven for thinking the house had been abandoned. It was as clean as I'd been able to make it, though it wasn't anywhere close to being decorated or feeling anything like a warm, welcoming home.

Maybe I should get a cat.

Yeah...I laughed at myself, because I could barely be trusted to take care of myself right now.

Dragging myself up the stairs, I turned the taps on the bathtub and smiled to myself. I hadn't bought the house for the neighborhood, the yard or the square footage. I bought it for the ancient, enormous clawfoot bathtub, the size of which strained the aging hot water heater each time I filled it. In hindsight, it was a really bad reason to buy a house, but it was hard to convince me of that when I sank into the tub each night.

Cursing my shortsightedness, I wrapped myself in a robe and went back to the kitchen for a glass of wine. Ahmad wasn't there to criticize me or to remind me that drinking was unacceptable for a woman, I thought as I popped the cork on a passable red and filled the glass nearly to the rim.

We had established early on in our relationship that there would forever be a double standard.

Well fuck him, because I wasn't planning on moving to Saudi Arabia to live with the rest of his super uptight, fanatical family, and I never would. I raised a middle finger into the air, shaking it gleefully in my quiet little kitchen.

I had to take a few sips of the wine before moving back up the stairs, to keep from sloshing it all over the floor and I sank back into the bubbles contentedly, lifting the glass to my lips defiantly.

That lying asshole.

We'd been so happy...at first.

I remembered the evening I'd walked into Ahmad's office for a legal consultation and just about turned into a puddle on the floor. I'd barely been able to get out the story of a client trying to stiff me on a large contract, I'd been so bowled over by his sharply handsome face.

Of course, I'd been awkward and goofy, not at all by design but by some genetic defect that rendered me stupid around handsome men, and he'd pretended to be charmed.

He was tall and gorgeous, regal with his sharp profile and immaculately tailored suits. He looked like an Arabic Ken doll I could drop into one of my renderings, and I found that for a time my mood boards skewed progressively more Middle Eastern in inspiration. He made me stupid like that.

He'd been so proud of the fact that I ran my own successful design firm. It was small, but clients in the greater Boston area clamored for my services and I always had more jobs coming in than I could handle.

We became something of a fixture in the local social scene, the petite blonde designer and the austerely handsome corporate attorney.

I took another sip and allowed myself to revisit the snapshot my brain had taken earlier in the evening. I needed something to push my husband from my thoughts.

Obviously Thomas was a socially inept asshole, but he was a damn fine one–a blind woman could have seen it–and I hadn't seen such a fine specimen in a long time, according to the messages received from my overgrown lady garden.

I tried to remember the last time I'd found a man attractive, and couldn't. Ahmad had ruined me for all other men: graceful, seductive, attentive.

At first.

Allowing myself to think of the contractor's wide shoulders and muscled arms made me feel a little dizzy.

Maybe the water was too hot.

He looked like the cover of a romance novel, all long dark hair and leonine eyes. Phew.

He could strip my roof any day, thanks.

There were unfamiliar urges happening in my body. It had been such a long time since my husband had even been interested in touching me that I'd completely lost any connection with myself. I didn't recognize the stirrings of desire any longer, not that they were even welcome. I'd closed down that aspect of my life years earlier, when Ahmad started working such long hours that he couldn't be expected to do anything but sleep while he was home.

Many of my husband's nights were spent away from our shared home. He was forever on business overseas or at the bachelor pad he kept in New York, since he was legal counsel for an enormous company based out of Manhattan.

Though he worked out of the Boston office, he was still in New York at least two weeks out of every month. But that was Ahmad: firm in his decision. He refused to move, claiming my business was in Boston so that was where we would stay.

It took me a really long time to realize I was a convenient excuse, providing cover for him.

I pulled the drain plug and rose from the tub to grab the huge, fluffy towel on the floor next to my wine glass and I pressed it quickly into the curves of my body to soak up water. The last thing I wanted was for my contractor to find me sprawled out naked on my bathroom tile the next morning, dead from a slip-and-fall head wound.

The mirror was feeling bitchy that night, sure to point out to me that I wasn't getting any younger. There were faint lines beginning to settle across my forehead and if I smiled, I could see where the crow's feet were going to land.

Well, at least my hair was still good. I wound it up in the large towel and critically surveyed my body. I was a little softer around the middle lately, but the girls were holding up nicely. My backside was firm, my thighs were tight and my arms were nicely defined from months of moving heavy furniture and boxes.

He can go screw himself.

Oh goody, my husband had barged back into my brain.

I cussed out imaginary Ahmad. There had been no reason for him not to find me attractive, just as there had been no reason for Thomas to look at me like I was a damn leper, and I huffed.

Now I was mad at both men.

Slipping an oversized t-shirt over my head, I crawled gratefully into my enormous bed and said a prayer of thanks for cool linen sheets, crickets outside the window and the small ceiling fan that whirred furiously to stir up something of a breeze.

Tonight I was thankful for more, but I wasn't sure exactly what. The only thing that came to mind was *yummy muscles.*

I snorted at myself–*Stupid*–and rolled over to go to sleep.

TWO

Thomas

Merciful mother of God.

My Catholic mother would have dragged my ass to confession for the thoughts I was having about the woman who lived on Dothan Way. All it had taken was one look over my shoulder, at the curvy blonde dynamo standing in the front yard, and I had to hide behind the roofline.

I was grumpy on a great day, and today had not been a great day. Besides, what did she think she was doing in that tight little t-shirt? Sure her pretenses were decent.

Maybe.

It was kind of her to offer me something cold to drink, but did she not realize I couldn't stop staring at her tits through that thin shirt?

I had to admit to myself that just maybe that was her plan. It wouldn't be the first time a woman had flashed me her lucky charms.

My brain chanted "Magically delicious," and I slapped a hand over my face. No, no, no. Bad Thomas.

When it came to my social graces, I'd been told more than once over the past few years that I was "possibly on the spectrum."

I didn't bother to tell people why I'd turned into such an ogre, and I tried not to place too much stock in their opinions, but it went a long way toward explaining why most people didn't take to me easily.

What the hell had I been thinking, agreeing to fix this woman's roof?

If it hadn't been for Gerry, who seemed to be my biggest promoter around town, I'd have probably done one or two roofs a year. It was a holdover skill from my teenage years, when my dad insisted each of his children have a "viable skill" before they went out into the world. It just turned out that my skills set aligned nicely with the blue collar work he had in mind for me at the time.

My refusal of the warming beer in Natalie's hand was probably a little more harsh than necessary, but she made me uncomfortable. I'd felt her eyes on me when I changed my shirt and I was half tempted to ask her if she liked what she saw, just to knock her back a little.

As she leaned over to put both bottles on the ground, I thanked God I could knock out the job in only a couple days because that way I wouldn't have to see her again.

Most of the jobs Gerry got me into were charity cases for poor little old ladies. The ones who fussed and baked and plied me with chocolate chip cookies and then tried to set me up with their granddaughters. You know, the ones who were always "such a *nice* girl," which usually meant they were cross-eyed and living under a bridge with feral cats. But this time...well, this one sure as hell wasn't cross-eyed, I noted with some appreciation.

When she made eye contact with me, her shockingly blue eyes made something zing inside and I nervously licked my lips as I watched her mouth move. She was gorgeous, all dark lashes and soft lips, and her cheeks turned the softest shade of pink when I snapped at her.

I couldn't get away from her fast enough.

When she leaned over to pick up the bottles from the lawn, my pants started to grow tight.

Damn it, I have to cut this short.

So I made a complete idiot of myself and tore out of her driveway before I could get a second look at any of the things I really wanted to see.

I hadn't seen any that warranted a second look for quite some time and it really wouldn't do, to turn into a drooling mess on her front lawn, so I'd bolted.

Since I was already sweaty and smelly, I went upstairs to put myself through a punishing round of lifting in the front bedroom.

The old four-bedroom house had surprisingly large rooms and now that the house was empty, they were all mine to do with as I pleased. So now, rather than just an office in the front room with the large windows, I'd shoved the desk with all the monitors and gadgets into one corner and filled the bank of windows with machines and weights.

After my pathetic dinner, I spent some time working on a project on the office side of the room.

Then, since the clock told me it was nearly two, and because I knew Mrs. O'Shaughnessy had her binoculars out, I decided to call it.

I showered quickly and collapsed into bed, my eyes wide open, my arms feeling empty as I remembered yet again why my house felt so lonely.

Fuck, this was going to be another long night.

THREE

Natalie

A sharp pop, then a crackling electrical noise woke me from my sleep and I rolled over to see I'd only been asleep twenty minutes.

It took me a moment to decide what to do and I sniffed cautiously. Not smelling any smoke, I rolled over again and went back to sleep.

It was early when I woke again–too early to get up, and I lay still for a moment, eyes trying to focus in the darkness. Why was I awake?

The air was hot and still in the room and the t-shirt clung damply to my body.

I groaned.

Shit.

The ceiling fan wasn't running. Either the wiring had fried itself somewhere or a breaker had popped in the middle of the night.

Reaching to my bedside stand to grab my phone, I swung my legs over the edge of the bed. It was 5:12, which was too damn early to be up, but I was so hot there was no way I'd be going back to sleep. Instead, I flicked on the flashlight app and made my way down the stairs and through the laundry room to the small garage, where the breaker box sat on the wall. A single switch was facing the wrong way, so I reset it and let myself back into the house, glad to see that at least the light over the kitchen sink was back on.

After standing beneath the ceiling fan in my room for a solid fifteen minutes, sipping my lukewarm "iced" coffee, I was finally cool enough (and dry enough) to think about getting dressed for the day.

I grabbed a light linen skirt and a thin cotton t-shirt, skewering my hair up on my head with a couple of plastic pins. It was going to be hotter than hell today and I didn't care who saw me like this–even if he was really yummy–barely out of my pajamas, my hair piled up.

I was tired and cranky and I couldn't decide if I was enduring early menopause or just an Alabama summer. Because God knew Boston could get hot, but this was like living in a lobster pot all the time.

The sky was beginning to pink when I walked back down to the kitchen to pour another cup of coffee, and when my stomach roared I remembered last night's dinner hadn't exactly been nutritious or particularly filling. But to eat breakfast I was going to need utensils, so I snapped the lid of the dishwasher open and...you have got to be kidding me.

A burnt rubber smell drifted out to meet me and I eyed the bottom of the appliance with dread, noting the several inches of standing water. Even I knew what that meant: this relic had breathed its last and gone out in a blaze of glory. There was no way anyone was making motors for this late-60s behemoth anymore.

Fishing the utensils out of the basket, I dropped them into the sink with an angry clang, then retrieved the few forlorn dishes resting on the top rack. I was going to have to pull the bottom rack right out of the thing to scoop out the water, and I cursed myself for my lack of preparation. I had no shop vac.

Fetching a five-gallon bucket from my bedroom, I set to work scooping the murky water out with a drinking glass. It was slow going, and by the time the pail was half full I walked it to the front door and pitched the contents out across the lawn.

Back inside for round two.

Huffing in frustration, I finally hoisted the last pail of water and threw open the front door, flinging it out across the lawn.

This time something was different. The splash sounded wrong and I looked up quickly to see Thomas standing there on the bottom step, soaked, his lips working like he wanted to utter something terrible but I'd washed the words right out of his mouth.

My face must have gone whiter than my t-shirt. "I'm so sorry!" I sputtered, flapping one hand helplessly. I probably looked like I was having a seizure. "It's...I had no idea...I...what are you doing here so early? It's only six!"

He ran his hands over his face, smoothing back all that dark, wet hair and I swallowed hard. He had yet to say a word. Instead, he grabbed the bottom of his soaked t-shirt and stripped it over his head.

Sweet baby Jesus, my ovaries believe!

I tried to remember the man was not performing my own personal strip tease, but try as I might, my mind kept falling right back into the gutter.

Even if he was the town asshole, I had no problem with enjoying the view.

"Just tell me that wasn't toilet water," he said finally, his shirt dropping onto the porch with a wet slap. "If it was, we might be done here."

"Dishwasher." I squirmed. "But there was almost nothing in it...because I eat like a toddler."

Why was I telling him this?

He nodded shortly and then asked, "What's with the dishwasher?"

"Blew the drain pump out," I said, my mouth twisting downward. It looked like I'd be doing some appliance shopping today, which meant I'd actually have to leave my house. I'd have to talk to *people.* Ugh.

His eyebrows lifted in surprise. "Impressive," he said, and I got the feeling he was making fun of me just a little bit. "When ours blew, my wife called me in a panic to tell me the sucking thing had stopped sucking and apparently there was smoke *and* bubbles pouring out the bottom of the panel." He chuckled to himself, a thoroughly warm, delightful sound, but the sparkle in his eyes left just as quickly as it came.

I looked surreptitiously down at his left hand, noticing a thin band I hadn't seen yesterday. Shit, so Gerry had her facts wrong: this gorgeous god was married. Of course he was.

"You have a wife?" The words were out of my mouth before I could stop them. They sounded judgy, my tone incredulous, like it was impossible.

"You have a mute button?" His tone was decidedly cooler and his rebuke stung, since *he'd* been the first one to bring her up.

My lips twisted a little and I threw the bucket down on the porch, irritated that he'd seen the hurt on my face. "That was mean," I said, turning to walk the short distance to the kitchen, leaving the door open behind me.

I was putting the bottom rack back into the yawning mouth of the dishwasher when I heard footsteps behind me. "I can pull this out," he said quietly, and I turned to see him eyeing the hulking green monster.

An apology did not appear to be forthcoming.

"It's not supposed to rain for a few days yet, but I need to replace some of the underlayment on your roof–there are some squishy spots. If I can get a head start this morning, I can take you over to Smitty's this afternoon."

"It's fine, I'll figure it out." I was still upset by his comment. He'd made me feel small and silly.

"I doubt you're going to want to tow a dishwasher home in that fancy little car of yours." He disappeared under the sink and I could hear the sound of knobs being turned with some difficulty.

"What?" His head popped out from under the sink and he had just the tiniest hint of a grin on his face. "No more questions?"

I mimed zipping my lips, locking them and throwing away the key. It made an actual grin stretch across his face, slow and lazy, and my heart sank. He was devastatingly gorgeous. Asshole or not, this guy was going to feature in a few x-rated dreams, I was pretty sure, just as I was sure I was not going to survive a few more days with him around.

"I'm holding you to it." He gestured toward my freshly locked mouth.

He wrestled the green monster out into the front yard, his biceps straining, the thick chords in his back twisting. It was astonishing what this sweaty, grumpy man could do to me I thought, butterflies fluttering somewhere that was not quite my stomach.

Settle down, ladies.

"I left it out in front of your garage," he called as he walked back into the house and I was disappointed when he appeared in a fresh t-shirt. "You'll have to call the dump to come haul it away, but maybe you'll get lucky and someone will take it off your hands for parts or scrap. No telling what people are willing to scavenge these days."

I held up a fresh cup of coffee and a carton of half-and-half and he looked at me suspiciously. I could have sworn his eyes narrowed. "No, thanks. Just water, if you don't mind. I try to mostly stay away from addictive substances. General rule for my own good, these days."

He nodded shortly at me and walked out, shutting the front door behind him and when I heard a tap against the wall, I knew he was already back up on the roof. Since that signaled the start of his work day, I moved to the small room upstairs that I'd designated my home office and as his feet clomp-clomp-clomped over my head, I tried to churn out another article.

When my stomach reminded me I still hadn't eaten breakfast, I drifted back to the kitchen to see whether I had anything easy to eat. I sighed in frustration, knowing the cupboards held all of a bag of rice, a box of pasta and a few cans of tomato sauce.

Cracking two eggs into a hot skillet, I ate them almost before they were set. Then I grabbed my keys and handbag and let myself out the front door.

"I need groceries," I called up and his head popped over the ridgeline. "I left the door open in case you need to use the bathroom."

It was still early and there were only a few cars in the parking lot, which suited me just fine. I'd been living a hermit's life the past few months and though the locals seemed curious about me, I had absolutely no curiosity about them. I was on a people break, finding there wasn't a single question I wanted to answer or small talk in which I wished to participate.

Going off the list in my head, I piled produce into my cart, the squeaky wheel grating on my nerves.

"Well, you must be the lady who bought the Jacobson place!" The voice was far too loud and I had to wipe the wince off my face before turning to face the short older lady who'd rolled up behind me with a loaded cart, boxing me in against the dairy case.

"Natalie." I held out my hand and tried to smile, though it hurt my face a little. Socializing wasn't my strongest skill these days. Talking to people involved uncomfortable questions, questions they expected answered, and I didn't have most of those answers for myself just yet. Moving across the country to a place where I had no ties had only solved a portion of that problem.

"You can call me Libby," she said behind her hand, as if this were some big secret. "I live just across the street from you and I've been hoping to catch you for ages but you're a real homebody, aren't you?" She grinned. Her short gray hair was crazy, but it looked intentional, and oversize glasses covered half of her small face. "I see you got that Thomas man working on your roof." She'd leaned closer and her hand was up next to her mouth again. "You'd best be careful around him, young lady. He's a dark soul, bless his heart."

What was it with Thomas? Had he managed to offend each and every one of the people in this town, or had he offended them as a whole, collectively, and they'd all voted to never forgive him?

"I keep hearing that," I said, trying to keep my voice casual. "He can't be all that bad."

Libby pulled a face. "Don't go letting him fool you now. That pretty face is hiding a whole passel of trouble."

I wanted to ask what the hell a passel was, but I didn't dare. Libby was working herself up into a passionate frenzy, her hands gesticulating wildly. "He hardly sleeps. Lord knows what he's doing in that big house of his, all by himself. You drive by at two in the morning and lights are *blazing*. Something's not right in that man's head."

All by himself.

My brain seized on that as I remembered the thin band on his finger and his reference to his wife. This warranted further investigation, but I didn't want the answers from Libby. Something told me she didn't have them.

"Are you usually driving by at two in the morning?" I asked, a smile on my face so as to appear at least a little friendly. I wasn't sure I liked the guy yet, as a person, but I got the feeling he was being treated unfairly.

Libby sputtered for a moment, clucking very much like a little chicken, and I turned to pull a carton of milk and several containers of eggs from the case while she formulated her answer.

"Well, that's what I been told, you understand. There's people lives near him say that's the way it is. Have to say though, he *does* keep it neat as a pin–not to vouch for the inside. I never been inside." She switched subjects suddenly as she gestured around us. "I see him now and again.

Don't seem to eat much, big man like him. Shame." And she was shaking her head at a thought that remained mercifully trapped inside.

I didn't ask how she knew any of those things.

Finally extricating myself from Libby's gossipy clutches, I added a few more things to my cart and the teenage boy running the register rang up my purchases without looking me in the eyes. That was a welcome change after being cornered by the dairy case.

I started the car before unloading the groceries, cranking up the AC. The humidity was brutal and my hair was taking on a life of its own. Sitting in the cooling air for a moment, I pondered what Libby had said. What, exactly, was it that was a shame?

FOUR

Thomas

The look on her face when she'd doused me with the pail full of dirty dish water had almost been worth it. If there was a level somewhere below mortified, she had reached it instantaneously, stumbling and sputtering and stuttering as she tried to apologize to me.

I didn't tell her I'd been covered in far worse things while apprenticing to my dad. Dish water was pretty tame by comparison.

Her hair was piled up on top of her head again and when she wasn't looking at me, I tried to sneak a few more peeks of her legs. The skirt was longer than the shorts she'd been wearing the day before, but I was a leg man and this smooth pair was really doing something for me.

Which was a problem.

I had forgotten how much women could talk and when she came a little too close to subjects that made me uncomfortable, I couldn't help but be an asshole. I'd discovered a long time ago that the best way to get a person to shut up was to make them really uncomfortable, and it seemed a pretty easy task with her.

All those stupid questions. She acted like she actually wanted to get to know me, which was *not* what I'd signed up for. Of course, I also hadn't signed up to haul out her dishwasher, but my traitorous mouth had already roped me into taking her to Smitty's this afternoon to pick up a new one. I was cursing myself a little bit for that, but also kind of congratulating myself.

Maybe she'd wear the skirt.

Maybe it would hitch up her legs a little when she climbed into my truck.

Fuck, man. What are you doing?

I was so irritated at my inability to keep my shit together around her, I excused myself and went outside to work on the roof before it got too hot. Alabama in July was always going to be wicked hot, but at least I could get something done before the sun was set to "blister."

I turned my attention back to stripping the last few rows of shingles off the roof. All four damn layers. If I'd known what I was getting into...I examined a spongy spot...yeah, I'd have still taken the job. Maybe with more enthusiasm, if I was being honest. It was awful nice to have a job with a view for once.

There were a few sheets of roof sheathing and rolls of underlayment in the bed of my truck and since she was gone a long time, I managed the patching and underlayment pretty quickly. Since I'd stupidly committed myself to helping her select and haul a dishwasher this afternoon, I was really going to have to pick up my pace.

FIVE

Natalie

If he heard the car engine, or the door slam, he didn't acknowledge it. I could hear a pneumatic tool and I wondered if he was already lining the backside of the house with shingles. It certainly could be said he worked quickly for a crew of one.

After putting the groceries away, curiosity got the better of me. I drifted outside and circled the house, shading my eyes. The cicadas were already at full bore and I had to shout over their noise. "You're out of your mind."

The sound of the staple gun stopped and he turned to look down at me, saying nothing.

"It's hotter than hell up there. You can't stay there–you'll catch heatstroke and fall off my roof, and then you'll sue me for breaking your stupid neck."

He grinned, an actual tooth-baring grin. "You don't 'catch' heatstroke, Natalie. I'm fine. You don't have to worry about me falling off your roof *or* suing you."

"I'm making lunch," I called back up. "It'll be ready in forty-five minutes."

"I packed a couple sandwiches."

"Bullshit. Put them in the refrigerator for later–the least I can do is feed and hydrate you. Otherwise bad things happen. You know, like passing out and falling off roofs. And lawsuits." I nodded firmly, case closed.

He looked surprised that I'd argued with him and he chewed on his lip for a minute before it seemed he decided not to engage. He turned back to his work and I hurried into the house, because I had absolutely no idea what I was going to feed him.

Whatever I came up with in forty-five minutes seemed the obvious answer.

When the front door shut softly, I turned to find him standing in the kitchen in his socks, a fresh t-shirt pulled over his head, his hair slicked back with sweat. Somehow he still smelled absolutely divine, which was insanely unfair.

"You didn't have to change," I said, reaching into the refrigerator and pulling out a pitcher of the tea I'd left in there to brew. "It's just me."

"I keep a stack of clean t-shirts in the truck," he said, looking like he was unsure of where he should be standing. "It's just good manners."

"Makes up for your other, somewhat more severe shortcomings then," I said, and I turned from the oven to grin at him, but the look on his face was one of shock.

"I'm teasing," I followed up quickly. "Sounds like you have quite the reputation around here, though. Should I be concerned?"

He didn't answer, but he did load up his plate with more food than I thought I'd ever seen one person eat. He settled quickly at the island and I cringed when I realized this meant I had to sit next to him, elbow to elbow. He was going to smell the pheromones.

"I should have the back half done by three," he said between bites as I set a basket of warm rolls and a stick of butter in front of him and I swear his eyes lit up. "Then I'll take you over to Smitty's and you can pick out whatever suits you." He ducked his head down to start shoveling food into his mouth.

"There's more," I said gently and he swiveled his head to look at me. "You're eating like you haven't had food in days. There's plenty more and you're welcome to it. I can't eat all of it myself."

He blushed a furious red, some of the hair that he'd tucked behind his ear escaping to partially cover his face as he looked down at his plate. "Beats the hell out of dry turkey and cheese sandwiches," he finally said, and I took that as my point of entry.

"Does she pack your lunches for you in the morning, then?"

It was like watching someone turn to stone. He froze with the fork halfway to his mouth, then seemed to regain his composure. "No," he said with some effort. "I do. I'm not much good in the kitchen. Never took the time to figure out how to cook."

"She cooks for you though, right? Dinner?"

His warm brown eyes were horribly cold when he turned to look at me and I swallowed hard, a piece of chicken almost catching in my throat. "Right," I said, my face flooding with shame as I looked back down at my own plate. "Sorry. Mute button."

He smiled just a little.

He ate another, only slightly smaller, plate after that and scarfed down four bread rolls.

I refilled his glass of tea twice more and he grunted his thanks.

When I pulled an apple pie out of the warming drawer under the oven, his eyes grew wide and I hastened to explain. "I didn't make it myself–I just bought this one. But I couldn't pass it up." I shrugged, patting my hip with my free hand and he hid his smile behind a fist.

"This tastes like childhood," he said softly, and when I turned to join him at the island, he was staring at the pie but he was far, far away. I was quiet because to me it just tasted like pie from the supermarket, with that weird, cheap shortening aftertaste.

He scraped his plate clean and stood, rinsing it in the sink before his eyes traveled to the gaping hole where the dishwasher had been just that morning. "I suppose that means I'd better get to it," he said, scratching his head. "Doing dishes by hand for a couple days would be my worst nightmare–and you have all these dishes now because you made a nice lunch..." He looked a little guilty.

He crossed the kitchen and was almost out the front door before I heard him call back, "Thanks for feeding me–you didn't have to do that." I thought I heard him say "I never eat that well," but he was already out the door.

I wondered if it was nice enough to knock a percentage off what I knew would be a hefty bill from him. He'd obviously already far exceeded the materials he'd quoted, which meant I could make out a check to "Financial Ruin" in about two more days.

• • • •

TRUE TO HIS WORD, HE was back in the house by three, already in another fresh t-shirt. "Natalie," he called up the stairs, and I poked my head over the rickety banister. "We have to hurry. Smitty's closes at five on the dot, because the old man has a standing date with his favorite seat at the bar. Come on."

Hurrying down the stairs, I grabbed my handbag and followed him out the door, stopping only to lock it. It made him snort and I looked over my shoulder to see him with one hand in his hair. "First of all," he said, "this town is so small that no one has to lock their doors. Not even in this day and age. And secondly, this house is so old...that *handleset* is so old..." he pointed toward my front door. "You can bet half the people in this town either have a copy of the key or have the same damn one."

He opened the passenger door of his truck for me, removing a stack of folded t-shirts from the seat and opening the door behind me to relocate them. "Hop up," he said, and I kept my eyes straight ahead, situating myself while he closed the door behind me.

He seemed perfectly happy to drive in silence and I blew a puff of air out through my cheeks. "You're not a big fan of conversation, are you?" I asked finally, trying to keep my voice light. What was it about this jerk that made me want to *try*?

"People talk too much," he said out the side of his mouth, his lips twisting a little. "They should be listening more."

That effectively struck me silent. It was another rebuke I took to heart, so I clamped my lips tightly shut and watched the scenery unfold outside the window. The trees here looked old and gnarled, like they'd been there for hundreds of years and Spanish moss hung from some of them.

What an arbitrary choice Alabama had been. I'd found a charming old house for a really reasonable price in a small town that was coastal–if you could buy in the expensive part of town.

This was a fresh start in a place where no one knew my name or the humiliation I'd been through, and during one of Ahmad's business trips to London I'd packed up my things and moved.

I wasn't surprised when he didn't come after me. In fact, aside from his angry text about the sofa (his favorite, apparently–news to me, given the nuclear argument we had when I bought it), we hadn't spoken since.

I'd responded that his reaction to the sofa's disappearance exceeded his reaction to that of his *wife* leaving, and that was particularly curious.

He hadn't bothered to respond.

Thomas and I drove in silence the rest of the way to the store, an enormous rectangular building with a corrugated metal roof and huge windows, tremendously large panes of tinted glass. The small parking lot was wrapped with a chain link fence, razor wire strung along the top.

"What the hell?" I muttered as I stared at the huge box. "You'd think he was selling bondage gear and sex toys, or maybe he's an arms dealer. What's with the black-out windows?"

He chuckled beside me. "That would be an interesting side business, but this area is pretty conservative. Can't say many people want to see Smitty's place to turn into a one-stop shop for a microwave, an AR and a blue dildo."

I blushed a little, trying to suppress the snort that threatened to erupt. "That was oddly specific–a blue one? Also personal experience?" I teased, following him toward the double doors.

He smiled slightly and held one for me. I stepped through, greeted by a blast of mercifully cool air.

"Aw, nah hea come a sweet little lady." The voice boomed across the store and I looked around in alarm, expecting to find a giant waiting in ambush behind one of the floor model wash machines. Instead, a man shorter than me appeared from one of the aisles, all ninety pounds of him, and most of that was his nose.

"J'miah Smith, ma'am." He held out gnarled fingers to shake my hand and my mouth flapped uselessly.

Words. For once I had no words.

"Smitty." Thomas came up behind me and took the man's hand cordially, giving it a solid shake that rattled his small bird bones. "This is Miss Natalie. She needs a dishwasher–a good one–like the one I got a while back."

"Holdin' up well then, m'boy?" Smitty asked him, squinting up myopically at Thomas.

"Better than expected," Thomas said. "I put it through its paces every so often and so far it's working like a charm."

"You knows better than to think Smitty sells trash." The man clucked, shaking his head at Thomas, and I thought that the longer I looked at him, I couldn't decide whether he was Gollum or a Hobbit.

"Do Miss Natalie know what she lookin' to buy?" His yellowing eyes were kind and friendly, his demeanor jovial, even if I found him a shocking personality crammed into an oddly tiny body. I didn't know what to do with him. My brain was absolutely refusing to catalog.

"Well..." I looked around the store hesitantly. "Maybe you could just show me where you keep the Precious."

Cough.

"The Bosch. So sorry. The Bosch dishwashers."

Thomas choked behind me, then wheezed, and as we followed an unfazed Smitty through a warren of aisles, I turned to look at him. His shoulders were shaking with barely contained laughter, his face so screwed up with silent hilarity that I didn't know how he could see where he was going.

"Dis one." Smitty thumped the top of a gleaming chrome box and I looked closely at how his lips moved when he talked, because I suspected most of the teeth in his mouth were not his own. "Dis one be on clearance. I give you a real good deal–discontinued. Got parts in back I throw in free."

That was my favorite word these days.

I leaned closer to inspect the sticker on the unit, then examined the inside. Then I gestured wordlessly to Thomas, who was wiping at his eyes with his t-shirt. He stepped forward to stick his head inside the box, examining God knows what, and when he emerged he started to haggle with Smitty in some kind of broken language I thought might be Creole.

"Aha!" Thomas exclaimed suddenly, the first word I'd been able to identify in the last seven sentences. "You have yourself a deal, Jeremiah!" He stuck out his hand, rattling the little man soundly.

Smitty beamed from ear to ear and beckoned us to follow him, leading us deeper into the bowels of the store, where he rang up my purchase on a cash register I suspected was older than him. It chugged and thunked and finally dinged, three figures popping up in the display and I handed over my credit card.

"Aw, Miss Nat," he said, and he looked mournful. "Don't got no c'nections in dis hea building. Maybe you has a check?" He looked hopeful and I raised my eyebrows, digging into my handbag to retrieve the checkbook issued to me in prehistoric times.

Thomas loaded the dishwasher onto a dolly with a heave, then rolled it out of the store behind me while Smitty trailed after us. The two of them wrestled it into the bed of the truck while I looked on dubiously, aware that getting the machine *out* of the truck on the other end of our trip would prove a most interesting experience.

Smitty hurried back into the store while Thomas secured the machine to the pickup bed with a series of straps and bungee cords. He'd just cinched the last one and snapped the tailgate into place when the little man came bustling back out of the store with a large box in his arms. "No leavin' dis!" he hollered, and I handed the box from Smitty to Thomas with one raised eyebrow.

There were very few things in the box I recognized by name or function, but I thanked Smitty anyway and when I shook his hand he blushed violently. "Ain't anyting a'tall, Miss Nat. You need sumpin', you finds Smitty." He jerked a thumb toward his chest and I nodded solemnly, thanking him again before climbing into the truck.

"That was...*he*...was really something," I said as Thomas maneuvered the truck out of the parking lot, a huge grin on his face.

"I do believe you has an admirer, Miss Natalie," he drawled, and I reached across the space to slap his solid shoulder. It didn't budge him at all, and my palm tingled from the contact.

"I can't believe you asked him to help you find the Precious." He howled with laughter, pounding the steering wheel with the flat of one palm. He had to wipe his eyes again before he could see to drive, and little bursts of laughter kept finding their way through his lips.

"What?" I asked innocently, a small smile tugging at the corners of my mouth. "I've never seen such a tiny person, and that's saying something, because I'm pretty pocket-sized myself."

I liked him this way, I thought, observing the way that humor softened his features. He was beautiful when he smiled and downright panty-melting when he laughed, but it seemed he didn't laugh often.

Again I watched as the landscape tore past, trying to appreciate my new surroundings. This was my home now, whether I liked it or not. I needed to stay put for a while to rebuild myself, in more ways than one.

I could feel Thomas watching me out of the corner of his eye, and I finally turned my head. "You're awfully quiet," he said, and he sounded surprised when he said it.

"I'm l-i-s-t-e-n-i-n-g," I said exaggeratedly, and he quirked an eyebrow at me, a small smile still on his lips.

If someone had asked me how we got the dishwasher out of the truck bed even five minutes after we unloaded it, I'm not sure I could have said. But for whatever it was worth, I had a vicious new bruise on my shin, I'd scraped my forearm on the tailgate, and Thomas had sweated through another t-shirt while muttering terrifyingly vociferous curses under his breath. The last one involved Mary and Joseph and a couple exotic animals I thought had no business being grouped with saints, especially in the confusing positions he'd mentioned. I wasn't eager to hear another, the mental contortions of the last one already too much to sort.

He heaved the shiny box up the two steps of the front porch, then over the sill and across the short space to the kitchen.

While he scooted the dishwasher into place and hooked it up, I poured more tea for him. I set it on the counter before pulling leftover chicken out of the fridge.

By the time he popped out from beneath the sink, I'd pulled together four fat chicken salad sandwiches. I set three on a plate and one on the other, grabbing a tub of store bought potato salad to heap on the sides of the plates, finishing our indoor picnic with potato chips.

His eyes got big again when he saw the food. "You expecting company?"

"I'm feeding you," I said, pointing toward the island where he'd been sitting hours before. "You went out of your way for me. This isn't anything fancy, but after everything you did today I'm not going to send you home to cook for yourself. After what you told me, I don't trust you to do a very good job of it."

His eyes filled with something I thought might be gratitude and he turned away from me quickly, washing his hands briskly in the sink.

"I won't be able to finish up tomorrow," he said as he took a bite of the first sandwich. "There's something I have to take care of, so I'll be back the day after. I don't expect it'll take me a full day to finish, and it should be done right before rain moves in."

That was a relief, I thought. Finally, I could collect all the five gallon pails dotting my bedroom, the ones I left out "just in case," even on sunny days.

I crunched through my chips and ate most of my potato salad, polishing off the sandwich quickly. Then I pulled the cold pie from the fridge and I swear his eyes lit up.

"Ice cream?" I asked as I plated another large slice.

"Aw no, I shouldn't..."

I took that as a yes and I pulled the tub from the freezer, scooping two huge mounds onto the slice before setting it in front of him. For his part, he looked like a five-year-old staring through a candy shop window: paralyzed with delight.

"I should skip tonight," I said with a rueful smile, tucking the pie tin back into the fridge. I patted my softening middle with one hand. "When I don't have anyone to cook for, ice cream is sometimes–oftentimes–dinner."

He looked startled and I realized I'd just left the door wide open for the questions I did *not* want him to ask.

Who do you cook for?

Why are you alone?

How long has it been?

But to his credit, the pie went into his mouth and no words came out.

He *listened* so damn much, it was going to make me crazy.

Leaning back in the chair, he folded his hands over his stomach and groaned contentedly. "You saved me from a couple frozen pizzas." One hand patted his stomach and I couldn't help but notice how nicely fitted his t-shirt was; nicely enough that I could see the tight lacing of his abs. It made my mouth water unexpectedly.

I'd like to lick some ice cream off that.

"I've been known to succumb to the charms of freezer case items from time to time," I said, collecting our plates and rinsing them in the sink before slotting them into the dishwasher. Adding in the dishes from lunch, I dropped in a detergent pod and decided to start the load although the racks weren't entirely full.

"I'll just hang out here for a minute to make sure it works," he said, leaning back in his chair.

"Whatever," I teased. "You're so stuffed, you couldn't move if the water line broke and was flooding the house. Don't try to hide it."

"You're right," he groaned. "I can't even feel my legs."

He sat quietly while I cleaned up the small kitchen, wiping down the counters, refilling his glass of tea, scrubbing out the sink. I could feel him watching me and when I finally caught his expression, I thought he looked terribly sad. Alone. It made my heart twist a little. I would recognize that look anywhere, because it was my default expression these days.

"Are you okay?" I asked as gently as I could, trying to keep the tremble out of my voice.

He shook himself suddenly, drawing a deep, shuddering breath. "What?"

"Are you alright?"

Something went hard in his eyes again and he curled his upper lip in a sneer. "Yeah, sure. Why wouldn't I be?"

I didn't say anything. My learning curve with him was short, and since he used silence and hurtful words as a weapon against me, it was the only thing to use against him. I shrugged then. "If you say so."

Something in my chest hurt, but I didn't know whether it was for myself or for him.

Glancing up at the clock, I realized it was just after seven. I was beginning to understand this man had nowhere to be. Maybe the normalcy of a humming dishwasher in a cheerful kitchen, combined with a pleasantly full stomach, was what had put that look on his face. Something like nostalgia.

His eyes followed mine and he easily read my thoughts. "I should get going," he said, pushing himself quickly to his feet and tucking the stool beneath the countertop. "Thanks for feeding me again." His smile was forced, nervous and uncomfortable.

"I enjoy cooking for people." My own smile was warm and genuine. "I haven't been able to do it for a really long time. Any time you're hungry, my door is open."

Shit, that was a loaded sentence.

I blushed, hoping he couldn't read that thought too, as it ran through my mind.

"Uh, thanks." He looked uncomfortable. Maybe he'd known exactly what I was thinking. "I'll see you the day after tomorrow, then."

I nodded, not moving from my spot against the sink. He knew where the door was and he looked like he wanted nothing more in that moment than to run through it.

When I heard the door close I crumpled onto the stool, dropping my head down to the island countertop. "Oh crap," I moaned, banging my forehead on the counter with a hollow thump. "I am in so much trouble."

SIX

Thomas

Raven was waiting for me on the front porch when I got home and I scooped up the tiny black cat, cradling her against my chest as I unlocked the front door.

"You're as good as it gets these days, little girl," I told her as her little body reverberated with a purr and her brilliant green eyes drifted shut while I scratched her chin. She was the only reason I bothered to come home most days, as her very minimal care kept me tethered to some sort of routine: Make dinner.

Work out.

Write code.

Check in with my team on the West Coast.

Feed the cat.

My stomach was so full, I decided to put off working out for a bit. Instead, I stretched out on the sofa and Raven curled up on my chest with a contented little rattle. It was unusual for her, since I typically didn't see her until I was brushing my teeth at night, when she'd wind around my legs and jump up to sleep at the foot of my bed.

Maybe tonight I'd try sleeping in my room again, I thought uncomfortably, my eyes having grown heavy despite the fact the sun had only just set. God knew I hadn't been sleeping well for a very long time.

I didn't have the energy to pull up my email tonight. I didn't want to put out fires or schedule meetings.

I didn't want to read progress reports or the latest findings from the three new business analysts who'd started on only six weeks earlier.

I didn't want to read code, or write it, or review the latest upgrade engineered by one of the teams.

Instead, I showered and washed a small load of laundry. Then I fed the cat, drank a glass of water and climbed back up the stairs.

I passed two of the other bedrooms on my way down the hallway, avoiding the master, since I could still feel the icy chill coming from that room.

The next room, though...I let my hand trail down the side of the door frame as I gazed into the space. It was dark, and my brain searched for all the right things in the shadowy shapes: the small bunk bed, the toy chest, the book shelf, the train set, the pair of ballet shoes hanging from a brass hook on the wall.

This space hurts me.

Raven got tired of waiting for me and I heard her squeaky little chirp from down the hallway, as she jumped up on the bed in my room.

Physically tearing myself from the almost-gravitational pull of the room, I fought the panic that always rose in my gut when I allowed myself to peer in on the life I'd so briefly had.

They were never yours.

The ghosts followed me into my room at the end of the hallway. It was the smallest room of the house, the walls painted a deep shade, so dark it was almost black.

The only furniture was from an old wedding set, the furniture I'd purchased when Lydia and I were planning a life together. It was the set we'd shipped around the world more than once, every nick and ding and dent a story from another exotic location. But the set was mine now and I didn't even care to replace it, since some of the memories were pretty sweet.

I threw myself onto the bed and the ghosts climbed in with me, snuggled up close, wrapping their bony fingers around my memories and ripping at my heart while I tried to close my eyes and forget.

It would be a kindness to wake with selective amnesia. Merciful. To wake completely unfamiliar with my surroundings, with no memory of the faces in the photos I kept sorted in boxes in the living room ottoman.

Though I didn't pray often–sorry, Ma–that night I prayed the prayer that had been constantly on my heart for the past several years.

Please help me forget.

SEVEN

Natalie

The next day I painted the bathroom and the paint was the first thing Thomas smelled when he walked into the house the following morning, a bag in his hand. He must have followed his nose, because when I peered around from the kitchen I could see his body halfway inside the bathroom and I heard him whistle appreciatively. "Hey, nice job–this looks great."

I blushed a little under the unexpected praise. "Thanks," I said. "I was just feeling super-productive yesterday and it made for a good, quick story for today's post, so..."

He looked at me weird again, but he didn't ask any questions.

"You hungry?" I asked, spinning toward the oven. My own breakfast plans hadn't taken into account that I was only feeding myself, and the leftovers were copious.

"You offering?" he asked, and from the small smile on his face I could tell that was exactly what he'd been hoping.

"Duh. It's the way to a man's heart," I joked as I pulled a plate from the cabinet and when I turned to catch his expression, he had gone completely white. "I'm kidding!" I exclaimed. "Do you think I'm such a desperate soul that I'd try to lure a man with food?"

"I've seen some do worse," he said quietly, and my face dropped.

"Well..." I couldn't think of a single thing to say as I piled the plate high with hash browns and scrambled eggs, turkey bacon and toast. He was practically drooling on the countertop as I handed the plate over to him. "I'm not that girl, my friend."

I refilled his plate and when he finished he rinsed it in the sink, leaving it on the sideboard. "Guess I'll go see what I can knock out," he said, patting his stomach with both hands. "If you don't hear anything in an hour, throw up a rock–I might be asleep by the chimney."

What was that, some sort of humor? From the man who had no room for jokes? I stood slack-jawed for a moment. What a different person he was from the person I'd met a few days earlier. Apparently a little food really softened this guy up.

"You know the drill," I said as he washed his hands at the sink. "I'll have lunch ready by noon."

"Shit, Natalie. You keep feeding me like this and I'm just going to start ripping off a few more shingles every day so I can come back the next day to 'fix' them." He hung some giant air quotes.

"You don't need an excuse, Thomas," I said gently. Something in him needed kindness and my own broken places recognized this. "You know you're welcome here any time. You're not so bad when you're not grumpy, and it'll encourage me to do a better job of cooking for myself anyway, if I have someone else to feed. After all, I really shouldn't try to exist on ice cream forever. My ass will be the next thing to go." I cast a quick glance behind myself and I felt his eyes follow.

He hung his head, but I saw how his eyes twinkled before he did. "You've saved both of us from ourselves. I should mention it to the priest at Mass; maybe he'll put in a recommendation to have you canonized. Saint Natalie." He thought about that for a moment. "Hmm." He tapped his chin. "I'm not a good Catholic; there might already be one."

"Oh, I'm definitely getting in," I shot back as I scraped a pan into the trash. "He'll saint me for my unwavering patience. You, my child..." I intoned as I made the symbol of the cross in the air. "You have undertaken a great good in nourishing the bodies of the woeful, perpetually crotchety folk."

He wheezed with silent laughter. "Crotchety? What am I, ninety?"

I lifted an eyebrow. "Morose? Maudlin? Cynical? Grouchy? Cross? I can do this all day, buddy. Pick your favorite."

He smiled a real smile and I thought to myself that he handled teasing well, though I doubted he was teased often. Teasing was supposed to be gentle and done with affection. Affection was something he wasn't receiving, if my neighbors were any indication.

"Crotchety." He mumbled the word to himself with a chuckle, turning to leave the kitchen with a small wave.

Seeing him like that relaxed me. I breathed easier, feeling that perhaps he could be just a little more open. More human.

None of this mattered, I tried to tell myself. He would finish my roof today and he'd disappear back to his big, tidy house, wherever that was, and I'd be stuck here with my buckets and paint rollers, eating ice cream for dinner.

But I didn't want to believe that. I wanted to believe he'd drop by whenever he was lonely, under the pretense he'd stopped by to see what was bubbling away in my kitchen.

I really just wanted him to drop by just to see me. I liked his company and I liked teasing him.

When he didn't come in at noon, I went to find him. It was calm and still outside, except for the cicadas.

He was in the yard, picking up scraps that had fallen from the roof the past few days, throwing everything into a bucket. "All done," he called and I shaded my eyes quickly to look up at the roof. I hoped the action hid my disappointment. I'd come to enjoy the company of this cranky ogre in the past few days and though I knew he'd never say it, he was warming up to me. I was sure of it.

"Already?" I asked. I hated that I could hear disappointment in my voice. "I thought it would take you all day!"

"Nope," he said, stepping closer to look up with me. "She's tight now. No more squishy spots and definitely no more leaks. Should test that theory by tomorrow, too. Rain's coming."

I said nothing, making a motion that indicated he should follow me and when he sat at the island and I slid his plate in front of him, I thought his eyes actually watered.

He wasted no time, picking up his burger with both hands and shoving it into his mouth, sighing contentedly as he chewed. "Are you sure there's not something else you need done around here?" he asked around a mouthful. "I'm going to die of starvation if I have to go back to feeding myself with any kind of regularity. I only cook out of necessity and I'll be honest: What I do can't really be called cooking. It's only taken you a few days to completely wreck the pathetic rhythm I had going."

Actually, that was something I wanted to talk to him about, and I grabbed a sketchpad from one of the kitchen drawers. I sat next to him and quickly sketched the shape of my room, pointing to where I wanted to install two skylights.

"I just put shingles on that damn roof and now you want to cut holes in it?" He looked incredulous.

The man had no vision, that much was clear. I tugged at his arm to get him to follow me and he carried his plate with him as we climbed the stairs, clearly unwilling to be parted from his fries.

"Can't you see it?" I asked. "The room will be so bright and airy. It'll make the space feel so much bigger and more gracious."

What would have been more gracious was if a bra wasn't hanging on my bedpost. Oops.

"Skylights leak," he pronounced, cramming a fistful of fries into his mouth.

"Not if you do the job," I said with finality, and he arched an eyebrow. "Come on, I know you know how to do it. I also know you'll do the best job for the fairest price. And besides, you were looking for a reason to be here: You just admitted you can't cook." I snagged a fry from his plate. That uncomfortable look was back on his face.

"Thomas," I laughed finally, "I'm not trying to proposition you." There was a part of me that desperately wanted to do just that. "It's an even exchange: serious work for money and food. Isn't that normally how this works?"

"Nothing about you is normal, lady," he muttered under his breath and I caught mine, a little taken aback. I wasn't sure how he'd meant that, but it felt a little cruel.

"That wasn't very nice," I said, stealing four more of his fries and giving him a pointed glare. "And we were doing so well."

"Hey!" he exclaimed as his fries disappeared into my mouth.

"Asshole penalty," I said around the mouthful. "Because you're being mean to me and I don't deserve it."

He set the plate down on the dresser and scrubbed both hands down his face. "Fuck. I'm sorry."

"See? That wasn't so hard."

He grimaced. "I don't have a lot of practice with...people...lately. When I'm here, I live my own life and do my own thing, and I guess I've hidden myself away and turned into..."

"A *crotchety* old man." I grinned, waiting for him to roll his eyes. "I understand. I've been hiding from people and from the things I want to forget, too. I just haven't lost *all* of my social skills yet. But you, my friend..." I whistled. "You might be too far gone. I don't know if we can bring you back."

He swallowed hard and though my words had been teasing, I was pretty sure he was taking them to heart.

"It wasn't supposed to be this way," he said quietly, obviously lost in thought.

"I know a few things about that," I answered softly. "Sometimes changes hit you so fast that you can't even pull yourself back up. There aren't many people who understand that, either. Close friends, neighbors you've had for years–family...it's like being trapped in a soundproof room and no one comes to let you out. You're stuck in there, screaming, all by yourself." I swallowed hard, surprised to find my eyes were watering.

"Yeah...something like that." His expression was so filled with heartbreak that it hurt to look at him. I had to fight the urge to close the distance between us and throw my arms around him. But since that would have really freaked him out, I just nodded and turned, walking quietly out of the room in order to leave him with his thoughts. He needed a minute.

It took me a while to clean up the mess I'd made in the kitchen. I'd had plans for the afternoon, but suddenly I couldn't remember what they were. I was too busy straining my ears, waiting to hear his footsteps on the stairs and I began to wonder if I shouldn't have left him up there by himself.

There was a pressure change in the house and I looked up suddenly, putting the sponge back in the holder by the sink. I hadn't heard footsteps, but the front door had just opened and closed.

Opening the door quietly, I found him sitting on the front porch, his feet on the steps. He didn't turn to look at me, and I eased myself down onto the step next to him.

"If you don't want company I can go," I said quietly. The words hung in the air for a long time and finally he shook his head.

"It's fine."

It wasn't fine and we both knew that, but I wrapped my arms around my knees and rested my chin on them. I didn't want to pressure him into anything. I had those raw moments too, and I knew I was nowhere near done having them.

Sometimes it helped having someone who was just *there*.

"I've been in your way long enough," he said finally, wiping a hand roughly across his face. "I'll work up an estimate for you on the windows and get you some specs. Then it's up to you when you want them put in–well, you and the weather."

"I want the ones that are this big." I held out my arms for width, then stretched even wider for length. Something popped in my right shoulder. "Two of them, on that part of the ceiling I showed you."

"Thank you for those incredibly specific details," he said, finally looking at me again and though his eyes were red there was a small smile on his face. "That will help tremendously when I place a custom order and tell them I want them 'about so-wide-by-yay-long.'"

I bumped his shoulder with my own. "Eh, you're getting the hang of me."

He scrambled up from the porch quickly and I realized it was the first time I'd really made pointed physical contact with him. Maybe I had spooked him? I had to fix it.

"If you're in a hurry, let me wrap some pie to send with you. You didn't even get your dessert."

His eyes narrowed. "You are an evil temptress."

"It's lemon meringue. No sane person says no to that."

"Well, *I* certainly won't."

I hurried back into the house and cut the pie in half, depositing it on a large dinner plate and wrapping it carefully with plastic. Then I grabbed the tub of whipped topping from the fridge and hurried back out the front door.

"Here," I said, shoving both things at him. "There should be enough to hold you until dinner, or maybe it will *be* dinner, if you can restrain yourself for that long."

He looked at the pie and the topping, then up at me. He wasn't smiling. In fact, I thought he looked a little suspicious.

"Why are you being nice to me, Natalie?"

Uh...why *was* I being nice to him? Because I was a nice person?

Yes, one point for me.

Because I felt like he needed someone to be nice to him?

Yes, another point.

Because he was gorgeous?

Duh.

Shit, no points for that one. In fact, maybe a subtraction.

"Everyone needs someone who cares," I said lamely. "I've gotten the impression there aren't many people who are kind to you."

"Because I'm the asshole nobody wants!" he yelled suddenly, the air thick with his rage and I startled, the plate slipping out of my hands and shattering on the front walk.

I stood there staring at it stupidly as he threw himself down on his knees, collecting the bits of shattered porcelain. "I'm sorry, Natalie. I'm sorry, I'm so sorry. I didn't mean to scare you. I..." He crumpled, dropping the shards to the ground and covering his face with his hands. His shoulders shook silently and I stood staring at him stupidly, completely frozen.

It took a moment for my brain to catch up and I stepped carefully over the broken glass and obliterated pie, dropping to my knees next to him. I wrapped my arms around him tight and held on for dear life, one arm around his back and another around his opposite shoulder, a hand curled up into that glorious hair.

His heart is breaking and you're being a pervert, copping a feel.

I snapped back to the moment, shame flooding my cheeks.

He *was* nicely solid under my fingers, and they wanted to explore, but this was not the time.

The outburst didn't last long. I felt him move to wipe his face, though my face was over his shoulder and at an angle, so I could only go on the movement. And though he was collecting himself, I felt him soften into me just the tiniest bit, and he rested his head on my shoulder like he'd lost the battle.

"I'm sorry, Natalie." His voice was steadier and calmer. "That was a kind gesture and I fucked it up."

"Hey..." I patted his back awkwardly. "Lemon meringue pie is a trigger. Duly noted." He chuckled a little, and his hair tickled my neck.

"You know," I said quietly, loath to pull away from him but aware that we were probably the neighborhood's living room window daytime drama, I did so slowly.

I tucked a piece of his hair back behind his ear just because I couldn't help myself, and it made my fingertips tingle. "There is another half of the pie in the house. If I can manage not to jump like a rabbit at loud noises, I think I could plate up another couple slices."

He nodded at me gratefully and we rose together, managing between the two of us to scoop most of the pie onto the broken plate pieces and he grabbed the container of topping.

He followed me into the house, where we carefully deposited the unfortunate mess into the trash bin and washed our hands at the kitchen sink. Then I took down two new plates and pulled the pie from the refrigerator, cutting a small slice for myself and dumping the rest on his plate, cutting it into three equal slices only after, because God knew his muscles would burn it off by the miracle of their existence.

He was watching me out of the side of his eye, silent, as I dolloped generous portions of whipped topping onto each. Then I fetched forks from the drawer near my hip and handed him one. "This is the more delicious side, anyway." I grinned at him. "It's totally why I was keeping this half for myself."

He shook his head and rolled his eyes at me, but I could tell he was relieved. Why exactly, I wasn't sure, and whatever his reason he kept it to himself, leaning back against the sink and lifting the plate closer to his mouth as he used the fork to cut small bites. He grunted a little as he ate it, little sounds of happiness, and I grinned at him as I chewed my own. "That's my super-secret, award-winning recipe."

His eyes got big. "You *made* this? That makes me an even bigger ass!"

I sighed, reaching around him to set my plate in the sink and licking the crumbs off my lips. "What's past is past, Thomas. Every day is a new choice and today I'm not getting mad over silly things, like a broken plate and dropped pie–which was *my* fault, anyway. I'd rather lose a plate than lose a friend."

He looked at me cautiously, the fork halfway to his mouth. "Friend?"

"Yup." It came out with far more bravado than I felt. "You have been designated my friend–my first one here, which I'd say is great, but I've been living here for months. And by most standards, I suppose I've not been trying very hard. So buckle in, *friend*." I knew my eyes were twinkling, because I liked teasing him.

He cut another bite, his eyes wary.

"Friends are people I *like*, Thomas. They're the people I can trust and count on. People I'd help out of a jam whenever they need the help, because I know they'd do the same for me. And besides Gerry," I pointed across the room in the direction of her house, "there aren't many people in this town that I like yet. So this is a designation of honor. I mean, really, who else would have taken me to find the Precious?" I gestured toward the shiny new dishwasher with a grin and his lips quirked a little.

"There aren't many people in this town I will ever like," he grumbled. Then he looked up at me. "I guess I'll make an exception for you."

"I'm very likable," I assured him. "But maybe a little jumpy."

But I didn't tell him why and he didn't ask.

I didn't have the energy to tell him how the smallest things turned Ahmad into a raging monster toward the end, so that my skittishness was earned.

He laughed a little, shaking his head and turning to set his plate in the sink.

"Besides," I said quietly, "everyone needs a friend who won't hold the past over their head."

There was that look again, and I decided to ignore it. I certainly wasn't about to start asking him questions and risk him having another breakdown. Whatever it was, I was pretty sure it would come out when he needed it to.

EIGHT

Thomas

⁂

How completely embarrassing.

While I drove home, I spent the entirety of the short trip berating myself for my temper and my complete inability to control *any* of my emotions that day.

What had gotten into me?

Not only was it unlike me to openly snap at someone who was completely undeserving–I saved my temper for the purposefully stupid–but what the hell had happened on her sidewalk? When she jumped and dropped that plate, I had genuinely lost my shit. I'd collapsed on the sidewalk at the strength of the memory I'd never be able to explain to her.

Lately it had been coming to me in dreams, as if that had been the pivotal moment in my life when I could or should have done something differently.

Maybe, if I hadn't let her leave–if I'd yelled back and hurled awful accusations...or if I'd been faster.

If I'd marched out to the car and pulled their bags out; taken the keys from her hand and refused to let them go...

All things I'd considered thousands of times.

I parked in the driveway and sat with a hand over my eyes as the movie reel of memory unspooled sharp images of the awful moments again, the memories as jagged and painful as they'd always been.

It took me a minute to stop shaking, bracing my forearms against the steering wheel of the truck as I tried to wipe the vision from my eyes.

My knees were a little unsteady when I finally climbed out of the truck and made the short trip to the kitchen door. I unlocked it and let myself inside. In my mind's eye I could still see the wreckage from the stack of plates Lydia had thrown at me, and how it had taken me three days to pull myself together enough to clean up the mess, feeling like I lost more with each piece I stacked into the trash bin.

It wasn't lost on me that there were some people you could never really know. I'd met Lydia on the first day of third grade and had fallen instantly in love with her dark hair and deceptively sweet smile.

Dumb little shit.

I'd been hopelessly devoted to her for nearly thirty years before she'd let it slip that her mistake hadn't been a mistake at all, it had been a conscious choice. She'd chosen Harrison, my childhood friend and business partner, over me years earlier.

She just forgot to tell me.

Anger burned in my gut, a feeling that had shown up only recently and though Gerry was convinced it was healthy–it meant I was "advancing through the stages of grief," she said–it was annoying. It just meant I walked around ready to punch things at the slightest provocation.

It meant I was hard on gentle people, like Natalie.

It meant I didn't have many friends and though my pursuits had almost always been solitary, it might have been nice to have a few more decent humans in my life.

The cat let herself in through the small door and blinked up at me in confusion. She wasn't used to me being home so early and she sauntered down the hallway toward the laundry room to check her food bowl. I could hear her crunching away at leftover kibble as I climbed the stairs to the second floor. It wasn't yet time for dinner, but I could punish myself with a hard workout and some angry music.

So I did.

NINE

Natalie

I didn't hear from Thomas the next day.

Or the next.

Or the next.

I started checking my mailbox, thinking maybe he'd done another stealth estimate for the skylights, but there was nothing there.

A million things were running through my head: *You scared him away.*

He's ashamed and now he doesn't want to come back.

He's figured out what a mess you are.

I threw myself into the quick, temporary redo of my bedroom. I pre-drilled everything for curtains and put in the anchors, then I threw down a dropcloth and painted it. It took all day for the paint to dry, with the poor little fan cranking away, and in the waning light of day I installed the chandelier I'd pulled out of my office in Boston.

The afternoon of the fourth day after Plategate, Gerry showed up at my door with a pie in her hand. Curiously, it was lemon meringue. I invited her in and gestured toward the pie. She nodded eagerly, so I pulled some iced tea from the fridge and cut the pie into generous slices and pulled the whipped topping from the fridge, noting ruefully that there was a dusty smear along the front of the label.

"How did you know lemon was my favorite?" I asked, and her eyes twinkled.

"I have my ways," she said sweetly, and she proceeded to tell me she was of the opinion my new roof was solid and weatherproof, completed with an attention to detail one didn't often see.

"That storm that blew through a couple days ago had me nervous." I smiled. "But I'd already taken all the buckets out of my room, so thank God it stayed dry."

Gerry asked if there was a lot of water damage and I told her the discoloration on the ceiling of my bedroom had inspired me to institute a temporary fix known as painting. Then, finishing my pie, I led her up the stairs to show her my project of the last few days and she caught her breath. "This is beautiful, Natalie! It's elegant and serene. This is a real oasis." She was admiring the large painting hanging across from the bed, a cityscape of Florence, painted from a snapshot I'd taken during spring break my junior year of university.

When I mentioned I'd asked Thomas to install skylights and pointed out where, she chuckled a little. "You'll be waiting for a little while yet. When he's here he keeps himself pretty busy: lots of odd jobs, and then he has a garden, and he works on his place...but he travels a lot for business."

I had no idea his roofing skills were in such demand. I shrugged a little, feeling marginally better about the silence of the past few days. My heart didn't flutter in a panic over the thought I might have driven him away and I heaved a sigh of relief. "Thank God," I admitted to her with a shaky laugh. "He's so...withdrawn. I thought maybe I was too much for him and I scared him away."

Gerry's expression took on something knowing and I didn't like it. "Natalie, deep down he is a wonderful man. He's kind, protective and caring, and he loves hard. I've known him for a long time and I can tell you that he hides behind anger and bluster because he's been deeply wounded. He's been hiding it for so long, I don't know that he knows how to find himself again. He's been going through the motions, keeping people at an arm's length while figuring things out. It's going to take a lot of time and patience." She paused. "He's...well, the best way to describe it is that he's best treated with the caution you might reserve for a wild animal. He has to be tamed again."

"Tame him?" My laugh came out as a snort. "Gerry, I think I may have given you the wrong impression. I am in no position to be chasing a man I've just met. I think he just needs a friend."

She looked at me thoughtfully, as if I'd said something that had never occurred to her, and a slow smile spread across her face. "You're right. That is something he most certainly needs, but be ready for him to put up a fight. I'm not sure he remembers how to be a friend, he's been a loner for so long."

I shrugged again. "I totally get that."

The wife must have left him.

I crossed the room to straighten a picture frame that was hanging at a slight angle and driving me nuts. "I've been having a hard time with people lately, too. It takes a while to ease back into the social expectations most people have of me."

"I think you're doing just fine." Gerry smiled kindly. Then she trailed back down the stairs and I thought she was heading for the front door, but she walked into the living room instead and plopped down on the sofa. I took one of the club chairs across from her, feeling like I might be settling in for an interrogation.

She went fairly easy on me, asking about my family background, my education and work experience. She mentioned she'd accidentally gotten a piece of my mail and that led her to Google me, which brought her to my site. She'd been impressed by what she found and asked gently if she might recommend my design and staging services to some friends who were considering redecorating their very large home.

I should have been overjoyed, I knew, but I was hesitant to say yes. I'd become comfortable hiding out in my little house on the edge of town, only venturing out for food when it became absolutely necessary.

Even I knew I had to get back on the horse at some point. My bank account wouldn't hold up forever and living under the looming threat of an expensive divorce made me realize I was going to have to abandon my solitary ways and get my ass out there. My posts hadn't been regular and revenue wasn't exactly pouring in, so it was time to stop sulking and get back to it.

Over the course of the next week, I posted an update to my site about my bedroom refresh, complete with some before and after photos.

Gerry put me in touch with her friends and I met with Christa to tour her palatial home and to view, photograph and measure the rooms she wished to revamp. We spent an afternoon discussing color, pattern and texture preferences, lighting, accents, furniture and how the rooms would flow with the rest of the house. By the time I left, I'd provided her with a sweeping estimate and we shook on it. I told her I'd provide her a more detailed estimate over the next few days, as there was a considerable amount of research I needed to complete, thanks to the notes I'd taken regarding finishes.

It was a full week later–two weeks since I'd last seen Thomas–when I pulled into my driveway late one evening to find him up on my roof. I parked the car in front of the garage and walked around to the side of the house, my heels sinking into the sandy dirt.

"You're back," I called up to him and he snapped a tape measure shut.

"Sure am," he answered, scrawling something quickly onto a scrap of paper and tucking the pencil back behind his ear. He disappeared then, over the ridgeline, and I heard the metallic clank of a ladder being loaded into a truck bed. It was enough to draw me back to the driveway and I found him leaning against the tailgate with a pad of paper and a serious look on his face.

He looked up quickly as my heels tapped on the concrete and he didn't try to hide the look of surprise. "You're all cleaned up."

"It's like being struck by lightning." I looked down at my navy pencil skirt, white silk shell and nude heels. "Statistically improbable, but it has been documented." I grinned.

My favorite tortoiseshell sunglasses held my hair off my face, tiny diamond studs winking at him in the waning light of day. I hadn't dressed this way in months, but today I'd been on the job, poring over websites and catalogs with Christa, placing custom orders.

"I was on a design job today," I said, setting my heavy shoulder bag on the tailgate next to him and leaning in to see what he was sketching. He smelled warm and clean, like sandalwood soap and dryer sheets, and I left only a few inches between us as I watched while he worked.

"You smell nice," I said easily, and the corner of his mouth lifted a little.

"My laundry detergent gets the ladies every time. Who knew mountain freshness was such an aphrodisiac?"

"That's not your laundry detergent," I said, finally close enough to recognize the smell. Australian sandalwood and black pepper. And something else I couldn't place: something warm and delicious that probably didn't have a name at all.

He flipped the paper so I could see his quick sketch of the roof of my house, complete with measurements, two yawning rectangles on one side. "How do you know that?"

I answered without thinking. "My–uh, someone I used to know...he wears the same one."

Thomas took an experimental sniff of his underarm. "That's surprising. This one's pretty fancy. My wife used to buy it for me at this ridiculously overpriced little apothecary in New York every time she went to the city. Somewhere in Soho, I think. She'd bring back like six of them in her suitcase." He was smiling, and then he wasn't. "Now I just order it online."

"You must like it then," I said, afraid to push but wishing he'd disclose just a little more.

"Nah," he said. "It's probably just habit. It's what I know. She liked the way it smelled and it works well, so there's no sense in changing it up."

I'd been picking up on the past tense for a while, but he hadn't asked about my slip so I wouldn't ask about his. It was eating me up inside, though.

"Sayad," he said suddenly and I snapped to attention, all my nerve endings crackling with an uncomfortable electricity. "That's an unusual last name for someone who looks like you." He was looking at me down his shoulder. "If I had to guess, there's not a drop of Arabic blood in you, Blondie."

I swallowed hard. He'd gotten my check, then.

A check I'd mailed to him for the invoice he'd never sent.

A check that remained uncashed.

Folding my arms over my chest, I motioned with one finger toward his sketch. "Tell me where to order the windows."

He was still looking at me, something on his face that might have been amusement when I didn't try to respond to what had been carefully worded as a non-question sort of question.

"I have your skylights. The people I bought my house from left some sitting in the garage. They left me the plans and everything, but I thought they looked stupid, so I never put them in. Turns out they're the perfect size for your house."

My eyes grew round. I didn't want favors. "I'll pay you for them," I said firmly, and he laughed.

"What for? They're just sitting in my garage. If anything, you're helping me clear out some space. About time, too. I was too lazy to sell them and I want to turn the garage into a decent workshop. I just haven't gotten around to that part yet."

It was almost too good to be true: two expensive skylights for nothing but the cost of labor. "That's ridiculous," I sputtered. "You know how much those windows cost and you should be trying to sell them to me to make a profit."

"Are you trying to talk me out of it?"

I fussed a little, my hands drawing frantic circles in the air. "That's...it's too nice, Thomas. There's no reason to do that."

"Well..." he stretched slowly and a wicked grin crept across his face. "Then we'll swap. How about you trade me some dinner for my windows?"

I glanced at the face of his watch and rolled my eyes. "Well played, sir. Well. Played. Show up at dinnertime to give an estimate? You knew exactly what you were doing." I slapped his shoulder with an open hand before I thought about it and I winced. Touching him was a bad idea and even the briefest contact sent currents of electricity up my arm.

"What?" His tone of voice suggested I'd done him injury. "I wasn't just going to show up and barge in, but I flew in this afternoon and...well, there was a frozen pizza in my freezer and it just was *not* calling my name today. It seemed like the perfect time for an estimate."

I seized on the tiny morsel of information, though it wasn't really news, thanks to Gerry. "Flew in?"

"Yup. I travel with some regularity."

"I had no idea your roofing skills were in such demand," I teased, hoisting my bag back onto my shoulder.

I'd already caught sight of the small number on the paper and I couldn't help but think he felt like he owed me something because again, his estimate was laughably low.

He didn't say anything, lifting his shoulders in a tiny shrug and he stood to latch the tailgate, following me toward the house with his paper and pencil in hand.

Unlocking the door, I let him in behind me and sniffed the air experimentally. It smelled obnoxious, like an entire box of dryer sheets had spontaneously combusted somewhere in the house.

Thomas almost had to sit down when I pulled the crusty loaf of bread from the refrigerator. "You *made* that?" He said it with such awe–reverence, really–that I wondered if I'd somehow negotiated world peace.

"Don't let my secrets out," I laughed. "Before I decided on design school, I actually completed a year of culinary training. Apparently it took me a whole year to realize that I liked cooking and baking for fun, and to feed the people I loved, but I didn't actually want to work in a restaurant–and no way in hell do I have the patience or the skill to be a personal chef."

Popping the bread into the oven to warm, I took a stick of butter from the fridge and slid the pot of soup onto a burner. "Sorry it's not exciting," I said. "Tonight is all about easy comfort food, because it was a long day and I'm tired."

There was a thoughtful expression on his face. "My little sister is a personal chef, and home cooked food has always been something comforting to all the kids in my family. Then again, it's probably because I'm appreciative of something I don't have."

"Come on, Thomas. Your wife doesn't cook at all?" By now I was eighty-nine percent certain there was no wife.

"She doesn't...didn't...uh..." He looked down at his shoes and I knew he was waiting for me to jump all over him with questions. Instead, I stirred the soup and gave him the out he was searching for.

"Want to grab the bowls out of that cabinet? I'm short," I said, pointing, and he rushed over to grab bowls, small plates, glasses and silverware before walking everything out to the dining room.

Oh, we're going fancy tonight.

I heard a startled exclamation of surprise from the dining room and I waited for him to reappear in the kitchen. When he didn't, I poked my head around the doorway and was punched in the nose by the offensive smell.

Sitting on the table was the most enormous proliferation of stinky flowers I'd seen in my life. They were so voluminous that no matter where one sat at the small dining table, the petals obscured the view in every direction.

"Wow," he said as I walked into the dining room. "Someone must have screwed up really, really, *really* bad. My guess is that whoever the asshole is, he wants you back."

My heart fell. He was right about the screwing up part and I knew exactly who they were from. The question was how they'd gotten to my dining room table when I'd been gone all day.

"Let's eat in the kitchen," I suggested quickly, wanting to turn my back on the half-assed apology flowers as quickly as possible.

Ahmad wants something, but it sure as hell isn't me.

We ate quietly, and this time the silence was comfortable, which was weird considering the questions the flowers probably should have invited. He sat beside me, spreading butter across yet another piece of bread and sighing contentedly when he bit into it.

I stole a sidelong glance at him. I was far too messy. The flowers on the table proved that. They proved that my husband had finally figured something out: the money I made was no longer being deposited into the joint account he ruled with a despotic fist, denying me access to my own earnings.

It meant he'd finally figured out I'd sold my business and hadn't deposited the earnings into our shared account.

Maybe he'd finally figured out that I'd opened a separate bank account and had slowly funneled my revenue stream into it in increments before leaving him. Right now he couldn't touch it and though the flowers suggested he was attempting a reconciliation, I knew it was something else entirely: Ahmad was on the warpath.

TEN

Thomas

The air in the room changed the instant Natalie saw the flowers. She went from sweet and playful to freaked out and withdrawn inside of three seconds flat and it finally, *finally* occurred to me that she might not be all sunshine and rainbows. That kind of made me like her more.

I was back to California only two days later for an emergency board meeting, the skylights still leaning against the wall in Natalie's garage.

I'd had to leave quickly, with very little notice, and Gerry called just as I checked into my hotel room to tell me to get my ass back to Natalie's place as soon as I got back to Alabama. She'd been to see Natalie, she said, and the woman was convinced she'd scared me away.

"Who is this?" I teased after Gerry completed her diatribe and, as it always did, it pulled her up short. She'd never gotten used to being teased; she said it was my dry delivery.

"You very well know who this is, young man," she huffed.

Uh-oh, *young man*, which I was not anymore. That meant I was in trouble.

"There is a sweet, beautiful, seemingly unattached woman living next door to me and it's about time your miserable, grumpy, moping ass got *off* your ass and took notice of the fact."

I really hated it when Gerry tried to convince me I was wasting my life on no one and nothing important. Besides, I had work to keep me busy.

Projects to complete.

Weeds to pull.

Programs to write.

Meetings to convene.

A cat to feed.

Serious decisions to consider and votes to cast.

I didn't have time for many things, and I wasn't going to *make* time for more. Besides, Natalie's windows (where had I come up with this stupid idea?) were already going to cut into a large chunk of time I'd scheduled to finish up a project I was working on with a graduate team at Stanford.

"I'm an adult now, Gerry," I reminded her, slightly less afraid of her when I was over two thousand miles away. "I don't need someone to run interference. I don't need projects or distractions, and I sure as hell don't need a girlfriend."

She made a noise in my ear. "That's exactly what you need, you foolish boy. You're one of the smartest, most successful people I've ever known, but you have the social skills of a rabid cat. Stop biting every hand that tries to pet you, Thomas."

I decided to forego the reference to what I saw as obviously sexual, because she wouldn't have found it funny anyway.

Having seen the flowers firsthand, I questioned Gerry's assessment of Natalie's relationship situation, as it hadn't initially appeared Natalie was remotely attached. She didn't wear a wedding band or an engagement ring, but I knew one thing: Those were *I Fucked Up* flowers. They were *Take My Sorry Ass Back* flowers. They were tall and showy and smelly and probably just the sort of thing a woman liked: Dramatic.

I snorted, because I was being ridiculous.

She hadn't swooned or exclaimed in happy surprise. In fact, thinking back to the look in her eyes when she'd poked her head around the corner...yeah, that hadn't been a happy look. I'd never seen a woman look at flowers like that before, like she wanted to light them on fire and dropkick the flaming mass out of her house.

I sighed, shelving the memory as I considered tacking a few days onto the end of my trip, to drive the short distance to the Sonoma house. It was where I felt the most at peace, shut away from the traffic of Palo Alto.

Cocooned from the bustle of San Francisco.

Just me and the quiet house and the huge, rolling vineyard.

Well, and the Jensens of course, the home's caretakers. The two of them were quiet and efficient, the house kept neat without the fuss and clatter of banging pots or a whirring vacuum.

Perfectly mixed drinks always awaited me in the living room at five p.m. on the dot. (Personal research led me to conclude that Jensen himself mixed the drinks, but how they materialized in the living room I still had no idea. That part required additional research.)

I thought about sitting in the large hot tub at night, gazing up at the burning white stars before climbing the polished ebony stairs to crash into the huge four-poster bed. I slept well there, dreamlessly, the ghosts that followed me everywhere typically too jetlagged to find me in the big bed until I'd been there for several days.

In the end, I decided to keep my original flight back to Alabama. If anything, I needed to dispense with the obligation I'd created for myself: I needed to get the skylights in and then I needed to shut the tailgate on my truck and Drive. The fuck. Away.

ELEVEN

Natalie

While Thomas worked on installing skylights the next few days, I plotted as to how I was going to rope him into Christa's job with me. I needed manpower, and though I was reasonably capable and we weren't knocking down any walls or running new wiring, I had zero feel for the local labor market. I was still learning local codes and I had no crew.

Thomas put up no fight whenever I called that food was ready, and his appetite was good for my ego. There was nothing I put in front of the man that wasn't met with an expression of absolute delight, especially desserts, and I found myself devoting more and more time to cooking and baking between projects.

I'd been avoiding the flower arrangement for days, knowing there was a carefully worded card buried somewhere in that monstrous proliferation of blooms. They were stinking up my house, filling it with a cloying smell I'd never liked: lilies. Ahmad knew I hated them. I hated the way they smelled and the way they dropped pollen everywhere, so it made perfect sense that lilies comprised the bulk of the arrangement.

This was his warning shot.

It had been almost ten days since the arrival of the flowers, followed shortly by Thomas's total disappearance for five days. But he was upstairs, in my room, making some last adjustments when I finally decided to read the card.

I needed to know what I was up against.

"Natalie," he called on his way down the stairs, his footsteps heavy and the third step creaked. "I know it's killing you. Come take a look at these beauties. It's like they were made for your place."

He wandered into the dining room, looking for me, and I heard him swallow hard when he saw my face.

I was on the floor, my head leaned back against the wall, my eyes closed.

I was just going to hide here for another minute.

Sinking down beside me, he said nothing. He just sat there and waited. I could feel his discomfort and I tried to swallow, dashing the moisture from my cheeks with the back of my fingers. "Sorry," I croaked. "Stupid fucking flowers." I crumpled the card in my fist and pitched it toward the table.

He said nothing, wrapping warm fingers around my bare knee and squeezing gently. It felt good to be touched by another human in a comforting way, even if his fingers made me all tingly. It reminded me that we were very careful not to touch one another at all times: no hugs or accidental brushes. We were exceedingly cautious not to bump into one another in the kitchen, which meant this was intentional.

I ran my fingers through my hair and huffed a frustrated sigh. "I thought I'd run far enough. I didn't post any details about where I landed. I don't do my banking here, all my bills are in my maiden name, and I haven't switched my car registration. I use an IP address randomizer. The house is in a trust...the only thing I can think of is that he hired a P.I." I rubbed the heels of my hands into my eyes, remembering too late that I was wearing mascara.

"You're hiding from someone?" He sounded incredulous and I laughed a little.

"I think I might be hiding from everyone," I responded. Then I pushed to my feet, holding out a hand to help him up. He ignored it, pushing himself up with a fist pressed to the battered hardwood.

"I've been hiding for a while too," he said finally and I turned to look at him. I was already halfway out of the room and into the kitchen, but he stood where he'd risen to his feet. "I can tell you right now that it won't do you any good to live like you're waiting for the other shoe to drop. Trust me on this."

He held out a hand to me and I looked at him in surprise. "Come see."

Following him up the stairs, it occurred to me that under any other circumstances I'd have been delighted to be holding his hand as we climbed the stairs to my bedroom. But as it was, my face was swollen and I'd just alluded to a sordid past.

I also hadn't waxed in a month and the sight of my neglected bare feet would probably send him running.

Thomas had sealed off the door to my bedroom two days before and told me I wasn't allowed to peek, so I'd slept on the tiny twin daybed shoved into the corner of my office. It had been miserable, the air flow even worse in the smaller room, and I'd dragged another box fan up the stairs from the garage.

"No peeking," he warned as he reached for the doorknob, and I put one hand over my eyes, not at all eager to let go of his big hand. Something about such a small point of contact was weirdly comforting.

"Okay," he said finally, shuffling me carefully into place and I suspected we were along the wall at the far end of the room. "See for yourself."

I opened my eyes slowly, trying to get used to the extraordinary amount of light in the room.

When I looked up, my mouth dropped open and I couldn't catch my breath. Not only had he installed the skylights, but he'd also put in two large windows along what had previously been a blank wall.

How had he known?

The room was bright and airy and while I tried to find the right words to express my gratitude, my jaw just randomly opening and closing, he dropped my hand to give me a remote.

"This way you can shut the blinds when it gets too hot." He leaned a little closer, pressing a button and I watched slats drop into place across the skylights. "And these..." he gestured toward the new windows along the wall. "I kind of made a big assumption." He looked a little nervous. "I saw the drawings on your desk, and..."

"You had more spare windows," I laughed, aware that it sounded a little hollow.

"No, you did. That little shed behind the house is packed with all kinds of crazy stuff–I guess now I have to admit I snooped. Haven't you ever checked it out? I'm going to dig through more of it later.

"The realtor who bought this house years ago, right before the crash, was stockpiling stuff in the shed. I have no idea why he left all of it, but you've got some neat things in there. Including these beauties." He gestured toward the windows which, from what I could see, were pristine double-panes.

I didn't know what to say and before I could catch myself, I felt a fresh rush of tears making their way down my cheeks. It made me feel like an idiot. He was going to think I didn't like it, but I didn't trust my voice to say anything.

"You okay, Natalie? Did I do something wrong?" He was looking at me uncomfortably, like he knew I needed a hug but he'd rather give me a kidney than touch me again. I wrapped my arms around myself instead and shook my head, closing my eyes again and leaning back against the wall. He'd done something kind and I'd needed something kind, but kindness reminded me of just how alone I was.

This beautiful bedroom was mine and mine alone. No one else would ever see it. All I could think of was how lonely I was, and had been for a really long time, even if I was less lonely outside the confines of my dead marriage.

"I'll just go dig through the shed a bit," he said uncomfortably, excusing himself from the room.

He was back in the house an hour later, cobwebs in his hair and dirt smeared down his handsome face. "Natalie!" he called as he rushed in through the side door, into the kitchen. "You're not gonna believe the stuff in there!"

I had been sitting at the desk in my hot little office, staring at the screen of my laptop. Today the words weren't coming and though I had plenty of story ideas and articles to pitch, videos to make and a few things to edit, it felt like I had nothing to work with. I had no inspiration or confidence or focus, whatsoever.

Now seemed like a good time for a tall glass of iced coffee, so when he came tearing through the door I was already assembling things.

"I think some of the things in there are original to the house," he was babbling excitedly. "Casement windows and some really gorgeous stained glass...there are some pocket doors and original knobs, too."

Now was my moment and I knew it.

"Thank God you're as interested in this stuff as I am," I grinned, pulling a pitcher of cold coffee from the fridge and watching his face wrinkle in confusion as he tried to figure out what I was going to do with it. "Because I could use your help. I've taken on a project for Christa Masters and although I know how to paint and hang curtains on my own, she has this insane chandelier that I need help hanging. Oh...and she wants the French doors ripped out and replaced with pocket doors. I wouldn't mind some help with those monsters."

Thomas was looking at me like I'd grown another head.

"I don't know anyone here," I explained, pulling a tall glass from the cabinet and filling it with ice. "I don't have a feel for the local labor market, not at all. I don't know any other contractors or their prices, or whether they can do half the things they'll certainly promise. But you..." I added whole milk to the glass, and a glug of maple syrup, before pouring in the coffee. He was still watching the process in fascination. "You're my guy."

"What?" That shook him out of it. He looked startled.

"I need to borrow you for an afternoon to help me hang a chandelier and I can't very well install the doors by myself. I'll pay you for it."

He had moved closer and his hand shot out to take the iced coffee from me, bringing it to his mouth for a long chug before he handed it back.

Now it was my turn to look shocked, and I looked down at the half empty glass in astonishment.

"I haven't had an iced coffee since..." he thought back for a moment. "The IMPACT conference. Wow...that one was something." He was a million miles away again.

Where the hell had that come from?

I handed the glass back to him. "It won't kill me to make another. You can finish it."

I didn't point out the obvious, that he seemed to be intentionally ingesting an addictive substance, and while he took a solo trip down memory lane, I mixed another.

"So, why no addictive substances?" I asked slowly, wondering if I was going to get another lecture about minding my own business.

"Long story." He looked down into his glass and I knew that was his way of telling me nicely that he didn't want to talk about it.

I filed the outburst away in my memory banks for later, when I could Google the IMPACT conference. It felt like the first clue he'd given me as to who he really was. Or maybe, I thought with a start, it was a clue to who he *had been*. Either way, there was a clue and since he didn't exactly sprinkle those around like a kindergartener with glitter, I held onto that one tight.

"So, when do you need me at the Masters' place to help out?" he asked suddenly, setting his glass in the sink.

"I've already packed up both rooms and most of the orders are starting to trickle in–you should see her garage right now. I told her I'd be there to paint and start styling things by Friday.

"She's doing two rooms and they're big, so I'd say it's going to take me about a solid week between the two of them and I figured I'd hang the chandelier last. Do you need a firm date?"

He looked weirdly uncomfortable. "I can help you paint, but I'm no good at the girly stuff. That's all you. But if we work together we can cut the time in half and get the whole thing done before I have to leave."

That part, where he went when he left, was still a baffling mystery.

"I'm flying out for work again in ten days, so if you want this job done fast I suggest we do it before I go. I don't know how long I'm gone this time–not yet, anyway."

I wanted to ask him where he was going and why, and he knew it, because he had that *Don't ask* look on his face, so I left it at that. If I started prying he had every right to do the same, and there were a lot of things I wasn't going to be ready to say out loud for a long time.

TWELVE

Thomas

Why did I keep roping myself into this shit? She asked for an inch and I gave twelve damn miles, like I had all the time in the world to just donate to Natalie's charity. And I didn't, in fact. I had deadlines to meet, and some of them were pretty solid.

I did not miss deadlines, and I wasn't about to start now.

I couldn't be honest with myself without getting scared, because I didn't like the way Natalie was worming her way into my days. (For the record, I was a little more ok with the way she'd wormed her way into my nights. I'd had a couple really interesting dreams already that had resulted in being unable to look her directly in the eye for a few days.)

But we were friends. Friends helped one another. Besides, she'd practically turned her house into a soup kitchen for my sake and God knew I couldn't get enough of her cooking.

I'd been starved for real food and care for years, subsisting on takeout, conference food, sandwiches during board meetings, continental breakfasts...and as for care, well...sometimes Lydia threw me a bone, but more often than not I was left to my own devices.

When I got home that afternoon, I set up a video conference with my legal counsel. Then I dove straight into several hours of video chat with my Stanford team. We were finally testing a new program we'd written, at some considerable personal expense. I expected to present it to the world in a few months, a collaborative software program to be used within the medical field.

I had designed the integrative app myself, which dovetailed into the larger program to be housed on server space I would donate and maintain, to major medical institutions. The cost was tremendous, though I could write off most of the expenses.

That wasn't why I was doing it, though. This project was my baby and every student, every professor, every tech consultant involved in the project, had signed an NDA.

It wasn't so much about the leaking of proprietary information as it was that I didn't want the *idea* of it leaked, or even whispered about, before it was one hundred percent complete and flawless.

It would be my legacy, the culmination of two years of slavish work.

It was a memorial project of sorts.

It was long past dark by the time I turned off the monitors in my office and I spent just a few minutes lifting and going through some basic stretches and calisthenics, just to keep the machine well oiled. A day without a workout left me feeling cagey and restless, and like Smitty hit the bar at 5:15 every night, I could be found in my home gym.

There were worse addictions, I supposed.

As usual, I slept fitfully that night. Natalie didn't visit my dreams, but the ghosts did.

How could even the living souls haunt me?

I was up early, back at the weights because I couldn't sleep and instead of coffee or breakfast or anything that made sense, I pushed myself to exhaustion on the giant machine before I moved to the treadmill to run until the sun started to creep into the room.

Natalie had noticed I wasn't sleeping. She hadn't said as much, but I'd seen the disapproving look on her face when she tried to hand me the coffee I almost always refused. She didn't like that I showed up at 6:30 to start working on the projects I kept inventing for myself at her house, although she was an early riser too.

My phone buzzed suddenly and after hitting the three-mile mark on the treadmill, I slowed for a moment, just long enough to consider myself cooled down before I turned the machine off and moved toward my desk.

I couldn't imagine who would be texting me so early.

It was my sister, Finn, working her way toward her own happily ever after and if I hadn't been so damned happy for her, I'd have been insanely jealous.

I responded quickly and went downstairs to make something I could pretend was breakfast.

Dropping into the chair behind the six monitors, most of them mounted to the wall, I flicked on two of them and tied up a couple loose ends before I made a phone call to schedule a flight.

I confirmed a noon takeoff and rushed down the hallway to shower and pack a bag.

THIRTEEN

Natalie

Thomas left me alone the rest of the week, though I texted several times to check on him.

I began to worry that he thought I was trying to lure him in and he was successfully resisting.

Was I trying to lure him in?

I knew my kitchen was the key to his very damaged heart, or at least one of the keys–the only one I'd figured out so far. But it seemed unfair to use something so basic against him, so I reminded myself once again that we were *just friends*.

On Friday morning I arrived at the Masters' home a few minutes early, totally expecting to be stood up after Thomas's radio silence of the past few days. I didn't know why it surprised me or, really, why it sort of hurt my feelings. I mean, I knew the man needed his space and I was starting to understand that if something made him feel uncomfortable, he needed to back away for a while.

His truck pulled up next to my little Subaru and I looked over to see him climbing quickly out of the cab. Something about him didn't seem right, I thought as I caught a glimpse of his face. There was something hollow about his expression and though I'd been feeding him well up until Monday, there was a gauntness to him, as if the last meal he'd eaten had been in my kitchen days before.

I got out of my car and piled my hair on top of my head, skewering it with a pencil. Today was not my most glamorous, I thought, looking down at the battered overalls I always wore for painting, simply because they provided great coverage. They were soft with age and frequent washes, some places hardened due to repeated paint spills.

When I opened the hatch to start pulling out supplies, he came up beside me without a word and grabbed two of the five-gallon paint buckets, trailing behind me as I carried brushes and rollers and trays toward the house.

We made the trip again and again, until I had emptied the car of all my supplies.

The drop cloth was already down in the sitting room, since I'd come over the previous afternoon to tape things off.

As I peeled the lid off the first paint bucket, Thomas poured it into two separate trays and handed me the extension handle for one of the rollers. He still hadn't said a word, and I nodded to him in thanks. Somehow, speaking first seemed like it would either break the spell or grate on his ears and I wasn't sure I wanted either of those things to happen.

We painted in silence, each starting at opposite ends of the room. The *whoosh-whoosh* of the rollers was hypnotic and we worked quickly, meeting in the middle eventually. Without communicating that we were at a stopping point, we both wrapped our trays to keep the rollers moist while we broke for lunch.

The cicadas clacked lazily as we walked toward our respective vehicles and without asking if I could join him, I retrieved the cooler from my car and lowered the tailgate on his truck while he fished around for something in the cab.

By the time he'd closed the door and realized I was unloading food, I had a neat pile of containers drawing an imaginary line between where I would sit and where he would sit.

He still didn't say anything, walking slowly around the truck and hoisting himself up to sit on the tailgate on his side of the line. He set something beside him then, partially hidden by his thigh, and I thought they were two sad little waxed paper-wrapped squares.

He didn't eat nearly as much as I knew he could, his shoulders folded forward, and when he set down his dish and leaned back on his hands, I opened the cooler again. His eyes followed as I reached in and pulled out two glass containers, both stuffed to the top with rhubarb pie.

Handing him a container and a fresh fork, I dug into my own without waiting for him to start. Out of the corner of my eye I could see that while he seemed to be eating, it was swallowing that was causing him great difficulty and I kicked myself for not packing something to drink. Unless...that wasn't what was causing the problem.

He cleared the trash while I packed the dishes, and when he snapped the tailgate closed on the truck it was understood it was time to get back to work.

Again, he trailed after me into the house and I tried not to let him hear me sigh. Whatever this was, there had to be a way to break him out of his funk.

I slipped my phone from the center pocket of my overalls to text Christa about her sound system.

While Thomas unwrapped the trays and filled them with another dose of paint, I located the expensive control panel and said a prayer of thanks for Def Leppard. At least the music would eat up the painful silence, and if he was really lucky I might just break into song as I painted.

He hardly looked surprised when the first notes rang out over the expansive speaker system, and I grinned at him as I stuck the roller into the tray and coated it with paint. He had no idea what kind of a good time he was in for, as when I listened to Def Leppard I danced really, really badly. It was more of a hip shuffle, really. Weird gyrations and wiggles, because I had absolutely no sense of rhythm.

So while Joe asked if we were ready to get rocked, poured some sugar on me and got hysterical, I painted with weird twitches that suggested I was suffering a seizure. But then...shit. I'd forgotten about the slower stuff, the songs I supposed people called ballads.

In a cruel twist of fate, "Love Bites" played back-to-back with "Have You Ever Needed Someone So Bad."

There was a stretching, aching feeling in my chest when I saw his shoulders sag and I wanted to crawl under the drop cloths and hide. Instead, I did the very mature thing and looked away quickly. I didn't look back until I heard something over the music that sounded like a curse, and I looked over my shoulder to see his roller on the floor and him rapidly retreating from the room.

When I finished painting, satisfied we'd done a thorough job of it, I wrapped the trays again and turned down the music. The house went silent for a long stretch between songs, almost eerily so, and I let myself outside to go in search of him.

Not to my benefit, the Masters had a huge property that backed right out onto the beach. It meant I had several acres of intricate landscaping to search if I hoped to find him, and when I didn't find him near his truck, I started to wander down toward the waterfront.

There was a fairly dense wall of trees and hedges between the beach and the house, which likely acted as a deterrent to drifting beach walkers, and as I neared them I heard a repeated, muffled sound and a sharp curse. I caught sight of Thomas just in time to see him execute a vicious jab at a tree trunk.

"Hey," I called softly and he spun around to face me. His hair was a mess and his eyes were wild.

Maybe Gerry had been right. He certainly did *look* feral. His shoulders were heaving with deep, hard breaths and I looked down at the fist he hadn't relaxed, not surprised to see blood dripping from his knuckles into the mixture of weedy grass and soft sand.

"No," he hissed when I finally stopped in front of him. "Don't touch me."

My eyes widened in surprise. That was probably exactly what my intent had been, I thought, and he'd interpreted my movements before I'd even registered the thought. It pushed me backward, some unseen hand, and I staggered a little as I put distance between us.

I felt like an ass, chastised and small, without knowing what it was I'd done to offend.

I had been the one to open the windows to the sitting room, to allow the paint to dry without stinking up the house, and Joe's voice drifted down the lawn.

But if Joe was two steps behind, I was about ninety. I had no idea how to reach this guy; how to draw him out of his shell. He kept tucking himself back into it, tightly, every time I thought he'd started to relax with me.

Turning so that I faced the water, I sank down at the edge of the lawn and planted my butt in the sand. This was the first time I'd seen the beach since moving here and I tried to find the peace that usually came over me when I was near water.

It turned out peace was on vacation today, probably bound for some stupid landlocked state, I thought, rolling my eyes to myself. It had been exceedingly elusive of late, and I wondered quickly how long Thomas had been searching for it.

Maybe he hadn't begun.

I sat there for a long time, doing my best not to look behind me. At that point, I wasn't even sure he was still there. He'd been silent since I plopped down and, rather than turn to look for him, I finally made two fists to push into the sand as I struggled to my feet.

He was there, leaning his back against the tree he'd been trying to murder. The blood had dried on his hand and I shook my head as I looked at him.

When I moved closer, so that he had no choice but to look at me, he flinched. "I told you not to touch me," he growled, and the sting of his words made me angry.

"I'm not touching you," I snapped, motioning to the distance between us that could have fit another person. "See? You. Me." I waved my hand between us. "Holy Spirit."

He rolled his beautiful eyes at me, damn him.

"Look...clearly you're going through something that's really got you messed up, and I'm sorry. I'm trying to be your friend, Thomas. I'd like to be able to help but it's pointless for me to ask questions you won't answer, so...I'm going to finish cleaning up inside."

There wasn't a lot left to clean up in the house and I folded the drop cloth, moving it to the dining room, the room I planned to paint the next day.

Christa wasn't home yet, so I closed the windows, turned on the ceiling fans and shut the doors to the room, leaving a note for her taped to the door.

No peeking! I'll be back tomorrow by nine.

After locking up the house, I crawled into the car. I waited for a moment, listening carefully and watching the yard. It worried me, to think of him sitting there by himself, and it did occur to me he could have thrown himself into the ocean. So I sat there pretending to go through my phone and respond to a few messages that had come in over the course of the day. But out of the corner of my eye I was watching to see whether he walked up from the beach.

When I caught movement in my peripheral vision, I lifted my head to see him opening the door to his truck. He wasn't looking at me–wouldn't look at me–and he started it up, pulling it quickly around the circular driveway and out onto the road even before he'd clipped his seatbelt.

I put pot pie in the oven when I got home, to warm it while I showered.

Since I wasn't trying to impress anyone, I swapped out my dirtied t-shirt and paint-splattered overalls for an old, soft pair of shorts and a baggy t-shirt. I felt bruised on the inside after being ignored all day and the soft old clothes didn't rub up against me and chafe my hurt feelings.

Dropping my smelly work clothes into the wash machine, I started the cycle before drifting back to the kitchen. It was already after seven and the sun's rays were growing longer as it crept toward sunset. It was unusually beautiful, the humidity holding onto the warm rays and turning them into something viscerally golden. It made me want to sit out on the tiny concrete slab off the kitchen door with a glass of wine, so I poured a crisp glass of white and sat on the step with condensation rapidly forming and running down the bowl of my wine glass.

The mosquitoes came out like a Mongolian horde as the sun dipped lower and as I shooed and swatted, the evening light began to lose its magic. I let them chase me inside and I added more to my glass as I looked at the clock. It was already after eight and dinner had been warm and waiting for a long time.

I fought against the urge to text him. It was obvious he wasn't coming. It filled me with frustration, because again I felt like I'd done something to chase him away.

I cut a portion of the pot pie to scoop into a large bowl. Then I put a large serving into a glass container and texted Gerry.

Gerry's response was quick and I shoved the bowl back into the oven to stay warm, grabbing the container and my keys off the hook by the door.

When my GPS indicated I had arrived, I put the car into park at the curb, looking up at the tall Colonial set back only a short distance from the road. It appeared freshly painted and there were flower boxes on all the windows, each filled with cheerful little blooms.

Getting out of my car with the container in hand, I froze as I realized that I wasn't absolutely, one hundred percent sure there *wasn't* a wife somewhere in that house.

I was in the middle of texting Gerry a very awkward question when I heard a door squeak open and I looked up to see Thomas backlit in his entryway. He'd showered too and was also wearing beaten old shorts and a t-shirt, only his clothes were fitted on account of the fact he was built like a freaking Greek sculpture.

Licking my lips self-consciously, I pushed myself off the fender of my car and marched up the short walk. Every step seemed obnoxiously loud as I grew closer to his porch and I climbed the stairs quickly, half convinced he might start to berate me right there on his front porch.

"You have to eat," seemed to be all I could get out as I shoved the container into his hands. "It's still warm." I held up a small plastic wrapped packet of disposable utensils, dropping them on top of the dish.

Turning quickly, I ran back down the steps and down the walk.

I didn't realize that I hadn't looked at his face even once until I was in the car, already starting the engine, and I glanced quickly up at the house to see him still standing in the door.

It took only a few moments to get home and, picking up my glass of warming wine, I splashed a little more in and retrieved my bowl from the oven. The pot pie would be dry and crumbly by now, I thought, but it seemed worth it. I felt like I'd done something nice for someone in need, even if he didn't recognize that he was in need.

After eating at the kitchen counter, I rinsed the few dishes and slotted them into the dishwasher.

It wasn't late, but I was tired, so I closed up the house and climbed the stairs, slipping out of my shorts and bra before washing my face and brushing my teeth.

Climbing right into the center of the bed, I stacked up pillows behind me and settled in with a book I'd been meaning to read for months. But the intro was slow and my eyes were heavy...and at some point I sank deeper into the pillows and the book took a wild flight toward my night table.

I didn't even care that the lamp was still on; tonight I needed a night light to keep the demons away.

FOURTEEN

Thomas

By the time I showed up at Christa's house, I was even more exhausted than usual. I had taken the last four days to travel to the west coast to meet with my lawyers, then attend an emergency board meeting.

While I was there I dropped in on a powerful friend who could perhaps exert some necessary influence.

The shittiest part of the whole awful trip? The day I left, I got an email from one of my lawyers. The one I'd employed to keep Harrison at an arm's length and off-balance.

I'd been walking around in an angry daze ever since.

Thomas, please know that we've done everything possible. We have exhausted every legal contingency and appeal. But, despite our efforts, the judge has sided in Harrison's favor and we have no further recourse.

Please take some time to brace yourself for what is to come and advise what we might do to be of assistance.

Assistance? Was he fucking kidding? I paid him and his team exorbitant amounts of money to keep things moving in my favor.

Smoothly.

Quietly.

This was unacceptable and I considered asking for my money back.

It wasn't Natalie's fault I could barely speak when I showed up to lend a hand. In fact, I was probably largely useless, considering what had transpired over the last few days. But if anything, I would keep my word to her. There was no reason to punish her just because my life had imploded again.

But that's exactly what I did. I couldn't tell her what was going on, because I couldn't talk. In fact, I could barely look her in the eye. She had enough of her own shit to handle without trying to make mine better too, because that was exactly what she would try to do and I knew it.

If I was learning anything about Natalie, it was that she was the sort of person who would cover your wounds with her own hands, even as she bled out.

I didn't know what to do with someone like that: gentle, caring, giving...I just didn't trust it.

I was such a wreck on my first day back, I took my anger out on one of the palm trees at the bottom of the property.

And her.

She'd looked so hurt when I snapped at her that I felt momentarily guilty. But only for that moment, because she was sticking her nose where it didn't belong. She was seeking me out when I didn't want to be sought, or found, or comforted, or...whatever.

I just wanted her to leave me alone.

But really, I didn't. So I went home that night to clean up my self-inflicted wounds and let her comfort me in my dreams.

FIFTEEN

Natalie

Since I suspected Thomas hadn't been eating at all the past few days, I took the chance he'd be hungry *if* he showed up at the Masters' place the next morning.

When I pulled into Christa's driveway to find him already there, we performed an awkward container swap as he handed over the dish I'd taken him the night before, and I handed him breakfast.

What was my obsession with feeding this man? I tried to think back, to pinpoint when it had come to signify caring. But examining my motives involved some uncomfortable realizations, and immediately I thought of the sour expression on Ahmad's mother's face the first time I'd met her, standing in his kitchen, cooking dinner for her.

I was too blonde, too short, too western and far too curvy.

Entirely too far beneath his station and completely unaware of my own.

She made sure I heard every word later, when she took Ahmad to task for not allowing her to find him a nice Saudi girl, and her voice rang out with acerbic clarity from the gracious living room he'd contracted me to decorate before we'd begun seeing one another.

The only thing his mother ever begrudgingly approved of was that I could cook. But even that received a sniff of disdain, because I didn't bother to cook the traditional Persian or Khaleeji dishes.

It's not that I never tried, but that I never tried when she came to visit, because that woman could find imperfection in God, Himself. I knew better than to subject myself to that level of scrutiny and derision, because that was all I'd ever get from her.

Thomas was already finished eating and I suspected he'd inhaled the breakfast wrap while I'd been spaced out on Memory Lane.

Since it was clear that we were still participating in Advanced Levels of Silence, and what a fun-filled game that was, I tucked the empty container into my car with a sigh and hurried toward the house. The faster we could paint the slightly smaller dining room, the better, since he could go home to finish his sulk.

Christa had left a note next to mine, letting me know that she and Jonesy had decamped on an impromptu scouting trip to Texas for a few days and they wouldn't be back until the middle of next week.

I handed the note to Thomas, rolling my eyes. Who names their kid Jonesy Masters? What was the guy, a yacht captain?

A golfer?

An artist with a secondary home in Chelsea?

"His real name is Jonas. Used to play for the Falcons. He's head coach for the Crimson Tide now. You know, U of A."

Well, that explained the scouting part.

I was shocked to hear Thomas's voice and I wondered if he'd said something because he'd been reading my thoughts. I just held up my hands in a shrug before turning to snap on a fresh roller and open a bucket of paint. After all, I was pretty sure he had spoken by accident.

This time I didn't make the mistake of cranking up the sound system, though I did crank open the windows. It made for an interminable quiet between the two of us as we dipped our rollers, then swished them across the walls.

We finished the first coat quickly and it wasn't even past eleven, but I was already hungry. So I wrapped up my roller in its tray and let myself out the front door to fetch the large cooler I'd packed full of lunch. Again. Because clearly I was a glutton for punishment.

I parked my butt in the middle of the room, right on top of the drop cloth, and unpacked the cooler.

He tried to feign disinterest as I kept reaching into the depths to bring out more and more, but he failed and eventually he wrapped up his own tray, walking over slowly to sit several feet away from me.

The BLT's were delicious, but the bread kept catching in my throat as I tried to swallow. I was nervous, the silence yawning and empty between us, and silence always activated my natural instinct to fill it up with words. But since Thomas had an adversarial relationship with talking, I filled my mouth with food to keep the words from falling out.

It was clear that I would be quite successful, because I was about to choke to death.

When he'd finished three sandwiches, a helping of macaroni salad, a handful of carrot sticks with hummus and a huge slice of chocolate silk pie, he groaned and stretched out right where he sat, leaning slowly until he'd stretched out on the floor.

When I returned from stashing the cooler in the car, he was still and I could tell by the rhythmic rise and fall of his chest that he had fallen asleep.

It made me think back to the nosy little lady at the supermarket, telling me that the lights burned in his house at all hours.

His face was relaxed, the tension finally gone from between his eyebrows and his lips parted just a little, showing his even white teeth hidden just beyond. He looked peaceful–and a lot younger, since he wasn't frowning, one hand splayed over his nicely broad chest.

I barely resisted the urge to crawl over to him and rest my head over his heart.

Giving him plenty of room, I lowered myself to the drop cloth covering the hard floor, rolling so that I was very nearly on my stomach, my forearm beneath my cheek. Just a few minutes of rest wouldn't hurt anyone, I figured. After all, we needed to give the first coat a few more minutes to properly set, and it wouldn't take us long at all to put up the second one.

When I woke again, it was to the sound of a paint roller swishing across a wall and I blinked slowly, stretching out and trying to shake off the confused fatigue of a deeper sleep than I'd expected.

Rising slowly and working some kinks out of my compressed rib cage, I unwrapped my tray and joined him. He paused as he heard the sound of my roller, but he didn't look back.

After two days of almost complete silence, I needed him to be the one to break the silence (again) first. He needed to extend the olive branch.

He didn't.

We finished the job an hour later and took the equipment outside to clean up and pack away in the back of my car.

The instant the hatch was closed on the Subaru, he was moving away from me and toward his truck, and I caught my breath a little, angry with myself that I allowed his actions to hurt my feelings. "Okay," I said to his back, desperate to say anything to him. "You can send me an invoice for your time, or I'll just calculate our hours and bring you a check."

He stopped, his hand on the door of his truck and he shook his head at me shortly. But since I didn't know what the hell that was supposed to mean, I just shrugged helplessly at him. "Thanks, Thomas. You saved me a lot of time. If you have time on Monday, we could put up the chandelier and just be done with it–I don't have to finish the rooms before we do that part. I can get someone else to help me with the doors."

He nodded just as shortly, getting into his truck and slamming the door and I waited for the engine to start up as I walked back toward the house. I needed to shut the windows and doors, to turn out the lights and make sure I'd locked everything up tight.

It took me a few minutes to get everything in order and as I let myself back out onto the expansive front porch to lock the front door, I noticed his truck was still sitting there. I could see his arms crossed over the steering wheel and his forehead resting on his wrists.

I walked over slowly and stood for a moment, waiting for him to look up. When he didn't, I tapped gently on the window and his head flew up. He looked angry and lost.

"You ok?" I asked, my hands shoved deep in my pockets. I'd already decided against inviting him over for dinner, knowing he wouldn't come anyway.

It didn't seem possible, but he seemed worse today than he'd been yesterday.

He scrubbed a hand down the side of his face and, without answering me, turned over the engine and tore down the driveway. It didn't startle me, but the unwelcome discomfort was back in my chest, like a gnawing that wasn't quite pain. I was starting to realize that if he treated me this way, he probably treated others even worse.

That made me mad at myself, for making excuses for him.

The drive to my house took about fifteen minutes, as I had to cross town. I lived on the shabbier, far less expensive side, and I couldn't even see the beach if I stood on the roof of my house, much less from my backyard.

As delightful as I found the beach, I wasn't jealous of what the Masters had. Someday I would have the option, I thought, as I considered how my site had taken off over just the past three years, and I hoped someday life would be a little easier.

Initially, my website had been a side venture. It was something I did for fun, mostly on the weekend, to document the projects on my own home. Every now and then I asked a client if I could feature my work for them on the blog and very rarely was I turned down, though there were a few who were fiercely protective of their privacy and their personal spaces.

What started as a small venture eventually started generating modest ad revenue, and I curated a few shops with online retailers and commission began coming in that way, too. But then retailers began approaching me about collaborations, and that was when things had really begun to explode.

Whether Ahmad started getting weird before the blog started showing signs of success, or after, I couldn't remember. I'd been so busy with back-to-back jobs and building up my readership, then my social media numbers, that I hadn't really noticed when he started to watch our personal bank account like a hawk.

Suddenly, things that had been routine expenditures for me: a gym membership, drinks with girlfriends, a trip to the spa, a hair appointment...all became things I had to answer for when he questioned the necessity of the expenses.

He'd sit on the sofa with the month's statement, glasses perched halfway down his straight nose and make disapproving little harrumphs as his finger moved over the evidence of my financial indiscretions.

Purchases made with the money *I* was earning.

Let's not pretend I wasn't furious, because I was. My business was generating enough that I was finally drawing a salary comparable to his bloated corporate salary. That was nothing to sneeze at, and that was before I factored in my blog revenue.

In fact, my site afforded us an upgrade to a very posh home in Beacon Hill–his insistence, not mine. I'd wanted something old and rough and in need of love and a good coat of paint. That was the very thing I'd built the blog upon.

He wanted new and flashy, with tall ceilings and windows, marble everything, and a chef's kitchen. That meant expensive, which may have been why he was watching my spending so closely, but I bit my tongue rather than point out the hypocrisy, because he'd certainly done nothing to curtail his own.

Suddenly he seemed to have something to prove, and we sold the small house he'd bought as a bachelor. It was the one I'd spent years bringing up to date and polishing until it was an absolute real estate gem. But when we sold it, he reminded me that his name was the only one on the deed. (That was when I should have left, but you know what they say about hindsight.)

My husband seemed to think it fair that despite my years of work on the home we'd shared, he should invest the proceeds of the sale–the entire amount–on his own. So the money disappeared into a murky brokerage account, or at least that was the story, and I wasn't allowed to question it.

When my side venture started to *really* generate revenue, I started to bring in more money than he was and though it started small, eventually it turned into a *lot* more money. And since he was watching my expenditures like the chair of the Federal Reserve, I started repaying the favor, reviewing bank and credit card statements with disdainful noises. We had surpassed Comfortable, drifting into Ridiculous, so why did my expenditures carry so much more weight than his?

That was when my subconscious told me I'd be wise to start a separate bank account, and quietly I did, funneling a small percentage from my revenues at first, and bumping it up by several points each month.

The real infusion was when I sold my business to my assistant, on the downlow, but rehabbing the house I'd bought with cash was eating through that sizable nest egg faster than I'd have liked.

Had I been preparing myself for an end? Of course I had. If I had been honest with myself, the cracks in our marriage were evident even before we said I Do.

The problems went back to the first time I met his family, when they looked down on me as some tawdry little girl who'd managed to entice their handsome, successful son/brother/cousin.

What an idiot I'd been, blinded by his beauty and success, rushing into a marriage with a man I hardly knew.

What I knew now was that getting to know the real man *after* exchanging vows had been one of my less brilliant ideas.

What I hadn't known at the time was that I really hadn't enticed him at all, because he wasn't the one in any rush to marry me. It was his parents who pushed. I wasn't their first choice, or even their last one, but times were desperate because his mother was hellbent on him settling down and producing an heir, considering he was already 35 when we met.

Then she wanted granddaughters to spoil (just so long as the grandson came first), and she was the sort who didn't give a person room to argue.

There was money in it, I came to understand later: His parents would see to it that our son was educated in the finest schools and with the best teachers.

In Saudi Arabia.

Away from me, the corrupting influence that was his hypothetical western mother.

When our son turned twelve we were to put our fictional child on a plane to Riyadh, where his grandfather would retrieve him from the airport, to be doted upon and essentially raised by his grandmother, until he graduated college ten years later.

Much to Ahmad's consternation, my uterus was even less cooperative than I was, and each month that I bled he was angrier than the last.

It could be said he could have shown more enthusiasm–a little more effort might not have hurt–but from his family's perspective, and maybe his, his prize cow was a big dud.

After all, his family had shown him a great honor, to commit in advance to the expense of raising and educating our firstborn. He would be a testament to the family, placed in the best schools and given the highest religious education with the best local clerics.

Honestly, I think that was when my reproductive system put her foot down and simply refused to get pregnant. I may or may not have helped it along with a secret IUD and just endured the monthly tantrums, as I was not about to generate a child who was trained to treat women the way Ahmad's father treated his mother.

While Farida had strong opinions, she had no real voice. It was her job to be decorative. She dressed in modern designer clothing, but she wouldn't leave the house without her abaya, covered from head to toe, even when visiting us in Boston. Her husband wouldn't stand for it–and oddly, neither would she. She tried to convince me, just once, that wearing one would make me a dutiful wife and I informed her that I had no interest in being called any such thing. There was no reason for me to commit myself to customs of oppression, I explained. (That earned me a withering look and you can guess what she sent me for Christmas that year, the devious bitch.)

If there was one thing we did not discuss in our household, it was Ahmad's family dynamics. His phone calls to his parents were brief, perfunctory affairs conducted every Sunday morning from his study. The calls were never longer than twenty minutes and few pleasantries were exchanged. Overhearing his calm conversations with them was like listening to a weather report in Farsi.

As time went on, Ahmad seemed to lose interest in having kids at all. He stopped trying to please his mother and that blame was immediately heaped on my head. But as he explained, he had decided children would be a disruption to the lifestyle he had come to enjoy: late dinners; trips to the symphony; Saturday mornings spent rowing the Charles River and weekends spent attending art shows in New York or jetting to Hilton Head for a few days at the beach.

Not that he needed the tan, of course. He was olive-skinned and gorgeous and putting him on the beach in a pair of board shorts was like advertising free sex. Women flocked to him like starved seagulls.

Considering the attention constantly thrown his way, and the way he brushed it off, I'd been surprised by his violent reactions to men who so much as looked at me. Women were allowed to fawn all over him, to send him drinks and slip him their numbers. But if a man looked at me for a second too long or, God forbid he smiled in my direction, Ahmad was ready to rain down the wrath of Allah on the poor, unsuspecting soul.

Once I'd been running late at work and told my husband I would meet him at the restaurant for dinner, as it would take me less time to get there than it would to go home first.

It was raining that night and the sidewalks were slick. When I stepped from the cab just a few feet from the restaurant, my heel slipped and I went down hard on the sidewalk. One of the patrons had been out front, standing beneath an awning as he smoked a cigarette and he witnessed my graceless ass plant. He rushed over to help me, pulling me up and retrieving the shoe that had gone flying off my foot. He'd just held it out, Prince Charming style, when my husband emerged from the restaurant and split his lip.

When I burst into tears, Ahmad was baffled. He had defended my honor, he insisted–his honor, really–and I hailed the next cab to take home, hardly surprised to find I had no appetite.

That was the first night I slept in the guest room.

It became easier and easier to sleep in the guest room, and as time went on I made peace with the fact that he hadn't come after me.

He didn't stand outside the door to apologize or plead.

He didn't try to slip in during the middle of the night to carry me back to bed, or to slide in next to me and hold me close.

Sleeping apart was easier than facing the fights he wanted to pick, or the sex he didn't want to have. After all, I slept better on my own, I decided. I told myself that it made more sense to sleep apart since I suffered such vicious insomnia and was a light sleeper, while he twitched like a dog.

Even in sleep we were incompatible.

The thought occurred to me as I pulled into my driveway that I could refuse Ahmad's demands: the short list printed with tiny bullet points on the card, sent with his cloying flowers.

The florist taking the order must have been horrified.

The last thing I wanted to do was to continue to play the part of his good little wife, keeping up the show for his family, even though he was trying to hold my own money over my head.

He'd changed the password to our joint account and had reported my bank card stolen. Since he was the primary name on the account, my calls to the bank to discuss the account containing my own money were met with disdain.

At this point, I thought, it was likely he'd drained the account and stashed the funds in various places: stocks, real estate...I wouldn't have put it past him to have been wiring funds to his parents overseas for "safe keeping."

It was seeming more and more likely that if I planned to get anything back, I was going to have to file and a judge would force the issue. And God save me from the shit storm that would follow.

• • • •

THAT NIGHT I REALLY didn't feel like cooking. I contemplated mixing wine and sorbet in my blender for the ultimate adult smoothie, but I managed to talk myself into a slightly more responsible dinner–not without a good glass of red, though.

Settling in front of the TV, I didn't even bother to take off my gross work clothes. The sweat and paint had dried and I was too worn down to care. After all, I told myself, I would shower before bed. No one was going to see me like this.

I let myself get caught up in an old black and white film and before I knew it, it was long past sunset and I was stretched out on the sofa, contemplating starting another movie or just falling asleep right there.

My obsessive-compulsive nature got the better of me and I walked my dirty dishes to the kitchen, rinsing and tucking them into the dishwasher. Then I walked down the hall to the laundry room and stripped, throwing everything into the open, empty tub.

Flipping the lights off behind me, I checked the locks on the doors before walking up the stairs and twisting the tap on the bathtub. I could think of nothing nicer than a soak in the enormous beast, and I poured a heap of bath salts in before lowering myself into the hot water.

I must have fallen asleep, because a clattering noise woke me and I startled violently, having slipped down into the water past my chin. It was cooling rapidly and I stood quickly, yanking the drain plug and throwing a towel around myself as I reached for the phone that rattled across the countertop.

"Hello?" I answered cautiously. The number that flashed up on the screen was identified simply as "Thomas," and I couldn't imagine why he'd be calling me after midnight.

"Miss Nat, is J'miah Smith. You recall?"

Did I ever. Smitty was just about the most unforgettable person I'd ever met.

"I do recall, Jeremiah. How can I help you?"

"Well, Miss Nat, you see..." There was a lot of noise in the background and a vague, irritated mumbling that I suspected might be Thomas. "I–Missuh Thomas–has bit o' trouble tonight. He ain't in no fit shape to be drivin' an Miss Gerry not be answerin' her phone...you's the only other person I recognizes on Missuh Thomas's list."

I toweled off quickly with one hand as my brain fought hard to keep up with Jeremiah's thick, unusual speech patterns. Clearly I needed a crash course in Backwater Bayou.

"He can't drive?" I asked, putting Smitty on speaker so I could twist a towel around my hair. I was fairly certain that meant only one thing, and it was something that surprised me, considering Thomas's vehement avoidance of two of my favorite vices.

"You knows where to find Bubba's Grill and Pub?" he asked hopefully, and I flicked through my phone to plug the name into the map application. It was nearly half an hour away and I groaned internally as I thought of walking into a room filled with drunken men, in my pajamas, at one in the morning.

"How bad is he, Jeremiah?" I asked, and there was a rustling noise, like the phone was being held against a shirt.

"'Bout to be whole lot worse," he said quietly into the phone when the scratching noises stopped. "Cuz ladies been buyin' him shots, an he was a whole mess already, before dem shots showed up."

"Jeremiah," I said in my most authoritative tone. "Keep him awake and away from the trashy ladies. I'll be there as fast as I can–no sense in compounding the regrets of a rough night."

"You hurry now, Miss Nat," he urged, and I wondered if he drank with Thomas often. "He be mighty hard to carry. Lot easier gettin' a man out on his own two feet."

I hung up and dove into underwear, jeans and a thin shirt. Then, shoving my phone and driver's license into my back pocket, I hurried down the stairs and grabbed the car keys off the hook in the laundry room.

The drive was long and dark and I passed through several small towns before I found Bubba's, a derelict building out in the middle of nowhere, surrounded by what must have been three acres of parking lot. I didn't like the look of the place, with its burned out bulbs and peeling paint. There were at least forty Harleys parked out front too, leading me to believe the folks who frequented this particular bar were regulars and they were quite probably from harder walks of life than myself.

The door swung open and I swallowed hard as a noxious wave of cigarette smoke and stale beer just about knocked me over. Several grizzled bikers at the bar turned to look me over and one lifted his chin slightly. I looked away immediately, not wanting to invite any trouble or attention to myself, since I'd never had any trouble attracting attention from the wrong kinds of men.

My eyes quickly scanned the room and I found Thomas almost immediately, his face down on his arms at the bar, five women clustered around him cackling like hens as they tried to convince him to take just one more shot.

"I think he's had enough, ladies." The strength of my voice surprised me and several of them whipped around, their lips curling back as they took in my bare face, damp hair and very plain clothing. Compared to Ms. Leopard Pants and her cantilevered boobs, a dangerous precipice upon which she'd rested a cheap string of beads, I was dull indeed.

"Who are you, makin' decisions for him?" she whined, raking a hand through her teased hair and performing a quick adjustment of her best assets. They were impressive, I had to give her that, but they were about to swallow her necklace whole.

"He called for a ride home," I told her. "I'll see to it that he arrives there safely."

"Aw darlin', he's comin' home with me. I'll make sure he experiences *everything* safely." Her lips pulled back in a predatory smile, which was ill-advised, as there were several gaps in places that should have held teeth. I ran my tongue across my own teeth before realizing what I'd done.

"Listen, Tits–Toots." My temper was short and I heard a muffled giggle from the bar that I thought might have come from Thomas. "I outweigh your scrawny butt by twenty pounds and I grew up playing baseball, so my aim is good and my arm is strong. You can fight me for him, but it would be a shame to lose more teeth. If you know what's good for you, you'll give us some space." My hair was practically standing on end.

Right on cue, Thomas sat up and turned his head to throw up down her chest. She shrieked in dismay and I threw her a stack of cocktail napkins, working myself under Thomas's arm in order to lift him from the barstool. Best to get him out before things got any uglier.

One of the bikers, the one with tattoos creeping all the way up his neck, was already making his way over.

I managed to get him a couple steps before he seemed to right himself and we made a straighter line for the door. Somehow he seemed more stable and I finally realized it was Smitty, tucked under his other arm, helping to guide him out toward the car.

"Need a minute," Thomas mumbled when we stepped out into the humid night air and Smitty spun him quickly as Thomas vomited again.

Smitty helped me wrangle him into the front seat of my car and I giggled as he fumbled with the button to scoot the seat back. It was almost laughable how little the car looked with Thomas stuffed inside of it.

"Thanks, Jeremiah," I said as I shut the door carefully after checking to make sure all hands and feet were accounted for and out of the way. Smitty blushed bashfully in the weak parking lot lights and it occurred to me that the little hobbit drank because he was lonely and probably had nothing better to do.

"Can I give you a ride home?" I asked gently and he looked down at his feet, shaking his head slowly.

"Aw, nah, Miss Nat. Kind o' you. I lives jus' over dat way." He pointed into the darkness beyond the parking lot. "I jus' walk on home gone closin' time."

Smitty wandered off toward the bar again, in a remarkably straight line, while I crawled into the driver's seat and immediately rolled down the windows. Thomas reeked of spilled liquor, stale cigarettes, cheap perfume and vomit. It was enough to turn my stomach and I pulled up my texts from Gerry to retrieve his address, plugging it into my GPS. I turned down the sound and watched the map on the small screen so I knew the few turns I had to make to get to his house.

Thomas snored as I drove, and I pulled up right into his driveway. I didn't have Smitty to help me on this end of things and when I opened Thomas's door, the only thing that kept him from falling out of the car was the seatbelt–and that could just barely handle him.

"Thomas," I said gently, leaning close to his ear. He hardly stirred. "I'm going to need a little help to get you into your house."

"Nobody in my house," he mumbled, and I leaned my shoulder into his to push him back into the car while I unclipped his seatbelt.

"Come on," I said, putting both arms around his ribcage and trying to turn him to pull him out of the car.

Something I hadn't counted on was that Thomas was almost a foot taller than me and he outweighed me by what must have been eighty pounds of solid muscle. I could hardly budge him, and I jabbed a thumb into his ribs to startle him awake. "This way," I instructed, putting a hand over his head so he wouldn't slam it into the car frame on his way out.

The car beeped when I clicked the fob and I tucked back under his arm to try to steer him toward the house. It was slow going, weaving as we were across the lawn, and by the time I got him up to the front door I was panting from the exertion.

His head fell forward, resting against the pane of his front door and he brought up a big hand to slap at the glass. "Lydia!" he howled, his voice suddenly remarkably clear. "I know what you did." He made a fist, pounding against the door and I shoved a hand carefully into the pocket of his jeans to retrieve his keys. It made him giggle like a little girl. "Hey...careful, lady." *Hiccup.* Apparently that had been enough to distract him. "Stop tryin'a grab my junk and keep yer hand outta m' pants." He was slurring his words again.

"Your junk *and* your pants are all yours tonight, my friend," I assured him as I cycled quickly through the few keys on the ring, the door finally swinging open, and he lurched into the entryway. "You can thank me for that gift tomorrow."

I thought of the woman at the bar with a shudder. Yeah, she'd have been the sort of gift to keep on giving, all right, through at least four cycles of penicillin.

Shit, I really hadn't thought this through. I'd gone to collect him and I'd seen him safely home, but I couldn't leave him in this state. He was so drunk, it was possible he was a danger to himself.

"Here," I said, holding up both of his hands so he could brace himself against the wall while I ducked down to untie his boots.

"What're y'doing?" he laughed, and I placed the arch of my foot at the heel of the first boot.

"Step," I commanded, my foot pulling down at his boot so he could step out of it. I did the same for the second boot and he braced an arm against the wall, leaning and sliding against it as he began to weave down the hallway and into the darkness of the house.

"Thomas, wait," I commanded and I heard his footsteps falter. I followed the sound, holding my phone toward the floor and flicking the flashlight so we could see where we were going.

"Natalie makes me iced tea–none of that stupid fancy crap you drink," he informed me with another hiccup as I led him back toward what I thought might be the kitchen. "She makes chicken salad an' macaroni an' roasted asparagus an' salmon with blackberry sauce..." he trailed off slowly, licking his lips.

I was beginning to wonder where he was going with this. Maybe he was hungry?

"She's s'nice to me, Lydia." He sounded plaintive, like a little boy. "Doesn't 'spect nothin' from me. 'S weird, right?"

Sloppy was *such* a distant memory by now.

There were tall stools at his kitchen island and I leaned him onto one as I hurried to the sink, searching the nearby cupboards until I found a bottle of painkillers. Then I drew a large glass of water from the tap and took it to him, shaking three pills from the bottle.

He let me pop the pills into his mouth and he chugged the glass of water with a grimace. "Gotta use the...thing..." his hands were making an indistinct motion and I finally understood he meant I hadn't used the filtered tap for drinking water.

"She makes pie," he continued, and I began to wonder if this Lydia person was upstairs sleeping in his bed. If so, at least one of us was in for a rude surprise.

I refilled the glass from the proper tap, then helped him back to his feet. This next part was going to be tricky, I knew, and I let him slide along the wall as we moved toward the staircase.

"Who's Lydia?" I asked quietly as he reached out for the newel post and pulled his foot up onto the first step.

"Silly," he hiccupped again. "The wife." He chuckled to himself like it was a great joke and I blew out a big breath. At any moment I expected a bright overhead light to snap on and to find an angry woman in tiny underwear waiting for us at the top of the steps. A man like this would surely have a gorgeous, bitchy wife who was understandably angry another woman was helping her husband up to bed.

There were pale bars of moonlight illuminating the hallway and I looked into an open bedroom door to see huge windows and a large bed. The bed appeared to be empty and I breathed a sigh of relief, trying to direct him through the doorway.

"Nah," he said, bracing himself against the railing that ran the length of the open hallway. "This way."

We passed several more doors before he turned and in the faint light I could just make out a small bunk bed. There was a rug on the floor and a low bookshelf crammed with books. There was a toy box shoved up against one wall, with a collection of cars and trains lined up across the top. A pair of ballet shoes hung on the wall and there were princess sheets and a huge teddy bear on the top bunk, trains on the bottom.

I was confused. "Thomas, this isn't your room." I set the glass of water on the dresser near the bed.

"This...where I'm sleeping," he said, pulling his arm from my shoulders and yanking his shirt over his head. Then, with a quick movement, his pants were on the floor and he sprawled gracelessly on the bed in his boxer briefs.

It was enough to make me wish I had covered my eyes, because I couldn't stop staring. I gawked, telling myself I needed to find him a blanket and then take myself home.

It was a little easier to talk myself into the going home part, since he still smelled pretty terrible.

"Don' leave." His voice was muffled by the pillow and he turned his head slowly, one arm flopping across the bed in my direction. "She doesn't want me."

I had no idea what to say, and I sat gingerly at the edge of the bed, completely unsure of what to do other than to drive home or to curl up on the rug next to the bed and try to sleep. I had real concerns that he might just lean over the edge of the bed and throw up on me during what was left of the night.

Reaching toward the end of the bed, I found a small blanket that I unfolded and draped over him when he rolled onto his back. Then I stood, smoothing his hair off his beautiful face. "Sleep well, Thomas," I said. I contemplated rolling him back over, in case he threw up in his sleep.

"No." His hand shot out to grab my wrist and pull me back down. "Need *you* t' sleep, baby."

My own eyes were heavy. I'd been up since six that morning and it had to be two. I contemplated finding another bedroom to sleep in, or crashing on the sofa I'd seen in his living room when we'd walked past.

But his hold on my wrist was increasing in strength and I sat back down slowly, curling up along the very edge of the bed, wildly uncomfortable. I was fairly sure this big, completely shitfaced man thought I was his wife.

Thomas scooted slowly, backing himself up against the wall and his other arm snaked around me, dragging me back to him. He wrapped himself quickly around me from behind, the big spoon.

"Better," he mumbled into my hair and I could feel him drawing slow breaths as he nuzzled into me, one arm still under me and the other over my ribcage, pinning me tightly against him.

"My Natalie's not like you, baby." His voice was growing quieter with sleep. "She takes...care of me. Needs someone t' do it for her, that stubborn, irritating, nosy little..." The air was punctuated by a quiet snore.

My brain spun tiredly: *My Natalie.*

Who needed someone to take care of her? Lydia, or me?

Drunk Thomas was even more confusing than sober Thomas and, completely exhausted, I skipped over the insults that made my heart ache and allowed myself to drift off into sleep.

• • • •

I WOKE TO A NOISE AND a heavy weight across my chest. At first it filled me with panic and my eyes snapped open, but as I took in the unfamiliar room the events of only a few hours before began to play through my head.

I cringed as I realized I was being held tightly against Thomas's mostly-naked body–not that the thought in of itself was in any way upsetting. In fact, in just about any other set of circumstances I'd have been thrilled. But in this case I had a hunch he'd be pretty upset to wake up and find things as they were, even if it had been of his own doing. Chances were very good he wouldn't remember much of the night before.

While part of me just wanted to stay curled up against him, common sense told me I needed to put distance between our bodies–and quickly. I could feel his response to my nearness and as much as I wanted to stay and explore that situation, I carefully, slowly, gently peeled his fingers from my ribcage and lifted his arm, scooting in slow motion to minimize my disturbance of the bed. He mumbled something when I lifted myself from it and he rolled to scoop up the pillow, burying his face in it.

He was going to have one hell of a hangover, I thought, despite the painkillers I'd managed to get into him in the wee morning hours.

Lucky for him, I had endured a few doozies of my own and had developed a failsafe breakfast combination.

I just hoped he had a few things in his fridge.

I didn't close the bedroom door entirely, but left it cracked open so that my noises in the kitchen wouldn't startle or wake him. I was a born disaster and fully anticipated breaking a dish or banging my head on a cupboard door.

It took a minute to locate the coffee (in the freezer and with an expiration date from the days of the dinosaurs), and I was impressed to find a decent grinder in one of the cabinets.

Diving into the lower cabinets, I prayed to find alcohol–any kind–just enough for a serving, or he'd be throwing up before he'd had breakfast.

The clock said it was nearing nine when I heard cautious movement and running water upstairs, and I wondered if he would come charging down with a baseball bat.

He finally shuffled through the doorway bare chested, in fitted joggers that showed off his muscular legs and made my lady parts do funny things. His long, dark hair was wet and scooped over his ears, one thick chunk hanging in his face.

"I smelled coffee," he explained in a gravelly voice and if he was surprised to find me in his kitchen, he didn't look like it. "It seems like a good idea this morning."

"Here's another good idea," I said, hardly able to keep my eyes off his impressively broad shoulders as I handed him a tall Bloody Mary. "Hair of the dog. Drink this first and I'll feed you breakfast."

I took a deep breath to calm the somersaulting feeling happening low in my stomach. I was trying to recall the last time my stomach had done gymnastics over a *friend* and was coming up with nothing.

He groaned. "I don't think it's a good idea to put anything into my stomach right now."

I pointed at the beverage with a wilted piece of celery peeking from the top. "Start there and sip very slowly."

He disappeared again and when I had breakfast ready I went to look for him, finding him sitting on the living room sofa with his feet up on the coffee table as he stared out the front window.

"I fucked up last night, Natalie. Was I an ass to you?" he asked suddenly, and I sat down on the coffee table so I could see his expressions. I had to look away though, suddenly and intensely aware of what else his fitted pants were showcasing, and I felt the blood rush to my face.

Holy hell, he's packing.

I blamed it on years of unwilling abstinence.

"You were nicer to me last night than you have been the past couple days, so... no, you weren't an ass last night, specifically."

Oh thank God, my words still worked.

Then I stole another peek, kind of on purpose, and lost my train of thought again.

"I didn't do anything that...uh..." He looked guilty. "I didn't do anything stupid, did I?"

"Well, Jeremiah managed to keep most of the ladies off you, so I'm fairly confident you didn't do anything that would have required treatment."

He winced and I grinned. "Miss Leopard Pants was really gunning to take you home. She wasn't my biggest fan when I showed up and told her you'd be keeping your parts to yourself."

He chuckled a little. "Now that part I sort of remember. You called her something funny."

Yeah, at the height of what was not my finest moment. I can't be going all jealous crazy bitch like that again.

"You were really upset with someone named Lydia–you seemed to think I was her some of the time," I said gently and I watched his eyes immediately go flat and hard. The smile fell off his face and he lifted the glass to his lips to drain the last of the boozy tomato juice. He muttered something I couldn't make out, but it didn't sound like it was complimentary.

"Where did you sleep?" he asked suddenly, his face lined with concern, and the bottom of my stomach dropped out.

"Uh...you got pretty upset when I tried to leave," I said, suddenly and intensely interested in a small snag in my sweatshirt. I could feel the blood rushing to my face.

Understanding dawned in his eyes. "Shit, I'm sorry." He swapped his glass for the coffee mug, wiping one hand across his face. "That had to be weird. I was really, really shitfaced." He looked down at his feet. "I'm not...I'm not like that, Natalie. I swear. I don't go out to tie one on anymore and I don't bring women home. There were...extenuating circumstances I can't really explain. I was upset and I have a...challenging...relationship with alcohol and I slipped."

I sat quietly for a moment, trying to determine whether he'd lose his shit if I tried to ask him a question. As a rule, he didn't seem to like questions, so I decided to lead with telling him one of my truths in hopes it would get him to open up.

"In my former life," I started, "I lived in Boston, in a big, beautiful house with four bedrooms."

He looked up curiously.

"One was the bedroom I shared with..." Nope, not going there. "One was an office and the other two bedrooms were officially guest rooms, but over time, one of them became more of my own bedroom than the one I shared. It was where I went to hide; the place I could sleep the best, because there was no one angry sleeping next to me. It was filled with things that made me happy...things that calmed me." I stopped, gauging his facial expression carefully. "Is that why you sleep in that bedroom, Thomas?" I asked quietly. "Is that where you feel at peace?"

His glass banged onto the coffee table and he shot to his feet, rounding the sofa and moving away from me quickly, disappearing through the dining area and into the kitchen.

As far as timing was concerned, maybe it was for the best that he was running away from me, because I'd been seriously considering leaning in to hug him.

Okay, then. I sighed deeply, pressing the heels of my hands into tired eyes. I hadn't had nearly enough sleep or coffee, and I took his abrupt disappearance as a clue that I'd overstepped yet again. It wasn't quite fair to say that he moved the mark, because he hadn't, but I never knew just what was going to set him off.

I was really tired, and since I'd already cooked breakfast, I decided he could figure that out on his own and I dug into my pocket for keys as I let myself quietly out the front door. It seemed obvious he needed still more time to himself.

The drive to my house was short and stupidly, I felt guilty for leaving him to fend for himself, so I walked over to Gerry's place to ask her if she'd be willing to help me retrieve Thomas's truck. She raised an eyebrow at me, but she hopped into my car without a word, and I dangled his keys at her.

Gerry drove his truck back to his place and I followed behind.

Thomas did not appear, though Gerry disappeared into his house for a moment with the keys.

Her expression was troubled when she crawled into my passenger seat and when I dropped her off in her driveway, she grabbed my hand and squeezed tightly.

She turned her face quickly as she let herself out of the car, but I thought I saw moisture standing in her eyes.

I let myself into my own house and kicked my shoes off at the door. Then I walked right up the stairs and collapsed into my bed.

Mercifully, sleep welcomed me quickly.

• • • •

THE ROOM WAS WARM WHEN I woke again–I had forgotten to turn on the fan–and I knew by the light slanting in through the windows that it was already afternoon.

I'd slept for several solid, uninterrupted hours but I still felt tired and a little kicked around on the inside. Something about interactions with Thomas caused things to hurt in ways I didn't think they should.

There was a soft knocking at the front door and I realized that was what had awakened me, so I swung my feet over the edge of the bed and padded down the stairs to peek through the side lights. Thomas stood there, with something in his hands, a look on his face that wasn't quite one of contrition.

"I'm sorry, Natalie," he called and I heard a soft thump that sounded like his head hitting the front door. "I was an ass."

"Am," I corrected through the door. "Very much in the present tense."

"Am an ass. Will you let me apologize to your face, or do I need to kiss and make up with your front door?"

My eyes widened. Thomas, *wanting* to apologize?

Offering?

I wasn't sure what to do with that.

And what was this about kissing? Because I'd open the door naked for some of that.

I pulled the door open cautiously, aware that I had sleep creases in my face and my hair was probably crazy.

I'd ripped off my light sweatshirt at some point during my nap and though I wore a tank top, I wasn't wearing a bra, so I quickly crossed my arms over my chest, as flashing him the high beams seemed to be a particular talent of mine, and when he was around they were *always* high beams. My body hadn't yet gotten the memo that I'd slapped the label of "friends" on our relationship, because all of my parts sure as hell wanted to be besties with all of his.

Bad friend. Stop it.

"Ok if I come in?" he asked, a paper bag in his arms.

Only if you start taking off your clothes.

"Only if you promise not to puke on me," I said, trying to summon a small smile, and he looked alarmed.

"I didn't, did I?"

"No, but you barfed on Leopard Lady, so I figured at some point I would make the list. In fact, I'm kind of shocked you didn't throw up on me during the night."

He walked through to the kitchen and set the bag on the countertop.

I was sure that by now half the neighborhood was standing outside my front door with water glasses pressed against the outside, trying desperately to hear every word.

Sitting at the island, he steepled his fingers and sat waiting as I brewed a press of coffee. My thoughts were fuzzy, interrupted as I'd been from my nap.

Without asking whether he wanted a cup, I fetched a strainer from the drawer and poured two large mugs, adding half and half and sliding one in front of him. At the very least, I figured, it would give him something to do with his hands.

It would also give him a reason not to look at me.

What could I say? I was a very accommodating hostess.

Sitting beside him, I was careful to look into my coffee and not at him, afraid he would spook.

He didn't look over at me and I noticed he was keeping a careful distance between our arms on the countertop.

"I got some bad news a couple days ago," he said finally, and I heard my Adam's apple drag when I took a sip of coffee. "My lawyer let me know that a petition was overruled by the judge."

It took everything I had not to look at him and I worked hard to keep my voice calm and neutral, fixing my gaze instead on the fridge. "Does it have something to do with a divorce?"

"No, not directly. It's worse–I can't..." He took a deep, shuddering breath. "I can't even say it out loud."

He had to know how hard it was for me not to barrage him with questions and he took another big breath. "I've been fighting this for the past two years, and this was it. The judge made a final ruling and there's nothing left to do since my legal team has exhausted every option."

There didn't seem to be words to fit the situation. He had been walking around absolutely wrecked for days and now I had something of a reason.

Instead of saying anything, I took another sip of my coffee and set down the mug. Then I reached over the short distance between us and squeezed his forearm gently. To his credit he only flinched a little, so perhaps I was only mildly leprous today, of the non-contagious variety. "I'm sorry," I said. "I don't even know what to say."

"No questions?" he asked, a touch of humor creeping into his voice.

"A lot of questions," I said slowly, "but none of them are any of my business and you've made it clear you're not the type to be pushed, although that might be exactly what you need. So it doesn't mean I *won't* ask those questions, but not today."

Thomas got to his feet and opened the bag he'd set on the edge of the counter, pulling out a nice bottle of wine, followed by noodles and sauce, a clamshell filled with greens, a bottle of dressing, a small loaf of crusty bread and a box of chocolate cake mix.

"I'm afraid to be home by myself right now," he said, his back to me as he braced both arms on the counter. "Everything tastes better at your house anyway–probably because I'm not the one cooking it. I never could cook for shit and now...well, now I guess I'm really stuck."

"Why *are* you home by yourself, Thomas? I kept expecting your wife to walk in and start cursing at me. You...you said 'She doesn't want me,'" I revealed, wondering if I was pushing too far just after I'd told him I wouldn't.

He took a really deep breath. "I'm not ready, Natalie. I haven't talked about it with anyone and I'm not ready to start now. It still hurts too much." He was still leaning against the counter, his head hanging down below his shoulders.

"Okay," I said, pushing up from my stool and crossing the short space to rinse my mug in the sink.

I stood there for a moment, wanting desperately to step up behind him and wrap my arms around his middle, to press my face against his back in a tight hug. I knew what it was to hurt all on your own and to have no one there to help you hold all the pieces together.

I tried to push the thought away and glanced at the clock on the stove, surprised to find it was actually later in the afternoon than I'd expected, and my stomach rumbled as it reminded me I had skipped the breakfast I'd made at his place.

Leaving him to boil the noodles, I mixed the cake and popped it into the oven, then tossed the salad in a bowl and chopped additional vegetables into it.

While I chopped, he unwrapped the bread and popped it into the oven with the cake so it could warm, and I was impressed when he sifted through my herbs and spices and created a dipping oil for the bread.

"Not a complete barbarian," I observed and he looked up quickly, tucking his hair over his ear.

"I used to travel a lot for work–far more extensively than I do now. My favorite was always Italy, but I learned some interesting things in Japan. Not many things I wanted to replicate at home from Finland or Russia, though..." He shuddered and tested the oil by swirling a finger through it and popping it into his mouth.

I watched in fascination, a lurid fantasy popping up behind my eyes and I felt the blood rush into my face again.

"So, then you must be some kind of barrel tile expert," I said, trying to distract myself as I pulled wine glasses down from the cupboard, and I felt the air change immediately in the room. "You know...Italy...all those gorgeous old terracotta roofs."

He looked confused.

"All the traveling you do for business," I prompted, feeling very much like I was leading a horse to water.

"Uh..." he located the corkscrew and worked the cork out of the wine, only pouring into one glass and handing it to me. "No, not exactly. I'm pretty handy, but the contracting work I do is mostly to keep myself busy when I'm here. I don't take that show on the road."

Whatever that means.

The dining room table was finally put to real use, now that it no longer hosted The Flowers of the Apocalypse.

I pulled the nicer plates from the cupboard and my grandmother's silver service from the small credenza pushed up against the dining room wall.

He asked to see my mock-ups for the Masters' house as we finished dessert and I hurried up the stairs to fetch them from my office.

While I talked him through the drawings–something I couldn't imagine he could possibly be interested in–he stacked up the dishes and carried them into the kitchen. It was completely natural and without prompting on my part, and I followed behind with the few small serving pieces we'd had out on the table.

The room tilted a little as I carried things into the kitchen and I looked at the wine bottle on the counter, realizing I'd had quite a lot of it all on my own, and most of that before I'd begun to eat. That, I thought with some consternation, was not a good thing.

When I drank too much, I became effusive. I offered up information freely and no one could shut me up. It was very similar to when I was sober, only that when I was sober I asked questions instead.

When I was drunk I just started barfing out personal information at no provocation whatsoever.

"My husband was keeping a lover in another city."

Oh fuck, that was out there now.

I snapped the dishwasher closed, wishing I'd taped my mouth shut right after eating the cake.

Maybe before, in fact, if my butt got a vote. It seemed to be going through a growth spurt lately.

Thomas nodded like I hadn't just dropped a bomb in the middle of the room.

Why was he nodding? What kind of a response was that?

"He wants me to pretend for his family that we're happily married. He's demanded that I return to Boston for Thanksgiving, when his parents fly in for a visit, or he'll maintain his stranglehold over our joint bank account."

He raised an eyebrow at me as he grabbed the sponge and wiped down the countertop.

That was weird.

"His parents haven't been stateside in almost seven years, but this time they're coming for Thanksgiving and they're staying past Christmas. Do you know what that means? Do you know what he expects me to *do*?"

"Well, judging by your last name...um...I have assumptions. I'll take a crazy guess that it means he expects you to stay in Boston until they leave and put on the show of a dutiful wife for his parents, who probably have pretty particular ideas about what a marriage should be."

"It's a farce!" I hollered, pounding my fist against the cheap laminate countertop and it made a hollow thumping noise. "He wants nothing to do with me, Thomas! He couldn't even stand being in the same bed as me. I slept in our guest room almost exclusively for the last few years of our marriage, until I decided to leave him.

"Do you know the last time that we actually..." Hiccup. *Whoa, whoa, whoa. Hold on. Wind it back in, girlfriend. You almost threw that one right out there and we are not going for pity. Not today.*

Thomas looked really uncomfortable and I winced. Clearly there'd been no point in trying to stop that train of thought: the damn thing was in the station and the passengers had already disembarked.

I shoved my hands through my hair to hold my head onto my shoulders. My face was hot and my knees were suddenly weak as adrenaline and shame coursed through my body.

"He's an idiot," Thomas said shortly as he wrapped up the rest of the cake and put it in the refrigerator without looking at me.

I laughed suddenly, disgusted with myself. "How come when I drink too much, I give up all my secrets? When you drink too much, you're still a freaking vault."

His face clouded over and he lifted his shoulders in a noncommittal shrug. "I've never really been able to talk to anybody. No one would have listened anyway, so I never got in the habit. Gerry tries sometimes, but even she knows there are certain subjects that are off-limits. There are a lot of things I just can't talk about. Not yet." He wrapped his arms around himself and I sighed, sad for him again.

Sad for me too, maybe, as I recalled briefly how nice it had been to have those big arms wrapped around me while I slept, even though he had no recollection of doing it.

"Maybe you've just never given anyone the chance because you're afraid of judgment."

"I should go, Natalie. I'm sorry if I just stirred up trouble."

Stirred up trouble? Oh, he had no idea how much trouble there was to be had. It involved a length of rope I kept in the junk drawer, and my bed.

Yes, please.

Nodding, I sighed, feeling my face fall as I did. "Sorry I got sloppy and chased you away," was all I could manage, and he laughed as he dug into his pocket for his keys.

"*You* got sloppy?" He chuckled as he reached over and tucked my hair behind my ear, and my heart stopped. He didn't make any further movements toward me, though. Instead, he turned slowly and started walking toward the front door. "You didn't make someone pick you up at a bar early in the morning because you were too shitfaced to drive and I'll just stop right there, because you know the rest of that story. But you didn't get sloppy, Natalie, I did."

He turned to face me, one hand on the doorknob. "Thank you for being so patient when I didn't deserve it."

Then he touched two fingers to his eyebrow, like an abbreviated salute, and he was gone.

First of all, you'd better believe I finished that bottle of wine. There was a good cry to be had and thanks to my good friend from–hang on, the label said it here somewhere–Montepulciano–I was going to find it. It was going to be an ugly cry, the kind that left me heaving and sobbing convulsively until I fell asleep, because I needed something to knock me out.

When I heard a tap at the door I rushed to it, thinking foolishly that maybe he'd changed his mind and come back.

Gerry stood on my porch with a sweet smile on her face and a bottle of crisp white wine in her hands and I groaned. "Oh Gerry, I think I might already be hammered. Thomas brought a bottle to have with dinner...and I drank it all by myself.

"Then I turned into a big-mouthed idiot and chased him away with all my stupid words."

"You're still mostly making sense, darling, and without slurring your words. Therefore, you are far from shitfaced. And now here I am, ready to discuss why we drove out to retrieve Thomas's truck this morning.

Since I saw it here not all that long ago, it leads me to believe there's a story you just might like to share with me–since I have more wine, of course."

I shook my head at her even as the grin spread across my face. Gerry was old enough to be my mother, but in just weeks I felt closer to her than my own. Besides, something told me she already knew the end from the beginning because the woman was pretty damn astute.

She hurried into my kitchen–or maybe she didn't, but it felt like everything was moving faster than I was. So I followed her slowly, retrieving two fresh wine glasses and handing her the corkscrew, even if it was a bad idea.

We curled up at opposite ends of the sofa in my living room and with no preamble, Gerry started to tell me a story about a little boy who'd grown up in the northern part of Washington state, almost British Columbia, she said.

The little boy had fallen in love with a beautiful girl when they were still quite young.

The boy's mother had warned him the girl would break his heart.

The girl's mother had warned him the girl would break his heart.

But they were married young, moving around the world as the boy chased one job after another, trying to keep up with his wife's demands for money and status and adventure.

He collected jobs from Hong Kong to London to Palo Alto and along the way she collected Chanel, Fendi and Prada.

There was a sickening feeling coiling in my gut as Gerry continued her story and I clutched my wine glass to my chest, only occasionally remembering to sip. She was telling the story in broad strokes and I knew she was being cautious not to give away details that were not her own, but it was plain who she was talking about.

"Where is she?" I asked finally, aware I was prying back the lid without permission. "He's still wearing a wedding ring, Gerry. Where is Lydia?"

Gerry's face turned sorrowful. "You know something about her already, then."

No, I really didn't. I didn't know nearly enough.

I told her some of what had happened the night before, leaving out the part about falling asleep in his arms, in what I was pretty sure was his son's bed.

"The end of that story isn't mine to tell," she said gently. "He'll tell you when he's ready and it'll break your heart. I warned him a long time ago that she was no good." She sighed heavily and something reached through the fog in my brain to prod at my deductive reasoning.

"A long time ago? If you know all of these details, then you've known him for a long time. What does that make you to him?"

She reached down and retrieved the wine bottle from the floor, filling up my glass before emptying the rest into her own. "You don't have any guesses, dear girl?" Her face was kind and a smile played around her mouth.

I sat looking at her hard, my brain trying to piece together information I felt I'd been gathering since I first met her.

"You're his mother," I said finally, sinking back even deeper into the sofa as I stared at her, though I didn't see any resemblance between the two of them.

"Well..." she lifted her glass toward the light and gazed through the golden liquid for a moment. "Not quite, or not exactly–but maybe the closest thing he's had to a mother since he was twelve."

"Let me guess," I said, holding up one hand to make my point. "There are still more details you can't share, because it's not your story?" It came out all pissy.

"Oh no, part of it's my story, just not all of it. You see...Thomas's father has a bit of a wandering eye..."

She had a faraway look and I settled in for her tale of many women scorned, and she'd been the first in a long line. As it turned out, she was the second wife, long since divorced. Stepmother Number One in a lineup of six, last she knew.

"What about his mom?" I asked. "Where is she?"

"That's why I was the second wife," Gerry said gently. "Thomas's mother died when he was still quite young–cancer, as the family decided to call it. That way they didn't have to explain she drank herself into the grave. Broke Charles's heart.

"Of course, if I'd known at the time that he'd never love another woman the way he loved her...well, I don't know that I would have wasted my time, because something in him died with her." She sighed. "It wasn't all bad, though. As it was, the children and I have remained very close.

"It was when Thomas and Lydia...well, that was when I moved here. He needed someone and I wasn't *all* he had, but I was about all he could get. His brothers are darling but they're useless and his sister is a dear, but she has significant troubles of her own."

This was fascinating information. I knew about *one* sister, but Thomas had a real family–brothers *and* a sister!

I was an only child, so siblings were something I had never known.

I sat thoughtfully as Gerry finished her wine, one arm wrapped around my knees while the other held my glass.

"Thank you for your kindness toward him," she said softly and I thought I saw tears in her eyes. "Most women see a beautiful man–that face melts hearts and that body seems to incinerate their common sense–and they go crazy trying to pin him down.

"Not one of them has been kind or patient or caring, always just chasing after him to satisfy their own agenda. They want his body or his money, or both, and he's become extremely jaded.

"You've been good for him, Natalie." She held up a hand before I could protest or even interject.

"I teased him about spending so much time at your place and he had to confess that you were feeding him, for no reason other than to be nice, as far as he could tell." A big smile broke out across her face. "Lydia wasn't much of a cook, and he's hopeless in the kitchen, but that boy has always loved to eat."

I leaned over to put my empty glass on the coffee table. Now that I felt like I had something of an ally, I wrapped my other arm around my legs and fixed Gerry with an earnest look.

"I know what it's like to have your heart broken," I said softly. "I think his has been broken far worse than mine and I don't know if he can be helped through that, but something makes me want to. And...I'm not trying to be his friend to get into his pants." I struggled with what I wanted to put into words. I knew I wasn't being quite completely honest with myself, or with her.

"He deserves to be happy too, just like I do, and so as silly as it is, it makes me happy to do things for him. He just...lights up every time." There was so much more, but words were insufficient.

"That's what makes you perfect for him," she said, lifting herself from the sofa and setting the empty wine bottle and her glass on the coffee table next to mine. "He's always needed someone who would think of him first, and he's never had that. He just has to learn to trust you, because he's learned the hard way not to trust women." She shuddered, shaking off a thought. Then she winked, reaching out to smooth my hair. "Whether you decide you just want to keep things friendly, or maybe more, you have his attention. In the meantime...food is his love language. But it would seem you've got that figured out." She grinned.

I followed her to the door as she began the process of seeing herself out, and I invited her over for dinner on Thursday night, when I knew Thomas would be out of town on business.

My brain ached as it tried to catalog all the new information Gerry had plugged in over the course of an hour. It didn't seem possible, but her story raised even more questions in my mind.

I still didn't have a definitive grasp on Lydia, and I was sure there was at least one child in the mix, but some of the important facts were still nebulous.

I still didn't have a handle on why Thomas was such an angry mess all of the time. All I knew was that he was alone. Somehow, for some reason, his family was gone.

Checking all the locks and turning out the lights, I used the banister as a tow rope to pull myself up the stairs and toward my bedroom.

That night, when I fell asleep I dreamed of a little boy who looked like Thomas, with dark hair and golden-brown eyes.

In those dreams, I spent the whole exhausting night trying to protect him from a faceless monster.

SIXTEEN

Thomas

I had known the instant I opened my eyes that morning that something was wrong. The throbbing in my head slowed my thought process, but I tried to think back to the last thing I could remember...and I couldn't remember getting home.

I couldn't remember getting up the stairs or getting undressed.

I couldn't remember getting into bed–this wasn't even my bed, but I'd been sleeping in here since my lawyer delivered the devastating blow.

I gagged, instantly aware that I smelled disgusting and I rolled carefully, catching a whiff of something sweet from the pillow next to my head. It smelled familiar, clean, comforting, and a lot like a woman.

Dragging myself into the shower, I scrubbed the awful smells from the night before off my body and quickly washed my hair.

Why did I smell coffee?

Somehow I had gotten home and it seemed unlikely I'd done that on my own.

Somehow I had gotten into bed and I didn't feel half as shitty as I should have, so someone had probably convinced me to hydrate.

And the pillow–don't forget the pillow.

Shit, had I brought a woman home?

Most mornings I walked around the house in my underwear or gym shorts, checking my emails, maybe frying a couple eggs after a workout. But today...well, just in case Gerry was in my kitchen again–woman showed up whenever she damn well pleased–I put on a pair of joggers.

Finding Natalie in my kitchen was a little scary, because she was the last person I'd expected.

My heartrate picked right up when I walked into the room and found her stirring away at something on my stove, and the domestic scene almost brought tears to my eyes. I couldn't remember ever finding Lydia making something that hadn't come from a takeout container. She typically left me to fend for myself, since she hardly ate more than carrot sticks and fucking rice cakes. She'd avoided fat like it was the antichrist and as forty crept closer she ended up paying big bucks to have the shit injected into her face, since her anorexic diet made her look haggard.

When I walked back out into the living room to discover Natalie had gone, with breakfast hot and waiting on the stove, I actually felt guilty.

I'd managed to chase her away.

Gerry walked into my house just over an hour later and threw my keys down on the island countertop. She stood there glaring at me while I leaned against the sink, having made a second cup of coffee after carefully eating a pile of greasy hash browns, bacon and toast. Finally, I didn't feel like throwing up–at least until I saw the expression on Gerry's face.

You fucked up something bad, boy.

"Don't take it out on her, Thomas," she finally snapped. "She didn't have to pick you up in the middle of the night.

"She didn't have to stay over to make sure you didn't choke on your own vomit.

"She certainly didn't have to make you breakfast." She gestured sharply toward the stove. "She could have left you to figure out how to get back to your truck, but she didn't. And my very psychic sensibilities tell me you were far less than generous toward her this morning."

She stood there a second longer, gauging my expression. "Yeah...that's what I thought."

That's how I found myself slinking through the aisles of the grocery store, filling my basket with a half-assed apology: food, wine. I even looked for flowers, but I was afraid that would send a confusing message, because everyone knew what flowers meant–even me.

That's also how I found myself standing on her front porch with absolutely no words in my head and a little fear in my throat.

That's how, when she let something slip of how her husband had neglected her, I started to hope we might have a few more things in common than I'd thought. Like maybe she could *see* me and understand some of the clawing, sucking anger that threatened to steal my every breath.

Gerry texted me later that night to tell me she'd had a long, boozy talk with Natalie and would I please start answering some of the questions the woman was dying to ask? It was time to put myself out there, she said. Trust another human.

I shuddered when I thought about it. Even Gerry didn't know *all* the details, and if I could help it I would never tell the whole story, in every gory detail, to another living soul. Because the less others knew about the details, the less they would pity me.

Did they think I didn't see it?

Poor man lost his family.

His wife left him, you know. Women never leave–something must be wrong with him.

Maybe he couldn't satisfy her, or maybe he was mean or spiteful or abusive.

Maybe he wasn't worth the effort it took to love him.

That was it, wasn't it? The fear that dogged me all day long and ate me alive at night: Maybe I wasn't worth the effort it took, and I'd done a damn good job of making sure no one got close enough to try.

I barked and snapped and snarled like a rabid dog.

I refused to engage in conversations, to attend church, or to show up at social gatherings.

I only went grocery shopping when it was absolutely necessary, and even then I showed up as the store was just opening its doors, running through the market in a panic as I threw convenient freezer items into my cart.

My muscles were fueled by TV dinners with more cheap fat and calories than flavor or nutrition. Even I knew I was buying trouble if I kept eating that way.

For whatever reason, Natalie just kept feeding me. She expected me to show up at meal times and more often than not I did, even if I wasn't working at her house that day. I just couldn't stay away, knowing she'd gone through the trouble and had probably made something spectacular, because she always did, and with a regular feeding schedule of good quality food, I felt better.

Slept better.

Put on muscle faster.

I was a little less hair-trigger angry all the time, so maybe her cooking was kind of saving my life. (I didn't like that at all, because that meant I owed her something, and probably more than just undying gratitude.)

That night when I crawled into bed, I actually took the time to say a prayer. I asked for the same things my brain was always screaming about: Help me get over what *she* did.

Help it to stop hurting.

Help me to stop missing them.

Help me to learn to trust someone deserving and let me be deserving of her *trust.*

Hold up, that was new.

Not Natalie–no God, it can't be her. Because once she learns just how empty I am, she'll want nothing more to do with me.

SEVENTEEN

Natalie

Thomas didn't show up at the Masters' house until Wednesday, the day before I knew he was leaving on business. He wore a grim, determined expression and I walked him through the completed sitting room and the mostly-completed dining room so he could see the living designs, rather than the flat sketches I'd shown him only days before.

It took us longer than I'd thought it would to hang the chandelier. The angle was awkward and the ceilings were tall, and I learned quickly that despite the fact Thomas walked on roofs like he was a mountain goat, he hated ladders. So that was what found me on the skyscraper ladder, twenty feet up, holding the wiring caps in my teeth as I lined up the wires and twisted the appropriate colors together. Then very carefully, at the risk of upsetting the ladder or dropping the chandelier–thankfully a deceptively airy, lightweight confection–I mounted it to the ceiling.

Thomas was sweating by the time I got back down to the ground, and he gave my arm a quick squeeze. "Watching you up there made me so nervous." He shivered, and I wondered if I should ask him if he was all right.

I'd brought a check for him, based upon the days he'd put in helping me paint. "I'm a little short," I explained as I handed him the small scrap of paper. "I didn't count on it taking so long to put up the chandelier, so I'll bring you a check for the difference."

"You'll do no such thing." His voice was gruff and I looked up to see a frown creased between his eyes. He crumpled the check in his hand and reached over, shoving it into the front pocket of my overalls, careful not to let his fingers brush my chest.

"Thomas!" I shrieked. "When you did my roof and I asked why you didn't have help, you said it was because you couldn't afford help. You need to cash this check!" I pulled it out of the pocket and tried to smooth it with my hands.

He hadn't cashed the one for my roof yet either.

Or the one for all the work he'd done on the windows.

He was grinning at me like he knew a secret I didn't, and I folded the rumpled check in half with a frustrated huff and tucked it into the pocket of his t-shirt. I was not so careful when it came to touching his chest and it put a goofy grin on my face. Touching the man made me absolutely stupid, like his skin just siphoned off my active brain cells.

"Truth is," he said slowly, helping me to collapse the ladder, "that I can afford plenty. I just don't like dealing with *people*."

He didn't elaborate and I didn't ask, but I did roll my eyes and shake my head.

Maybe that meant I wasn't people.

An idea came to me as I packed up my gear for the day, my project at Christa's house finally completed, and I grinned to myself as I formulated the plan and before starting my car I shot a quick text to Gerry to ask if I could count on her cooperation.

Gerry's gleeful cooperation immediately secured, I waved cheerfully to Thomas and pointed the Subaru down the driveway. I'd invited him to dinner, though I knew he wouldn't come–I could read his moods better than he thought–so I could get started tonight.

By the time he arrived home from his trip, the man wouldn't know what had hit him.

EIGHTEEN

Thomas

Natalie had no idea what I could afford and what I couldn't, and there was very little I couldn't. That was something I kept a secret, though. Once women recognized me: recognized my stock options, my holdings, my investment portfolio, my bloated account in Switzerland and the smaller account I kept stateside for liquidation, things got weird.

Every time.

In fact, that was a large part of the reason I didn't trust them, especially since my own wife had once admitted to me that I was her meal ticket rather than the love of her life.

Eventually Natalie would find out. Then she would look at me the same way all the others did.

It always started with sympathy. Then, if Google was summoned, it morphed into avarice.

Sometimes there were lustful looks, but greed always seemed to trump lust, because I wasn't nearly as pretty as the number of zeroes attached to my name.

I kept watching Natalie for the signs, surprised that I was starting to consider things with her that I hadn't considered doing with a woman for a long time.

But in this case, it didn't seem to be happening. Natalie was good at keeping her distance lately and I didn't often catch her stealing looks at me, even though I kind of wanted to.

She didn't play coy. She was straightforward and sweet, but I never felt like she was flirting.

Maybe she really has *put me in the Friend Zone.*

That was sobering and, if I was a little honest, really disheartening, because already I hated that I wanted her to think about me in the ways I couldn't stop thinking about her.

The weird part was that she seemed genuinely mad every time I tried to do something nice for her. They were things any other woman would have flat-out expected of me.

She'd gotten so upset when I didn't cash her checks, and it was everything I could do to keep from telling her the materials...the labor...it was all so inconsequential, I didn't have the heart to charge her for it.

After all, I knew she was struggling in her own way. It must have been hard to leave such a dominant, controlling prick, and she'd admitted he was doing his best to tie up her finances in complicated knots.

Speaking of her asshole husband, was it wrong for me to be thoroughly jealous? Because shit, I was.

I'd looked the guy up and found pictures of them at events together. She was beautiful, her smile dazzling, a real knockout in whatever she wore.

That body...holy shit.

But her husband, by comparison, shared none of her warmth or her draw and the nicest word that came to mind was *imperious*. He was stiff and formal, never so much as a flash of his teeth.

The guy looked like he had a sharp poker up his ass.

How the hell did he land her?

I sat staring at one picture for a long time. The smile on her face was so dazzling, I wanted to climb into the picture and ask her how her lips could lie when her eyes told the truth. Her eyes were hollow and hard. She was smiling brilliantly, but she looked so sad.

The next morning I packed a small bag and made the routine trip to the airport in my truck. I found it kind of humorous to park a work truck in the long-term parking, and I made sure to lock the huge tool chest in the back before I walked away from it.

There was no reason to feel guilty for leaving.

There was no reason to feel guilty for not telling Natalie where I was going or what I was doing, because it was best if she continued to think that I was just a lowly contractor, whatever the variety.

The truth was that I didn't want to give her the opportunity to disappoint me.

I'd been so shocked when she announced I was her *friend*, for a second I wondered if she thought something was wrong with me. Maybe she wasn't attracted to me and that bruised my pride a little.

That Natalie was feeding me made me her charity case.

Not to sound stereotypical, but food was definitely the way to my heart, considering how long I'd gone without the care a good woman typically provided.

Was that sexist of me? Eh, maybe. But when I thought about what I wanted my home life to look like, it involved a clean and welcoming house filled with delicious smells, laughing children...and later, once the kids were in bed, a woman who wanted me as much as I wanted her.

Warm.

Fragrant.

Soft.

Teasing.

Loud.

Fuck yes, loud.

A woman who trailed her fingers down my chest and kissed me frantically, just as desperate to tear off my clothes as I was hers.

In my mind's eye I could picture Natalie's slim fingers wrenching my shirt open, buttons flying, because she was too impatient. She would have *that look* in her eye: a wicked gleam.

Shit.

I pulled the tray table down over my lap just as the flight attendant leaned over to ask if I wanted anything to drink. Thank God I did it then, or I'd have poked her damn eye out, she got so close.

About the only thing that could have gotten me out of the funk I'd been in the past few days were the cute little overalls Natalie wore while we were painting. Maybe *she* thought they were baggy and forgiving, but they hugged her in all the right places and even though I acted like I wanted her to leave me the fuck alone, I also wanted to back her into a corner and slip my hands into the sides to smooth over her skin while I kissed her silly.

Damn it, you idiot. Get it together.

The flight attendant carefully set a hot cup of tea on the tray table, her smile a little more than friendly. "Here you are, Mr. Atholton. Please let me know if there's anything else I can do for you."

I smiled at her, knowing my expression was tight.

It won't be you, that's for sure.

Women like her were the reason I hated flying commercial, though I did on occasion and this time it was because my pilot was in Arizona, caring for an ailing parent.

What the hell was wrong with me? Was I so broken that I couldn't appreciate the advances of a beautiful woman?

Yes.

Was I such a mess that I couldn't put the past behind me and lose myself in a few meaningless encounters?

Yes.

I looked down at the thin band on my left hand and wondered why I still wore it.

Oh, right: guilt.

I clenched my fingers into a tight fist. I was never really going to be rid of Lydia, was I?

I sighed in frustration and sipped my tea, irritated with myself. I had no way to take the edge off and ordering a drink, which would turn into six, was a bad idea.

Instead, I would make the trip from one coast to the next. Again. To meet with my lawyers and Lydia's.

Then there was a meeting of the board, for *my* company, the one Harrison had stolen from me.

Then a meeting with my team at Stanford.

The only reprieve from all these meetings was to fall into bed in my hotel room, alone and exhausted, wishing I could kiss my babies goodnight just one more time and fall asleep in the warm, comforting arms of the woman who loved me.

Whoever that was.

NINETEEN

Natalie

This guy wasn't going to take my money, that much was clear. He held three checks from me: roof, windows and painting, and he hadn't cashed a single one. It irked me, making me feel like I was up to my eyeballs in debt to him, though it was clear he considered us even, and probably since I kept him fed.

And let's be clear: The man could *eat.* Like a starving refugee.

After unloading my car, I hurried into the house and synched up my phone to my laptop, so I could pull the pictures the next day when posting a piece about Christa's house.

Then I practically skipped down to the kitchen to take inventory of my cupboards, quickly compiling a meal plan and a grocery list on the small notepad I kept in the junk drawer.

That night I drew up a batch cooking plan and I took stock of the storage containers I could stand to spare, adding all manner of supplies to my list.

Then I sent Gerry a text detailing my plans, as she'd agreed to help.

She was waiting for me in my kitchen when I got back from the market the next afternoon and I stared at her stupidly as I hauled in the first paper bag stuffed with groceries. I was entirely certain I'd locked all the doors before I left.

She held up a set of keys, grinning at me as she sipped from a glass of something that looked stronger than the wine we'd had the last time she'd been over.

"We have the same handleset," she said with another jingle of the keys, and I rolled my eyes.

Holy crap, Thomas had been right.

We cleaned and peeled and chopped, then stirred and sifted and cooked and baked, well into the night. The foil pans I'd bought at the market began to accumulate in my refrigerator and on the island countertop as we labeled and added a date to the top of each sealed container, and it was past midnight by the time we finished.

By then we were both a little goofy, having ingested several of Gerry's "top secret family recipe" Old Fashioneds. I was pretty sure she'd poured straight turpentine into the last one, since my throat felt like I'd swallowed fire ants.

"I'm fine to drive," Gerry insisted and I looked at her curiously. "Besides, by now Sheriff Landry is home and in bed."

"It's after midnight. Won't it be odd if we show up at his house and just start carrying in a ton of stuff? Someone will see us."

"Sweetheart, if there's one thing people in this town need to learn, it's how to mind their own business. You can bet that won't be happening anytime soon, so it's best to live your life the way you want because they'll talk no matter what."

She had a point.

We loaded all the containers into tote bags and slotted everything carefully into the back of my car, then made a slow trip through the quiet streets to Thomas's house.

Gerry fished her key ring out of her pocket and selected a key, fitting it to the lock of the front door and swinging it wide. Then we tag-teamed, with me bringing bag after bag from the back of the car to hand off to her at the front door as she walked everything in.

Once the Subaru was empty, I joined her in the house. She had stacked everything on Thomas's island and I giggled when I saw how much we'd managed to put together in just a few hours. "Holy shit, Gerry. Where are we going to put all of it?"

"That's why we made the freezer meals first," she said, grabbing a bag in each hand and disappearing down a back hallway. I grabbed two bags and followed, finding myself in a neat, spacious laundry room at the back of the house. The walls had been tiled with clean, shiny white subway tiles and there was a sorting bin next to the front-loading washer and dryer, with clothes neatly sorted and awaiting their turn through the appliances.

This guy's not normal.

"Over here." Gerry redirected my attention to the chest freezer sharing a wall with the door, and she tipped the lid open as I started to unpack the bags, handing her one container after another.

"Not bad." She surveyed our work carefully. "We could do another round and then we'll get to the baked goods. I don't need to tell you the man has a taste for homemade bread and chocolate chip cookies."

I grinned gleefully to myself, trying to picture the look on Thomas's face when he arrived home to find a house full of carefully prepared food.

I wished for a moment to be a fly on the wall, when he realized we'd filled his house with food so that even when he locked himself away in his house, hiding from the world, I could be sure he was being well fed.

"He'll be gone for a week this time," Gerry said as she trailed back into the kitchen, looking around her thoughtfully. "You'd hardly know anyone lived here."

She was right, I thought, looking around at what could be seen from the light over the stove. Everything was immaculate, not a thing out of place. There were no dirty dishes in the sink and the dishwasher's light indicated a fresh load was contained in its trays, the counters scrubbed clean.

"It's because he doesn't really *live* here," Gerry said thoughtfully and I looked at her quickly. "He's barely living at all," she said, still more to herself than to me and her expression was one of deep sadness.

Something in her tone of voice had me rushing across the distance. I pulled her into a tight hug and she squeezed me back with just as much strength. "You love him like his real mom," I said into her shoulder–she was quite a bit taller than me–and she squeezed harder.

"I do," she said. "But I'm not enough. I can't fill the deepest cracks in his heart. That's a job for someone else, and he has to let someone *in* to do it."

We drove quietly back to my place and parted ways for the night in my driveway. She promised to come over the next evening in order to complete round two of Operation Feed Thomas.

That night my heart felt lighter than it had in a while. I showered quickly and brushed my teeth, crawling into my bed feeling genuinely tired. Maybe it was my reward for a good deed, I thought as I drifted almost immediately into sleep: Tonight I'd earned my way out of insomnia.

TWENTY

Thomas

Since all my meetings were in Palo Alto, this time I booked a hotel in Half Moon Bay. It was something I did when I needed time on the beach to decompress. It was something I couldn't easily get if I stayed at Maren's in Sonoma, being a little too far inland, and I knew this round of meetings would be tough. Harder than usual, since Harrison still had something I wanted desperately.

There was no way in hell he'd give it to me, either. He'd already found a way to ensure I stepped down as CEO of my own company, the one I'd founded and brought him on as a partner.

I had no bargaining chips left and he knew it. He had me right where he wanted me.

I couldn't begin to pinpoint the moment our friendship had begun to rot in his mind. There weren't any reasons I could come up with that helped explain why he so desperately hated me.

I'd managed to maintain a seat on the board, after a great deal of negotiating and tremendous legal action, and it drove him nuts to know I had a vote in how he was running *my* company after all he'd done to shut me out.

Why hadn't I fought harder? I asked myself that question for the millionth time as I rolled up my pants to walk along the beach. The sand was packed hard, cool underfoot despite the relative warmth of the late summer day.

The answer was simple: I'd needed to get out. I'd already lost too much and it was time to focus on rebuilding my relationship with my family.

I'd needed to take them far away, away from the distractions and the constant noise.

Away from the social responsibilities and expectations.

Away from Harrison.

It had been two years already, during which time I'd made countless trips out to fix Harrison's fuck-ups.

The other board members were over him. He'd demonstrated stunning negligence and since I was no longer there to cover up for him, to fix things, to make sure the things he was doing weren't going to damage my company or drag it into the legal turmoil of a federal investigation, things were taking a nosedive.

The roaring surf was a welcome soundtrack, though it did little to soothe my boiling thoughts: For a handful of years, I'd had it all. I was the golden child, blessed by the gods of Fortune, Connections and Hard Work. I'd had the houses, the cars, the beautiful wife...I stopped myself with a Talking Heads lyric.

I was tired of playing out the old memories in rapidfire snapshots in my mind's eye. That life wasn't exactly what I wanted anymore, I realized, my ambitions still strong but my need for peace and quiet shaped by the time I'd spent in the deep south.

My stomach roared angrily and I squinted at the watch on my wrist. The inn served a great breakfast–I stayed here often enough to know that–but for the rest of the day people were on their own.

Rolling my pant legs down and slipping into my shoes, I walked across the parking lot to the little Italian restaurant that sat near the road.

My favorite waiter was on duty, the guy who always cracked dry jokes and remembered my name every time I came in.

"Thomas!" Bill's face lit up with a genuine grin, and I grinned right back at him, noticing that he was wearing better quality shoes this time.

I'd made sure of that the last time I visited, tossing a few hundred extra dollars into the tip and telling him he needed to be taking better care of his feet.

I knew he was diabetic, thanks to the countless hours of conversation we'd had in brief snatches over the past few years, and though he'd never complained, it had bothered me to watch him. It was clear he didn't take a single step without pain.

Bill was a big guy–not so much that he was tall, but he was solid, with a barrel chest and not much of a neck.

Built like a brick shitehouse, Da would say.

When Bill leaned in to throw an arm over my back in a hug that ended with loud clapping noises, I tried not to let the surprise show on my face. I would never get used to people seeming genuinely happy to see me.

"You look good," he commented as he slid the plate of lasagna in front of me and grabbed the glass I'd already drained of water. "Your face is fuller–in a good way. You finally learn how to cook?"

I couldn't help but snort. He and I both knew the chances of that were slim.

His face lit with understanding. "Ah, you found someone who knows how to cook." A grin stretched wide across his face and he punched me gently in the arm. "Only other explanation. Good on you, boy."

I nodded, shoveling a forkful of the lasagna into my mouth and chewed quickly, hoping to quiet the roar my stomach had just put up. "She found me, I suppose, and she's an amazing cook–went to culinary school for a while."

Bill's eyes went soft and dreamy. "My Nora did, too. I'd blame her for this..." he gestured toward his expansive middle. "But most of this happened after she passed. I missed her cooking something terrible, and I still do, but I miss *her* more than the food." He struggled to swallow and I felt terribly out of my depth. "No amount of store bought cookies replaces a woman's love and care and believe me, I've done the homework."

"Don't I know it," I sighed. But then it hit me: No, I *didn't* know it. I had no idea what Natalie felt for me, and if Lydia was the ruler against which I measured love, I didn't want *anything* to do with it.

Clearly, I'd never actually had a woman's love.

Bill knew my weakness and without asking whether I wanted dessert, he slipped into the bakery case and brought me a huge slice of wild blueberry pie.

I'd have said I was too stuffed to eat it, but I could *always* make room for pie.

"Hannah made this one fresh, just this morning," he said, sliding the plate in front of me with a huge grin on his face. He stood there too, waiting for me to take my first bite.

"It's amazing," I said around a mouthful and he clapped me on the back before hurrying off to another table. And it was good, I thought as I continued to chew.

But the crust wasn't as flaky at Natalie's.

The flavor was flatter, more bland.

Uh-oh.

A warning chimed in my gut just as a fierce wave of a foreign emotion balled up in my throat.

I miss her cooking.

But even I knew it was more than that, because I was pretty sure I missed *her.*

Snapping a quick photo of my plate, I fired it off to her with a text: *Not half as good as the pies you make, but at least I didn't drop this one on the front walk.*

Her response was quick, the three little dots bouncing on my screen almost immediately.

You haven't had my Banoffee yet. It's my mother's recipe, and the only thing I've ever seen her make, unless we're counting cocktails. I call it "Conflict Diamond Dessert," because every man she's made it for has proposed within a week.

Why did that make me uncomfortable? It wasn't a warning, was it?

I decided to go for witty banter.

How many proposals have you racked up with this heavenly pie?

She didn't answer right away and I paid my bill, tucking a few hundred dollars behind the receipt for Bill.

I walked back across the parking lot and let myself into my room, trying to decide whether I should open my laptop and throw myself into work or put on some swim shorts and lie in the sunshine on one of the deck chairs near the small pool.

The lure of the sunshine was too strong to resist and the phone vibrated gently on the chair next to me as I soaked up the rays. I held up a hand to shade the screen, my sunglasses hardly enough against the bright sunlight.

That pie? I make it in secret. And then I eat all of it. My recipe is far better than my mother's and I would never purposely employ such a fierce weapon against the weak and unprepared.

My lips turned up in a smile. So that was why she hadn't made it for me.

Weak and unprepared, huh? Yeah...bring it on, baby.

TWENTY-ONE

Natalie

Though I filled up the week with tasks, including several more nighttime trips with Gerry to Thomas's house, the week seemed to drag by interminably. I began to realize just how much I'd isolated myself, if I was counting on Thomas for company. And though Gerry was dropping by with some frequency, I knew it was unfair to foist all my friendship needs upon her.

Thomas's silly, almost-flirty texts dwindled and I knew it was because he was insanely busy, but I still checked my phone every five minutes like an idiot. I didn't want to admit that every time I heard a chime, my heart jumped into my throat.

Maybe it's him.

Because I wanted it to be him. He was almost playful, and I got a little charge every time I realized one of his texts could be taken in a completely different way.

Friends, Natalie, I reminded myself. *Your idea.*

I worked hard to keep my days full of activity in order to beat my body and brain into submission. That way I slept at night, as soundly as I had in a long time. I was too tired to startle awake every time the crickets stopped chirping or a raccoon knocked over a trash bin somewhere down the block.

With increased attention to my content generation, readership and ad clicks were beginning to tick upward again. My social media numbers were climbing and I considered adding a few simple YouTube tutorials to my ever-growing list of endeavors.

Once I'd created a storyboard for myself for the rest of the month, I pitched a few more articles to magazines geared toward design and DIY.

Then another idea, only somewhat related, hit me.

I walked across the yard, crossing into Gerry's and knocking at the back door. Her house was similar in layout to my own, with the back door opening right into the kitchen and she opened it even before I had the chance to knock a second time.

My face felt hot and I knew it meant I was glowing with excitement. I hurried into her kitchen behind her and talked quickly, gesticulating wildly because I couldn't keep still.

She quickly handed me a piece of paper and a pen so I could draw out what I'd envisioned and she shook her head at me with a small smile on her face. "He's home in two days, Natalie. Do you think that can be accomplished in that short a period?"

I gestured for Gerry to follow me and we hurried across her yard, back into my own, where I propped open the door to my back shed. Thomas had called it a treasure trove and I hoped it held at least most of the materials I needed, since driving to a big box store and shopping for the essentials would eat up a lot more time than I had left.

The two of us collapsed the back seats in the Subaru and started piling in lumber and the beaten up boxes of sturdy wire shelving I'd found at the back of the shed. Then Gerry tied everything in place, since I'd have to drive over with the hatch open, and I rushed inside to grab my toolbox. I had no idea what kind of tools Thomas had in his garage, and I wasn't going to leave anything to chance.

Backing the car into his driveway, leaving a few feet to open the garage door, I shook my head as Gerry retrieved her keys and unlocked the side door to the building.

"Do you have keys for every place in town?" I asked as she grinned at me through the panes of the garage door, the locks squealing as she shot them back and hoisted the creaky old door.

"My key probably opens the doors to a quarter of the houses in this town," she said. "Yours too, remember? If you want any privacy, you might want to consider changing that handleset." She wiggled her eyebrows at me, and I knew she'd been the one to set the horrid flowers on my table.

We unloaded the supplies onto the lawn and Gerry sat just inside the back gate of my car, staring down at my rough plans. "I don't know how much help I can be," she said as she squinted into the garage, and I took a deep breath as I stared at all the crap piled into what was actually a very large space.

"Holy cow," I said, wondering for the first time if I'd had any idea what I was getting myself into. This was going to involve a lot of hauling, a lot of sorting, then building and organizing.

There was no way I was going to get this done in two days.

"I'll start hauling things out," Gerry said, eyeing the mountain of paint cans stacked along one wall. "I can handle most of it while you get in there and start measuring.

"There's a work table buried somewhere in that mess and if we can unearth it, there might also be a circular saw." She eyed the pile of lumber. "Maybe not the best answer, but we can make it work."

True to her word, she hauled things into the driveway, sorting them into neat piles so that reorganizing later would be faster.

I took measurements and made notes on my paper, switching around a few of the plans until I was satisfied that what I had on paper would not only be functional, but it would save the most space.

Neighbors drifted past occasionally, most under the auspices of walking their dogs, and each called out a friendly greeting to Gerry. She ran interference so I could continue to work uninterrupted and whenever I heard my name, I raised a hand in a distracted greeting.

By the time the last rays of sunlight had disappeared, I had assembled most of the shelves and built a sorting system for some of his larger items. Then I got to work hanging a pegboard on the wall while Gerry disappeared into the house to warm up one of the meals we'd left in his freezer.

We sat on the cement floor while we ate and Gerry looked around the room, more shadows than light thanks to the weak light of the single bulb.

There was a smile on her face. "You get an idea, people better get out of your way."

"There's no way I'd have gotten this far without you," I said, and she clanked her fork handle against my own like one would clink glasses.

"I'm going to stay a little longer if that's ok, so I can get paint on the walls. That way, when I show up tomorrow morning, I can just put all the shelving in place and start organizing. It's going to be a much brighter, more usable space." I paused, biting my lip. "I hope he likes it–he said he wanted to turn this into his workshop."

"You're accumulating points," she said as she shoveled another forkful of her enchilada into her mouth.

"That frustrating man won't cash my checks for the work he's done!" I exclaimed. "I have to find some way to pay him back for all the work and the money he's already put into my house!"

Gerry smiled knowingly as she looked anywhere but at me, and I felt a prickle of discomfort.

"I'm not doing this to get into his pants," I blurted, suddenly unable to eat another bite of my dinner. I wasn't sure she'd believed me the first time I'd told her, because I hadn't believed myself.

"It's just...this helps me to have something to focus on that's not myself. It keeps me busy and it makes me happy to feel like I'm being useful...helpful...or something."

"He's not going to know what to do with you. He already doesn't." She tried to hide her smile by popping the last forkful of food into her mouth and I sat puzzled, unsure as to what she meant.

She set down her plate, stretching her long legs out in front of her as she leaned back on the heels of her hands. "He doesn't know what to do when people are nice to him. You understand that," she said, fixing me with an appraising stare. "You're a beautiful woman. When a man goes out of his way to do something nice for you, don't you suspect his motives?"

My face flamed instantaneously when I realized no man other than Thomas had done something nice for me in a very long time.

Was Gerry trying to insinuate that either of us wanted to be more than friendly?

Were we trying to one-up the other in this silly game of ingratiating favors we were playing, trying to see who would cave first?

"You don't think *he'll* think I'm trying to be his girlfriend, do you? That's not at all what I meant!"

Was it?

I dropped my own plate to the floor and slapped a hand against my forehead. "Ah, shit," I moaned, dropping my face between my knees. "That asshole broke me."

That was the in Gerry had been waiting for, and I knew it the instant the words were out of my mouth.

That was how we spent the next hour sitting on the garage floor, too deep in conversation about the demise of my marriage to even consider working.

Well, I wasn't–but Gerry was probably working, being that she was the shrink.

Gerry seemed weirdly happy when she finally pushed to her feet to stretch out the kinks, slapping her butt vigorously to restore circulation. "You were sent here for a reason, Natalie," she said as she scooped up both of our plates. "It could be that you're an answer to my prayers–his too, if he'd bother with them once in a while. Stubborn ass thinks he has to figure out and fix everything on his own."

That felt weird and I didn't know what to say, so I got to my feet and grabbed the supplies I needed to start painting the wooden walls.

While Gerry washed our few dishes and cleaned up the small amount of mess, I poured paint into a tray and began vigorously rolling it onto the walls. The light was weak and I'd need to cut in the next morning, before applying a second coat, but at least I could get the job started.

She waited patiently while I finished, swatting at errant mosquitoes while I wrapped up the tray for the night.

"I need to do something about this lighting," I said absently as I pulled down the main door and shot the locks back into place. Then she flipped the switch to kill the power to the single bulb and locked the door by feel.

I looked around at the enormous piles and stacks of things littering his driveway and she read my mind. "You could leave a stack of cash sitting here and it would still be here in the morning. It was probably silly to lock the garage."

She said so, but I wasn't so sure. It seemed to me that for being such a safe town, she was awfully careful to lock things behind her.

"Trust me. Mrs. O'Shaughnessy, across the street, is the best security system money can't buy. She's into her nineties and has decided she doesn't need sleep anymore. She'll be up most of the night, staring out the windows, watching for the hooligans who will never materialize."

I wondered if Mrs. O'Shaughnessy owned binoculars and was the one to blame for the gossip about the nighttime goings-on in Thomas's house.

It was late when we pulled into my driveway and though Gerry invited me over for a nightcap, I was too tired to do anything but fall asleep in a hot bath. So I declined her offer, telling her I would definitely take her up on it the next night, once I had finished the job. I would need the fortifications then, knowing Thomas would arrive home only hours after I left, and I had no idea how he would interpret my intentions. I didn't have a solid read on the guy yet and it was typical of me, I thought, to jump in without considering all the ramifications of my actions.

By some miracle, I managed to get through a hot bath without falling asleep and drowning myself, and as I wrapped myself up in a light bathrobe, a thought occurred.

I wound my hair into a towel and hurried down the stairs to the large closet in the laundry room, where I kept most of my staging materials.

It took me fifteen minutes to find what I was looking for and I made a note to myself to spend time organizing the disastrous pile in the closet over the weekend. But there, at the bottom of the pile, were the boxes I'd been looking for. I knew I'd had extras, I thought gleefully, piling everything up by the front door and hurrying back up the stairs.

I would have to be up early if there was any hope of finishing my idiotic project, and I tossed the robe and the towel over my bathroom door before crashing into bed.

• • • •

MY STOMACH WAS IN KNOTS when I woke up and I could barely choke down breakfast, brewing enough coffee to fill a large Thermos and loading it into the Subaru along with the boxes I'd pulled the night before.

Thomas was flying home today and the minutes were counting down.

It was before seven when I arrived and I fished the key out of my pocket, the one Gerry had wordlessly removed from her keyring the night before and handed to me. In fact, she'd handed me two, and I could only presume the other one was to his house.

Gerry had appointments throughout the day and couldn't come with me, so I resolved that if I needed food, or if I just couldn't hold off on using the bathroom any longer, it was easy enough to drive home. It felt too sneaky and invasive, thinking of letting myself into his house while he was away and unsuspecting. Somehow, I suspected he would interpret it as a breach of trust.

The building had several decently-sized windows and daylight was far better than the weak light from the bulb dangling in the middle of the room.

I worked quickly and by the time I had the second coat on the walls the room glowed with warm mid-morning light. The light paint had eliminated some of the dark shadows and the space looked fresh and cheerful.

It was going to be another hot one, I thought, having already sweated through my tank top, my wet ponytail hanging down my back and clinging to my skin. I wished I'd brought the box fan from my bedroom, and as I cleaned up all my painting supplies the cicadas began their obnoxious chatter.

The next step was to haul all the assembled shelving units from the center of the room to organize and mount along the walls. It was surprisingly quick work, and by lunchtime I choked down a few cups of hot coffee–which made me sweat even more–before starting to haul things back in from the driveway.

By early afternoon I had to pee mightily and I hurried home to use the bathroom and to retrieve some S-hooks from my own garage. I'd forgotten to pack them the night before and organizing the peg board would require the additional pieces.

The pegboard took longer than I'd thought it would. Still, I managed to get everything back inside, off the driveway, neatly organized on shelves.

I'd moved the huge wooden workbench, with grunts and sweat and curses, closer to one of the electrical boxes in the room. Then I daisy chained together some light bars, providing illumination on the underside of some of the shelves to brighten the room from the far end.

Putting floor lamps in a garage felt a little desperate, but I didn't have the time or the certification to rewire the building.

It was almost seven by the time I finished, and though I knew there were so many more tweaks I wanted to make, Gerry had warned me already that his plane landed early and he would be home in half an hour.

I pulled my initial drawing of the space and a stub of a pencil from the back pocket of my pants, scribbling a note across the top of my drawings and measurements and leaving the scraps on his work table.

Then I pulled the main door shut, shot the locks, and let myself out of the side door, locking it carefully before hurrying to my car and driving like hell to get home.

I was giddy when I pulled into Gerry's driveway, sweaty and smelly and grinning like my face would split as I pounded on her front door.

"Got it!" I sang as she swung open the door and her eyes crinkled as she smiled back.

"I had no doubt you would," she said. "But let me be the first to say you're quite possibly a bit manic–even so, I don't actually know *how* you did it."

A hand appeared from behind her back to pass me a tall glass of something boozy.

"I don't think you'd be the first to say that," I said, taking a grateful chug and coughing as the alcohol hit the back of my throat.

Five minutes later I was sitting in her kitchen while she chopped and stirred, directing me to rest my legs and feet while she cooked. I was only too happy to comply, already feeling a little fuzzy from the drink she had mixed, and I realized that I hadn't eaten anything since this morning. I'd been high as a kite on adrenaline and coffee.

That night Gerry fed me dinner, and as the sun set I stumbled back to my house, resolving to move my car from her driveway in the morning.

Or whenever I could see straight again, which would probably take a couple days.

I dumped my smelly clothes into the wash and drank a big glass of water before heading upstairs to shower.

What in the hell was I going to do with myself now? I wondered as I shampooed my hair. I'd been running on the fumes of excitement the last few days and while I'd been wildly productive, I felt the same slight letdown I felt every time I completed a really challenging project.

I'd changed into pajamas and unwound the towel from my hair when a wild hammering started at my front door. It made my heart stutter, because I knew who it was, and the noise was violent.

Angry.

Maybe, I thought as I hurried down the stairs, he was mad at me.

How is that possible? Crap. What did I screw up?

Without flipping on the porch light, I snapped back the lock and Thomas burst through the door, a paper bunched tight in his fist. He didn't have to flatten it out for me to read the message I'd scrawled for him: *Now we're even.*

"The hell we are," he snarled, shoving the note in my face and I stumbled back in surprise, suddenly eager to put a little extra distance between myself and the roaring monster who'd just charged through my door.

Rage made him seem even bigger.

"What the fuck were you doing in my house, Natalie?" he demanded, his voice still far too loud, and he slammed the door behind him. "You think that since you had to take my sorry ass home once, you can just let yourself in to snoop around while I'm gone? Maybe dig through my things to look for the answers to questions I know you're just dying to ask?"

My eyes filled with tears as he railed on and when his shoulders finally slumped, I understood he was done.

It was then that I turned away from him to walk into the kitchen, wiping my eyes on my shirt sleeves while my back was turned to him and I pretended it was utterly necessary to fill a glass of water.

I could feel the rage rolling off of him as he stood leaning against the island, the shirtsleeves of his button down rolled up over his forearms.

It didn't occur to me that perhaps he was angry about something more than me invading his privacy.

If I hadn't been so rattled, it would also have occurred to me that he was even more delicious in fitted dress pants, his long hair brushed back to fall neatly behind his ears.

"I didn't go to your house by myself, Thomas, and you know I wouldn't overstep like that. I had supervision and though I had the keys to your house while I was there today, I didn't go in because I didn't feel it was right to be in there without you or Gerry."

Shit. I winced. I'd just thrown my only other friend under the bus.

"What were you and *Gerry* doing in my house?" he asked suspiciously and suddenly I knew he hadn't yet discovered the freezer filled with meals, the fridge bursting with labeled containers, or the pie sitting under a glass dome I'd left on his counter the night before.

Maybe when he discovered it he'd feel like the ass he was.

"Gerry was kind enough to give me a lot of her time this last week," I said finally, wondering if he suspected I knew her link to him. "I'd never have been able to get it all done if she hadn't helped me."

His face didn't soften at all.

"You two are trouble together," he hissed and I pushed my hair back behind my ears, wondering how it was possible he could be so violently angry with me for having done something I'd thought was nice.

I shrugged slowly. "I'd hoped it would be something you liked, since you'd mentioned wanting to turn your garage into a workshop." I knew my face had fallen and I turned my head quickly so he couldn't see the disappointed tears crowding my eyes. The last thing I wanted was for this man to see me crying again.

"I thought some of the paint cans had exploded from the heat." He shoved his hands through his hair. "What the hell, woman? I get home after the trip from hell and I smell paint when I park outside my damn garage. I thought I had an awful mess to clean up, and instead..." He looked up at me, and for the first time it seemed to dawn on him that I was upset. His mouth hung open as he stared at me.

"Go home, Thomas," I said tiredly, rubbing a hand into my eyes. "I mean, that was obviously the exact reason I did it: so you could drive over here after a day of traveling and make me feel like I'm about this big." I held up my fingers so he could see the millimeters of space between them.

"I didn't look through your things or spend time alone in your house. I did find a box of paperwork in your garage, but I left it on one of the shelves–I didn't go through it. So whatever your secrets are, they're still just yours."

I set my glass in the sink.

"I'd offer to feed you dinner, but I'm worn out. You're welcome to whatever you can find in my fridge, but I'm going to bed."

I went upstairs and shut my bedroom door, sinking down on the rug to wrap my arms around my knees and sniffle quietly in the dark.

The front door closed more gently than I'd expected and I heard a car start up outside.

I didn't go to the window, but I did crawl into my bed and though I was exhausted, the stupid tears just kept sliding down my cheeks during the hour it took me to fall asleep.

TWENTY-TWO

Thomas

It wasn't so late that I couldn't find a liquor store that was open. It was a stupid, impulsive decision I'd regret in the morning, drinking to forget, but I was furious and I didn't entirely understand why.

Rather than drink myself stupid with Smitty, I picked up a bottle of my favorite Scotch. It was the one I used to drink, back when I'd been a more routine drinker and less an abstainer who suffered the occasional lapse, and drove myself home.

Maybe I'd find some answers toward the bottom of this bottle.

People said it wasn't healthy to drink alone, but I disagreed. When I *really* drank, things got ugly. I wasn't the sort to curl up and cry, to reminisce, to get sloppy over the past. No, I drank to let out the rage, which was the very reason I so rarely did it.

I'd already terrified Lydia one night, turning into a roaring monster and putting my fist through the drywall. It was after she'd made the first of several terrible admissions, and I tried to kill the pain in my chest with booze. If I could pour enough of the stuff into the cavity, maybe I could drown the beating, twitching thing in there that ached so much.

The house sat, dark and quiet, waiting for me like a softly breathing, hibernating animal.

I sat in the truck, trying to decide whether I wanted to pop the cork out of the bottle to drink and sweat in my truck, or go inside to share the libations with the ghosts.

It was hot as fuck and I could hear a horde of mosquitoes outside my window, battering their tiny bodies against the glass as they skittered and skated, trying to get to the buffet on the other side.

So ghosts it was.

Nothing good will come of this.

It was rare I sat at home and drank alone–almost never, since there was nothing here to distract me.

Nothing to keep me from the boxes of photos I kept in the storage ottoman in the living room.

Nothing to keep me from sifting through the box of keepsakes stored in the credenza.

Nothing to save me from the destructive wallow, and by the time the buzz started in my head, the blinding rage found me.

She did this.

They did this.

They took everything from me.

Eventually I lurched up the stairs, the bottle in my hand. I couldn't be bothered to refill a glass just now.

The trip had been awful, just as I'd expected it would be.

The meeting with the divorce lawyers yielded a new set of demands.

Then the meeting with my other lawyers, the corporate team I kept, yielded some truly distressing information about Harrison's mismanagement of my company.

The board was searching for ways to legally reinstate my position, since Harrison clearly needed a babysitter.

On top of that, my personal project–my labor of love–had hit a major roadblock and the team I was working with at Stanford wasn't sure they'd have the kinks worked out in time to release the app simultaneously with the main program, into which it was supposed to neatly dovetail. One without the other was a failure and one more failure was something I couldn't handle.

I'd spent the last night of my trip at Maren's in Sonoma, like I almost always did. It was both the highlight and the most torturous part of every trip, because there were memories there, and monuments to the dead that both soothed and tortured me.

I'd been sitting in my office long enough I decided, slapping shut the lid of my laptop. The code was a blur anyway, and if I didn't cut myself off now I'd start looking for Lydia. I'd see all the photos of her being happy and I'd just simmer with resentment.

How could she just move on like that?

Snapping off the light, I kept one hand on the banister as I walked toward my room. It wasn't where I really wanted to be, I knew that, and I heard the small voice in my head.

I can't sleep, Daddy. Read me a story?

Leaning against the doorframe, I thought of all the times I'd crawled into that little bed with a book.

Held a tiny body against my chest as I sang a lullaby.

Picked up toys and stuffed animals to toss into a bin so little feet didn't trip over things in the middle of the night.

Smoothed back hair, tucked blankets, kissed foreheads.

I peeled myself off the doorframe and forced my feet a few steps further, into my own room. It was a cozy little cave where I could hide myself away, even the moon afraid to dip her rays into the deep darkness that lived here.

Setting the bottle on my nightstand, I finally kicked off my shoes and stripped off my work uniform: Pants, shirt, undershirt, belt and socks, all on the floor in a sloppy pile. Then I crashed into the bed, my head spinning and hot from what had already been too much scotch.

Rolling slowly to lean over the edge, I fished my phone from the pocket of my pants and lay there on my back, staring at the ceiling. I owed Natalie an apology; a big one, for being a complete asshole.

I wasn't mad at her, but unwelcome thoughts of her had been frustrating me all week. I'd taken it out on her, emotionally emptied from my trip, anger the only feeling I had left when it should have been gratitude.

My garage was fucking pristine.

I picked a fight with myself as I tried to string together words to text her.

You are such a fuck-up. She's been nothing but sweet and caring and you made a point of driving over there to jump down her throat. You're just mad that you want her and you're scared she doesn't want you back.

I do not. She's making me crazy! I can't handle any more of her nicey-niceness. Everyone expects something.

It scares you that she doesn't? You should just ask her what she wants from you; get it over with.

Shut up. You're not helping. Of course she wants something. Everyone does.

I leaned over to grab the bottle off the nightstand, taking a careful swig. The room was spinning although I was still, which meant there was a slim chance I might actually fall asleep tonight.

I gave up on the words and tossed the phone onto the nightstand, closing my eyes. I waited for sleep to find me and in that space in between, my imagination found her. It was where she curled into me, hooking one leg over mine, curling her fingers against my chest. She was so warm and fragrant. I could smell her hair; feel the softness of the silky strands on my shoulder.

Her heart was thudding gently against my ribcage, keeping time with my own.

And her voice...it was so achingly soft and sweet.

"Sleep, my love. Here is where you are safe."

For the first time in a long time I slept through the night–thanks, booze–and I didn't have a single nightmare.

TWENTY-THREE

Natalie

When I woke the next morning, I huffed an angry breath at the numbers on my alarm clock and rolled over to bury my head in the pillow on the other side of the bed. The night had been too short and I knew I'd burn up all my energy long before the day was done.

There was nothing for it. Birdsong drifted through the open windows, as well as the noise of a few cars on the street as people left their houses to travel to work.

I was awake and there was no use in trying to fight it.

I don't know why I bothered to check my phone, because it's not like I expected a voicemail or a texted apology from Thomas. Still, I wondered if he felt sufficiently like an ass when he got home and found the pie on his kitchen island.

Sitting at my island with the French press and a carton of half and half, I drank the whole pot of coffee before I decided I'd worked up enough energy to make breakfast.

I had no ambition. No drive or zip or desire to do things that involved even the most basic self-care this morning. However, with three large cups of coffee on an empty stomach, it was a matter of mere moments before I started to twitch like a cracked out squirrel.

I grabbed a piece of pre-sliced cheese to shove into my mouth while I pulled things from the fridge to put together a semi-respectable breakfast.

With food in my belly and the dishes slotted neatly into the dishwasher, I took myself upstairs to pay a few bills online and to make sure the post I'd scheduled had actually posted across my various platforms.

The office was hot and I wondered for the fifty-seventh time since moving in whether I could have some unobtrusive, reasonably inexpensive ductwork run through my house to get an air conditioning unit running.

The humidity was brutal. I'd already spotted mold trying to grow in my shower grout and I'd flipped out and scrubbed the whole thing with hydrogen peroxide.

The window was open as wide as I could possibly open it and I sat at my desk for a moment, eyeing all the unused wall space, wondering if I had any other spare windows kicking around in my treasure trove garden shed.

I decided to find out, pushing up from my desk and hurrying down the stairs to let myself into the back yard through the kitchen door.

The distance between the kitchen door and the garden shed couldn't have been more than fifty feet, and as I tramped through the too-long grass I could hear muffled shouting drifting from Gerry's house. The voices rose and fell and from the pitch of each, I could tell Thomas and Gerry were having an explosive disagreement.

This was my fault.

I changed course immediately, tapping on Gerry's back door. The voices continued, considerably louder now that I stood right outside the house.

Since it was clear no one could hear me and would not be answering the door, I let myself in and followed the yelling, my hackles raising as he continued to holler at Gerry.

"Stop it!" I yelled, rounding the corner to the living room and nearly slamming into Thomas. "Don't you dare take it out on Gerry because you think I did something stupid. Yell at me if you're mad–she was just being my friend–which is something you seem to have a *really hard time* doing." I felt my face crumple as I said it and I was able to register the look of shock on Gerry's face just before the wall of Thomas's chest completely obstructed my view.

"You are complete shit at minding your own business," he said, and before I could formulate a response, I couldn't breathe.

It took a minute for my brain to process that he had me in a boa constrictor grip, banded tightly against his chest by his giant arms, and just as I started to sink into him, he released me abruptly. I staggered a little, trying to regain my equilibrium.

Apparently that had been my thanks and I wanted more of it, please.

"Don't you think that's going to get you off the hook, mister," Gerry was saying, wagging a finger in Thomas's face. "That's not nearly enough. Now sit down with her–take your time–and pull your head out of your ass or you're going to lose the one person who's done nothing but show you kindness." She swatted him gently.

Gerry disappeared into the kitchen and I could hear pots and pans rattling as Thomas stood staring at me with an expression I thought might be dread. He really wasn't very good at apologies, and it was slowly dawning on me that the argument I'd overheard without processing was Gerry dressing *him* down for ripping me a new one the night before.

He crossed the room to sit in a chair near the window, about as far away from me as he could possibly get without sitting on the lawn.

I considered parking myself on the coffee table in front of him just to irritate him, but I settled for the sofa instead, on the other side of the room.

"I'm sorry," he said quietly, and I could tell the words tasted bad. "I don't have any excuses for my behavior. I'm...not very good about accepting help or gifts from others and when I found your note and realized what you'd done, I completely lost my shit. I was so angry with you, for thinking that somehow I was keeping score. Because that's what *Lydia* would have done: she keeps score."

I sat up straighter, ready to interject my disagreement and he shook his head at me.

"I understand. Gerry set me straight: You were teasing. You were doing something nice for me and I was a complete dick about it."

I nodded as he said it, because on that point we were in total agreement.

He shifted uncomfortably in his chair, seemingly unable to meet my eyes. "I found the pie this morning, when I was looking for food to soak up a stupid hangover.

"Then I opened the fridge to see if the eggs were any good, and the fridge was full." He shook his head. "And then I got the crazy idea to check the freezer in the laundry room..." He swallowed hard. "Why are you being kind to me, Natalie?"

"If you're suspicious that I'm just trying to get in your pants or I'm after something that's yours, that ship never even made it into the dock," I said bitterly. "It's enough work just trying to be your friend and I can hardly even get you to accept that."

There was a cough from the kitchen and he looked up suddenly.

"You're right," he agreed, lacing his fingers together as Gerry moved into the room with a tray containing the fixings for coffee.

I held up my hand as she poured one, knowing that I'd rocket off into the stratosphere with another cup.

"To be fair," she interjected, "the people Thomas has considered close friends in the past–and he is selective with his friends, so there have only been a few–have royally screwed him over."

A look passed between the two of them and Thomas shook his head tightly at her, only once, his lips a tight, flat line. He held onto his secrets with the zeal of a practiced, dedicated hoarder.

"I'm done here," I huffed, irritated beyond what I knew was rational. "Everything is so top secret, like you're the only person who's ever had problems. No one's life is perfect, Thomas, and the fact people are interested enough to ask questions means that they want to know about *you*. Not everyone is collecting details to use against you for future blackmail."

He looked at me narrowly.

"Want me to prove it? I'll give you one of my secrets while I'm totally sober."

He grinned when I said that, and I took in a deep breath and steeled myself against the worst truth I had. "You remember when I got a little too tipsy and told you my husband was keeping a side piece?"

His lips hadn't relaxed at all and I saw Gerry's posture stiffen out of the corner of my eye. I was shaking, I thought, either from nerves or rage or both–or maybe it was the excessive amount of caffeine.

It was also possible I was having a stroke, thanks to that fifth cup of coffee.

I put a hand over my eyes as I remembered driving to New York on a drizzly afternoon while Ahmad was in Madrid. I had received a very delicately worded report from the investigator I'd finally hired after some nagging suspicions, and I had determined to show up and demand an explanation from the woman I knew he was keeping.

"I moved here after a private investigator confirmed...well, I confirmed it for myself, too..." I cleared my throat, aware that wasn't a full explanation.

"It took me a while to figure out that I'd been funding the lifestyle and the upkeep of my husband's toy, which you sort of already knew." My voice grew quieter with each word. The shame was starting to creep in.

I needed to sit down again, and I lowered myself carefully to the sofa once more.

"He has a live-in lover. A twenty-four year old boy toy who calls himself Sonny," I finished disdainfully, watching two sets of eyebrows skyrocket. "This boy has been living in my husband's New York apartment for the past few years and I was none the wiser. There were so many things I overlooked–maybe things I refused to see."

Thomas cleared his throat. "So that's definitely why he needs you back in Boston this fall."

"Yup," I said, far more brightly than I felt. "It would be the end of the world if his very conservative parents came to visit and suspected that his marriage was a sham."

"But it is a sham," Gerry said, and she was looking at me funny.

"It has been for a long time," I whispered, ready to curl up on the sofa and sleep for a thousand years. Saying the words out loud was physically draining. Admitting that I'd been thrown over for a man had been an extraordinary blow to my pride then, and it was still.

"Bet you can't top that," I challenged Thomas with an uncomfortable smile. He didn't say anything, his arms folded tightly over his chest.

"He might," Gerry said quietly and he quickly put one hand over his eyes.

I stood slowly, aware that Thomas's emotional vault was still tightly locked and closely guarded.

Since I was tired of putting myself out there and getting nothing in return, I hugged Gerry quickly.

Thomas's voice drifted after me as I walked into the kitchen, about to let myself out the back door. "We weren't exactly fighting about you when you came over," he called, causing me to stop in my tracks. I poked my head back around the corner.

"Just what every woman wants to hear." I tried for a tight smile. "That she's not worth fighting over. Trust me, I've been that girl for long enough."

"That's not what I said and you know it's not what I meant. Stop putting words in my mouth." He shot out of the chair like someone had released a coiled spring.

"She's upset with me for being hard on you and she's right." He gestured toward Gerry, who pursed her lips at him in response. "I didn't mean to be hard on you, but there's no point when talking about something doesn't fix it."

"Um, okay." I stepped back into the room, unsure whether he was going to continue his train of thought. "Don't tell that to Gerry," I said, gesturing to several diplomas hanging on the wall, and it made her grin.

He sighed heavily and stabbed a hand through his hair like he wanted to pull the fistful from his scalp.

"When I told you I got some bad news...before..." Gerry moved toward him and reached for his hand, and he took hers gratefully. "It had to do with my family."

I felt a cold chill run through me at the word and I stood staring blankly at him. The man was full of frustrating, anticlimactic non-answers and could gloss over details like it was his full time job.

I already knew it was about your family.

I couldn't think of anything more to say and he certainly wasn't effusive, so I slowly crossed the space to wrap my arms tightly around his chest. He tensed, as I'd expected, then relaxed slowly, bringing his arms up to hug me back.

Yummy, I wanted to stay right here...

It occurred to me, as I tried not to succumb to the fact he smelled really good, that he wasn't used to people doing something nice for him, because the people in his past had always expected something in return. Bartering goods or services for kindness hardly seemed like a friendship or a relationship of any sort, and I wondered just what had happened to make him so suspicious of the people in his life.

Finally letting him go and backing away reluctantly, I smiled weakly at Gerry. "It's possible I need a few more, far less dramatic friends in my life in order to level you two out."

She smiled back at me and rolled her eyes.

I needed a minute to process the sparse information I'd just ingested.

This definitely meant there was more to it than Lydia, and more than a divorce.

Custody?

I was back to my original suspicion.

I left the two of them standing in Gerry's living room, letting myself quietly out the back door so I could spend a few moments sorting my thoughts.

After wandering through the back yard for a while, and taking a dive through the garden shed (no more spare windows), I walked back to my house and let myself in through the kitchen door.

Thomas was sitting at my island with a stack of cookies and a glass of milk in front of him, and he smiled weakly when I raised an eyebrow at him.

"That was draining," he explained, snapping off a frozen bite with strong, straight teeth. "I hope I didn't scare you–and that this is ok." He waved the cookie at me before chasing the words with a long pull of milk from his glass.

Obviously he felt quite at home in my kitchen.

To be fair, I had just told him the husband I couldn't shake was, at best, bisexual; at worst, I'd been a beard for much longer than I'd known.

Did he really suspect I scared easily?

"It's really hard to be your friend," I said finally, leaning back against the counter near the sink, and he ducked his head.

"I know," he said, grabbing another cookie from the stack. "It's probably why I don't have any."

"Except me."

"Except you."

I could tell the smile he tried to shoot me took some real work and I thought I heard a couple of his facial muscles creak under the strain.

I pushed off the counter, wondering if I could get him to fill the silence if I were to refrain from talking for once. However, he seemed content to sit and crunch away at one cookie after another. It was exasperating, and finally I caved.

"You need actual food, Thomas. This is ridiculous. You can't just eat cookies and expect your muscles will be fueled by chocolate chips," I huffed, and I heard a chuckle from the general direction of the island.

"My house is fully stocked with real food, thanks to you. But right now I'm doing the chick thing: I'm eating because I need comfort food." He sighed, his shoulders slumping forward.

I didn't say anything, knowing he wasn't going to tell me why. So I pulled a cast iron pot from one of the drawers and filled it with milk, stirring in flour from a small container in the cupboard. I put it on the stovetop and cranked the burner. If he wanted comfort food, I would give him comfort food.

He finished his stack of cookies and sat quietly in his chair, watching as I bustled around the kitchen. His eyes followed me some of the time, the rest of the time staring down at the fingers he'd linked together on the countertop.

Stirring the roux and adding cooked noodles, I let it simmer for long moments before adding seasonings, then stirring in more cubes of cheese. Then firing up the broiler, I slid the pot into the oven while he sat, watching silently.

"How often do you have to travel for work?" I asked finally, unable to maintain the silence any longer.

He looked really uncomfortable and lifted his shoulders in a half shrug.

"Sometimes. It's not as routine as it used to be, but probably a couple times a month."

There was something big he wasn't telling me–maybe more than one thing–and I folded my arms over my chest as I stared him down.

"You don't talk about yourself *at all.* You don't talk about why you travel all the time, or your family, or what's happened to hurt you so much that you won't let anyone else in. It's like you're walking around hollow, like you have no soul. What is it that drives you?"

I didn't expect an answer and I didn't get one. He had his elbows on the countertop, his hands pushed into his hair to hold his head up as he stared down at the pattern.

I left him sitting there while I drifted into the laundry room to fold the small load I'd left in the dryer and I parked the laundry basket on the stairs to take up to my room later.

"When are you thinking about redoing the kitchen?" he asked as I walked back into the kitchen and I looked around slowly.

Ok, we're changing the subject because things got too heavy.

The kitchen was clean, but it was my least favorite room of the house. For someone who loved to cook, it was like living in purgatory day in and day out, surrounded by yellow pine and chipping formica.

"Once a judge awards me half the marital assets–or my fair share of what my husband has tried to hide from me. So honestly, probably never, because one of us has to file first."

He winced.

"Is that why you work so hard?" I asked, looking away from him in order to check on the macaroni's progress under the broiler. "Because you got screwed over in divorce court?"

"I got screwed over a long time before that," he said, tapping his knuckles against the countertop.

Shaking my head, I drew a deep breath. Forget it. Pulling information out of him was like wringing water from a rock.

Looking around the kitchen, I knew just how shabby it looked. With the disintegrating cabinets and the cheap hardware, the plastic countertops and a shallow-basin stainless steel sink, the kitchen was worse than basic. It was ugly as sin. None of my cheap hacks could disguise it.

Not the cheerful paint color.

Not the light bars I'd mounted under the cabinets.

Not the low-light plants resting atop the cabinets, their happy little green leaves trailing down the sides.

"I suppose it should be my next project," I said with a shrug. "I can do it on my own cheaply enough, if I'm willing to assemble my own cabinets. I've already got the design and I have almost enough tile collected for the backsplash I want to put up. It's just...going to take me a really long time, so maybe I'll just paint the cabinets and swap out the hardware instead. You know, buy myself a couple years' sanity while I save up to pay someone else to just gut it and start fresh. As it is..." I looked around slowly. "Yeah, it's pretty tragic."

He shook his head at me as I flipped the oven door down and shielded my hands with hot pads before pulling the bubbling, crispy mass of homemade mac and cheese from under the broiler.

"No way in hell," I said and his eyes snapped to me. I realized he'd been distracted by the perfection that was crispy, melty cheese. "Don't even think those thoughts, because I just saw them. You're *busy*. You're not redoing my kitchen."

He pointed at the pot and made a "Gimme" motion with one hand, a small smile on his gorgeous face and when he actually smiled–like really let go and committed to it–it was enough to incinerate a woman's underwear. If he'd been paying attention, he'd have seen the smoke pouring from my pants.

"I have short periods of intense busy-ness," he said, his eyes still not leaving the pot of macaroni. "Followed by long periods of absolutely crushing quiet and alone time. I don't do as many jobs in this town as you think and when I'm away for work...well, that takes all my time and concentration."

He attacked the bowl I set in front of him, scooping crispy bites into his mouth and talking through his teeth in order to vent the heat from his too-hot food. "Holy shit, this is *good*. Damn it, woman, I missed your cooking." He slapped the countertop with an open palm and it made me smile just a little. (He'd missed something about me! Squee!)

It was one of my favorites, too: it was the dish I'd made for myself every night for the first two weeks I'd moved to town, when I needed something comforting and familiar because I felt so empty and alone.

Pasta with cheese, bottomless glasses of wine and Moose Tracks ice cream were solely to blame for the fact I couldn't fit into most of my pants anymore.

He had two heaping bowls and when he groaned and patted his stomach, I put the leftovers in the fridge for my own lunch.

"I'll be back tomorrow," he said. "I usually deal with jet lag better...I'm still kind of a mess, even after a full night. I didn't work out when I got home and that usually helps me with the reset." He patted his stomach again. "But that was a great carb load and I should be out like a light."

He leaned over quickly, kissing the top of my head and I blushed all the way down to my feet. I was pretty sure he didn't even realize he'd done it. After all, it didn't feel to me like something friends would do, not unless they were *really* close, and I was pretty sure Thomas wasn't ready to be that close to me.

He snatched his dish off the countertop and rinsed it, leaving it in the sink.

"Have your plans ready; we're going to see what we can do when I come out of hibernation."

The house was too quiet after he left and I cast around desperately for something to do, feeling weirdly unmoored and even more out of routine than usual, especially considering I didn't have much of a "usual" routine yet.

I was unsettled and confused, which should have been enough to keep me from making any big decisions. But instead I sat down at my computer and composed a brief response to Ahmad: I had received his stinky flowers and even smellier list of demands. I refused to comply with any of his unreasonable bullshit, as he was clearly in the wrong and if he wanted to drag things out, I was pretty sure a judge would side with me.

I bullet-pointed my own list of demands: He would restore my access to my own funds and we would agree to the amicable dissolution of our marriage, or I would call a lawyer and his mother.

In that order.

All it would take would be five little letters: S-o-n-n-y. Even Farida would know, without the help of whatever was Saudi Arabian Google, that wasn't a woman's name.

Without rereading my angry diatribe even once, I hit Send.

• • • •

TRUE TO HIS WORD, THOMAS was back the next day. He looked somewhat less worn and haggard and he looked over my quick sketches before taking a series of detailed measurements. He was quiet and thoughtful, jotting down numbers on a small pad of paper.

"I don't even know if I'll end up staying here," I said, my back to him as I looked around the kitchen, trying to project the vision I had in my head.

He was quiet, so I turned just quickly enough to catch the expression on his face. If I hadn't known better, I'd have called it stricken.

I sighed, grabbing a screwdriver and setting to work removing the hardware from each of the cabinet doors.

"I pretty much just pulled up a map of the United States, closed my eyes and pointed. I wasn't even serious about Alabama–I just happened across the listing for this house." I was rambling and he was being remarkably patient. "I could afford it. It was near the ocean. I didn't know anyone here..." I spun to face him.

"Why did *you* move here, Thomas? After all that world travel, this must be a sleepy, boring little place for you."

He was suddenly, remarkably interested in something under the sink and I waited, certain he'd heard me, and when he finally extricated himself from the cabinet I was waiting, leaning against the island with my arms crossed.

"I like sleepy and boring," he said finally. "I'd had enough excitement and I was ready for something quiet and simple."

Oh, that wasn't all of it and I could see it in his face. Something about the word "excitement" tipped me off that what he really meant was that he'd been running away from something too, and maybe he still was.

I made a mental note to myself to do some serious Google searches on the guy later.

Thomas had brought one of the freezer meals with him and we warmed it up for lunch while we discussed plans and appliances, time lines and hardware. He was very concerned that my little kitchen should experience the shortest period of downtime possible, since he wasn't sure how I would otherwise cook. (He'd admitted to it with a small grin: it was a powerful incentive to complete the job quickly.)

By the time he left for the day I'd removed all the hardware, all the cabinet doors and hinges and I spent much of the evening packing my cupboards into boxes and laundry baskets, storing what I could in the walk-in closet beneath my main set of stairs.

Then, tired and a little grumpy, I closed up the house and dragged myself up to my room without giving dinner a second thought. I felt bloated and achy and cranky–stupid PMS–and I flopped down on my bed to surf my phone for a while.

I remembered that I'd meant to Google Thomas and I tried to string together something I knew would get a hit.

Thomas+California+divorce.

Nothing.

Ok, Technology+California+Thomas.

Still nothing. I sucked at this.

Palo Alto+California+Dispute+Thomas.

There were a few listings and something caught my eye halfway down the page. It was an old newspaper article from the Sacramento Bee, not more than three paragraphs mentioning that a Harrison Powell of Redwood City-Woodside had named a Lydia Voorhees in a paternity suit, the estranged wife of Mr. Powell's longtime business partner, Thomas Atholton. He was suing *her* to establish paternity, and skimming the article it looked like they had a history of odd lawsuits against one another.

Well, that was unexpected.

I dropped the phone onto the bed beside me, suddenly unsure how much more I wanted to know. The date on the article was several years previous and I sighed as I picked the phone up again, deciding to torture myself a little further by giving the mystery woman a face and pulling up images of Lydia Voorhees, my nemesis.

Image after image populated the small screen, of a statuesque woman with silky, jet black hair and aquamarine eyes.

I scrolled slowly until I found a photo of her with Thomas: He was in a tux and she in a deep scarlet evening gown slit up to *there*, a megawatt smile on her beautiful face. His arm was wrapped possessively around her waist and he was looking down at her with hot eyes, like he couldn't wait to get her home. I could *see* his smolder and I wondered if anyone had ever looked at me that way, like I was just a flaming goddess of sex.

I dropped the phone again, a jealous ache in my chest. I was jealous of a woman I'd never met, and I hoped to God in that moment that I'd never meet her, because clearly I would have to punch her in the throat. She'd held one of the finest men I'd ever met completely captive and God knew what she'd done, but she'd broken him.

I couldn't help but wonder what he'd been like before, before she got her claws into him and I imagined someone warm and passionate, not the angry, closed off person he was now.

It was enough for one evening. I had plenty to fill my brain and though it was barely past sunset and I was still fully dressed, I snapped off the lamp near my bed and rolled over to hug my pillow.

Tonight I felt alone in a way that made me wonder if I was going to be ok and somehow, I suspected, it was what Thomas felt with every breath.

• • • •

THE NEXT MORNING I woke with the same heavy feeling in my chest.

I laced myself into some decent shoes and went for a walk before breakfast, trying to clear the cobwebs.

The air wasn't as thick this morning, the humidity having backed off just a little, and without realizing I was headed for the ocean, I found myself on the beach an hour later. The sand was dense, coarse and flattened as if it had been rolled, packed down into the earth. I sat in it for a while, watching small waves roll in and out, my fingers digging absently into the grainy stuff, mindlessly sifting.

By the time I decided to head home, the sun was high in the sky and my stomach had some angry words for me. It was a long walk back, a slight ache around the edges of my eyes as my body protested the lack of caffeine.

I was beginning to see Thomas's point about avoiding addictive substances, because I felt like shit.

"Hey!" Thomas's face split into an honest-to-goodness grin as I straggled into my yard and I looked over my shoulder quickly to see if someone was standing behind me. He was damn near perky and there was no way he was that excited to see me, unless...crap. Had I forgotten a bra again? That would explain a lot. Guys had a thing for my boobs and usually preferred to talk to them rather than my face.

"I was starting to worry about you," he said and I finally realized that my garage door was yawning and he'd stacked piles of wood inside. I scratched my head as I eyed it up, confused.

"I needed to clear my head a little, so I walked to the beach this morning."

"Did it work?"

"No. I don't feel any clearer and I'd probably get on my knees for a cup of coffee right now."

His cheeks flamed a violent red and I realized just exactly what a loaded innuendo that had been.

"Prayer, Thomas," I snapped. "And supplication."

"Maybe the coffee I brewed will help," he said as he hauled a bulky table saw from the back of his truck. "Don't worry, I don't expect any...prayer." He laughed nervously.

I raised an eyebrow, but I didn't have the mental capacity for more words, so I held up two fingers to ask if he wanted a cup and he shook his head, chewing on his lip as he bit back a smile.

By the time I returned, a veritable jug of caffeinated goodness in my hand, he'd set up a makeshift workshop in my garage and he was quickly measuring, marking pieces of wood and writing something down on a corresponding scrap of paper. I waited for him to enlighten me, but he was concentrating so hard that he didn't even notice me until I came right up beside him and cast a shadow.

"So..." I lifted the coffee to my lips again, aware that I probably looked like a sweaty mess.

"Kitchens are expensive, which is why you haven't started a remodel," he said matter-of-factly and I rolled my eyes at him.

Thank you, Captain Obvious. Please, do gift me another of your sentient insights.

"Duh."

"Since you have the design..." he pulled my sketch from his shirt pocket and unfolded it quickly, "and I have the materials and the knowledge, we are going to build your cabinets. Shouldn't take more than a couple days to do this."

My jaw dropped. "You have better things to be doing. And this is still expensive–probably well beyond what I'd have budgeted anyway–all this wood...have you lost your mind?" I cast a glance behind me, at the stack of wood that was so solid, it couldn't even claim particle board as a distant relation.

There was that irritated expression from him again.

"I have the materials and right now I have the time. You have a kitchen in need, so I'll work on cranking them out while you go take that room apart. I've seen some of your work and you like to make a mess, so go demolish that eyesore." He grinned.

Great. If a *guy* thought my kitchen was an eyesore, it was genuinely gross.

I shook my head at him, setting down my coffee in order to grab the hair band off my wrist and pull the mess of sweaty hair up into a high ponytail.

"Cute," he teased, and I shot him a narrow look.

"It'll be even cuter in a couple hours when I'm all red in the face and covered in sawdust, cobwebs and dirt."

His grin grew wider. "Nah, that'll be pretty hot. You have this Marilyn Monroe-cheerleader thing going on..." His eyebrows lifted.

Was Thomas flirting with me? I didn't know what to do with that.

Since no witty banter was springing to mind, I clamped my mouth firmly shut and retrieved my cup, taking myself quickly into the house to hide.

Standing in my kitchen, I took a deep breath. I'd start with the upper boxes, I thought, in case they came crashing down, since I really didn't care about saving the gross countertops.

Retrieving my cordless drill and a crowbar, I set to work, careful not to put any dents in the drywall.

My kitchen plans were fairly simple, albeit far more open and airy, and I'd elected not to swap the locations of any major components, since the room already had a good flow–it was just uglier than sin itself.

I managed to zap myself when I disconnected the range hood and I eyed the suspect wiring job with dismay. My predecessor had hardwired the hood into the wires protruding from the wall, no box.

After I recovered from the surge of 120 volts running through my body, I walked out to the garage and killed the power to half the house.

"There's a problem," I called to Thomas over the sharp whine of the saw and he flicked a switch, pushing safety glasses back into hair coated with sawdust and wood shavings.

"The wiring in the kitchen is cloth wrap."

"Shit." He ran a hand through his hair. "That means the whole damn house needs to be redone." He stood for a moment with his hand in his hair as he thought, and I absently admired the fine planes of his chest and shockingly flat stomach. With his hand in his hair, one bicep bulged out in sharp relief and I licked my lips before realizing I was staring. Looking at the man did nothing to hurt my feelings, I thought fuzzily. Even if he *could* make me mad as hell inside of three seconds.

"Ok," he said finally. "Let me make a couple calls. You just go do what you can in there and I'll see what I can pull together."

I walked back into the house, shaking my head. Rewire my entire house...yeah, because that sounded cheap. I couldn't even handle the cost of a budget kitchen renovation, as buying this house had taken a vicious chunk out of my account.

How the hell was I going to pay Thomas for all those materials and his labor, and still have money left over to rewire the house? I should have known this was going to happen.

In my experience, there was no such thing as "simple." One straightforward job usually turned into three complicated, time consuming and often expensive endeavors. (Just ask me about my master bathroom redo in Boston.)

Thomas drifted in as I separated the first lower cabinet from the wall.

"Problem solved," he announced and I looked over my shoulder at him, suspicion written all over my face.

"Don't tell me you're an electrician, too," I scoffed and he grinned at me, sawdust sifting down from his eyebrows when he did.

"Nope, but I know a good one and he was able to fit in an emergency job, so he'll be here the day after tomorrow."

"Huh," I grunted as I peeled back a piece of cheap countertop from the shortest lower cabinet and leaned it against the island. "That sounds expensive."

Thomas didn't answer, but was standing there expectantly, so I cocked my head at him and waited. He tapped his wrist and I looked at mine, but I wasn't wearing a watch and there was no power in the kitchen, so I was coming up empty.

"You hungry?"

My stomach roared. I'd had coffee, but I hadn't had breakfast. And now...I looked around at the sad state of disarray. Well, it seemed unlikely I'd be making anything in here for a while. I really hadn't thought this through very well. Points for gusto, but not for planning, because I was usually better than this.

Once we stepped outside he combed the sawdust from his hair with his fingers and pulled the garage door shut, indicating I should get into his truck.

I was buckling my seatbelt when he opened the door behind me and I saw a flash of skin. He was changing his shirt, I realized, a little disappointed that my particular vantage point left me with no way to discreetly ogle him. I tried to turn just a little, to look over my shoulder, and my eye landed on something in the seat behind me.

A car seat.

His clean t-shirts were stacked neatly into it and just before he closed the door I caught the briefest gesture. His hand reached in to squeeze the low armrest, like one would give a comforting squeeze to the arm of a small child. It made me catch my breath and I turned away quickly, the emotion sharp, unfamiliar and unwelcome.

His truck took a series of several familiar turns and only a few moments later we were parked in his driveway.

"I hear there's a crapload of food in this house," he said with a sly grin, and he hoisted the cooler of perishables I'd packed and I followed him through a side door into his kitchen.

While he popped things into the fridge and then slid one of the containers I'd prepared into the oven to warm, I sat at the island and really looked around his kitchen. It was obvious it had been remodeled with great care. It was clean and bright and efficient, with a light tile backsplash running all the way up the walls where there were no cabinets to cover it.

I ran a hand across the smooth marble countertop of the island and finally asked the question that had been bothering me all morning. "Please tell me you didn't go out and buy all that wood just to build cabinets for me."

"Nope." He was putting ice into glasses and filling them from the filtered tap. "I have a top secret shed filled with magical things, too." He wiggled his eyebrows.

"Explain to me why you happened to have just the right materials lying around by chance," I said suspiciously as he slid a glass across the counter to me.

"Uh...long story," he said, peeking into the oven, presumably so he wouldn't have to look at me.

"You seem to have a lot of those and you obviously don't like telling them," I commented as I sipped my water.

He was right: The filtered stuff really did taste a lot better.

He leaned back against the counter with a look on his face that suggested there was a bad taste in his mouth. "Yeah, well...the shortest version is that my wife wanted to remodel the kitchen but I thought it was lunacy to spend over fifty grand on the stupid cabinets she wanted. Just because you have the money doesn't mean you have to spend it. So I went out and bought all the materials and I was going to make the damn boxes, but she wouldn't hear of it–had to have her way." His expression grew darker. "So we bought the cabinets. And the countertops she wanted. And the hardware that cost a hundred and twenty bucks for each stupid little piece–the big pieces were a lot more." He gestured toward a wide handle on one of the lower drawers. "Then the enormous farmhouse sink she wanted–for a woman who didn't cook a day in her life." He rolled his eyes and huffed angrily.

"Sorry," I mumbled. "I shouldn't have asked." I wanted happy, playful Thomas back and this wasn't him.

"Fucking kitchen is worth more than the damn house," he grumbled as I trailed a finger down the condensation on my glass.

"For what it's worth," I said quietly, "it's beautiful."

My eyes drifted to a set of plates displayed in one of the glass-front cabinets and I squinted at what looked like an imperfection. It took a long moment to realize the plate looked like it had been painstakingly glued back together.

"That's consolation, I guess," he said and I couldn't tell if he was teasing me or just flat-out mocking me.

There was a knock at the door and Thomas disappeared for a moment, stalking back into the kitchen with a delivery envelope he slapped down at the opposite end of the counter. It was stuffed full and I strained my eyes to catch the return address at the top of the envelope.

Titan Tech & Consulting.

He caught me staring at the envelope and something flashed briefly across his face, but he didn't address it.

We ate quietly and I rinsed the plates while he stacked things into the dishwasher. Then I followed him back out to his truck and we drove to my house, still quiet, as if we'd already used up all of our allotted words for the day.

It felt like something had changed; like he was waiting for something and he expected it to be unpleasant.

I stood in the kitchen, looking around at the yawning spaces around the stove and refrigerator. The only cabinet remaining was the box holding the sink and I sighed to myself.

"If you wanted to paint, now would be the time to do it."

I hadn't heard Thomas come into the house.

"What's the point?" I asked. "If we're rewiring, the house will be a complete mess anyway."

"Nah." Thomas reached into my fridge to pull out sparkling water and I realized he'd restored partial power. "My guy is good. He's neat, clean and efficient. If he can help it there will be minimal damage to your walls and he'll patch up behind himself. He's multi-talented, which is his only salvation, because he's a real pain in the ass." He grinned, popping the tab on the can.

I had little time to wonder about who this miracle worker was, as Thomas beckoned I should follow him.

In the garage there were already four large wooden boxes, clamps sticking out at odd angles. Again, I was struck by how quickly Thomas worked. He'd created the deep base cabinets I'd sketched, and short of a sink and peninsula base, this was already most of the kitchen.

"I have an idea," he said and I looked at him with some alarm. That was usually my line.

"Since you're eliminating so many cabinets, why don't we take this space over here..." he pointed to the edge of my drawing. "If you're not continuing the cabinets right out to the doorway, you could put a pocket door into that under-stairs closet thing you have and fit it out as a pantry. It could open right next to your countertop instead of into your hallway."

I looked at him suspiciously. Strokes of design genius were supposed to be my field, not his, and I slapped his shoulder. "Next you're going to tell me that you'll sew me new curtains and build a solarium on that sad slab I call my patio."

He shrugged. "The solarium I could probably pull off, but sewing curtains not so much. I'll let you figure that part out if it's really essential to your design."

We called it a little early that afternoon, on account of my unwillingness to start painting that late in the day. I was tired and sore already.

"Mrs. O'Shaughnessy is going to be suspicious," I said as we got out of his truck again and I followed him into his house.

"Mrs. O. is a sweet lady, but she's a hundred years old and there's no way she's still getting dick. It makes her a little obsessive thinking about the people who *are*."

I smothered a snort, but the giggle erupted around my fingers. I couldn't believe he'd just said that out loud.

"Your sweet little old lady neighbor is obsessed with yours then, huh?" I said quickly, ready to throw it right back at him. "You know Mrs. O. is going to think we're doing it over here...multiple times a day." I started to laugh, finding the expression on his face too funny to continue. I thought for a second he might say he *wanted* to do that with me, but he recovered quickly.

"She's probably saying the rosary for your soul as we speak; we both know I'm a lost cause," he shot back with a wicked grin and I was surprised he hadn't turned beet red.

This was definitely flirting.

After eating, I was in no rush to get back. I wanted to sit in Thomas's environment for a while and take in the stories I knew the walls could tell. So I sat in the living room, curled up on the sofa with a glass of iced tea, listening closely even during the spaces Thomas wasn't talking, which was most of the time.

A noise came from the kitchen and I looked up quickly, trying to catch Thomas's eye as he stared into space, lost in thought about something. He'd gone quiet and serious again and there was no more silly flirting or teasing.

"Do you have a ghost in your house?" I asked, not really joking. There were some hair-raising tales out of Gulf Shores, not all that far to the south. I wasn't eager to experience any antebellum spirits firsthand–modern ones, either.

Thomas raised his head, his eyes coming into focus. "Cat," he responded shortly and I twisted my neck to see a small shape moving down the hallway toward us.

"Since when?" I asked, surprised I hadn't seen any signs of a cat previously.

"Couple years now," he responded, ever the effusive wealth of information.

He patted the arm of the deep chair he sat in and the tiny black cat leapt gracefully onto the chair, rubbing her head against his arm as a low rumble rolled through the room.

I never would have taken him for a pet owner in the first place, I thought, watching as he leaned his head toward her and she responded by touching her nose to his. It made him smile just a little, and when she jumped into his lap and sprawled out for belly rubs, he settled back into the chair, his big fingers curling through her fur.

Huh. Never would have pegged him as a cat person. That was a little weird.

"She was Lydia's, I guess," he offered out of nowhere and I sat silently, waiting for more information. It seemed to work best when he didn't realize he was talking.

"This little girl was a stray. We found her in the backyard one morning, just a kitten, and brought her inside. She was probably left behind when the mama cat moved all the other kittens, so I got stuck bottle feeding her and Lydia announced we were keeping her for..." He made a face after cutting off his sentence.

"I'm not big on cats, but I was traveling a lot for work and Lydia and I were going through...I wanted her to be happy, so I agreed. I would have agreed to just about anything then." His eyes drifted shut and I could see the painful memory on his face.

"You may not be big on cats, but it looks like she's big on you." I gestured toward the purring furball in his lap.

"Yeah..." The far away look came over his face again. "This little girl *hated* Lydia, which was kinda ironic. Once she was big enough to eat on her own, she wouldn't have anything to do with her. At night she'd sleep...um..." He paled, swallowing hard before continuing. "If I was home she'd sleep behind my knees at night, or on my chest if I rolled over onto my back. But if Lydia tried to get anywhere near her, she would run and hide."

I bit my tongue to keep from commenting on the obvious: how animals were often considered excellent judges of character. Then I considered that the cat was sitting in *his* lap and not mine, which probably said something about me.

"So this is Raven," he said, rewarded with a loud rumble and a big stretch from the tiny cat.

There was a sudden tension in the air and it felt like an enormous elephant had suddenly squeezed into the room with us, sucking out all the air as if something was about to get heavy. I hadn't said a thing, but he knew I felt the shift and when he lifted his head, his eyes were glassy.

"It was her fault."

"The cat?"

"Lydia."

I waited for him to continue, finding it suddenly difficult and painful to breathe. For once he was answering something before I could form the question.

"We moved here to gain some...perspective. We needed distance from our old life, because *I* needed distance from our old life," he said mostly to himself, looking haunted. "I came home early from a trip to Tokyo...well, long story. I was coming from Washington and Lydia didn't know when to expect me, because she wouldn't answer my calls. I wanted her to know I was going to Maren's, to spend a few days by myself and get my head on straight.

"Instead, I found my closest friend and my worst enemy there, looking perfectly comfortable, like he'd been there for days."

He lapsed into silence for a long moment, reliving something in his mind and I caught a ragged breath. He'd finally referenced something I knew haunted him during all his waking hours.

"Harrison and I hadn't been on speaking terms for some time and it wasn't his house anymore, so I was surprised to find him there. Angry. And then when Lydia walked into the room, I just...knew. I could see everything on her face: She hadn't given him up at all. She hated Maren's place, so there was no reason for her to be there other than that she thought I wouldn't be..."

I set down my empty glass on the coffee table and leaned forward, elbows on my knees, straining toward his words though the picture in my mind made it hard to catch my breath.

Give him up?

Who's Maren?

It wasn't Harrison's house anymore?

"My bed smelled like them." He looked up, his eyes blazing with anger and I felt my own eyes growing wider. "She tried to tell me it was something that had just happened, but I knew better. History." He swallowed hard and dragged a hand over his face and the cat shot out of his lap, stretching on the rug before sauntering over to wind around my leg.

"I'm sorry," I whispered, reaching down to carefully pick up the cat.

"What are you sorry for?" He looked surprised. "Are you sorry that my wife was cheating on me for *years*? Or are you sorry that she killed my son?"

She what?

I knew my expression was dumbfounded and I forgot I had the cat in my arms until she squirmed to be put down.

"I made...arrangements. Sacrifices. Changes–big ones. I begged her to give our marriage a chance and we moved out here, to the middle of nowhere, to start over. But it wasn't enough for her. She missed her friends, the fancy parties, the openings, the events...she was bored and apparently I wasn't very entertaining.

"So she drank a little to pass the time. And then she drank a little more. And pretty soon she was at the very edge of functional, but she was still pulling it off, because I never would have guessed. She was careful."

Thomas leaned back in his chair and crossed an ankle over his knee. "I still had to travel for business, but I was doing it a lot less." He fidgeted. "It happened when I was in Milan and Gerry called to tell me. Second longest, definitely *worst* flight of my life."

He dashed a hand across his eyes and I sat frozen to the sofa, wanting to offer him comfort in some way but I knew he wouldn't get it all out if I interrupted him.

"It was a DUI," he said flatly. "Lydia had a concussion and a few other serious injuries, but Aden...my little boy...he didn't make it." His voice caught. "The injuries were too great. The medical examiner said the force of impact caused 'excessive internal damage.' Not extensive, but *excessive*. He wasn't properly fastened in his car seat, though the M.E. didn't know if that would have been enough to save him." He dragged in a deep breath. "She was doing a hundred and twelve miles an hour when she wrapped the Mercedes around a telephone pole. You tell me how she's still alive."

Devil didn't want her, flashed through my brain.

He clenched his fists, drawing another deep breath.

"The D.A. was completely taken with her. He was young and impressionable and she was sexy and glamorous–he slapped her with a fine, but she didn't get any prison time because he didn't bring charges. She told him I was leaving her and she'd been trying to end things, since she was depressed. It was a load of shit–I never threatened to leave her, she left *me*. But she blamed it all on me: I was never home. I didn't want to make things work. Blah, blah, blah."

I had missed a step somewhere.

"The D.A. said she'd suffered enough, having lost a child while going through a marital breakdown, and he ordered her to complete a live-in substance abuse program and pay the fine. She had to keep up with daily AA meetings for a year.

"One, Natalie. One fucking year." He stopped suddenly, but it looked like he wanted to say more.

My breath caught on an intake and it sounded like the sob I'd been trying to suppress for the last few minutes. It made him look up quickly at me and though tears were streaming down my cheeks, his face was hard again. He was shutting everything off, the only way he knew how to deal with it.

"I'm not telling you this because I want you to feel sorry for me." There was an undercurrent of anger in his voice and I sensed the shift: though it was misplaced, this anger was for me and my reaction.

"Pity and empathy are very different things, even if you think they look like the same thing from the outside," I finally croaked and he shook his head.

"It's my heartbreak, Natalie, not yours."

"I didn't realize you had the exclusive rights to suffering," I retorted quickly, regretting it the moment the words left my mouth.

He stood slowly, glaring at me like I'd just committed the unpardonable sin, and maybe I had.

So why not compound it a little more? I rose from the sofa, my movements clearly telegraphing my intentions, and I skirted the coffee table carefully.

I didn't stop long enough to consider my actions, and I felt his whole body tense when I threw my arms around him. He stood there woodenly while I squeezed him harder and harder.

I waited for his arms to come up around me and finally he asked, "Are you trying to comfort me, or yourself?" His voice was cold.

What the hell?

I dropped my arms quickly and stepped back, trying not to let him see that his cruel words devastated me.

"I don't like to be touched and I've told you that. I don't trust it," he said flatly, and I wrapped my arms tightly around myself to keep my own heart from breaking. In his grief he was terribly cruel.

"You're barely human if you can't accept tenderness," I admonished, gulping to keep hot, angry tears from following the ones I'd been crying for him, because here we were *again*. Then I backed away, spinning quickly and grabbing my shoes from the floor near the front door.

I have to get out.

I didn't even bother to put them on, slamming the door behind me and running down his front walk at a pace that reminded me I hadn't been running in a really long time.

I didn't get very far before I realized there were headlights illuminating the road and since my lungs burned and my knees screamed for mercy, I slowed to as dignified a walk as I could manage.

"Get in." He pulled up alongside me, keeping pace with my angry stride.

Stupid short legs.

"I wouldn't want to put you out," I retorted. "Riding in your truck means being in close proximity. That means I might accidentally touch you, and God save us all should that happen. You might have to *feel* something." I threw my hands up over my head, my shoes dangling dangerously.

"You're going to cut your feet." He sounded mad again.

"My choice and my injuries, then, not yours," I sniped back at him, winding up and pitching one of my shoes just as far as I could throw it. It landed in the distance with a far less satisfying *plop* than I'd wanted, so I wound up and threw the other one.

"Good arm," he said, still no inflection in his voice, and I stopped short.

"Go home, Thomas."

"Not until I know you're home safely."

"You don't get to worry about me," I spat and something flashed across his face that I couldn't identify. "I'm not allowed to worry about *you*. I'm not allowed to care or to cross any one of the nine thousand invisible boundary lines you've created for me, and from one day to the next, I don't know where the hell the lines are.

"God forbid I should have feelings and be soft-hearted toward your suffering, because I do have *some* idea of what loss is like."

I stood there, my chest heaving, as he sat less than two feet away, one hand resting casually on the steering wheel, the other arm lying along the open window.

"You done yet?" he asked, sounding bored, and that was it. Something boiled up inside of me and I pulled back, slapping him hard across the face.

"Now," I panted as he held a hand to his cheek with a look of shock. "Now I'm done."

Then I darted in front of his truck and across someone's lawn, winding my way through one yard after another as I tried to work out the birdseye map in my head, figuring my detour would put me somewhere roughly in the vicinity of my house.

As luck would have it, my patchy directional sense put me in Gerry's yard and I straggled through the hedge bordering our yards to find his truck idling in my driveway.

My shoes sat on the porch step.

I gave him the finger and the Furious Eye of Satan before opening the front door I'd left unlocked and slammed it behind me.

TWENTY-FOUR

Thomas

I don't know what came over me. My social skills were pretty rusty, but I'd been downright heartless with Natalie–again–and there was no reason for it.

I didn't drive home. Instead, I pulled the truck into Gerry's driveway and tapped on her door. She opened it, took one look at me and held her arms out so I could walk in.

I'm twelve again.

"What did you do?" she asked gently, dwarfed when I wrapped my arms around her. Gerry had always given the best hugs and I sighed against the top of her head as I tried to find the answer to that question.

She was quiet for a long time, squeezing like she was trying to press her love into me through my skin. She'd always been this way: intuitive, gentle, and her love ran deep. She was the only person I could go to when things fell apart because she saw my intentions without judgment, whereas other people just saw an asshole.

"Why don't you spend the night here?" she asked softly. "No sense in you going home to that big, lonely house of yours when I have a perfectly good guest room. You'll sleep better after we talk and in the morning you can just walk over and apologize to Natalie."

How the fuck did she know?

"I think she's gotten under my skin, Gerry." There, I said it. "And I'm not sure I like it."

"So you're angry with her because she's reminding you how to be human and feel things."

"Maybe."

"You're angry with her for being exactly what you need."

I could feel the muscles of her face move against my shoulder and I knew her lips were set in a firm line.

"She's created a safe space for you, son. She's been gentle and thoughtful and she clearly has absolutely no expectation of anything in return. She's not in this for home repairs. She's trying to reach you and you push her so hard, sometimes she has to push back...

"Do you have any idea what you stand to lose if you don't let her in?"

Dropping my arms, I threw myself down on the sofa. I knew exactly what I stood to lose and it was more than I'd *ever* had before. I knew she cared, but it scared me, because if she cared it meant I could lose her too. Friendship was an easy, deceptive term but going from having nothing to lose to having everything–possibly the only thing–was downright terrifying.

"It scares me," I finally said quietly, twisting at the watch band on my wrist.

"Losing her *should* terrify you, because you keep this up and you will." Gerry sat beside me. Something clinked and I looked over to see her draining liquid from a glass.

"Do you have any idea how excited she was, Thomas?"

I looked at her blankly.

"Filling your house up with food was her idea. She told me that she wanted to make sure you were fed and cared for, even when you couldn't bear to be around people, and she meant around *her*. She worries about you. She wants to see you happy again and putting just one smile on your face gives her more joy than you could know. You found a good one this time. Technically, I suppose you could say I found her for you."

"Damned shrink," I muttered and she grinned at me.

"Comes in handy sometimes."

She patted my knee with several sharp slaps. "You sit here as long as you need to. You know where the guest room is and the bathroom is fully stocked with whatever you need. Take the night off from beating yourself up for once. Then maybe you can go easier on her, too."

Gerry disappeared and I heard a door softly close. I tipped my head back on the sofa, staring at the texture of the ceiling, and fell sound asleep.

TWENTY-FIVE

Natalie

There was a soft tap on my kitchen door as I sat in the living room with my feet resting on the coffee table. My soles ached and damn him, I *had* cut one foot. It wasn't enough to warrant stitches, but I hobbled carefully to the back door, looking through the panes before I shot the lock, lest I risk letting the devil back into my home.

"I hear he backed himself into a whole pile of shit this time." Gerry's voice preceded her as she stepped into the wrecked kitchen and she stopped short, looking around at the mostly bare room. "Wow...now I know why."

I laughed a little, the thought weighing heavily that maybe I shouldn't have let my temper get the better of me just after I destroyed the kitchen he'd promised to help me put back together. He probably wasn't feeling quite so charitable toward me anymore.

The two of us curled up on the sofa in the living room again and I poured cold glasses of rose' for each of us–big balloon glasses–and only because it would have been rude to chug straight from the bottle.

"You're getting too close and he's scared," she said quickly, lifting her glass to her lips for a long swallow of the cold refreshment.

"I'm getting too close, or he's *letting* me get too close?" I asked, wincing as I shifted the injured foot I'd decided to sit on.

"Doesn't matter," she answered firmly. "This is a new pattern for him: give a little, then freak out and retreat. Blow up. Come begging for forgiveness with his tail between his legs. He'll be back to apologize once he's had a nice, long night to reflect on his sins."

"I gave it back to him pretty good," I admitted, thankful the lights in the room weren't brighter or she'd have seen the flush that had started to creep into my cheeks. I hated that. "I hauled off and slapped him because he was being an ass, and then I flipped him off when I got home and found him sitting in my driveway. Slammed the door behind me."

Gerry made a strangled sound I realized was a snort, and she held a hand quickly over her mouth to keep wine from shooting across the sofa. "No, you didn't."

"I did, too. You should have seen the look on his face when I smacked him. I couldn't help it; he was being a dick."

"Good. No one gives it back to him." Gerry set her glass down on the coffee table with a clink. "It's about time someone knocked some sense into that man. He's been moping around for the last two years and no one but me has ever given it to him straight. I don't count and I think you know why."

"I don't know that I gave it to him straight, so much as that I just gave it *back*. I spent thirteen years being...less...and I've had enough of that. I don't expect him to open up to me overnight, but he needs to try harder. I can't help a bleeding rock. I mean...what is he doing with me, Gerry? Is he trying to be my friend, really? Or am I just letting myself get way too close to a perpetual charity case?"

She leaned closer and patted my knee awkwardly. "He'll be good to you if he can ever get his head out of his own ass. Remember what I said about him before: he's a good man who loves hard."

I must have looked at her with some alarm, because she looked a little taken aback. I wondered if she was thinking back over her statement and realizing just how presumptuous it sounded.

"Before I get to exploring any of...that," I gestured in a circular motion, "I think I might need help finding a good lawyer."

It made her right eyebrow lift in surprise. To her, it was a total non-sequitur.

"I don't want to be left holding the short end of the stick when I file for divorce."

••••

THE NEXT DAY, I PAINTED the kitchen at a furious clip. I was possessed by the twin demons, Anger and Caffeine, and they seemed to be surprisingly great pals. They sure as hell got a lot done.

Then I called no less than four different law firms, sitting through a thirty-minute consultation with each before deciding which I thought would best represent my interests.

After that I conducted a quick search for a plane ticket. The plan was to fly into Boston to meet with my new legal representative and from there she would draft the initial filing. It was pretty straightforward, but I wanted nothing left to chance. This needed to be concluded quickly and I needed to put the past behind me.

I was tired of living in fear that I would be left with nothing, because God knew the vicious diva angling to be the new Mrs. Sayad was a petty little bitch. He wanted me left with less than nothing, according to the P.I. I'd hired, though it had been my money supporting his lifestyle for years. (Shortsighted, perhaps, but clever he was not.)

The morning bled into the afternoon and I drifted into the kitchen a few times to pull small things from the refrigerator and make coffee on my free-standing stovetop.

It was still early afternoon when I heard noises outside and I peeked out the laundry room window to see Thomas's truck in the driveway. I could hear him rattling around the garage–his movements sounded uncoordinated and angry–and I went back upstairs to my office to finish a couple storyboards and set things up to post on a schedule.

I'd snapped a few photos of Thomas hard at work on the cabinets when he hadn't been looking. Then I compiled a photo-heavy post showing my kitchen in a "before" state, followed by photos of the current shell, with shots sprinkled in of Thomas working on cabinetry and the massive pile of wood and glue that sat on my curbside, awaiting pick-up.

There were times that being angry made me really productive and today was definitely one of those days. I cranked out piece after piece and when I finished writing and formatting, I set things up to post across my platforms the next morning.

Thomas worked in my garage until it was nearly dark, but he didn't once try to knock on the door or come into the house.

Since the last thing I was going to do included engaging the enemy, I stayed inside and worked on anything that kept me away from him, even though curiosity nagged at me all day.

The next morning I was up much too early, and I drove myself over to Mobile to get a decent breakfast at a diner. I stuffed myself full of food and then ordered a sandwich to go, because I wasn't going to Thomas's place right now if he begged me.

By the time I got home, the six weak cups of coffee I'd had at the diner had introduced themselves to my bladder and I rushed inside to use the bathroom, well aware Thomas's truck was already in my driveway.

I hurried up the stairs and into my master bathroom and I was washing my hands when through the open window I heard a booming voice: "Thomas Daniel Atholton, you no good, lying sack of shit." A car door slammed loudly. "Where are you, you useless son of a bitch? Hey, ASSHOLE!" The voice was big and booming and continuously increasing in rather frightening volume.

Whoever this guy was, he sounded like he was going to kill Thomas.

I was alarmed and went flying down the stairs, throwing open the front door to find an enormous man walking up my driveway toward the garage.

I didn't think at all at that moment, terrified for Thomas's safety.

Because maybe this was Harrison.

Positioning myself so that I stood between the giant and the garage, I sized him up as he drew nearer and looked down at me.

You're not even so much as a speed bump.

There were suddenly warm fingers on my hip as Thomas pulled me flush against his side. I looked up my shoulder at him to find him grinning at the huge man and before I knew what had hit me I was sandwiched between two very large bodies, too many arms squeezing the breath out of my lungs at once.

"Noah, you ugly fuck monkey. What sorry-ass, second-rate airline brought your dumb butt to Alabama?"

I extracted myself from the crush, sputtering, pulling my hair out of my face as the giant pounded Thomas on the back so hard I thought it might stop his heart.

"That piece of shit rattletrap hazard you booked for me, you dried up old fart–like you couldn't do better," Noah laughed as he released

Thomas and I breathed a sigh of relief as I realized the litany of horrible curses were terms of endearment between the two.

"Flying private's not enough for you these days?" Thomas asked, his tone teasing.

Finally, Noah seemed to realize I was there and his eyes grew wide as he openly stared at me. "Holy shit, Thom. What have you gone and done this time?"

I held out my hand to Noah. "I'm Natalie–and no, Thomas has not 'done me.' I do give him shit, though, of the unholy variety." I gave him a significant look.

He grinned a huge grin and in that split-second I realized just how much he looked like Thomas. "Lord have mercy, big brother, this one's spicy."

"You don't know the half of it," Thomas mumbled and I shot him such a withering glare that he clapped his mouth shut like it was on well-oiled hinges.

"You should pick me," Noah stage whispered behind one enormous paw. "At least mine still works–I'm the *younger* brother. Better range of motion, you know." He cleared his throat and swiveled his hips just once, suggestively.

Thomas smacked him upside the head with an open palm and the two of them tumbled into the grass, rolling quickly before Thomas pulled Noah up into something I recognized vaguely as a martial arts move.

Noah grunted heavily. "Fuck, man."

"Is that a tap?"

"Whatever, damn it. Just let go before something snaps." Noah's voice was strained.

Thomas released him and Noah scrambled to his feet, rubbing his arm carefully. He shot me a crooked grin and I watched him glance at Thomas out of the corner of his eye.

"You just keep something in mind, Natalie: The old man bested me this time, but you can ask the ladies...not one complaint. I'll handle *whatever* you need."

It was obvious whatever he was offering to handle wouldn't require a tool belt.

He released a loud "Oof," doubling over from a shot to the kidney and I caught the briefest flash of something on Thomas's face: white-hot anger. It made me catch my breath for just a second, before chalking it up to sibling rivalry with no small amount of disappointment.

"Ah, shit," Noah coughed. "Maybe an ice pack and a beer for the mortally wounded, Natalie?"

I shook my head at him, rolling my eyes as I slipped into the house to grab an ice pack from the freezer and a cold beer from the fridge. I handed both to him as he stood in my garage, appraising Thomas's work with a critical eye.

He held the ice pack to his back for all of three seconds before cracking open the beer and taking a deep chug.

"So much better. I never drink anymore." He winked before handing the ice back to me. "You are a pint-sized saint."

"I had almost forgotten what a pain in the ass you are," Thomas said around the pencil in his mouth as he made another quick cut and Noah smacked his lips as he took another pull from the longneck. The bottle was dwarfed by his giant hand.

"Don't worry," Noah tapped the edge of one of the cabinets repeatedly with a knuckle. "I figure I've got three days to annoy the hell out of you. That should make up for a couple of the years you missed out on. Maybe when I go home I'll even have a new girlfriend." He winked at me, his lips curling up at the corners as he slammed the rest of the bottle. It earned him a low growl from Thomas.

"Fuck if you will," I heard Thomas mutter under his breath, and though I was still really mad at him, my heart sped up just a little.

I wasn't imagining it, was I?

Noah chuckled and walked back down the driveway to fish around in the passenger seat of the tiny car I couldn't believe he'd been able to fold himself into.

"Yeah..." his voice carried up the driveway as he drew closer. "The clown car was a great idea, by the way."

Thomas smirked and I heard the snort slam into his sinuses.

"Not like you couldn't have reserved something a little better, Mr. Money Bags. It's *so* much more fun to fuck with the brother who actually does you favors."

Thomas looked a little guilty, but not enough to override the fact he was plainly and inordinately pleased with himself.

"Whatever," he scoffed. "I'm just keeping you humble. Besides, I'm putting you up at least one of the nights you're here, and Natalie's filled my house with so much food that you'll be eating like the hog that you are. Try not to grunt when we have her over for dinner tonight."

Noah narrowed his eyes at his brother and oinked loudly, then solicitously crooked his arm and offered it to me. "I will be inside with this lovely lady, conducting my initial inspection and spitballing some plans. Also possibly continuing our family name, with her permission, since it would seem you're just wasting time with this delightful specimen." He grinned down at me wickedly. This brother was adorable and I wondered if the other two were half as fun.

Thomas's pencil nailed him in the back of the skull as we disappeared through the door and into the laundry room.

"I don't think I'd want to be in the middle of it if you two were *actually* angry with each other," I whispered as we headed into the kitchen, and he chuckled in a way that was very disconcerting for such a large man.

"There's three people in this world that fuck with Mr. High-and-Mighty." He took something out of his pocket and began running it over the walls, making slash marks with his own pencil as he went. "That's Gerry, my sister Finn, and me, and if you wanna join our little group, we have room for a fourth. He needs all the hell we can give him. Keeps 'im decent. Too big for his britches, otherwise. Too serious and..." He held his arms out from his sides and stomped around like he was blustering through the house.

I didn't know what to say, so I reached into the mini fridge I had in the dining room and pulled out another beer for him. I didn't know whether he was officially on the clock, but at his size I figured it was like drinking water.

He took it with a grin and tucked it into his back pocket. "You and me, Nat? We're gonna get along just fine."

TWENTY-SIX

Thomas

Fucking Noah. Most of the time he was my favorite brother. He was a hard worker, goofy and loyal, and he had a heart of gold. He was the labrador retriever of the family: all he needed was a toy and a scratch behind the ears and he could go for days.

I wasn't as complimentary about my other two brothers, because Asher was like me and Aaron was...well, less close. That was my fault, since I'd been isolating myself from them the last couple years when all any of them had ever done was be there for me when I needed it.

I knew Noah was teasing. For heaven's sake, even Natalie knew he was teasing. But damned if I didn't see red the instant he looked at her.

Mine.

He saw it, too: the way my face tightened when he swept his eyes over her curves. He saw the hot, possessive look I tried not to shoot at her when he held out his arm to lead her into the house. And he thought watching me struggle with it was absolutely hilarious.

I'll beat the crap out of him later.

At that point I was so worked up, I had to stop working on cabinets. I was afraid I'd get careless and either chop off my hand with the saw, or I'd screw up a cut and lose time on the boxes I wanted to get installed as quickly as possible.

Though he'd just arrived, if he was going to act like that I would drag his ass back to the airport myself.

Instead, I picked up the paint sprayer and filled it, hauling the boxes and the doors outside to rest on the lawn. I had to keep busy, because it was everything I could do to keep from trailing after them to make sure he wasn't hitting on her. After all, he was the better catch: bigger, stronger, younger, a better sense of humor, and God knew he didn't have half the issues I did. In fact, he was fucking perfect for her.

That thought was so infuriating, I barely kept myself from hurling one of the doors across the lawn.

I tried to calm myself and rationalize why I felt threatened by my own brother. He was the one person who would never betray me. He had *always* been there, him and our sister Maren.

The three of us were closest in age. Maren had been thirteen months older than me and Noah was eleven months younger.

It was obvious that *something* worked really well for our parents, even if it hadn't been the marriage part.

The windows to the house were wide open and I could hear Natalie's sweet voice drifting out, the words indistinct but her tone gentle and soft, like her. And since I wanted to know what she and Noah were talking about, I crept closer to the house, making sure to look busy in case either of them looked out and spotted me sidling right up to the flower bed out front.

"He looked like he wanted to kill you," she said softly, her words finally clear and I caught a glimpse of Noah through the living room window as he made marks on the walls.

"I'd do worse than that if I caught him flirting with *my* woman," Noah responded and from the way he garbled his words I could tell he'd tucked the pencil between his teeth.

"I'm not *his woman*." She sounded displeased. "That sounds so...colonial."

"No?" he teased and I turned just as he looked out the window, his eyes boring right into mine. There was no way he knew what she meant by that.

"Well then, Nat, let me tell you something from a man's perspective. Because no offense at all, but sometimes you ladies are blind as fuck when it comes t' reading us, even when we're givin' you *all* the signals. He *wants* you to be. And he wants it so bad, it's tearin' him up inside." He stared me down, grinning, victorious. "And you may have noticed he don't like sharin' his toys."

I heard an angry huff from Natalie. "He can barely stand to be near me, and I will never be someone's toy, not ever again." She spat out the end of the sentence.

That's my girl: sweet and spicy and feisty. A slow smile spread across my lips and I knew Noah could see it.

Somehow, I just knew he would make me pay for it.

• • • •

BOTH OF US INVITED Natalie to my place for dinner.

Noah actually got down on one knee, kissed the back of her hand and begged her to come babysit so that I wouldn't strangle him. (I nearly did when he kissed her hand, and he giggled when my hands curled into fists at my side.)

The three of us drifted out to my truck and Noah wedged himself into the front passenger seat. That left Natalie to sit behind me, next to the car seat I hadn't had the heart to remove the past few years.

I could feel her eyes on me as I swapped out my sweaty t-shirt for a fresh one. Then I gave the arm rest a quick squeeze, just as I always did, and rounded the truck to slip behind the wheel.

The drive was short, but all the way to my place I could feel her eyes on me in the mirror. All I had to do was look up and catch her eye, to let her see what was going on inside my head. But I couldn't, because she was learning how to read me too quickly for my comfort.

I couldn't meet her gaze, for fear something was going to crack open inside. Today was a day I needed to keep myself busy and distracted, and letting her see all the things I was keeping locked up would come to no good.

I'd still not apologized to her for taking her head off the last time she'd been at my house, and I could tell from the stiffness in her shoulders, as she walked through the front door, that she hadn't forgotten either. But as I closed the door behind us and started to unlace my boots, she squeezed my shoulder before following Noah into the kitchen.

Had I imagined that? Had she trailed her fingers up from my bicep in order to do it?

She insisted on preparing something fresh and Noah dug a frilly, lacy apron out of my pantry cabinet. He looped it over his head to peals of laughter from Natalie, who told him the only things missing were high heels and garters.

That pulled me up short, because it *did* look like that sort of apron, and I turned a little green. Where had it come from? Lydia hadn't worn aprons, because Lydia didn't cook–couldn't cook for shit, as a matter of fact. It was a miracle I hadn't starved to death during our marriage.

Noah chopped up vegetables at her instruction and she pulled out the grill pan and dug steaks out of a tote I hadn't noticed she'd brought with. "The least I can do is feed you two a proper meal after all the work you put in today," she explained as Noah decided the apron would look better on her and was trying to tie the belt behind her as she walked toward the sink.

He was right: It did look better on her and my brain ran riot with the visual she'd supplied, adding in the garter belt and high heels.

Then I had to take a quick seat at the counter or I'd have embarrassed myself the next time she looked over.

It was driving me nuts, how Noah kept flirting with her. Finding small, innocent ways to touch her, to be near her, to tuck her up against his side and almost under his arm as they worked together.

I was the odd man out in my own kitchen. It was a familiar, awful feeling and it was feeding the rage monster clawing to get out of my chest.

He queued up a Sinatra song on the portable speaker I kept on the kitchen countertop, dropping his phone back into his pocket before sweeping her into a slow, messy dance around the kitchen.

The fact he had two left feet had never been enough to stop him. He was a clown and a flirt, the exact opposite of everything I was, and his happy-go-lucky attitude drew people to him like ants to sugar.

I had to walk away or I'd have him in a choke hold, the blood threatening to burst from my eyeballs when I watched him holding her.

She was laughing and teasing and chattering right back, completely at ease with him and for a moment I wondered if I'd done this to myself: pushed her right into my stupid brother's arms.

TWENTY-SEVEN

Natalie

The two of them managed to get through dinner without any fights to the death, though Thomas did shoot a warning glance at Noah more than once when Noah started exaggeratedly flirting with me. And whether or not he realized it, Thomas kept leaning closer and closer to me in his chair.

When Thomas got up to retrieve something from the kitchen, Noah reached out under the table with his foot and scooted the chair to within inches of mine. He wiggled his eyebrows at me, hiding his mouth behind his hand as Thomas walked back in and took in the placement of his chair. He narrowed his eyes, looking at Noah, then at me. Both of us looked back at him innocently and finally, without moving his chair, he sat and we finished the meal.

Of course, at that point I could hardly focus and I swear I kept missing my mouth because Thomas was so close, I was distracted. I could feel the heat rolling off of him and I just wanted to lean my face into his neck and breathe him in. Instead, I relaxed my leg, letting it fall against his under the table and he swallowed so hard that his throat made a funny noise.

"Leavin' you to clean up, dickhead," Noah said as he pushed back from the table and held his hand out to me. "I need to go say hello to Gerry, and Natalie's going to make sure no crafty ladies waylay me in those dark bushes by her house.

"Besides...I need a minute without you there, so I can tell her all your secrets."

"Oh, I think that's going to take a bit longer than a minute," I said, scooting my chair back. "This one's a vault, so you're my only hope. I have *so* many questions about him."

Thomas's lips clamped down tight and I offered him a small smile as Noah carried his plate through to the kitchen.

"You know I'm teasing," I said gently and Thomas moved closer hesitantly.

I could hear Noah digging around in the refrigerator as Thomas leaned his face down to mine, resting our foreheads together and breathing heavily, his hands clenched into fists at his sides. He was panting like an angry bull but the air was thick with something else. It was decidedly *not* anger this time.

I sighed, trying to hold myself in check when all I wanted to do was to lean closer and wrap my arms around him.

Don't touch him or he'll freak out.

"I won't ask him anything and I don't think he'd say anything anyway. He teases, but he's really loyal to you." I stepped back before he did, confused by what I saw in his eyes.

"You comin', love muffin?" Noah hollered from the kitchen and I snorted in spite of myself, rolling my eyes.

"He's messing with you," I whispered, shooting Thomas a small smile, because he didn't look so sure.

"Come on, twinkle buns, you're drivin' Thom's heap. We can come pick up jerkface in the morning." He cracked the cap off another beer.

"You really are an overgrown toddler," I teased as I grabbed Thomas's keys off the kitchen island. "Come on, I'll take you to Gerry–and I'll get him out of your hair," I threw over my shoulder.

"Yeah, by the way..." Thomas hollered from the dining room and I heard chairs being pushed back into place. "You're staying with her tonight or she'll never forgive me for not sharing you. I'm not getting on her bad side."

Noah huffed a little, grabbing the duffel bag he'd dropped in the hallway. "Passing me off already, bro? I see how it is."

As soon as we got into the truck, Noah became serious. It was something I hadn't seen from him yet and I was surprised by the abruptness of the change. It was like he became a different man once the seatbelt was on. "You think you can handle my big brother, Nat?"

"Uh...what?" I had just backed out of the driveway and I turned to look at him as I put the truck into drive. My legs were too short and I had to scoot the seat forward. "Right now I'm just trying to be his friend and that's been hard enough."

He sucked in a deep breath. "Tell me about it. He cut everyone off a couple years ago–went radio silent. Then Aden...and that bitch, Lydia..." His big frame shuddered and I swear the vehicle shook. "It broke him, Natalie. It's not my place to say that, especially since I don't know how much he's told you. He's super private, so he'd never forgive me, but..."

"It's ok," I said, reaching across the small space between us to pat his arm, the front of the cab filled to capacity with his enormous body. "I know he's hurting and I'm just starting to understand how badly. You can relax, because I'm not trying to get into his pants or steal his millions." It was a joke and I rolled my eyes, but a look of surprise passed quickly across Noah's face.

"He might be a little slow on the uptake when it comes t' you, but he would not be mad if you did get into his pants. Probably do him a whole heap of good."

"I might not be mad about it either, but I don't think either of us is ready for that."

He giggled again. It was distressingly high-pitched and girlish.

"He needs a real friend," I said finally, flipping on my blinker and looking to my left before executing a turn. "I'm all kinds of screwed up myself, but I think I can offer him that much. I mean...I want to offer him that, because the way he's hurting is...visceral. I can *feel* it when I'm near him and no one should have to go through that alone."

Noah nodded thoughtfully, his head turned to look out the window at the quiet streets illuminated by the glow of street lamps.

"He's chosen to go through it alone, because he keeps all of us out," he said, more to himself than to me.

He didn't say anything else, reaching once for the beer he'd set in the cup holder.

"Thanks for letting me get a little silly today. The wife's got my nuts in a box on the fireplace mantel. She won't let me keep alcohol in the house because she thinks it's setting a bad example for the kid–says I get too goofy." He grinned at me like he wasn't in the least upset about it and

I rolled my eyes at him. Somehow I knew there was a whole lot more to that story.

All the teasing, all the outrageous flirting: it was all to drive Thomas out of his mind, because the man sitting next to me was the very definition of pussy whipped and my kitty was certainly not doing those honors.

"He doesn't remember," Noah said shortly as I turned onto my street and my eyes darted quickly to him. "Me 'n Eve got married at his place in California this spring. He wouldn't have missed it for anything if he coulda helped it."

There seemed to be more to that story too, whatever it was.

I pulled into Gerry's driveway and sat patiently while Noah untangled himself from the seatbelt and he punched my arm lightly as he got out of the truck. "You're good people, Nat. Make sure you brew a real big pot in the mornin', an' I'll make sure we knock things out tomorrow. The faster I get the wirin' and patchin' done, faster I can help him put that mess back together." He grinned, shutting the door and rapping sharply on the roof twice.

It was all of ten yards to my own driveway and I pulled the truck off to the side, right up behind my Subaru.

The day had been weirdly taxing and I was unexpectedly tired, though it was only just nearing ten.

Noah's boisterous personality demanded a lot of output on everyone's part if they wanted to keep up, I thought, letting myself into the house and hanging the keys up on the hook in the laundry room.

I was so tired, I didn't even bother pulling up my site to read and reply to comments, which was something I typically did every evening the day of a post. It would have to wait until tomorrow, maybe even tomorrow evening, since the next day would be a complete mess.

Showering quickly, I brushed my teeth while half asleep and smeared a cream into my face. Then, turning out the bedside lamp, I folded back the light cover and top sheet.

Though it was creeping toward October by now, the nights had only just begun to cool and it wasn't yet consistent. Most nights, the air in the house was still thick with humidity.

My head had just hit the pillow when I heard a soft tapping at my front door, almost directly below my bedroom window.

Instantly my eyes were wide and my heart hammered as I weighed the possibilities: Gerry, Noah, Thomas...Ahmad.

That none of them seemed very likely was not comforting–it made me more nervous–and I crept down the stairs to peek through the sidelight.

Thomas stood on the porch, pacing back and forth with his hands in his hair and my heart was immediately in my throat. I hadn't heard a vehicle and I had taken his, which meant he'd walked.

Throwing back the bolt, I pulled the door open and stood waiting for him to snap out of it. He looked up then and even in the low light I could see the anguish in his eyes. He looked completely wrecked.

I held out a hand that he didn't take, but he followed me into the house and I shut the door behind him.

"I can't handle it, Natalie. I thought I could, but I can't," he said, his voice breaking, and I swallowed hard. What couldn't he handle?

He didn't seem to hear me when I offered tea, vodka, tranquilizers, or cookies and milk, and I wondered for a moment if he was in shock or just lost in his own misery as he stood there, looking at me like I might disappear.

I took his hand and he didn't pull away as I led him up the stairs and into the cozy space that was my bedroom.

He stood there, halfway into the room, looking around himself as if he was waking from a dream and I squatted down to untie his shoes. He kicked them off restlessly, reaching down to yank at his socks.

I looked down at my tank top and sleeping shorts, thankful I'd put on any clothing at all. He was looking at them too, I realized, chewing on the inside of his lip like he was debating whether he should take off more clothing or just leave it all on.

The butterflies in my stomach voted for less, those crazy bitches, and at the thought my nipples went all high-beam, plainly giving me away.

He stripped off his shirt and pants as if on autopilot and stood shivering, despite the warmth of the room.

"Sleep," I said quietly, pointing him toward the opposite side of the bed and he moved toward it unsteadily, like a drunken man.

He hasn't had enough time to be drinking–not since we left–or has he?

I hadn't smelled it on him. He smelled like...Thomas: good and warm, like a woodshop and his deodorant and something that came from just his skin that was intoxicating. Probably pheromones, I decided, crawling back into my side of the bed a little more eagerly than I should have.

I could feel him shivering yet and it freaked me out.

"Do you need a blanket?" I asked gently and when he didn't respond I rolled up behind him, pulling the blanket with me in order to wrap it around him though the room was fairly warm.

But still the bed shook, so I pressed my body up tight against his, tucking my legs up behind his thighs and pressing my chest into his back. I was shorter than him by quite a bit, my knees bumping up against his thighs.

His skin felt cool and I wrapped an arm over his chest.

He took my hand in his own, pressing it over his heart and while the shivering slowed, his body took on a deep, rhythmic shudder. I was pretty sure he was crying and that scared me, because I didn't know how to put Broken Thomas back together. I froze in place, unsure of what to do. He was such a rollercoaster of reactions and emotions, I didn't know what I was free to do without freaking him out.

I started digging through my distant childhood memories, trying to remember what my parents had done when I'd been sad, or woke up from a nightmare...

I tried to move my head back just a little, so my lips wouldn't brush his neck, which was the only thing those little traitors wanted to do. Already I could hardly think straight, all my skin pressed to his, and quietly I tried out my rusty voice.

I hadn't sung in years–not outside the shower, anyway–and my voice was shaky at first as I tried out the first few bars, low and soft in hopes it would soothe him as I sang "Baby Mine."

As I sang, I felt him begin to relax, the deep shudders growing fewer and fewer, and as I made my way through the song a second time, they finally stopped. I finished the song, squeezing him just a little tighter as I whispered "Peaceful dreams, Thomas. You're safe here."

I wanted to tell him he was loved, because it was easy to see how much he needed it, but I was pretty sure it would scare the shit out of him.

His deep voice rumbled out of him and it startled me, because I'd thought he was asleep. "I just miss them so damn much...I can't lose more, Natalie."

I slept fitfully that night, wrapped tightly around Thomas even though I was a little too warm, just because I was afraid to let go.

He was mumbling in his sleep, my hand still clutched tightly to his chest, and as dawn began to steal over the room I pressed my face into his hair and breathed him in greedily. My throat ached and my eyes burned, from either exhaustion or stupid emotion, I couldn't decide which.

I was falling in love with this disaster of a man and I was pretty sure he was too broken to ever love me back.

My mother's voice scolded me inside my head: *"Natalie, you really do know how to pick them."*

• • • •

ONCE AGAIN, I WAS UNSURE what to do. This was a recurring problem, it seemed. I was awake again, tired enough that I wanted to drift back into the warmth of sleep. However, there was a warm, solid, very much human man in my bed.

Given the complete absence of one in my bed the past few years, this was a highly unusual occurrence, and I had no idea what to do about it.

Thomas fidgeted in his sleep. He'd been sleeping on his side all night, facing away from me and I loosened my arm from around him so he could roll onto his back.

I scooted back just a little as he rolled, and to my surprise his arm shot out, scooping beneath me to draw me closer. I came to rest with my body tucked alongside his and my head on his chest.

Now I really can't make a break for it without him waking up; there's no way he did that on purpose.

Deciding I may as well just go with the flow and face whatever reactions awaited me when he woke up, *when* he woke up, I rested an arm on his chest, next to my face, and closed my eyes.

I prayed he wasn't dreaming of Lydia as I remembered his words of the night before and felt jealousy stab through me.

There was a singsong voice outside the window, calling up, and my eyes snapped open to "Natalie, my beautiful darlin'! It's your strappin', virile man–far more man 'n your poor choice for a boyfriend'll ever be.

"When you decide to let me in we can start workin'. 'Til then, I'll just sit out here on your porch and serenade you. But...let me warn you right now, I sound better *after* coffee. So really, it's in your best interest to lemme in soon if you wanna stay in the neighbors' good graces."

I heard the clomp of heavy work boots and, true to his word, Noah plunked his big body down on the porch and started singing some of the most god-awful, twangy old country songs I thought I'd ever heard.

There was a big hand running up and down my forearm and it took me a moment to realize that had been happening for a minute.

How long had he been awake?

"I'd pay him just to shut up," Thomas's voice rasped and I pulled myself upright very slowly and very unwillingly, especially since I was pretty sure he'd be able to see right through my tank top in the early morning light.

His eyes were red and tired and I bit down on my lip, pushing a strand of hair off his face and brushing a thumb under one eye. Obviously I couldn't stop myself, I'd wanted to touch him for so long and finally it seemed I had permission.

Thomas's eyes drifted to my chest and a lazy grin spread across his face. "I would say you should answer the door just like that, because his brain would fall right out of his ass, but I don't think I want anyone else seeing you like this." He swallowed hard, suddenly having a very hard time meeting my eyes, and I knew it wasn't just because he wanted to sneak another look.

I was pretty sure he'd just admitted that Friend Territory was pretty far in the rearview mirror, and it made my heart kick with a violent hope.

I scooted back down into the bed and wrapped my arms around him, resting my head on his chest. This was new and scary territory, but he didn't flinch or tense or tighten or throw me off, and I breathed a contented sigh. It felt really good to wrap myself around him and to feel his arms come up to rest lightly around me as a shiver ran through him.

Maybe I'm being too easy on him. There are so many problems here...

I sat up reluctantly and pulled a light sweatshirt over my head, grabbing a band for my hair. Then I hurried from the room and down the stairs.

"You're so lucky you didn't show up two weeks from now," I called through an open window to Noah, still crooning away on the front porch.

His repertoire was impressive, and completely exhausting.

"Bow season is coming. Chances are good you'd have gotten about three lines into that first song and I'd have been cleaning your heart off my front porch and repairing the bolt hole in the frame of my house."

He stopped singing immediately, swiveling to look at me through the window. "Oooh, you are a *feisty* one early in the morning!" He laughed that insane little girl laugh. "My stupid brother isn't going to have the first clue what to do with you, because he likes his women boring and dumb."

Suddenly there was a voice over my shoulder: "Your stupid brother is going to rip off your dick if you sing *one more* of those hellish songs. Can't you be like a normal person and shut the fuck up until after you've had coffee? Give the rest of us time to prepare for your shit show."

Noah turned his head quickly, but I saw the look of delight on his face when he realized Thomas was standing behind me, shirtless.

I was equally delighted and I fought the urge to turn quickly and put my hands on his chest–purely for research purposes, you understand.

"Oooh, Natalie," Noah crowed, recovering quickly. "That wasn't even fair. You never even gave me a chance."

"You never *had* a chance with her, jackass," Thomas barked and I turned quickly, grabbing his chin in my hand.

"Easy, killer," I said, and his eyes quickly snapped to mine, his nostrils flaring.

"He's pushing your buttons because he's your brother." I dropped my voice to a whisper. "And he cares about you. He wants to see you happy, but you know he'll take every chance he gets to tease you."

Thomas mumbled something under his breath when I let go of his face.

Noah let himself into the kitchen and kept jabbing me with his elbow when he thought Thomas wasn't looking, and I shook my head quickly at him. It took him a while to get the message that I had not just spent the night rocking his brother's world, though he still seemed giddy that Thomas had spent the night at my place.

The two of them continued to trade insults while I poured coffee and, to my surprise, Thomas nodded when I looked at him and made a pouring gesture. I wondered if he'd slept fitfully as well.

I could hear the two of them calling each other creative names as I carried my cup upstairs with me, giggling when "You're a flea-infested monkey butt–the ugly, red-assed one!" drifted up after me.

Noah, I suspected, was really a six-year-old trapped in a giant's body.

Waking my computer, I opened the office window wider and sat down to catch up on what was surely a barrage of comments: some kind, some snippy, some just outright trolling.

I laced my fingers together and stretched them out, pushing my arms up over my head with a grunt. This was typically not the part that I enjoyed, but interacting with my base was essential, so after each post I gave myself forty minutes to respond to inquiries and comments and then I moved on to other things.

It was only three comments in that I sat up straighter, a jolt of adrenaline pumping ice through my veins.

OMG, Natalie! Is that Thomas "The Titan" Atholton building your kitchen cabinets? I always knew the man was a dreamboat. Send him my way–he can renovate me All. Day. Long!

It was followed by about a million heart-eyed emojis and I sat with my mouth hanging open as my brain started to fire on the caffeine.

Thomas Atholton.

Of Titan Tech.

The envelope on his counter...the business trips.

I'd gotten it *all* wrong. He had to think I was a clueless idiot.

Ignoring the other messages, I opened a new browser window and searched Thomas+Atholton+Harrison+Titan. The page lit up with results, some from reputable news sources but far more from gossipy rags and celebrity stalking sites.

Tech Billionaire Goes to Ground After Partner Files Paternity Suit.

Titan Board Dumps Founder; Atholton Ditches West Coast Homes In Fire Sale.

Sexy Lydia Voorhees Dishes: Atholton's A Dud; Powell's A Stud!

Ugh. I slammed the lid shut and dropped my head down with a bang, my arms stretched out on the desk in front of me.

My mother is going to have a freaking field day with this.

"You ok?" Thomas's voice was surprisingly gentle and I lifted my head just enough to see that the tech giant had brought me another cup of coffee.

"Maybe," I said, gratefully accepting the steaming mug. "I think I just tripped and fell into Pandora's box."

His lips twisted into a tight grin and I knew he misunderstood what I meant, but I really didn't have the energy to set him straight. I wasn't sure I wanted to, in fact, since I kind of wanted to see what he'd with the opening I'd provided.

"I'm sorry."

I spun toward where he sat, in a chair that was too small for him, not far from the door. It was where I piled things I didn't feel like sorting or putting away: papers, mail, catalogs, packages, and the precarious stack now sat on the floor next to his feet.

"Why are you sorry?" I asked, wanting to actually hear it from his lips instead of filling in the blanks for him and letting him off the hook time after time.

"I'm messy and angry and not very nice to you some of the time. You deserve better than that."

Okay, so that's where we're starting.

"*Some* of the time?" I raised an eyebrow, lifting the mug to my lips.

He had the sense to look guilty, at least.

"Tell me about Pandora's Box," he pivoted suddenly, and I debated how to handle the question. I wondered if he was hoping I would address what had happened the night before. Instead, wordlessly, I lifted the lid on my laptop and spun it toward him so he could see the post.

His eyes widened when he saw the first photo of himself and his jaw set firmly. It was a good one if I could say so myself: He was concentrating hard, his forehead furrowed as he brought the saw blade down on a strip of wood. He looked broad and muscular, capable and handsome. *Edible*, my brain interjected, and I shook my head at myself. I was still an idiot.

Stupid lymbic system. Stop sending smoke signals to my pants.

"I should have asked your permission before I posted it," I said quietly. "I didn't use your name, so I didn't think anything of it...I didn't know."

His eyes drifted to the comments and he scrolled down the page, reading for far longer than I had, his expression growing harder and tighter.

"Dirty vultures," he muttered, and I waited for him to look up and explain what was going on. "That's what I'm trying to stay away from." He pointed toward my laptop and I waited for him to continue.

"Those are women who think they see an easy opportunity, like I'm so desperate for a woman's attention that I can just be scooped up and hauled home." He made a disgusted sound. "I've been running from that since Lydia left. Before then. But it got worse once she left. She thought it was hilarious that women threw themselves at me–tried to seduce me–sometimes right in front of her."

He drifted quickly through stories of stalkers: women who showed up at events to throw themselves at him. Some showed up at his office, occasionally going so far as to make an appointment, while one had broken into his house in Portola Valley and crawled into his bed while he was away on business. It was Lydia who found the intruder, sliding in next to her in the dark, and I'd have given every last cent to be a fly on the wall and hear that scream.

The two of them had a very active social life and due to his prominence, both were involved with numerous charities. Because of the amount of money he could throw around, there was always another gala, another dinner, another benefit. It kept their faces in the news and women interested.

Many women sent him fan mail, or love letters, or pleaded to have his babies, and his secretary in Palo Alto was tasked with running full-time interference.

Though he'd largely been pushed out of his own company, something he didn't elaborate on, he remained a very active figure on the board (to Harrison's consternation, apparently), and thus the reason he maintained a secretary and an active travel calendar.

Suddenly I knew what the Titan Tech envelope that sat on his counter was stuffed with, and I waited until he stopped speaking. Then I asked, "What do you do with all the fangirl mail?"

"Burn it."

"And I just outed you..." I held a hand over my mouth.

"It's not like you've given GPS coordinates to my home. But yeah, this puts me on a very uncomfortable radar."

"I'm so sorry...I really didn't know. I didn't know who you were. I'm not really current on the Who's Who of Silicon Valley."

He didn't look angry. "You didn't know because I didn't tell you."

"You didn't tell me because you don't trust me. You probably figured I was a gold digger, just like the others." I waited for him to catch it and correct me, but he didn't. Instead he laughed a short, humorless bark.

"Can you blame me for being overly cautious? My track record with women hasn't exactly been stellar." He held up his hands in a shrug.

"I can defuse this and I will," I said, pointing toward the laptop. "The heartbreak will be heard 'round the world when these women find out that Thomas the Titan is *not* the man building my kitchen cabinetry."

There was a weird expression on his face. "Who is it that's building your kitchen cabinets then, Natalie?"

I squirmed a little uncomfortably. Things were different. He was softer, somehow. More human than he'd ever seemed before.

"My friend Thomas," I said finally, trying to answer in a firm voice but it came out lower and more breathy than I'd wanted.

He nodded once and pushed to his feet, replacing the precarious stack of items on the chair. "Yeah," he said, and I thought it sounded as if he was trying to convince himself. "Your friend Thomas."

So there we were...back to that.

TWENTY-EIGHT

Thomas

It made me crazy that I'd been outed to Natalie, and while she hadn't acted any differently toward me during those few moments, I wondered if she just needed time for it to sink in.

She would get awkward and uncomfortable around me.

She would develop certain expectations, and I wasn't looking forward to that.

Our relationship was slowly becoming easier and less complicated than most of the relationships I had even with more casual friends and I didn't want that to change.

It was in the way I could sit in a comfortable silence with her.

It was in the way she looked at me each morning when I walked into her house, something soft and welcoming in her eyes.

It had me on edge, wondering somewhere down deep if she missed me the way I missed her when I left her house each day.

That means you need to admit to yourself that she's more than just a casual friend. Stop playing around.

It took me a while to finish and stain the shelves she wanted in her kitchen, and as I sealed the first one, I finally had to admit to myself that I wouldn't have done something like this for just anyone. This went above and beyond my charity toward helpless little old ladies. This was something much bigger, in time and expense and effort. It also meant more to me than most of my charitable endeavors and I knew it was because I wanted to see her face light up with joy.

Yesterday had been hard. Not only was it the anniversary of Aden's death, but I received a firm date from my lawyer that pertained to a very unpleasant task Harrison wished to carry out. The one for which he'd been granted permission by a judge.

Noah's flirting with Natalie had pushed me over the edge. It made me frantic in a way I couldn't put into words and I'd been the freak who showed up at her door without an explanation, clinging to her like a child, looking for support and comfort.

She'd given it without reservation, holding me tightly the way I used to hold Aden when he had nightmares, and when she'd whispered softly to me, it calmed me like no one ever had.

It scared me how jealous I was of Noah, even though I knew the jealousy was unfounded. He would never do that to me and I was fairly sure Natalie wouldn't either, but how could I be certain?

Maybe she would break my heart by falling for him after all.

Maybe she just loved and cared for everyone like this because her heart was so big, and the unwelcome thought stabbed at my chest.

Maybe I'm not special to her.

She fed us lunch, true to form, and Noah sighed in delight as he licked his fingers. "Lord bless you, woman. That was ridiculous. No wonder the old man looks like he's finally puttin' some meat on his bones. If I ate like this every day, I'd hafta work out at least as hard as he does." He patted his stomach thoughtfully.

Noah was definitely not in the shape I was, despite the fact he was built taller and broader than me. I teased that he was carrying a couple extra beer pounds around his middle and he'd never bothered to correct me, but truthfully he was looking the best I'd seen him in a long time.

It was a miracle I wasn't in worse shape, I thought, figuring I'd averaged around six frozen pizzas a week for a long time.

But then Natalie showed up and suddenly I was eating like a human again.

Natalie was throwing a wrench into my plans. I was going to have to make adjustments that would make me even more uncomfortable. I didn't like what she was making me think–things I had no right thinking about another man's wife, even if that man didn't appreciate her the way he should have. *His loss, my gain,* my brain taunted in a sing-songy voice and I wondered if, just maybe, she could actually *be* my gain.

I hauled in cabinets while Noah worked his way through the house, hanging doors and pushing boxes up tight against walls so I could take measurements and call the stonecutters. This was a small job and one of my guys owed me a favor. By greasing the wheels a little, I knew I could get a rush order for something very similar to what I'd seen on the mood board she'd created. (Yeah, I snooped.) I wanted her to be surprised, but more than anything I wanted to apologize in the only way I really knew how: by doing something nice.

Doing was my strength, whereas words were clearly not.

She'd been gentle with me all day long, using a soft voice and taking care not to sneak up on me.

When she did come up behind me to inspect progress or offer help, she rested her hand softly on my shoulder and each time she did, I wondered what she would do if I turned and caught her in my arms.

I wanted to kiss her in front of Noah so he'd back the hell off. I was going to have to do the guy equivalent of lifting my leg in order to get it through his thick skull.

My only solace was that I'd noticed today that she didn't touch him. Not that she didn't touch him the way she touched me, but she was very careful not to touch him *at all.* It made me gleeful, and I wondered if it was making him nuts, because Noah was very touchy-feely with everyone.

"Stop messin' with her," Noah hissed at me once he knew she was out of earshot. "You gotta throw her a bone, man. No more of this 'we're just buddies' bullshit." He wiggled his eyebrows at me. "You know. Otherwise you're gonna lose that to someone less deservin', bro, and *that* is miiighty fine."

I was trying not to hear him. I didn't want him to say what I already knew. Because if I was just Natalie's friend, eventually the door *would* be opened to other men: Men who would line up to fill the vacancy in her life long before she advertised the position, and the thought of someone else in her bed made rage boil up inside my chest.

Smitty had already insinuated much the same thing to me yesterday, when I'd stopped in to pay for the delivery of the glossy black La Cornue range I'd special ordered for her weeks earlier. It was the very one I knew she'd been coveting since I'd put in her skylights and managed to snoop through the drawings on her desk, before I talked her into redoing her kitchen.

I thanked my lucky stars Natalie was walking the beach the morning the range was delivered. I'd cleared space deep in the garage and promptly stacked lumber and panels on and around it to hide it. Of course, it was the other reason I'd summoned Noah and she had handily provided me with a reason: the wiring.

I needed muscle and Noah had fifty pounds on me and was several inches taller, alternately described by women in hushed whispers as "utterly terrifying" or "a magnificent beast."

I mostly needed him for his ability to haul things, but unfortunately he came with the mouth attached.

I'd let Noah in on the plan as soon as I had a timeline in my head and he quickly switched his schedule around once I told him I'd fly him in to rewire the house. I'd had to swear him to secrecy because he had no poker face and his secret-keeping ability was rivaled only by that of toddlers at Christmastime.

He knocked out the rewire quickly, then went back to patch and Natalie, delighted with progress, was right behind him with paint brushes and rollers. It gave her a good reason to paint the other rooms in the house, she said, and when she disappeared to paint her master bathroom, Noah let himself out into the garage to give me his pep talk.

Leaning back against the pile of scraps covering the stove, he crossed his big arms over his chest. "Way I see it, bro, you're playing this one of two ways." He slapped a big hand down on the piece of plywood I'd slid over the top of the range. "You're either tryin' a' ride in on your overpriced white horse to rescue the damsel in distress, or you're testin' her by throwin' expensive things her way. That way, when she gets stars in her eyes, you can be disappointed she's just like the others an' push her away, too."

"She won't," I said shortly, and I was surprised to find that I was at least ninety percent confident in my own words. "She's not impressed by things. She *knows*, Noah, and she's still mad I haven't cashed her checks." I chuckled a little.

"You tell her yet?" he asked, peeking under the plywood sheet and letting out a low whistle when he saw the name on the box.

"Which thing?" I asked distractedly, sanding down a rough edge.

"Any of the other stuff."

"She knows some about Lydia. And Aden."

Noah looked disappointed. "She can't be what you want if you won't let her all the way in, dipshit. You're keepin' her in the dark on purpose."

"Are we really going to stand here and have a talk about *feelings*?" I asked him, barely turning. He didn't have to see my face to hear the disgust in my voice.

"Yup." He reached across the space to slap my shoulder. "Cuz you're catchin' 'em, and it's about damn time."

TWENTY-NINE

Natalie

True to what I'd thought was his overinflated word, Noah was a rewiring genius. He had the house completely rewired by the end of the day, the damage much less than I'd expected. He'd started back at the bottom of the house, patching carefully and some hours later Thomas set a piece of paper on the island with his signature at the bottom.

"It's after hours now," he said, gesturing toward the paper. "We can file that with the county in the morning."

"You're a code inspector, too?" I asked, staring at him in dismay.

"I am a man of many talents and even more connections," he grinned, and I had the overwhelming urge to wrap my arms around him and kiss him.

Something told me that was another of his talents.

Noah came up behind him and reached around to slap a spackle-covered hand on Thomas's chest. "This guy's even better with his hands than he is with his brain, Natalie. Lucky for you, maybe, 'cuz he's a damn genius." He wiggled his eyebrows and I blushed a furious, immediate shade of red. "I told him he was wasting his time in the technology sector."

Thomas looked at him disgustedly. "I suppose thirteen billion was a waste of time."

I choked. *What the hell?*

Noah's big hand slapped him a few more times for good measure. "Eh, you got lucky, bro. Thank goodness you got out before that asswipe tanked it all. But come on...that's not serious money, ask Forbes. Compared to Musk, you're playin' in the kiddie pool."

Thomas shot him a wicked glare and I had a feeling Noah had been goading him about something for a while.

Neither of them seemed to notice that I was standing there with my mouth hanging wide open, my brain churning frantically to keep up.

"All I'm sayin' is that Eve an' me never got a wedding gift from you. I vote you buy us a private island with all that money you made from government contracts."

Thomas's eyebrows raised and he turned toward his brother with a murderous expression. "Eve? So you mean to tell me you've been pulling my dick the whole time with this flirting bullshit? You *finally* got serious about Eve? Sole-control-of-your-man-stick serious?" He was suddenly gleeful.

Noah giggled and crouched down like he was waiting to absorb a body blow, wincing as he pulled a chain out of the neck of his shirt, from which dangled a large gold ring. "Took a while to convince her, but this?" He gestured between himself and me. "I had a theory to test."

"What theory was that?" Thomas asked, reaching over with a lightning-quick movement to smack the side of Noah's head.

"You don't want me to say right now," Noah grinned, looking pointedly at me, and Thomas chased him out of the room, but not before I saw the flush creeping up his neck.

It seemed he had guessed the theory.

The two of them carried in the cabinets from the garage and set them in their places without mounting them. Thomas looked around, his hand on his chin for a moment. "Yeah," he said. "I can see it now. Nice job, Natalie. This is going to look so much bigger and fresher and cleaner. Noah and I will get these in tomorrow and then start on the backsplash. I took countertop measurements off your old cabinets, since you weren't changing the configuration or sizing, and I sent my guy the measurements for the peninsula base. The job is pretty easy.'"

"You have got to be kidding me," I said as I shook my head at him. "Is there nothing you can't do? Next you'll tell me that you've written five successful apps, you're a cyber security specialist, you've developed server farms around the world and, oh–you're a master carpenter who loves to restore old houses using hand tools, but only when you're not busy transcribing ancient Greek."

Noah grinned at me and I knew what was coming.

"I *am* a cyber security expert, actually," Thomas said with a shrug. "But I mainly stick to software development when it comes to my own business ventures, even if I make the big money on the government contracts.

"Also, I've *produced* three apps, but I have no interest in developing server farms. And though I'm not quite a master carpenter, I really do enjoy woodworking."

"He does actually speak Greek. Pretty passable Creole too," Noah interjected, and I threw up my hands.

"What on earth are you doing here, Thomas Atholton? You should be working for some shadowy figure headquartered at the Pentagon. Like overseas. On some gorgeous, sandy-white island with blue rooftops and exotic women."

He really did have a James Bond thing going on, all broody and self-contained.

Noah hauled in cartons of tile from the garage, stacking them up against the far wall. Then he brought in the light fixtures that had arrived that day–the fastest order I'd ever placed–before disappearing into the garage again.

"Mind if I take some pictures of progress tomorrow?" I asked, and Thomas pulled a wry face. "I'll be careful," I promised, having spent a large portion of the afternoon doing damage control online.

Gerry had extended an invitation for dinner and I was grateful to her as I watched how both men relaxed in her presence and adopted an easier, gentler attitude toward one another. She truly was a miracle worker, I thought, observing the easy flow between the three of them. And to my surprise, she worked hard to make sure I was included, explaining the inside jokes and the silly stories with patience and kindness.

I'd slipped over to her place earlier in the afternoon to make Banoffee pie, which Thomas ate in concentrated silence, while Noah moaned that he'd married the wrong woman. He made me promise to give his wife the recipe.

"You're a good mama," I observed as both men cleared the table without being asked.

Gerry sat comfortably, a sweet smile on her face as the two of them loaded dishes into the dishwasher and wrapped food to put away. I had never seen anything like it.

"I was with them the longest," she said quietly, and I knew the look on my face asked the question, so she continued with more detail than she'd given me before: She had met their father shortly after the death of Charles's first wife and he, desperate to restore order to his household (and desperate to get into her pants), had rushed her down the aisle. They remained married for six years, until Thomas was eighteen and went off to college, at which point Charles began trading in for the newer model every few years.

She saw the look on my face as I sat back in my chair. "There are some people you have to let go of because they're not good for you, even if you love them and it hurts like hell," she said, and I knew she was purposely keeping her voice low. "I'm far more selective these days." The side of her mouth pulled up in a half grin, and I knew it was because of the expression on my face.

She eyed me for a moment, something obviously at the forefront of her mind. "There are a few people you'll meet in your lifetime who are worth keeping and they are sometimes the most work," she said, and I could feel a presence behind me, just beyond the doorway. I knew it was Thomas, pausing, listening quietly to our conversation as Noah kept up a steady banter with what was apparently a very ornery dishwasher. He had already heaped a litany of insults on it in what sounded like Russian.

"I saw him pacing on your porch last night, dear girl. He was frantic."

I looked up suddenly, my face warm, to find that her eyes were kind. "You have been gentle with him when he didn't expect it and kind when he didn't deserve it. You have managed to be there when he needs you most, and that's what a friend does. *And* a lover who's worth the effort. But he's prickly and scared, so go slow. Be patient and don't give up on him. He's just starting to figure out he wants you to be both of those things in his life." Her voice was purposefully quiet, low, so as not to carry into the kitchen.

"He keeps himself from me," I said quietly, my index finger absently tracing the rim of my glass. "It's his choice to make. I have offered my friendship and I can't promise more because I don't think I can be enough for what he needs. I've never been enough for anyone else." I blushed the instant the words fell from my mouth and hated that I was still so insecure.

There was a cough in the kitchen and Noah called Thomas something involving a farm animal and a confusing sexual position. It made me suck in my lips to keep from laughing, because it explained a lot about Thomas's more intricate, vociferous curses.

Gerry was looking at me thoughtfully, her head cocked slightly to the side. "I think you'll figure it out together," she said gently. "But I think you know he has a way of taxing one's patience. He has a tendency to purposely drive people away. He's learned to fear intimacy because he expects betrayal and if you expect nothing from someone, they will not disappoint." Her lip quirked a little. "Ask me how I know this is true."

I sat with my eyes downcast, thinking, a despondent feeling stealing over me. An unwelcome memory was clouding my vision, one of Thomas in my bed, wrapped up tightly in my arms.

I was tired of sleeping alone.

I wanted to be the little spoon again, something I hadn't had in so long that I almost wondered if I'd ever had it at all.

Gerry caught my eye and nodded knowingly, and I drew in a deep breath, terrified she'd read my every intimate thought, just as a large hand squeezed my shoulder.

I lifted my hand to his without even thinking, linking my fingers through his as I tipped my head back to look up at him. It was such an intimate, innocent thing, something reflexive, but I saw the shift in his expression when I touched him and I wondered how much he'd purposely overheard.

"I should get this big jerk home," Thomas said quietly, gesturing toward the kitchen with his other hand.

"I'm not staying with you, you asshole!" Noah howled from the kitchen. "Gerry makes me *real* breakfast, not donuts and freakin' burnt eggs! The sheets on the bed *match*, too, and there's a towel without holes in the bathroom! Hell, no. You'll find me right here in the mornin'!

"Right, Gerry?" His head popped around the frame of the doorway as he gave her a pleading look.

Thomas snorted, his forehead collapsing into his eyebrows as his face screwed up while he tried to keep from laughing out loud, and I only half wondered if he'd purposely tortured Noah in the past.

It seemed he could afford a lot more than just a matching set of sheets.

I reached up slowly with the other hand, curling my fingers around his neck almost without knowing what I was doing, and I smiled up at him. Something hot unfurled in his eyes and I had to look away, for fear of being burned.

"Dinner was amazing. Thank you, Gerry," I found myself saying, suddenly on my feet despite the fact I swayed a little. "These two are making record time in my kitchen and once it's back in any kind of workable shape, I owe you."

Gerry rose with me, though she wasn't at all unsteady on her feet. "You owe me nothing," she said with a smile. "But I'm grateful to have you as a friend." She cast an intense look at Thomas. "Now..." she smiled slowly. "You two call it a night."

Thomas said nothing, tucking my hand under his arm and moving toward the door.

I made no excuses and neither did he. It was understood we were all adults here.

We let ourselves into my house and he trailed almost hesitantly up the stairs after me.

But if he was waiting for a great seduction, he was in for my standard evening show: washing my face and brushing my teeth, since there was no way he was ready for me to start stripping off my clothes and climbing him like a tree, even if that was the only thing on my mind right now.

He hesitated slightly as I handed him a spare toothbrush from under the sink and he brushed his teeth next to me, watching me with a strange look on his face.

He stripped down to his underwear and I tried desperately to keep my eyes averted until he crawled under the thin sheet, lying on his back, one big arm thrown up over his head.

I could almost hear him thinking and by the pattern of his breath, it was obvious he wasn't sleeping.

"This is weird, I'm sorry. I should sleep on the sofa."

"Don't you dare. You like this as much as I do." I was already so tired, and I reached for one of his arms as I rolled slowly. "Besides, it's your turn," I said with a little laugh, and I felt him follow my movement.

My stomach flip-flopped when he pressed up tightly behind me, one arm going over my ribs. I hummed contentedly as I captured his hand and curled my fingers around his, pressing our joined hands into my neck.

My voice was weak with exhaustion and nerves. "There is still so much love in your life, Thomas...you just have to let it in."

Where the hell had that come from?

I felt him shift uncomfortably behind me and I wondered if I'd pushed too far. I had no skills in this department, I thought, drifting slowly into some spectacularly troubled dreams, and I heard him mumble something just before I drifted off.

"There's nothing left in my life, Natalie, and I don't know how to let you in."

• • • •

IT WAS DARK. TOO DARK.

I woke suddenly, gasping for breath as I clawed my way into consciousness. The nightmare had been gripping, real, terrifying, and I was surprised I hadn't awakened myself with screams or tears.

A strong arm squeezed tightly around my ribcage and I breathed a cautious sigh of relief, because I knew I wasn't alone in my tiny guest room in Boston.

Thank God.

It was such a relief to wake up in Thomas's arms that I let a few deep, shuddering breaths shake my body, and too late I realized that Thomas was awake too.

"I can't sing for shit," he rasped in a sleepy voice. "Or I'd return the favor. But, Natalie..." His voice dipped low and it was as dark and promising as it had ever been. "Whatever you need, just tell me."

His lips were so close to my ear, I could feel them, and I debated whether I should turn and kiss him or just burst into tears.

What I needed was something he wasn't ready to give me, because it was more than the tone of his voice promised.

I sighed, bringing his fingers to my mouth to press a slow kiss to his knuckles, tucking his fingers into my neck again, just under my chin.

You've been lying to yourself.

"It tears me up when you're upset and I don't know how to fix it." His voice was so low and quiet. I thought I heard something more, but I couldn't be sure. I was intensely aware of his nearness, his big body wrapped around mine, hard in places it hadn't been when we'd fallen asleep.

"I don't want to do this anymore," I finally whispered, and his whole body tensed. He was quiet behind me and I could feel his strong, steady heartbeat against my back.

"I want more than what I told you," I confessed quietly. "But friends don't do this...they don't feel this way."

Slowly I unwound his arm and rolled to face him, though I could hardly see him in the dark. I couldn't see his expression, only the outline of his face, and I reached up a hand to rest on his cheek. He didn't tense when I did it, though I heard his breath catch, and I trailed my fingers across the sharp ridge of his cheekbone to tuck his hair behind his ear with soft fingertips.

"What do you want, Natalie?" His voice wobbled like he was fearful.

I propped myself up on an elbow and scooped my hair over my shoulder, aware of the sound of my own blood rushing in my ears and the fact his breath seemed to be coming faster.

"Why are you so afraid of me?" I asked, my fingers curling into his gloriously silky hair.

"Because everyone wants something from me and there's nothing left to give," he answered quietly. "Everything's already been taken."

His breath hitched jaggedly and I trailed light fingertips across his face to trace a winged eyebrow.

He wasn't talking about money or power or status. And though I wanted to tell him that I wouldn't take anything from him, I was fairly certain he'd heard it all before. He'd undoubtedly been promised the world many times over, by every woman who'd ever tried to wriggle her way into the circle of his arms.

What made me think I would be any different; that I would mean anything more?

I tried to contain the sigh, but it escaped anyway. Even I could hear the disappointment in it, the way it tripped over the tight emotions stuck in my throat.

I leaned down to him, winding my fingers into the hair at the back of his head. My hair covered us and I pressed my forehead to his, holding for a long moment. Then I released the fistful of his hair and pressed the flat of my palm to the side of his face, lowering myself again so that our faces rested inches apart on our pillows.

There was a boundary line here somewhere–probably already somewhere pretty far behind me–but I'd be damned if I was going to break his shaky trust by forcing anything. He needed to take the literal step forward and show me he trusted me.

Thomas's hand lifted, smoothing my hair back, his palm warm on my cheek. "I should have gone home tonight," he whispered darkly, scooping his arm around me to roll me back as he raised up on one arm.

His lips were warm and soft on my forehead, and I shivered a little.

A kiss on the forehead: your consolation prize.

But as his hair drifted around my face, I realized he hadn't pulled away. His breath was warm on my cheek, his thumb sweeping slowly across my bottom lip, and I felt my heart hiccup.

My brain screamed, but my body wasn't listening any longer. I lifted both hands between us to hold his face, unable to control that my back arched as he slipped an arm beneath my shoulders, lifting me toward him.

Our lips met with a gasp–maybe mine or maybe his–and without knowing what I was doing, I quickly wound a leg around his hips to draw him closer. It reminded me how little fabric there was between the two of us as his hard body pressed into mine, and an eager sound slipped from my throat.

I felt his reaction to that sound. He cut himself loose with a growl and lunged aggressively into my mouth, bypassing any tender, experimental kisses in favor of hungry bites and deep, hard sweeps of his tongue.

Heat raced across my skin, a response faster than panic, and I met every thrust and lick by arching myself into him, his hair wound tight in my fists to keep his face pressed to mine. I was lost in him and I knew he'd lost himself in me.

For a moment, I knew, I could help him shut everything else out, so that he would only feel.

The need was like nothing I'd ever felt before, hot and demanding, and my fuzzy brain couldn't determine whether it was his need or my own that was driving the insistent pace of our mouths. All I knew was that my body's impulses had quickly overridden any self control and my hips began to shamelessly grind into him.

I needed this, I thought frantically. We both did. Each of us needed to feel desired after years of emotional and sexual starvation.

I needed to know I had been enough to breach that impenetrable wall he'd tried to keep around his heart. The damn thing was wrapped in barbed wire and though I knew I would take any chance he gave me, I would come away bleeding and possibly mortally wounded.

"Natalie," he groaned into my ear, his mouth trailing down my neck, his tongue dipping into the hollow of my clavicle and I anchored one leg to the bed, clamping the other firmly around him as I rolled him. I was so much smaller than him that he gasped in surprise to find himself on his back and I took advantage of the lull, nipping his earlobe with my teeth before finding the soft place beneath his ear I suspected would drive him mad. I licked with featherlight strokes, then drew the skin between my lips to suck. It pulled a soft groan out of him and he pressed his body into mine, his fingers squeezing into my hips and thighs to press me closer.

"Oh my heavens, Thomas! You are such a wild, hairy beast."

There was a groan from outside and a falsetto voice drifted in through the open window. "Your muscles are almost as impressive as Noah's, but this tiny little...oh, this is so disappointin'."

Hiccup.

Giggle.

Wait–what? What the hell? I paused, lifting my head slowly and Thomas's fingers dug convulsively into my backside.

There was a snort of laughter outside and I sat up straighter, suddenly in direct and shocking contact with the spectacular evidence of Thomas's interest. I looked down at him quickly and he lifted his hips, making me gasp.

"Those assholes are drunk–ignore them," he whispered. "He and Gerry are peas in a pod. They like to wind each other up after a few drinks and they thought they'd tease us."

"Care to turn the tables?" I asked, an evil grin stealing over my face.

"I'll do anything you want if it makes you kiss me like that again." His voice was desperate, and I swiveled my hips against him so that a growl burst from his throat.

"Just like that," I whispered, and I felt his lips curve into a smile as his mouth touched my neck.

"Maybe you're a little bit of an exhibitionist," he teased, and I leaned down to take his mouth as forcefully as he'd taken mine. It knocked the breath out of him and I slid my body down his, overwhelmed by the delicious friction.

How long had it been?

"Maybe," I agreed as I let him roll me onto my back, pulling my thigh up over his hip and directing the pace as he slid his body against mine. "But I don't care what anyone else thinks or hears or sees...

"I don't care what you do or how the world sees you. Here, it's just you and me, and I want *you*, Thomas...this." I laid the fingers of my right hand over his heart and tapped my fingers.

It was as if I'd doused him with cold water. He froze, his breath slowing as sense seemed to return, and carefully he unwound his arms from beneath my body, lifting to slip over the side of the bed.

He was up and moving across the room instantly, and I heard the lock click on the bathroom door.

What the hell had just happened? I sat up, panting, dragging heavy hair off my sweating face. My body was on fire, and I gave serious thought to finishing the job on my own while he took his time in the bathroom.

Finally, I heard the light snap off and the door shut, and the air in the room crackled with tension as he came over to sit on the side of the bed. I could hear the sound of his hands running across the stubble on his face, and he leaned with his elbows on his knees and his head hanging down for a long time.

It took everything I had to keep from crawling up behind him to kiss his neck and drag him back down with me.

"I can't stay, or you won't like what happens," he said finally, standing up and retrieving his pants, stepping in quickly and moving from the room as if he feared I would chase him.

What the hell?

If Noah's drunk ass had just gone to bed instead of wandering through my yard...I let my mind wander through the delicious possibilities, aware it was doing nothing to calm my raging hormones or hammering heartbeat.

There was a startled exclamation outside and a low grunt, like the wind had been knocked out of someone, and I could have looked, but I didn't. Instead, frustrated, confused and angry, I wound myself in the light blanket and buried my head under the pillow, praying to fall asleep.

THIRTY

Thomas

I barely pulled myself away from Natalie in time. The woman made me crazy and keeping myself under tight control when I was near her sometimes required sarcasm, insults, and hurting her feelings.

But when I broke...and she kissed me back just as wildly as I had kissed her...my damn brain stopped working. Not a single rational thought passed through for long moments while I tasted her skin, explored her hot mouth and absorbed her soft, sweet sounds.

These were the dreams that had been filling my days and nights, waking and sleeping, and I could hardly believe I was holding her in my arms without resistance from her.

It happened because I was an idiot. I had taken advantage of her in a weak moment. I hadn't even asked her what made her so upset–not that I'd have remembered her answer anyway, because when she held my face like that I'd come unglued.

Just one soft touch was all it had taken to unleash the monster who wanted to devour her.

I let myself out the kitchen door, furious with myself, but even more furious we'd been interrupted.

If Noah had stayed in Gerry's house, I'd still be in Natalie's arms, losing myself in her. Not thinking, just feeling.

Noah was trailing across the front lawn, weaving back toward the hedge that bordered the yard and separated Natalie's property from Gerry's.

I dug in, seeing red, sprinting toward him and lifting my arms at the last second to take him down in a rolling tackle.

The glass in his hand went flying as my chest slammed into his back, and his body slapped the lawn with a loud, painful exhalation.

We rolled, crashing through the hedge, coming to rest on Gerry's lawn.

"I should beat you senseless," I snarled at him, and he held up his giant paws immediately and hiccupped.

"Aw come on, br–didn't mean nothin'. I was just..." He lost his train of thought, giggling so hard that I knew he and Gerry must have hit the hard stuff not long after Natalie and I left.

Noah was a big dude, but he was a damn lightweight these days.

"You ruined my night, jackass."

He sat up quickly, pushing me off easily, and I ran a hand down my arm when I felt something warm and sticky.

One of us was bleeding.

"You have..." *Hiccup.* "Stick...or somethin'...so far up yer ass," he sputtered drunkenly. "You'n know what t'do with her, a woman like that takin' care of you. Drive your drunk butt home an' let you hold her all night so *you* can sleep. Pffft...selfish dick."

How did he know about that?

Shit, maybe he wasn't as drunk as I'd thought he was.

Was he jealous?

"What has Gerry been telling you?"

"Nuffin'." *Hiccup.* "Essept you loooooove her, so y'push her away."

Damn it. I didn't need Gerry connecting the dots for him. I didn't need anyone to know, because I hadn't figured it out for myself until a few minutes ago. I needed more time with it, to unravel the tight knots in my gut.

I stepped back and held out a hand, helping him up, and he wobbled unsteadily on his feet.

"Stoopid," he accused me, shoving a finger into my chest. "Scared. S'you walk away from her. Choose to be mis...misa...mis-ble...sad," he finally spat.

I held a hand over my eyes for a moment and tried to calm the feelings that battled for my attention: rage, panic, fear, exhaustion, desire. Everything in my brain and body ached and I wanted to be angry with someone else for it.

Noah had been a mess like this once too, I remembered vividly, recalling the night I'd chartered a plane because I couldn't get to him any other way. That had been the lowest point for him, and the beginning of the end for me. When I'd finally returned home, it had been to find Harrison in my house, with my wife.

He plopped down on the wide step in front of Gerry's house and I lowered myself down next to him, reaching for his wrist and the long white scar covered by the wide band of the watch he perpetually wore.

"You're stronger 'n I was," he said quietly, letting me slide the watch up far enough to see the scar and the tattoo of the two tiny birds.

Avery and Everly.

"But y'keep doing dumb shit. You break too, bro. Again. Worse 'n last time, an' I dunno if I can get t'you fast enough, th'way you did fer me."

Hiccup.

He leaned his head on my shoulder and sighed heavily, and I held my breath, knowing the fumes would knock me over.

"I thought you quit," I said softly, and it wasn't an accusation.

"'S happy drinks, Thom. 'Fore I did it cuz I was in a bad place. Now's just messin' around."

I didn't think any kind of drinking was a good idea as far as he was concerned, but I was living in a glass house if any stones were being thrown.

"Stop...fightin' her," he said quietly, and I let my head drop down, bracing my elbows on my knees.

"Let th'woman make you happy."

"I don't know how," I admitted finally, and he lifted his head slowly, slinging an arm over my shoulders.

"I can't git up." He hiccupped and burped at the same time, and I rolled my eyes, pushing to my feet and dragging him up with me.

I pointed him in the direction of the front door and waited until he'd fumbled the latch open and was walking through. Then I turned to walk across the lawn.

"Thom," he called, and I looked back over my shoulder.

"She'll sh-show you, if y'let 'er."

I heard Gerry's voice from inside the house and Noah's insane, high-pitched giggle. Then the door shut and I shook my head to myself.

I could have taken my truck, because it was a long walk home, but I could use every minute of that walk to think my way out of this mess.

THIRTY-ONE

Natalie

To say I slept like garbage would be generous.

To say that I laid awake in my bed all night, with brief interludes of delirious exhaustion allowing me to think I was sleeping enough to dream, would have been closer to the truth.

The birds weren't even up yet when I rolled out of bed and dragged my butt into the bathroom to fill the tub. My entire body ached from the lack of sleep, and I sank gratefully into the warm embrace of the cast iron monster.

The hot water must have been enough to lull me to sleep for a while, and when I opened my eyes again there was sun shining through the bathroom window and the water was growing cool.

There was a noise downstairs and I was fairly certain that was what had awakened me. It sounded like shuffling, and I wondered if the two of them were already working in the kitchen.

I considered refilling the bathtub and staying longer. I wasn't ready to face Thomas yet this morning, and I was seriously tempted to punch Noah in the balls after last night.

Pulling the drain plug and drying myself, I put on deodorant and lotion before brushing my teeth. Then I dressed quickly in work clothes and followed the noises I heard in the kitchen.

Noah was fitting drawers into drawer slides when I walked into the kitchen and Thomas had his back to me, pouring coffee from a small espresso pot into a mug. He added a generous splash of cream before turning and handing it to me, his eyes downcast.

Ah, apology espresso.

Well, this was just great.

"Aren't you just fresh as a wilted daisy?" Noah grinned at me, and I considered slapping him.

"Some jackass decided to traipse through my yard last night." I gave him the finger.

I knew I looked like hell, but so did Thomas. He had deep shadows beneath his eyes that told me he'd spent a similarly difficult night once he'd left my bed.

"Aw, come on, Nat." Noah looked just a little contrite. "I was just messin' with you two."

"Yeah, well..." I made sure Thomas wasn't looking before I mouthed the rest. "You messed everything up, instead."

I pointed toward Thomas's back and raised my arms in a frustrated, exaggerated *What the hell* shrug.

"You know," Noah turned back toward the cabinet, and I heard the slide locks click into place as he tucked the drawer into the box. "I was just saving you from making an enormous mistake with the wrong brother."

I could hear the laughter in his voice.

"This old man obviously doesn't know what to do with you, because now he's had, what, three opportunities? You don't look like a satisfied woman to me."

I ran a hand across my face and realized how sore it was from scraping against Thomas's stubble the night before. Surely I had a vicious case of beard burn, and the color rushed to my cheeks when I caught my reflection in the window. Yup, it looked like I'd exfoliated my face with the sidewalk.

Thomas's practiced avoidance was driving me insane and I slammed back the rest of the espresso before setting the cup on the island counter.

"Let me know when you want that out of here," I said to no one in particular as I pointed to the island. "I wouldn't mind taking something apart today."

There was an angry, frustrated edge to my voice.

I heard Noah mutter something as I left the room, and Thomas's deep sigh was enough to stop me in my tracks.

"No," I heard him respond quietly to whatever it was that Noah had said. "...biggest mistake of my life."

His words leveled me and I sank to my knees in the narrow hallway, halfway between the kitchen and the entryway.

I was stunned, the damage immediately done, and I clutched at the invisible bolt in my chest and drew a deep, painful breath.

Noah almost tripped over me when he came rushing down the hallway with an armload of empty boxes. I looked up at him and he must have seen the misery on my face, because he dropped the boxes immediately and pulled me up so quickly that my arm nearly popped out of the socket. "What happened, Nat? You ok? You trip?"

I shook my head, unable to trust my voice. "I'm the mistake," I whispered finally, and my eyes brimmed with burning tears that felt like lava.

Noah looked really uncomfortable. "That's not what he said."

I hurried into the laundry room to grab my keys off the hook and I was out of the house before Noah could stop me or protest further.

I threw my handbag into the car and backed down the driveway at a pace that would have flattened anyone stupid enough to get behind me.

I had no idea where I was going and I really didn't care, so long as it was *away from here*.

Driving and crying and raging didn't seem to go together well, and when I finally admitted defeat, the Subaru and I were in Pensacola and I couldn't see straight any longer. I'd cried so hard as I drove that my eyes were swollen and my vision blurry, so I parked in a public lot and shoved huge sunglasses over my face. Then I walked and walked and walked down the beach until I worried I might actually be lost.

Peace wasn't here either, that sneaky bitch.

I didn't do much other than sit on the beach and think, bought some bottled water and a sandwich, and it was deep into the evening before I felt brave enough to face Thomas again, so I made the drive slowly home.

There was a light burning in my house and I let myself in through the garage, surprised to find Noah in the kitchen. He was looking around, checking off a small list he held in his hand, and I realized by some miracle they'd not only managed to complete the backsplash that day, but I had countertops.

"Not bad for a day's work, huh? Good thing you don't have a monster kitchen." Noah grinned. "Water's on again, so everything's ready to go." He pointed to the hole where the island had been. "I let Thomas take it out today 'cuz he needed to go ape on something and we didn't know if you'd be coming back, so...I hope you didn't have your heart set on destruction." He looked contrite and he shifted from one foot to the other, obviously uncomfortable.

"It'll be fine, Noah. Thank you. You've worked really hard on this and there's no way it could have been done without you."

He was chewing on something, his forehead furrowed with concentration. Then finally he blurted out, "He didn't mean it, Nat–not the way it sounded. You only heard the last bit of the sentence. He said keepin' you at an arm's length for so long was the biggest mistake of his life.

"He was so confused when you took off, and I smacked 'im for you–told him nice job, you thought he'd said somethin' hurtful.

"He's gotten real good at fucking things up for himself. He's sorta self-destructive, if you hadn't noticed. He's got...some problems."

I got the distinct feeling Noah was uncomfortable telling me these things. Guy Code or something.

"He's been a mess all day: can't focus for shit. Almost put an anchor through his stupid hand. I mean, I'm...yuck...I'm not good with this mushy stuff, Nat. Ask my Eve–drives her crazy." He paused, running a hand over his face, and I realized just how tired he looked. They'd really beat themselves up to get the job done.

"I wanna see him happy, you know? He's my big brother and I can't tell him stuff like that 'cuz he'd kick my ass. But he deserves to be happy. He's been through so much crazy shit, and no matter what's goin' on with him, he's always been there for the rest of us." He rubbed a hand across his face again and I heard the scrape of stubble.

"I'm tired of knowing he's hiding out here, sad and lonely and keepin' himself that way on purpose. But...then you got here..." His face twisted with an uncomfortable expression. "And he started callin' me again." A small smile pulled up the corners of his mouth. "You made him *nuts* with all your questions and all the things you did for him without bein' asked, or actin' like he owed you for it. You noticed things and paid attention. You made him *laugh*. You got *mad* when he did nice shit for you–you didn't expect it from him, like most people do. And I think the problem is that he's forgotten how to be happy, and it scares him to think that he could maybe be that...with you. You help him feel kinda normal again. Hopeful, maybe."

I pulled a shiny new leather barstool up to the peninsula and sank cautiously onto it. His words were swirling around my brain and I didn't know what to do with any of the things he was telling me.

"I was teasing last night," he said guiltily, plopping heavily onto the stool next to me, and it squealed in protest. "I didn't know it was...uh...a bad time."

"It was two in the morning, you moron. What else are people doing then?" I laughed a little and he flushed, running a hand through his dark hair, much shorter than Thomas's.

"You're gonna have to fight for him, Nat. No one's ever done that for him before. He needs it, to know that he matters. You'll have to get in his face and holler and yell and maybe smack him around a bit. He needs to know that you care enough not to give up. He was always the one making things work before, when no one was looking out for him and what he needed."

I nodded slowly and Noah got to his feet, wrapping a big arm around my shoulders.

"Go on then," he urged. "I'm crashin' with Gerry again, so don't worry about me...I doubt he's sleepin' anyway. You're too far under his skin, you sneaky little minx." He grinned. "Somehow you ladies worm right in there without us noticin'." He rubbed the spot over his heart in a reflexive motion. "Damned inconvenient sometimes."

Noah let himself out after giving me a quick hug and I dragged myself up the stairs, trying to decide whether I should just crawl into my own bed or whether I should take the initiative and go to him.

Allow no arguments.

Push him harder.

I drifted back to the kitchen before getting ready for bed and turned slowly, taking in the details that I'd glossed over while talking with Noah.

The backsplash tile had been my one splurge: handcrafted fireclay pieces from a small firm in Italy that I'd stumbled across on clearance.

Running my hand over the sink, I admired the smooth, glossy finish. It was an enormous cast iron farmhouse sink, with the same brass fixtures I'd wanted.

How did he get my list?

The schoolhouse pendant that hung over the sink had been on my list too, and I wrapped my arms around myself as I looked around at all the thoughtful touches and details. A lot of effort and expense had gone into making my dream kitchen and I sniffled a little.

He was planning this for a long time.

This meant I had a garage filled with things to return, because my few preparatory purchases had been much cheaper, modestly suited to my small budget.

A shower did nothing to settle my thoughts, filled with wild conjecture, though I tried to be reasonable–and failed. And rather than continue to second guess myself, I toweled off and pulled a soft boatneck dress over my head, hurrying down the stairs before I could change my mind.

There was a light burning in the garage when I pulled up to his house and I killed the headlights before I pulled into his driveway, parking right behind his truck.

At the very least, I thought, I needed to know *why*. His efforts went way beyond being a good or thoughtful friend.

He didn't hear me let myself in. He was sitting on a stool at the low workbench, his elbows on the table and his head in his hands.

"I'm still mad at you," I said softly as I closed the door behind me, and his head flew up. His face was haggard and drawn, dark shadows beneath his bloodshot eyes.

"Gerry was right," I said, walking slowly toward him. "You let people in just a little, then you push them away really hard. Sometimes I feel like I'm back farther behind the line than when I started and you burn the stupid bridge every time."

He didn't say anything, but I saw his chest shudder with a large intake of breath and I moved closer, wedging myself between him and the table to stand between his knees.

"It would be so much cheaper to just stop yourself before the words came out, wouldn't it? Instead of putting all your money into my house to show me you're sorry. Are you crazy? I mean, like would medication help level this out?"

He looked up at me slowly, with what I thought was a hopeful expression. "It's what you wanted, though?" His voice was hoarse, and I wondered if it was because he'd been fighting with Noah all day.

It was more than what I'd wanted. It was probably eight times the expense I could have actually managed on my own. But all I could do was nod and swallow hard, because I couldn't trust my voice or the moisture in my eyes.

He wanted me to be happy, and this was the only way he knew.

"I didn't see this coming," I said softly, gesturing between our two bodies. "I wasn't looking for anything...or anyone...I came here to hide. You screwed it all up for me." I rested a hand on the side of his neck, breathing in his warm, clean smell.

He leaned forward slightly in his chair, turning his head so that his cheek pressed into my chest and slowly, with effort, brought his arms up to wrap around me. I let him, holding him gently against my chest, one arm cradling his head, the other around his shoulders.

Somewhere in the back of my mind, I suspected he'd received very little tenderness in his life and he had no idea what to do with it.

"Come on," I said finally, helping him up. "We're good at this part. I'll tuck you in."

That drew a soft chuckle from him. "I'm not a little kid, Natalie, and we clearly don't have great luck with beds."

"No," I responded in agreement, flipping off the garage lights and closing the door behind us and I led him out. "Not exactly. But you are going to require careful handling for a while, like a child, because you've been broken many times. You also have the uncontrolled temper of a four year old, but we can work on that." I half-turned to grin at him, running a gentle hand down the side of his face to cup his chin. I *really* liked touching him when he didn't flinch.

He didn't say anything. He didn't even disagree with me for once, and he followed me as I led the way through the door and into his own kitchen. There I drew a glass of water for him and as he drank it, I tucked under his arms and hugged him tightly. This man's heart was empty, I thought, and it needed to be filled up.

Though it felt like my own heart was running dangerously low on affection, I had more than he did to share.

He set the glass down on the countertop, but he didn't pull away from me. He rested his cheek on top of my head and let me hold him, sighing deeply in a way I hoped was contented, but maybe it was resigned. Whatever it was, I could finally feel him relaxing. His body softened against mine as I held him and I swayed gently, rocking him where we stood.

Finally, his hand came beneath my chin, and I lifted my head to look at him. His eyes were on my mouth and I pushed up on my toes, taking his face in my hands and pressing my lips softly to his. He let me, bringing his hands up to cup my face, and I could feel the deep emotions warring just behind the lips he wouldn't open to me, a tender kiss that he wouldn't deepen.

We walked side by side up his wide staircase and he paused halfway down the hall, obviously conflicted. I knew what it was, and I laced my fingers carefully through his. "It's just sleep, Thomas. I'm not here to desecrate your memories; choose where you are most comfortable."

He shrank away from the master bedroom and I could feel his heart stretching toward the room I now knew was Aden's. He paused then, glancing down at me with hesitation in his eyes.

"I'll wait here," I said, releasing his hand and leaning back against the railing. It gave him time to disappear through the door of what I thought might be another bedroom and I heard running water and drawers opening and closing. When he reappeared he was in thin pajama pants and nothing else.

It was hard to remind my body that I was here for his heart when he was so damn tempting. But since that wouldn't make me any better than the others who'd set a trap for him, I simply smiled and held out my hand and his features relaxed again.

I could feel his hesitation as we entered Aden's room, and I knew it was because he was worried about what I was thinking. He was a huge man sleeping in the narrow twin bed, in a room decorated for a toddler when he had a spacious, comfortable bed only one door away in either direction.

I'd meant what I said, that I would tuck him in, but I didn't intend for anything beyond that. I thought a beat ahead, deciding I would sleep on his living room sofa, but when I brought the light blanket up around his body he opened his arms in an unmistakable plea.

I wasn't about to deny him something that brought him comfort, so I slipped out of my flats and folded myself carefully into the too-small bed. My back pressed against his front and he pressed his face into my neck, his arms wrapped tightly around me.

His needs were simple, I thought as I focused on the rhythm of his deep breaths and the gentle tapping of his heartbeat against my back.

Right now he needed to know I wouldn't leave.

His face was in my hair and I knew he was finally drawing comfort from my closeness. I felt my heart swelling with an emotion that scared me and I closed my eyes, because I knew something with absolute clarity: My only remaining ties to the man I'd been married to for thirteen years were legal.

What I felt for *this* man was painfully deep, wrapping around my heart without my permission.

Protective.

Frustratingly complicated, as he could make me violently angry in the space of three heartbeats and only seconds later I wanted to tear his clothes off.

That night I finally fell asleep crammed into a narrow little bed, smashed up against the huge body of the man taking up most of the space.

I tucked a leg behind me, to wind through his, and he hummed contentedly into my hair as I drifted into something that felt like peace.

THIRTY-TWO

Thomas

What I didn't dare tell Natalie was that when she let me hold her, I slept like a baby every time. The nightmares didn't come for me and if I woke during the night, it was to the comforting warmth and softness of her body tucked into mine.

It was kind of terrifying, how calming it was to be near her.

When I woke in the morning, my face in her soft hair, I understood just how dependent I'd become and the thought was absolutely terrifying: *Now I have more to lose.*

I'd spent the past several years distancing myself from everyone. I did it consciously, knowing that if I didn't need someone, they couldn't hurt or disappoint me. In fact, Gerry, Noah and Finn were the only people who hadn't given up and allowed me to do it. Everyone else had been pretty easy to convince.

While Noah and Finn texted and called (and I had largely ignored them), Gerry had picked up and moved immediately when Lydia left, close enough to keep an eye on me without being right next door.

After what Noah had been through when he lost Avery and Everly, I think she was afraid desperate actions ran in the family.

I'd never admitted it to her, but she had probably been the one to save me. She made sure I got semi-regular meals and that my clothes weren't too shabby, since I was probably not the best judge.

When Gerry worried I was in danger of self-destructing, she found something outside of my house to keep me busy: Iris Jenkins needed her porch rebuilt.

Ned Jackson needed some drywall ripped out and replaced after a plumbing catastrophe.

Natalie needed her roof replaced.

Thanks to my upbringing with the jack-of-all trades contractor I begrudgingly called Da, I was capable of all those things.

Natalie hardly moved during the night, that night. The bed was so small, it didn't allow for much adjustment, and by morning she was still tightly wrapped up in my arms. She had snuggled right up against me and dropped off to sleep and though the movement was involuntary, I squeezed her tighter when I felt something uncomfortable building up behind my eyes.

Stop pushing her away. You could have this every night.

She stirred slowly and I knew she was awake when her fingers curled around mine. She pushed her legs out straight to stretch before curving them back against mine and I hoped she wouldn't scoot her butt back against me, because I would embarrass myself. But she did, and I felt her still when she realized what was pressed up along the soft curve of her backside.

But then she wiggled her hips into me. I mean, you could have beaten me to death with my own hard-on. *She fucking wiggled,* and a soft giggle came from her lips. "Just checking," she teased, and I wanted to be angry when I heard laughter in her voice, but I paused. She wasn't making fun of me.

"What are you checking?" I finally asked, my face still pressed to the back of her head.

She reached back to hook a hand behind my knee, bringing my leg up over her thigh and pressing me against her even harder.

"Hmm." She was grinning; I could feel it. I could hear it in her voice. "That's better."

This was not going to end well if I didn't put some distance between us. She was going to gently tease and I was going to lose my mind. I would end up flipping her over and begging, grinding against her, tearing at her clothes.

Because for all my self-control, when it came to her, I was slipping. I was doing stupid shit to keep her at a distance when all I wanted was to hear those soft sounds she made when I kissed her. They stirred a fire in me I'd thought long dead, reminding me of what was supposed to happen when a man wanted a woman.

The burning question was whether Natalie wanted *me*. The real me, and all of me, because a lot of it wasn't pretty. I was terrified of the answer, having convinced myself that I was just her Lost Boy project.

She was kind to me because that was who she was.

She cared for me because she was nurturing. Her heart ached with mine because she was an empath.

It didn't mean she could love me in the way I was beginning to understand I really needed.

I was starting to sweat. The room was cool but her skin was warm and sweet. I was hard as a rock and I could feel a little hitch in her breath each time she inhaled, like just maybe she was turned on too, waiting for my response.

She cupped her fingers around my knee and squeezed before sliding her warm palm up the back of my leg, unabashedly palming my ass. It made my breath catch and she heard the sharp sound, slowly slipping her hand between my legs to cup my balls from behind.

That got my attention. My hips surged forward all on their own and my hand slipped down to her hip to pull her tighter.

I couldn't stop the groan. I couldn't help that I was mere breaths away from losing my tenuous grip on sanity. She was rattling the cage that contained a very dangerous monster.

A whisper from her: "Did you buy me an expensive French range because you felt guilty about wanting to sleep with me, Atholton?"

Oh, shit.

I pulled back from her hair and loosened my fingers on her hip.

Cleared my throat.

She took that moment to slide from the bed, twisting to face me as her knees hit the floor and she crossed her arms along the mattress and set her chin on her forearm. She was gazing at me curiously, but she didn't look angry or scared or insulted.

"What if I did?" I finally asked, terrified by the potential answer.

She smiled and rose slowly, stretching, her rumpled dress pulling even further up her smooth thighs before she leaned over to rub my cheek with her thumb, her eyes something warm and liquid.

"You can't buy me, because I don't find your money interesting or attractive."

I sputtered a little and she moved two fingers to cover my mouth, leaning her body over mine to kiss my earlobe.

"I was already yours." She straightened and smiled down at me as I stared at her in shock.

While I tried to calm the sound of blood raging in my ears, to find words, language, sounds and breath, she left the room.

THIRTY-THREE

Natalie

Noah came over that morning to say goodbye to Thomas and I watched the two of them grapple with uncomfortable emotions as they clapped backs and squeezed shoulders and tried desperately to keep stiff upper lips.

"You keep this horse's ass in line for me, Nat," Noah said with a grin, dashing an arm across his face quickly. "Stupid damn allergies. This humidity is bullshit, bro. Got me all kinds of congested."

It wasn't at all humid, for the first time since I could remember, and I moved in to squeeze under Noah's huge arms to hug him goodbye.

"You come see us sometime," he said as he squeezed me. "You and my girl will get along just fine–you can even bring this miserable old man with you."

That earned him a slap.

Noah folded himself into the tiny little rental car and stuck one big arm out the window as he drove away. I worried the car might tip from the weight displacement.

Thomas was quiet, which was not unusual for him, and as he stood on his porch watching his brother drive away, I circled an arm around his waist.

"You can call him tonight to make sure he got in safely. You've got enough time to think of at least seven devastating insults."

I heard him snort and he looked down his shoulder at me with a small smile. "I can do better than seven." Then he put an arm around my shoulders and pulled me in, dropping a kiss into my hair.

"Prove it." I swatted him halfheartedly and he chuckled into my hair, wrapping the other arm around me so that I was completely engulfed by his arms and chest.

"But..." My protest was weak. "Mrs. O'Shaughnessy!"

He released me just slightly and lifted my chin with his fingers. "Yeah? Should we teach her a few new things? Give her binoculars a real workout? Steam up the lenses?"

Hell, yes. I threw my arms up over his shoulders and grabbed the sides of his head with both hands, pushing up on my tiptoes to fan the flame already burning in my belly.

"See?" he mumbled, his lips only a breath away from my own. "I told you: an exhibitionist."

I kissed him until I couldn't see straight, which honestly didn't take long.

There was no elaborate dance.

There were no carefully chosen words or intricately planned seductions, because he seemed just as shocked by our volatility as I was.

Neither of us seemed capable of thinking ahead five minutes when it came to the other.

This man made me a walking, talking, hormonal fire hazard.

I spent most of the day at Thomas's house, since I wasn't eager to go home, and he didn't seem interested in letting me. Instead, we spent hours lying on the sofa in his living room, kissing and talking about the parts of our lives that we could stand to share.

Some things were still too painful and each time one of us drew a ragged breath, the other reassured with a gentle touch.

The sun moved across the sky and as the early afternoon rays began to drift in through the living room windows, I looked around the room and was struck again by the absence of *anything* on the walls: no art or family photos.

"Why aren't there any pictures on your walls?" I asked finally. He had lived in this house with his family. It seemed unusual that a woman wouldn't have tended to the decoration of her home.

Thomas turned his head to scan the walls as if it was the first time he was seeing them. "She didn't want to put anything up. I think she hoped this was a temporary exile," he said finally, making a movement as if he wanted to sit up. I let him, curling next to him on the sofa but giving him the space to move toward or away from me.

He was on his feet suddenly with a determined look on his face and when he rushed out of the room I hurried after him, a little alarmed.

Quickly unlocking the garage, he hurried from the pegboard to the shelves, collecting a hammer and small nails as he went. There was a huge grin on his face and he held up the nails and nodded toward the organized shelves. "For all the hell you give me, sometimes you really do make life easier."

"I make *everything* easier," I teased as I trailed after him back into the house. "You're the one who complicates stuff."

He dumped the hammer and box of nails on the living room floor and threw open the lid of a storage ottoman, pulling out neat file boxes as I looked at him askance. "You've *organized*?"

He grinned and pulled open the lid on the first heavy box, and not only were the pictures organized, they were also already in frames of like size, slotted in neatly, like a deck of playing cards.

Gently setting the first box on the floor, he reached in to retrieve a stack of four or five frames and as he set them reverently on the rug, his fingers trailing slowly down each one, my breath caught in my throat.

The little boy in each photo was a blond angel, his sweet face lit up with smiles of wonder, joy and love.

There were several boxes inside the ottoman and I watched his selection with interest, noting that he hardly seemed able to touch some of them. He shuffled them to the side with a grimace and I wondered what was in them–wedding pictures, maybe.

"He's beautiful," I said softly as he leaned back into the ottoman and retrieved a second box, the larger frames containing a few photos of him holding his son, a joy on his face I'd never seen before.

He was staring hard at the photo in his hand. "I came from a big, loud, crazy-dysfunctional family and Lydia was an only child. I don't think she planned on having kids exactly, not until we were getting old enough that it started to become a problem. Then she had trouble getting–and staying–pregnant."

The photos spread out before me spanned infancy to about the age of three, and I reached for one of the photos of Thomas cradling Aden in his arms, the little boy beaming up at him as he smiled down.

"He was so tiny, but what a beautiful little boy," I commented absently and Thomas looked at me strangely for a beat too long, his fingers wrapped protectively around one of the frames.

"Natalie..." He was looking at me like I'd missed something so obvious, and I glanced back down at their faces in the photo. "Don't you see it?"

I stared harder at the photo, knowing something was different, but I couldn't quite grasp it. Aden's features weren't quite sharp, as if his face had been smudged or blurred just slightly, and I looked up quickly at Thomas, who had scooted closer to look down at the picture with me.

"He had Down syndrome," he said softly. "We had the amnio done and Lydia wanted to terminate the pregnancy, but I couldn't let her. I became attached to the *idea* of him the instant I knew he might survive and I begged her not to. In the end, I told her I would *pay* her not to. That...is why the house in Portola Valley is now deeded to her." He lapsed again into silence and I set down the frame, reaching out for his hand.

"She bore the brunt of parenting, at least at first," he continued, letting me hold his hand but bracing the other on the floor as he stared across the array of frames he'd scattered.

I sucked in a deep breath and pitched forward to crawl on hands and knees across the rug, sorting through frames as I went until I'd grouped them into several different piles. Then I stood, offering my hand to him. "Come on," I said as I waited for him to take my hand. "Let's put them *all* up."

• • • •

WE SPENT SEVERAL HOURS that afternoon putting up the pictures all over Thomas's house.

The living room boasted a gallery wall and a few smaller prints went into the kitchen.

The stairwell got a few, and when we walked down the hallway I was surprised when Thomas walked right past Aden's bedroom and passed instead through the door at the end.

"Maybe this was why I couldn't sleep anywhere else." His voice drifted out and I stepped through the doorway to find another bedroom. The walls were dark and the furniture masculine, the walls as bare as the rest of the house had been.

"I had to sleep in his room because that was where I could be closest to the memories. I should have surrounded myself with these the instant she took them from me."

What?

He was already driving nails into the walls and as he hung photo after photo, I took in the unfamiliar space. This was his room–only his room–and I understood with a rush that the large master had been Lydia's, which was why he didn't sleep there.

"You were sleeping apart," I said as he swapped two of the frames, standing back to appraise his work.

"She said it was too disrupting." He shrugged, driving more nails into the wall that didn't have any pictures yet. "I was constantly traveling and she didn't like the inconsistency. Said it freaked her out to wake up and find someone in bed with her."

I made a face. That was some bullshit if I'd ever heard it.

"How long?" I asked, and he stopped moving, his fingers resting on the corner of one frame. I could see his face in profile and I watched his eyes drift shut.

"Not long after the birth," he said quietly. "We started keeping separate bedrooms in California and when we moved here I had hoped things would change. I was traveling so much less...I was really trying to help..." He dropped his hand and crossed the space to sit beside me on the bed.

"I suppose I knew for a long time before I *knew*," he said, and I turned my face to his. "I wanted to make Harrison work for it, but I know now that Lydia confronted him about it before he filed. She was considering leaving me and she couldn't figure out how to get Harrison to accept legal and financial responsibility, other than to file suit. She was worried I'd cut her off and if I'd wanted to be a real dick, I could have. It's what he'd have done in my situation."

"He filed first," I said quietly and he nodded.

"He wanted to crush me."

"But you loved Aden anyway." My voice sounded only half as incredulous as I felt.

"You loved him even though he would take a lifetime of care and he wasn't your own–even though his biological father wouldn't give him the time of day..." I had to stop because I was about to start crying again and God knew we'd had enough of that lately.

"You have such an incredible capacity for love," I said finally, the terrible ache in my chest creeping up into my throat as I leaned into his side, resting my head on his shoulder.

"You were exactly what that sweet little boy needed, Thomas. For the time he had you, *you* were his father. No one can take that away. *He* can't take your memories and he can't change what your little boy knew. You were the only one who didn't abandon him."

It was obvious this was a thought that had never occurred to Thomas. It changed the weight of the very air in the room, as if someone had thrown open a window to let in the sun and fresh breeze.

He leaned back suddenly, an expression of soul-deep relief washing across his face.

"You're right." His voice was barely more than a whisper. "I was all he had...and I loved him with everything I had."

I rose from the bed and squeezed his knee, returning from Aden's room with several things in my hands. I was mightily overstepping, I knew, and I set several of the toy train pieces on the low dresser before draping the small throw across the foot of the bed.

"You can have him in every room of the house," I said as I smoothed the creases out. "He doesn't have to stay in his little bedroom."

Thomas stood quickly, catching me in his arms and squeezing until I could hardly breathe.

"Thank you," he whispered into my hair. "I couldn't have done this on my own."

I squeezed him back, hanging on like I was clinging to him for dear life, and in a way I was, I supposed. I'd lived more in the past few months, arguing with this stubborn ass and trying to find ways to reach him, than

I'd lived in years. He was difficult and irritating and generally a pain in the butt, but I was hopelessly addicted.

When he smiled, it reached the darkest corners of my heart and watered a tiny seed of hope.

He loosened his hold and stood looking at me with something dark and hot in his eyes.

Uh-oh.

"Nope." I kissed his cheek quickly and backed away. "You've had a very emotional day. You need time and space to process all of this. You need to be ok with a lot of things that have come up for you today, and having me here much longer is going to confuse you and redirect all those emotions into something you're not ready to handle. You need to deal with things for real–no substitutions."

His lips curled in a wicked grin. "You seemed to think I could handle you just fine not all that long ago."

"I know more now," I said, backing slowly toward the door. "And I'm not the kind of girl to take advantage of emotional situations, because I won't win. And you, Mr. Atholton...well, I wouldn't mind winning you." I grinned. "And when I win, I'm *keeping* you. Now that I've seen what's hiding out underneath all that crotchety fuss and generally miserable behavior...let's just say that Leopard Pants doesn't stand a chance."

He moved like a flash to scoop me back up. "That trashy woman didn't ever have a chance, even in the state I was in that night. *I* told Smitty to call you. I knew I was wrecked and you were the only person I could trust, other than him, to save me from myself. Thank God you came. Thank God you were patient." He curled his fingers against my cheek before pressing his lips to my temple. "Please stay."

Oh, I would stay all right, but long-term, not tonight. Tonight he needed to himself, to make peace with hurts he hadn't been able to deal with the past several years.

"I'm going to make you dinner," I said into his shoulder. "And then I'm going to go home. You know where to find me if you need me, but right now you need the time alone, to process things that cannot be rushed. You need to take this time, Thomas. For both of us. We both need to be ready when we decide to make this *more.*"

We ate dinner together though it was still only early evening, and I cleaned up the kitchen while he sat at the island, gazing at the few photos we'd hung in the room. The pain was still there, palpable and sharp in the air, but the look on his face was less haunted. His expression was more peaceful than I'd ever seen.

He leaned through the window of the Subaru to kiss me before I left and I could have sworn I heard Mrs. O'Shaughnessy squawk in dismay from the living room window across the street.

"You're really giving the neighbors something to think about," I said as I ran my thumb across his full lower lip. "By nine tonight, Mrs. O. will have informed the whole town we were making babies on the front lawn."

His eyes went hot and he leaned in to whisper in my ear. "You wanna come back at nine and we can practice? We'd make some pretty babies."

"Hell, no!" I laughed, swatting his chest. "I'm not such a desperate soul that I want to share that glorious view with the neighbors." I gestured toward his general person.

"Glorious view?" The corner of his mouth lifted.

"Lord bless me, yes." I licked my lips as I mentally undressed him. "When that time comes, I'm not going to be rushed by mosquitoes and crickets and people taking the dog out for one last tinkle. Consider this your warning–you only get one."

Then I grinned at him, pulling him in for one more kiss before putting the car into reverse and backing down the short distance to the street.

It was a wise decision, I told myself as I drove home. I would give him time to put his heart in order while I took the time to put my legal affairs in order.

I had a cheating husband to divorce.

THIRTY-FOUR

Thomas

I could hardly sleep that night. I'd stayed up late drifting from one room to the next, drinking in the joy and contentment I saw on Aden's face, and my own, in the photos that now hung on the walls.

Why hadn't I done it sooner?

The ghosts were still that night.

Aden's laugh didn't echo in my memory.

My arms ached, but the ache didn't spread all the way to my heart.

Something felt a little better–not even close to healed, but better, like a wound that had finally stopped oozing and scabbed over.

I fed Raven and dropped a kiss on her small black head as I held her against my chest, and she rattled with a violent purr that threatened to shatter her ribcage. I had definitely lost my man card to this little ball of fluff. She leaned trustingly against me and when I set her down, trailing a hand down her back and all the way to the tip of her tail, she blinked up at me with what I swore was a smile.

The cat followed me as I checked the locks on all the doors and turned out the lights. Then she followed me up the stairs and jumped onto the bed, curling into a tight ball at the foot while I slipped into the bathroom to shower.

Spending the day with Natalie, just holding and kissing her, talking and laughing...I couldn't remember doing that before. Not ever. It had been the perfect day, and when she helped me put up the pictures of Aden and brought things of his to put in my room, I knew I was hopelessly gone over her.

Fighting her had done me no good, because she'd managed to find her way in after all. She'd gently battered at my defenses with her regular meals, her thoughtful ways and her crazy, intrusive questions, until I crumbled. I couldn't withstand the gentle assault and I had caved.

I braced myself with one arm against the shower tile, letting the hot water run down my neck and back, and it soothed some of the aches that came from sleeping in a too-small bed.

It didn't, however, soothe the ache that had been in my pants all day. Holding her, kissing her mouth, drinking in the soft sounds she made that told me she wanted me the way I wanted her...all of it had poured gas on the fire and suddenly all I could think about was what it would be like to have her in my bed.

Turning into the water, I let it run down the front of my body, wetting my skin as I closed my eyes and imagined the fingers touching me were hers. It was almost unbearable agony, to imagine her pressed up against me in the shower and I kept my eyes tightly shut to entertain the fantasy.

I'm only a little ashamed to say that my knees went weak when I imagined lifting her in my arms to press her back against the tile. She would tip her head back and I'd kiss her jaw, her throat, her gorgeous breasts.

The imagined sounds of her pleasure were what filled my mind as I told myself how much better it would be with her in my arms. The thought was enough to get me there, and the tension in my spine released as I came under the hot flow of water, still braced against the tiles with my other hand.

I stood for a moment, letting the water swirl around my feet, catching my breath and cursing myself. It was a poor substitute for what I knew Natalie would be. But months of watching her, fighting with her, swallowing down the desire I felt every time I saw her...I didn't want to do it anymore. I wanted to shower with her at night and wash her hair, tipping her chin up to kiss her as the water ran between us.

Then I wanted to carry her to my bed, our bodies wet, slipping and sliding against one another as we fought for the upper hand. She would give in to me eventually, I thought, smiling to myself. She would let me roll her under me and open her mouth, her heart, and her body to me in all the ways I needed her to take me in and hold me close.

I toweled off and brushed my teeth, crawling into bed naked and covering myself with a light sheet.

My last thought was *I hope she's loud.*

• • • •

THE NEXT DAY I SPENT the late afternoon and early evening doing some research and consulting with my Stanford team.

I also read through the brief my lawyers sent, preparing myself for another hellish trip.

I was tired of these emergency meetings and I was tired of cleaning up Harrison's messes. I wondered how much harder he had to push in order to get the board to remove him and reinstate me.

Harrison had worked hard to turn the board against me, and only one thing had worked in his favor: Lydia.

My memories of that time were terrible, followed by one bad decision after another.

When Noah called me to say goodbye, I panicked. It was three a.m. in Tokyo and I was scheduled to be there for another week on business.

Immediately I'd called the paramedics in Olympia, then our youngest sister Finn, then Gerry. With the two of them alerted, I had called Lydia and gotten her voicemail. I left a message that I was going to find a flight to Washington and didn't know when I'd be back home, since Noah needed me.

Then I started calling airlines, and when no one could get me on the next flight (it was cherry blossom season, after all), I paid through the nose to charter a flight to London, where I could catch a commercial flight to the States.

It took twenty-three hours of travel to get me to Noah's hospital bed, and when I got there, his room was empty but for him. He was sedated, sleeping peacefully, his huge body dwarfing the tiny bed and I slumped down next to him, grabbed his big hand and fell asleep face-down, kneeling next to him on the hard floor.

Lydia never called me back.

When I walked into the Sonoma house almost two weeks later, finding Harrison in the living room made my head spin. I had called him from Hong Kong, before I left. He was supposed to fly in to manage the last week of the enormous project I'd been overseeing, yet there he was on my sofa, looking inordinately pleased with himself.

"I thought you were going to the Portola house." Lydia's voice sounded weak as she stumbled into the room and I wondered why her eyes didn't look right, just as it occurred to me that she looked guilty–maybe even drunk–and Harrison looked smug.

So they were still a thing then. Message received.

The Hong Kong project exploded about three minutes after I got home, right after I screamed raw obscenities at Harrison without caring who saw or heard. Then I punched him in the face and, being a much bigger guy than him, lifted him by the collar with one hand and walked him out of my house to dump his ass on the driveway.

My life was falling apart. I'd taken a few weeks to deal with a family emergency and Harrison had managed to single-handedly destroy my business and my marriage while my back had been turned. Though to be fair, he'd been working on both for far longer than I'd have ever guessed.

Lydia stood in the entryway, white-faced and shocked when I stormed back into the house, but I didn't have time to deal with her because my phone was ringing.

It was Inez, the girl only three months out of grad school that Harrison had hired. I suspected he'd hired her because he wanted to bone her, not because she was highly competent.

In his place, he sent her to oversee the project.

Not only did Inez not know how to manage people, she didn't know how to set expectations, meet deadlines or establish quality control. She had absolutely no management experience, and I'd not have been surprised to find she had no knowledge of the industry whatsoever. I'd had to call her back to California and return to Hong Kong to clean up the mess myself.

Of course, the damage was done, and I was instantly on the hot seat with my board when they saw how far over the projected timeline and budget the project had run.

I was reminded the deliverable was simple; that we were running a business and not a charity, which rankled–they'd used my own words against me. Words I liked to introduce every time I found out Harrison demanded underbidding on more contracts, selling us short.

Over the course of a few weeks, my life had imploded, my eyes now wide open: I'd abandoned my business to rush to my dying brother. Then I'd returned home, hoping to take comfort in the arms of my wife, only to find she'd been in the arms of another man–the one I had once considered my closest friend.

I was back in Hong Kong by the end of the week and that was when Lydia texted to let me know she'd moved all of my things to Sonoma, which was where I'd be staying permanently. She'd let me know if managing Aden on her own in Portola was too much, since I might have to come pick him up for therapy appointments if she couldn't handle it.

I spent months of weekends driving between Portola and Sonoma, exhausted by slow-moving traffic and scheduling constraints.

Eventually, completely done, I made a standing appointment for a chartered helicopter, which made our trips much faster and more bearable.

I flew into LAX when the call about the crash came from Gerry, rushing to LA General as quickly as an Uber could take me. I didn't trust myself to drive, scaring the shit out of the driver when I spent the entirety of the drive alternating between cursing into my phone and openly weeping into my hands.

I rolled in my bed, the memory painful as I recalled the look on the surgeon's face when he entered the room and told us Aden needed more blood, and a lot of it. I had immediately rolled up my sleeve. "Take mine," I'd insisted. "Take as much as he needs."

"Are you O negative?" the surgeon had asked gently, and my brain refused to process what he was asking me.

"I think I'm B," I responded, shaking my head to clear the cobwebs. "B positive. But that shouldn't matter, right? He's my son."

The surgeon shook his head at me. "Your blood types are not compatible and you are not a universal donor." He looked at Lydia then, lying in her hospital bed. She had gone pale and clutched her hand to her chest. One of her arms was in a cast and she'd suffered a concussion, as well as some lacerations to her abdomen. But she'd lost hardly any blood.

As far as I was concerned, she could give him every last drop of her own, since she had caused this.

There was a familiar voice in the hallway and one of the nurses shoved a consent form in my face. "Sign this so he can receive blood," she barked, and I did it without asking where it was coming from.

Harrison strolled into the room an hour later, his shirt sleeve rolled up and a small bandage stuck to his arm. He strolled right past me and crossed the room to kiss Lydia, who was in and out of a sedated haze. I watched him do it, feeling nothing but contempt for the two of them, the twisting feeling in my chest something between jealousy and hatred.

I had no idea what I'd done to make him hate me so much that he'd stolen my family from me and was working to destroy my company.

"They can't be seen with me," he finally said. "The press will be too intense. I'll have a nurse sent to the house while they recuperate. Besides, how could I handle kids on my own while she gets better?" The way he looked at Lydia was almost disgusted.

My family flew in for the funeral and it was Noah who literally kept me on my feet throughout, holding me up when I had no strength of my own. He wept with me as my son's body was lowered into the ground, because if anyone could understand, it was him.

Then...after Lydia was discharged from the hospital and Harrison's driver dropped her at the Portola Valley house...

After I spent eleven nights drinking and sobbing myself to sleep, locked in my room, clutching his tiny blanket...

After I realized Lydia wasn't going to come to me even once...

Reason finally found me, and I went in search of the paperwork I had filed away from the tests conducted when Lydia became pregnant.

It was then that I paid attention to blood types...and confirmed what I already knew: Aden hadn't been my son at all.

I hadn't lost everything; I'd never had it in the first place.

THIRTY-FIVE

Natalie

Stepping off the plane at Logan, I knew I should feel like I was home. This had been my home airport for years, the one I flew out of and back into time and time again. Returning to it always meant returning to the beautiful home I loved almost as much as a person. That might have seemed odd to some people, but to me each house had a soul and I always listened until it spoke to me, telling me what it needed to be beautiful again.

Renting a car, I drove through Boston's notoriously bad traffic on narrow, clogged roads. This, I thought, was one thing I really hadn't missed.

Flipping the blinker to turn onto Devonshire, I crept toward a parking garage as quickly as traffic would allow.

This would be quick, the lawyer said.

This would be painless.

The worst part about it would be the trip would be the travel.

So far she was right.

Jeanine was no-nonsense. Her receptionist set me up in a small conference room and when a redheaded whirlwind burst through the door, I knew this was a woman who didn't waste time, money, or words. She shook my hand quickly before smoothing her sharp navy pantsuit and dropping into a chair. She launched immediately into rapid-fire questions, noting things quickly with a vicious slash of her pen.

When I shook her hand again, an hour later, I felt a bit shell-shocked. She'd gathered more than sufficient information, she said, and I'd paid her fee.

"Even if he contests, the court will determine division of property and this should be concluded, worst case scenario, within fourteen months.

"If he doesn't put up a fight, or you two reach an agreement in arbitration, both of which seem unlikely from what you've told me, this may conclude much faster.

"I'll provide you with information for a reliable process server so we can get things rolling."

I stumbled out of her office and walked back to the car in a daze.

Fourteen months.

If I'd known how long it would take, I'd have filed even before I left Ahmad. He was going to spend every day of the next year and longer making my life a living hell, of that I was certain.

My phone clattered in the cupholder as I pulled out of the parking garage. It was cold already and the days were growing shorter, and all I wanted was a hot meal, a warm shower and a comfortable bed.

I plugged in the address for The Liberty, the traffic just as crushingly slow as always. It made me chuckle to myself as I considered my very ironic choice of hotel. It was fitting that as I try to escape the prison of my marriage, I should spend the night in what was a renovated jail.

Dumping my small bag on the bed, I read quickly through the menu for one of the restaurants downstairs and booked a reservation for seven, just before hopping into the shower.

As I dressed again, I realized I hadn't checked my phone, and I tapped quickly on the screen to find a text and a missed call from Thomas.

Please don't believe everything you see, or read.

Well, that was frickin' cryptic. What the hell was he talking about? I resisted the urge to Google him, instead tapping on his number and waiting for him to answer. When he didn't, I dried my hair and applied some basic makeup, letting myself out of the room to walk down to dinner.

It wasn't any more fun eating alone in an expensive restaurant than it was in my own kitchen, and my waiter quickly gave up trying to ply me with *more*: more drinks, more bread, more dessert.

I was inordinately tired, worn out by travel, anger and other high emotions. If I was being honest with myself, I hadn't slept well since the day Thomas had driven away without so much as a goodbye. I'd known he was preoccupied, but it had taken every fiber of my being not to look desperate, texting and calling him or showing up at his house the night before he flew back to California.

The trips seemed to be increasing in frequency and duration, and there was an underlying current of worry that seemed to run through him. In fact, this had been his first communication in several days and it wasn't the warm, sweet kind I'd been hoping for.

It was always one step forward and two steps back with him.

Flipping on the TV for some background noise, I washed my face and loaded up my toothbrush. I drifted back into the room as I brushed my teeth, rolling my eyes over the salaciously gossipy piece that had just aired.

The woman was bubbling over with excitement as she introduced the next bit and my eyes focused sharply on a very familiar profile as a photo splashed across the screen.

"Associates of Thomas Atholton, the former face of Titan Tech, say he's looking to re-establish himself in Silicon Valley. The tech giant sits on several major boards, but has been quietly working on a new project while he's been hidden away, nursing a broken heart."

"Mmm," the host salivated and another photo appeared in the background. "I'd be more than willing to play nurse for him. But he's hardly the sort to be hurting for company. Sources say he's been hiding out in the south, playing house with someone in order to keep his mind off his impending divorce."

I looked closer at the photo behind the presenter, my heart catching in my throat as I recognized the long, dark hair and blazing blue eyes. It was Lydia who held Thomas in a tight hug, her smile victorious over his shoulder.

I'm going to be sick.

Rushing to the bathroom to spit out the toothpaste, I waited for my stomach to stop rolling. It was right on the edge, and I wiped the sweat from my forehead as I tried not to throw up while the announcer's voice bounced around the space.

"Close friends have indicated Atholton's travel to the west coast has increased lately, and it's said the estranged couple may be attempting a reconciliation.

"It's suspected that Mrs. Atholton has grown weary of Harrison Powell and his wandering eye."

I looked over my shoulder just in time to see a brief clip of a gorgeous blond-haired man on screen. He looked so much like Aden, I gasped.

The woman on screen pouted prettily. "I'd take either one of them, personally, but it looks like Tall, Dark and Handsome is off the market again. Don't cry yourselves to sleep though, girls, because it looks like Harrison's back on. I'd call him a very acceptable consolation prize."

His very important meetings–had they been with Lydia? After what she'd done to him, how could he even consider taking her back? And was he really just playing house with me, working secretly to win back the woman he professed to hate?

My head spun and sweat beaded as I sank gracelessly down onto the bed.

Mrs. Atholton.

Yeah, that was pretty real. Thomas *was* still wearing his wedding ring, and I'd never asked whether he'd considered going back to her.

All I could remember, suddenly, was the night I drove him home and the heavy word "wife" had been used in a very present tense.

I plugged his name into a search engine, unable to stop myself though my heart ached, and I looked over a handful of photos obviously taken at a very recent event. He was tall and delicious in his dark suit, his hair slicked back off his face to fall behind his ears. His expression was firm and implacable. It was his mask, the one he wore to keep people out.

Several photos of him with Lydia were available for my perusal and I scrolled through them slowly, noting her hand on his arm.

The seductive way she smiled at him.

Her fingers curled possessively in his hair.

He hadn't told me he would see her.

Anger coiled tight inside my gut. She wasn't allowed to touch him–to look at him–to be so familiar with him after what she'd done.

I searched his face in the photos, looking for some hint he found her unpleasant. He looked angry and aloof, but that wasn't enough for me, because he usually looked that way.

My head was beginning to pound and I took two nighttime painkillers, crawling into the big bed and turning off the lamp. My brain boiled with the "what if's," and when my phone buzzed with an incoming call twenty minutes later, I silenced it. My voice was too heavy with tears to risk talking to him, so I rolled over and cried over the loss of something I'd never had until I fell asleep.

• • • •

PULLING INTO MY DRIVEWAY, I sat for a moment with my hands wrapped around the car's steering wheel. I needed something for the restless feeling that bubbled inside of me and rather than walking into my house, I got out of the car and crossed the lawn to Gerry's.

Her face was sympathetic when she opened the door and took in my defeated posture.

"I was just letting him know you arrived home safely," Gerry said, holding a hand out to me and I hiccuped loudly, holding a hand quickly over my eyes as they started to leak again.

Stupid dang design flaw.

"Come here, baby girl," she clucked, pulling me through the door and into a crushing hug. "He obviously didn't do a very good job of warning you."

"Warning me?" I sputtered, pulling back from the wet mess I was making on her shoulder. "There's no way to warn a woman that you're actively working to get your ex back, or that you'll be hitting the social circuit with her like the two of you are still a thing."

Gerry snorted, taking me by the hand to lead me into her kitchen where she pointed toward a chair. I sat as she chopped and swirled and muddled and shook, then handed me a very large glass of something topped with greenery.

"He wouldn't take that woman back if he needed a kidney and she was the only match. He hates her, Natalie, and she damn well earned it."

I pulled my phone from my back pocket and pulled up the offensive images that were emblazoned on my brain, holding it silently toward her. "This doesn't look like hate."

She took it, flipping through each with a hard expression on her face.

"I know what it looks like," she said softly, hanging the phone back to me. "But there's an explanation. He doesn't love her anymore, and you need to trust that he knows what he's doing."

"What *is* he doing?" There was a tiny flare of hope in my heart at her words, and I looked up at her with shining eyes. "I can't compete against that, Gerry. I'm not tall and graceful and connected. I'm short and clumsy and a totally hot mess. I don't have a designer dressing me, because most days it's a miracle I even brush my hair. Any man in his right mind would choose her over me."

"Any man in his right mind would see right through her, Natalie. She's all surface. She's cold and calculating and cruel. You have been nothing but warm and caring and kind. Why would he choose her–go back to her–when he has someone like you? Why would he throw away real connection for a soulless mannequin?"

"I'm easy to throw away," I sighed deeply. Gerry was struggling here too, and if she didn't have answers for me, this was worse than I thought.

"I have nothing to go on," I said softly. "He pulls me close and then pushes me away, and when I ask for answers, I don't get any. I don't understand him or what he's doing or what he wants. I've tried to tell myself I'm nothing more than his friend for so long, but it's more, Gerry. It's a lot more, even though I've tried to stop it."

She smiled at me knowingly. "You know what his nickname is for you, sweet girl?" She handed me another tall, high-octane glass and I sipped carefully, slowly shaking my head.

I have a nickname?

Her smile grew wider and more Cheshire. "Well," she drawled lazily in a very un-Gerry-like way, "that does seem to depend upon the day and his moods. On the days he's in a good mood, you're 'Dynamite.' But on the days he's hurting and I know he's struggling with those pesky things we call feelings, you're 'Kryptonite.'"

She leaned back a little and watched my face. "Either way," she said softly, "I think it means that he can't stay away from you even though he knows he could blow everything to shit."

• • • •

GERRY TRIED TO GET me to stay for dinner, but I made an excuse about being exhausted, which was turning out to be true, and I pulled my bag from the car before stepping into my house.

The air hummed quietly and the smell of new paint still drifted from the kitchen.

I was surrounded by him, I thought, shivering suddenly. The things he'd done for me were not something a disinterested man would take the time to do. Then again, perhaps his magnanimous behavior was simply the result of a guilty conscience: He had led me this far and now he was going to disappear.

I drank a glass of water and quickly unpacked, starting a load of laundry before putting myself through a punishingly hot shower.

More than anything I wanted to crawl into bed and forget the past several days–particularly the past twenty-four hours.

I played out every scenario in my head: Lydia showing up at Thomas's hotel room.

Lydia shoving him against a wall to kiss him.

Thomas throwing her down on his bed to punish her with hands and teeth.

With each new scenario I wanted my brain to explode. An ischemic episode was a welcome thought, for once, because it would end everything.

Crawling into my bed, I silenced the ringer on my phone and placed it facedown on my nightstand. I heard it clatter across the top and a buzz alerted me to a missed call as I drifted into an exhausted, uneasy sleep, interrupted by the ding of several texts I didn't bother to check.

• • • •

I WOKE LONG BEFORE my alarm the next morning, a sick feeling in the pit of my stomach. It took only seconds to remember why I felt that way, and I dragged myself to the closet to pull out something to wear for the day.

It was better to have my heart broken early, right? Before I did something I'd really regret, investing more time and effort into something I would only find out, the hard way, wasn't going to work.

Maybe I had been a distraction: tail he could snag under the radar while he wooed his errant but beautiful wife on the other coast.

Brewing a full press of coffee, I took a cup with me to the garage, where all the finished shelves waited. Today was my day, I thought, taking a fortifying chug. I was angry enough to use power tools and risk breaking things, and I searched through the toolbox I'd devoted entirely to drill bits. It was an exotic collection–one to rival any contractor's pickup truck toolbox–and I'd watched more than one handyman's eyes go all soft and shiny at the beautiful sight of such organized perfection.

Bringing the laser level into the kitchen, I made marks for myself on the walls, moving a couple of them until I felt satisfied I'd just decided upon my final shelving configuration.

I was driving a heavy anchor into the wall when I felt a rush of warm air hit the back of my bare legs, and I turned quickly to see Thomas stepping through the kitchen door. He was in a rumpled dress shirt and pants.

He looked like hell.

"Damn it, Natalie, don't shut me out. I told you not to believe what you heard." His voice was raspy, the way mine got when I'd been crying too much, and I expected he was exhausted.

I set down the mallet and turned to fully face him. His eyes were bloodshot and there were dark smudges under them, like he hadn't slept in days.

"Self-preservation," I answered slowly. "You have too many secrets you can't seem to trust me with, and some of them are too big for me to handle when I find them out on my own."

"There are things I can't talk about yet," he said tightly, pushing at the sleeves of his shirt.

I looked pointedly at his wedding band. "Is that one of them? Because I'd like to hear that whole story. I'd figured there was a possibility you were still overcoming your hopeless love for her, despite the fact she was a horrible human. And you told me you were divorcing her, but according to nationally syndicated gossip shows, she is very much still a part of your life." I had to turn my face away, because the feeling in my gut was one of rising hysteria and I knew better than to think it would come out any way other than tears.

"Judging by the photos I saw, neither of you seems terribly finished with the other."

A small tremor ran through him and he took a step closer with a strange light in his eyes. "Lydia and I have been locked in contentious arbitration for a very long time. She has done everything in her power to fight me on every point and once again, we are at an impasse. This is simply making our lawyers obscenely wealthy."

"What is there to fight over?" I asked, pressing my butt up against the counter and leaning against my hands. "Money? I can imagine she's clawing for every cent she can get."

"I can't tell you that," he said flatly, and his expression was devoid of any emotion.

"Fine," I said quietly, feeling ice rush through my veins. I knew my posture was defeated. My shoulders slumped forward and I drew deep breaths through my nose, half terrified he was going to say he was considering giving in.

I don't want to share any part of him.

"And what does Harrison say to his girlfriend trying to win back her husband?"

There was a wicked gleam in his eyes. "They're not together anymore. They haven't been for some time now."

Then what was stopping him?

He sighed heavily, shoving a hand through his hair before looking up at me. "Every child should be raised in a home filled with love and care and laughter. The parents should be able to stand one another. Preferably love each other. Passionately." He looked down at his feet, his cheeks suddenly pink, and he twisted at the ring on his finger.

"Are you trying to tell me something?" I asked slowly, unsure of what he meant by that, but he didn't respond. Simply stood there looking at me like he was agonizing over something.

"You should be home, sleeping," I said, realizing his appearance meant he'd taken a very uncomfortable red eye flight home.

He scratched at his jaw and tucked his hair behind an ear before looking up again. "I couldn't," he said shortly. "You wouldn't talk to me and it was tearing me up. I know I suck at communicating, and when the shoe is on the other foot, I get frantic. I had to see you."

"It looked bad," I said, moving toward the stove to pour another cup of coffee.

"It only looks bad to people who have a personal interest."

"Is that so?" I asked, startled by his smug comment, and I knew he could see the way my jaw set.

"I hope so," he said, pushing off the countertop and coming to stand behind me. I froze, pretending to drink my coffee though it was entirely too hot, as his hands settled on my hips. It was enough to make me set down the mug and swallow hard. I was too easy: he could read me.

"I sleep better when you're with me," he said into my hair, dropping his forehead to the back of my head, and I didn't know whether that was a statement or an invitation. "You help chase the ghosts away."

I didn't know which ghosts those were, but I turned slowly and slipped my arms around his middle, pressing my head to his chest. He was so beautiful, it made my heart ache, and while I slipped my fingers into his hair he wrapped himself around me, hiding me in his arms.

"I didn't sleep with her, Natalie, and I'm not trying to win her back. We occasionally cross paths at events I have to attend, but she's nothing to me. But you..." His voice trailed off and I looked up. "You're the one I can't lose."

"Come on," I said gently, taking his hand and leading him up the stairs. I pointed to the bed I'd made only hours earlier. "In."

"Only if you're coming with," he said, unbuttoning his shirt and I waited, my brain completely incapacitated by the sight of this big man stripping in my bedroom. I thought of the nights I'd lain in this very bed and tried to remember the planes of his body the times I'd seen him without a shirt, or the night he'd crashed into the tiny bed in his boxers.

His t-shirt came off and all I could say was "Um."

Then he dropped his pants, walking toward my bed wearing only his boxer briefs.

This was not helping.

I couldn't think straight, admiring the fine view.

"I need to know I mean something to you, and you need something I can give you," I said, slipping in beside him and reaching up to touch his beautiful face. "You need to feel cared for and I can do that, but it hurts me, because I know you're not ready to give it back. And I just keep freaking doing it."

"I'm your charity case?" he asked, his eyes going from soft and hot to hard and glittery.

I shook my head slowly, my hair making a sliding noise on the pillow. "It would seem I've been *your* charity case." I smiled up at him.

"I haven't done anything I didn't want to do," he answered, still studying my face.

"Neither have I, and I want to do a great deal more," I said, reaching up with both hands to bring his face down to mine, and I felt his hesitation melt away the instant our lips met. It was as if it unlocked something inside of him, and he slid a hand beneath my head to angle my mouth, slipping inside with deep, soft licks. It was enough to make me combust, the knowledge that he was barely restraining himself, holding back though I could feel the tension coiled in his powerful body.

He nipped at my lower lip, pulling back, and I opened my eyes to see him staring down at me, his expression intense.

"Take what you need," I whispered back, and relief washed across his face. He dove into my mouth again, the stroking of his tongue encouraging me to writhe against him impatiently.

But he was slow. He kissed and licked his way down my neck, stopping to nuzzle under my ear as he drew deep breaths through his nose, and it made me giggle. "Are you *smelling* me?"

He hummed against my skin. "Drinking you in; you're delicious."

"We have lost time to make up for," I said quietly, turning the tables on him as I pressed my face into his neck to tease the soft skin I found there. It made him breathe faster, and I pressed my pelvis shamelessly into him as my own breathing grew labored. I'd wanted to lick this man the first time I saw him, I remembered, and I giggled as I moved down his chest to flick my tongue across the points of his nipples.

He pushed up and I straddled his hips. It put his mouth in the perfect position, and he lifted my breasts in his hands, kissing his way from one to the next.

"These," he said finally, dropping one more kiss over the thin fabric of my shirt, "have been very distracting."

I sat back just a little and made a sweeping gesture to encompass him entirely. "This...has been very distracting."

He chuckled, his hips swiveling in a small motion that reminded me how urgent other things really were and I looked down at him suspiciously. "What other tricks you got?"

He grinned lazily up at me. "If you behave I might show you."

"I'm the one misbehaving?" I pouted down at him, and the smile on his face stretched wider.

I grumbled against his shoulder, trying to twist my body in order to reach him, to drive him to the edge of the same madness. But he knew what I was doing and he kept himself out of my reach, straightening me back out with patience, continuing his tender assault.

"I want this all the time," he whispered, his lips back at my neck. "You were all I could think about while I was away: touching you and making you call my name. *Mine*." His words were fierce, but I couldn't see his face. "The way you melt into me when I hold you. The sounds you make drive me insane."

"This is hardly fair. Why can't I touch you?" I asked, breathlessly and he raised himself up, rolling me quickly and tucking one arm under my head to brace himself as he looked down into my face. His expression was heartbreaking, and he smoothed my hair back with his other hand. "You told me I needed time to process," he said with a smile, and I wriggled my hips impatiently.

"Don't use my words against me, Atholton."

He shook his head, the long strands of dark silk swirling around his face and tickling my cheeks.

"I have no intention of using anything *against* you, James," he whispered into my hair and I thought for a moment that I'd never told him my maiden name. "Except..." Something very large nudged gently against the sensitive place between my legs.

Bullseye.

"Except maybe this," he teased, rocking against me and I gasped a little.

I leaned up to kiss him, every muscle in his body tense and straining. I made it slow and wet, licking into him at a pace I knew our bodies would replicate, and his hips pressed into mine.

His hands shook when he cupped my face gently and I felt the familiar stirring, the ache. "Not yet, baby," he kissed me softly. "You're precious to me," he murmured against my lips. "I don't ever want to hurt you and I've done enough of that just this week. I have to earn you."

"Why do you have to be so chivalrous?" I complained grumpily, irritated he wouldn't let me seduce him the way he did me.

The weight of his body was oddly soothing, I thought, though I struggled for breath beneath the crushing mass of muscle and bone.

"Natalie." His voice caressed my name, and he slid his arms beneath me and rolled us so that I was lying on top of him again. He bore my weight without complaint, breathing easily beneath me. His arms were tight, wrapped around me like steel bands, pressing me to his chest with ferocious strength.

"Stay with me." His voice was low and urgent. "I sleep better when you're near me. Without you, it's..." He paused, looking uncomfortable again. "Lonely."

I pressed my face into his chest to breathe him in, warm skin and pheromones and desire. I didn't want to sleep. He smelled phenomenal and my body ached to feel him in all the soft, warm places that had been neglected for so long.

I curled tightly into him, my breathing still ragged from his kisses and he wrapped the blankets closer around us. He kissed me again before settling into the pillow and began to take long, deep breaths.

I willed my body to quiet and eventually followed him into a troubled sleep.

• • • •

THE SHADOWS WERE LONG when I opened my eyes again and a smile tugged at my lips as I listened to Thomas's soft snore, one arm thrown over his face as he slept.

I shifted slightly, wrapping myself tighter around him and he hummed a contented sound, one eye opening lazily as he smiled down at me.

"I haven't slept that well in...I don't even know. Maybe not ever." His voice was still thick with sleep. I suspected he hadn't slept for several of the nights before he'd come to me and had a large deficit to satisfy.

He slid one hand into my hair and leaned across the space to kiss me gently. I felt something crack inside when he did it. Something hot and gooey and dangerous.

He kissed the tip of my nose, his face inches from my own, and his warm brown eyes stayed locked on my own as he confessed, "I've wanted this–you–for a long time. You kept calling us friends...and I knew that wasn't really possible. But you know when I knew I was in serious trouble?"

It took all my effort to shake my head.

"The night I came home and found you'd completely redone my garage, so I drove over here to yell at you, because I was mad. I was furious with *myself*. What I really wanted to do was kiss you and haul you up to this big bed and devour you. And then you pretty much kicked me out, and I realized I'd come across all wrong. So I went back home with my tail between my legs and found a house full of food..." His voice trailed off and I was surprised to see his eyes looked a little watery. "I felt undeserving. I was–am. It was the first time I felt like maybe someone could...care for me with no ulterior motives. *You* were taking care of me." He turned his head to wipe his eyes on his shoulder. "And I didn't deserve that."

I didn't like these vulnerable-moment confessions, not when my brain couldn't be trusted to formulate thoughts properly and my heart was willing to just vomit emotion all over him. No, I needed a distraction before I blurted out something stupid, and I reached up to kiss him again.

"You are deserving," I whispered in a rush, terrified that I couldn't stop the flow of words as they fell from my lips. "And I do care–more than you could know."

Oh crap, what have you done?

"My Natalie." There was a tenderness in his eyes I'd never seen before when he finally settled back into his pillow, curled up beside me, his big body wrapped around my much smaller one. He seemed unable to talk, or maybe just unwilling, stroking his thumb over my cheek again and again with the smallest, sweetest smile on his face.

"Gerry was right," he said finally, dropping his face into the curve of my shoulder. "You're the answer to the prayers I refused to say."

"Whatever." I slapped his shoulder playfully and he lifted his face, his eyes bright and glittery.

"I'm serious. I've been crawling my way deeper and deeper into depression and despair. I've shut people out because I couldn't stand to feel anything–just ask Noah. Everything hurt. Ached. And I kept going only because I didn't know any other way. You kept finding ways to draw me out and it made me mad as hell." He chuckled.

The moment was intensely tender and my heart swelled and ached with what I felt for him. It terrified me, ghosts from both of our pasts trying to steal the brief moment of happiness.

"Just tell me I'm not going to be your small-town secret," I whispered, cringing as the words left my lips. It sounded desperate and small. "I have to be more than a toy."

"You're not a secret; not a toy," he said firmly, dropping his face to mine to kiss my eyes, my cheeks, my lips. "In fact, the next time I have to go to California, I want you to come with me. There are events I'll need to attend and things I want to show you."

"You just want me to help keep Lydia at an arm's length," I teased, and he swallowed slowly, his eyes never leaving mine.

"Those pictures you saw...we were not at that event together. She's a publicist now. She's always been good at worrying about her own image, so it makes sense she'd get paid to worry about someone else's." His eyes took on a faraway look.

"That picture of her looking over my shoulder: I know what you thought when you saw that. I know exactly what it looked like and that's just what she wanted. She propositioned me seconds before the photographer snapped the shot, '*for old time's sake.*'"

That horrible bitch.

"She needs to find a way to keep herself tied to you, since she's grown accustomed to...a certain amount of money."

"I suppose. She's probably arrogant enough to think I'm still in love with her, even after what she did...she doesn't like to lose." He put a hand over his face.

There was a determined knocking at the door downstairs and I groaned a little, unwinding myself from his arms and quickly slipping on a bra under my shirt as he watched with hot eyes.

"Natalie Sayad?"

I didn't recognize the young, clean-cut man standing on my porch.

"Hopefully not for much longer," I said, opening the door a little farther to step out.

His lips quirked a little and he shoved a thick stack of papers at me. "You have been served. Have a nice day, ma'am."

I stared after him in shock as he hurried down the steps, jumping into the car that sat behind mine, and backing hurriedly down the driveway.

Thomas found me seconds later, the papers in my hands and a look of total disbelief on my face. He glanced down at them quickly and I saw his forehead draw into a deep frown. "Separate support?" he asked, skimming the heading.

"He's claiming I've abandoned him and cut him off financially, for no reason. I know he's going to try to get to my separate bank account through the court system. I guess his boy's such an expensive hobby, he really does require two incomes to support."

"Put your lawyer on speaker," he demanded, and I fished in the pocket of my shorts to pull out my phone, quickly dialing Jeanine. Her assistant put me on hold for a moment and then Jeanine's distinctly New England accent grated across my ears.

"Natalie. What's going on?"

I quickly explained the situation as I sifted through the thick stack of papers, and she sighed heavily. "Put them into an envelope and have them sent to me." I heard her tap at a few keys.

"The process server probably hasn't served him yet, but your suit was filed before his. This will muddy things a bit, but your filing takes precedent. In fact, he might decide to withdraw this one once he's served, since it's likely he'll file a response and include his demands.

"Besides, it will be very inconvenient for him to travel to Alabama to pursue this, as he's already in for a very uncomfortable explanation regarding why he cut you off from your primary bank account in the first place."

"How long before he's served?" I asked, irritation making my skin hot.

"Legally, as long as the papers are served within the next five days, we're fine. In fact, this may work out to your advantage–knock him a little off-balance."

"He's doing this because he wants to control me," I said, and I could feel Thomas tensing next to me. "He doesn't want a divorce, but he does want the money I bring in, because it helps to support his expensive cupcake's lifestyle.

"*I* want the divorce because I refuse to live like this any longer. It's a lie and there is no benefit, not to me."

Jeanine snorted. "Sounds to me like the boy toy's going to have to get a job." Then she rang off abruptly.

I dropped the stack of papers onto the porch, feeling a little dizzy, and Thomas's arms went around me. He held me tightly, until he felt me relax into him, and when he released me I realized he was standing there shirtless. Not that I was complaining, but I'd watched a curtain flutter across the street, so at least my nosy neighbor, Libby was appreciating the very fine view.

Thomas picked up the stack to bring inside, setting it on the peninsula and paging carefully through them with one arched eyebrow.

"I have some experience with this," he said quietly, and I handed him a glass of iced tea. "Lydia dragged me into court for spousal support after she left me. I got lucky: the judge told her if she wanted any kind of division of property, she'd have to file for divorce." He tapped at his lip. "As it was, she'd walked away willingly. He didn't think she should be rewarded for that."

I was quiet while he read through the pages, twisting absently at the ring on his finger. I hated what that band symbolized, because it reminded me of what stood between us yet. He was taking steps, but it was obvious his largest hurdle was mental.

Every time he told me a little more about his past life, I stored the information away inside my brain to build a more complete picture. But the more he told me, Lydia was looking worse and worse, even when I hadn't thought it possible.

"I can have my legal team take a look if you'd like."

"You have a legal *team*? As in, more than one person?"

"Of course I do."

"I mean...not that I know much, but I thought you were mostly just serving on boards these days."

"Hmm." He took a long chug of his iced tea. "And other things."

Well, here we were again: something we weren't going to talk about.

"Are you afraid to tell me things because you think I'll use them against you?" I asked, and he looked up with a startled expression. "Because the last thing I want is for you to feel like you're not safe with me," I hurried on, "and I know it's...well, it's stupid-early days and like you don't even know my middle name yet..." This was getting weird and rambling.

"Elizabeth."

"Wait...what? How did you...I didn't tell you that."

"Says it right here." He grinned at me, driving his index finger into the paper, just beneath the heading *Respondent*.

"Ok, well...so you do know it. Now." I was flustered and he knew it.

He stood carefully, pushing the papers to the side before stepping in front of me, taking my face in his hands. "You talk a lot when you're nervous." He smiled down at me. "I know I don't...act like a normal person. I don't do what's expected of me, and you already know most of the 'why.'" His thumbs were smoothing back and forth across my cheeks. "I'm learning you, Natalie, and I've been studying hard. I think your heart is too big to ever intentionally do me harm and I still don't know what to do with that. I've never known someone like you before: someone who doesn't want *things* from me. Everyone has a reason and an ulterior motive, but you seem to be someone who just wants...*me*." His last word was a whisper and I understood this was a startling revelation to him, so I lifted my face to kiss him.

Smiling against his lips, I said, "Well, there might be a couple things I want from you," and he pulled back slowly, the look on his face indicating he didn't know whether he should be worried or whether he was being teased.

"This." I placed a hand over his heart and patted softly.

"And this." I leaned up to kiss him again, a very different kiss from the ones I'd given him upstairs. This one was soft and sweet, lingering long enough that he could read my meaning. It was enough to make him wrap me in his arms and squeeze almost convulsively tight and just maybe, I thought, I was starting to fill his empty heart just a little.

When our lips parted, he stood staring down at me for a long moment, his hands cupping my face. He blinked slowly before stepping back only a few inches, lowering his hands and twisting off his wedding band.

His arm shot out and I heard the metallic clink as he dropped it onto the windowsill over the sink.

"You have me," he whispered.

THIRTY-SIX

Thomas

Natalie's admission to me, in her kitchen, was almost enough to stop my heart. She was so guileless and earnest. I could see in her eyes that she meant what she said and it had taken every fiber of my being not to burst into tears and throw myself at her, sobbing like a child.

I'd waited to hear those words for so long.

I'd waited for someone like *her* for so long.

She lit me up on the inside, filling me with warmth and my heart with hope. And damn it, the woman made me *pie.* If that wasn't love...well, then there was no such thing.

So there it was: I left my wedding band on her windowsill, where it still sat days later.

I hadn't really meant to mention California to her, but she'd lit up when it tripped out of my mouth and I knew immediately that I had the chance to make her really happy. She wanted to know everything about me and California held a lot of those details.

She fed me dinner and I stayed a little longer to help her clean up.

Then held her close.

Then kissed her while thinking some deliciously dirty thoughts.

It was still fairly early in California, so while I drove home I placed a call to my secretary and ran a few things past her. There were a couple things I needed her to research and offer personal opinion on and she said she'd be in touch by the next afternoon.

With Natalie's permission, I sent a copy of her filing and Ahmad's to my lawyers, asking them to run a review through their Boston office for any little state-specific oddities, and to offer their commentary on how to speed the process, preferably with an outcome in her favor.

If he really wanted to pursue her money, I would make sure he had a hell of a time doing it.

Suddenly, I had renewed interest in finalizing my divorce with Lydia, and I told my lawyers I would agree to all of her terms. I was done arguing with her, and her arbitrary list of ridiculous demands were no longer worth the expenditure of my time, money or emotions.

A thought flashed through my mind and I picked up the phone to make one more call. I had work to do on my Stanford project tonight, but first I needed to put some of these nagging matters to bed.

It was late when I finally drifted back down to the kitchen. My house still felt empty and alone, and I let my memory drift back to scooping Natalie up as she loaded the dishwasher. She'd squealed, her hands dripping with rinse water, but her squeals turned to soft sighs when I leaned down to kiss her and she'd wrapped her arms around my neck.

I loved that, the way she responded to me so eagerly, opening to me immediately.

I felt more at home in Natalie's house than I did in my own. In fact, one of the best parts of the day was walking through her kitchen door to find her at the stove, delicious smells already warming the kitchen.

Pulling a tub of frozen chocolate chip cookies from the freezer, I grinned to myself. I'd told Gerry that I called Natalie's cookies Love Bites, for obvious reasons. A certain someone had taken the time to fill my freezers with food in order to show she cared for me and needless to say, lately I'd been eating a lot of the Love Bites while trying to come to terms with the confusing feelings that warred in my brain.

I hit the weights for a while before bed. I'd watched Natalie go wide-eyed when I took off my shirt.

How had I never noticed that before?

She'd licked her lips and pulled her bottom lip between her teeth with an expression that made me jump into her bed before she could see what it did to me.

It was obvious she liked what she saw, and I was going to do my damndest to keep it that way. It was something I'd always done for myself, but I hadn't felt wanted by a woman for the right reasons in a really long time.

I'd make sure the one who did want me for the right reasons had full access to all the perks.

The shower was killing me. I was just going to have to stop showering at night. Or maybe showering at all. Because every time I got into it I pictured Natalie naked, and today I'd spent some serious time with her partially naked.

Sweet mother of God.

My imagination ran rampant thinking of the way her small waist flared into gentle hips and smooth thighs. Everything about her was perfect and soft and beautiful and I leaned into my hand as I thought about dipping my tongue between her thighs and hearing her sigh.

Feeling her hands in my hair.

Making her scream for me again and again before finally allowing myself to sink into the bliss of her body.

The thought drove me into a shattering finish and I beat a fist against the tile wall as I groaned harshly.

Soon.

Soon you'll have her screaming for you.

It couldn't be soon enough.

THIRTY-SEVEN

Natalie

Thomas had informed me we would spend a week on the west coast, ending our stay at "Maren's place," and I wondered briefly if he'd unloaded all of his west coast properties so there was less to bicker about when it came time for a divorce settlement. Something told me Lydia wouldn't find her Portola Valley home sufficient.

There were two events to attend, one a launch party for something he said was super top secret, and the other a charity gala, as it seemed he was deeply involved in supporting research for Down syndrome.

I couldn't say no to that. I couldn't tell him I didn't want to attend his very important event with him because I had nothing to wear, but...well...I had nothing to wear.

Gerry found me digging through storage bins in my closet that afternoon, pulling out formalwear from my prior life. I held up one dress after another, none of them speaking to me, all of them associated with things I'd rather forget.

I collapsed on the floor in despair, looking at the mess around me.

"I'm going to embarrass him," I whispered to her. "Even if half these things fit, they're not right. Nothing seems right." I threw myself backward with a groan, arms stretched out.

Gerry smiled indulgently at me before stepping out of the closet and from the muffled words I could hear, I knew she'd stepped out into the hallway to use her phone.

"Is there anything else you need to get done today?" she asked, poking her head back into my closet, and I shook my head.

"You mean other than buy a new body? Nah, I'm good."

Her eyes twinkled a little. "None of my business, but a certain someone seems to like that body just fine."

I blushed. She'd totally busted Thomas and me a few days earlier, sitting on the back slab, watching the sun go down. I'd been in his lap, completely wrapped around him–not that he was complaining.

Thomas had been slow to initiate much beyond heavy making out, and the hesitation on his part was making me crazy. I didn't want to push, but I was hoping this trip was a catalyst for some serious sexy time. Otherwise it was possible my lady bits were going to finally and officially rust from disuse, or incinerate due to frustration.

Driving through town with one casual hand on the wheel, Gerry said little. But I was comfortable with her–comfortable enough to turn off the constant stream of conversation–and I looked out the window, realizing the route seemed familiar.

It was when we pulled up in front of Christa Masters' palatial residence that I gave her side eye. "What the hell are you up to, Gerry?"

Christa met us at the front door, all smiles, as polished and put together as she always was.

"Natalie!" she sang, holding her hands out to me. "I cannot tell you how much Jonesy and I love what you have done to the house! We hardly leave the sitting room, it's so fabulous. We've been talking about doing more soon."

I nodded dumbly, pretty sure Gerry hadn't brought me here to drum up more business.

She led us up a wide staircase and into a large sitting area on the second floor where a petite, curvy woman with almost-black hair rose from one of the overstuffed sofas. She was beautiful in a doll like way, her thick, glossy hair falling over fine porcelain features and softly flushed cheeks.

"This is my daughter, Daphne," Christa said with pride, and I tried to keep my eyes from bugging out. Christa hardly looked old enough to have a daughter who was clearly an adult–like *my age adult*.

Daphne stepped forward and took my hand and it was when she smiled that I saw her likeness to Christa.

"Daphne is divesting herself of some underperforming assets," Christa drawled with a cheeky smile, and the woman looked quickly down at her feet.

"What Mama wants to say is that my useless husband and I are divorcing." She drew in a deep breath, and I got the impression there was something more to the story.

Christa reached out to pinch Daphne's cheek. "Don't let this baby face fool you. My Daphne's brilliant: Just sold her design business to her assistant, and she's starting a new chapter in her life."

Daphne blushed a sweet shade of pink and she gestured between the two of us. "We're why I started designing," she said softly, and my head fell to the side. "Tell me you've ever had luck walking into a store and just grabbing something off the rack," she explained.

"Uh...not very often." I scooped a hand over my hips and butt. My latest dietary indiscretions aside, I'd always been weirdly proportioned. My mother called it "the Hollywood starlet curse." I had boobs and a butt, a tiny waist, and not a lot of height to distract from any of those facts.

Being built like an actual hourglass really sucked sometimes.

I heard a pop behind me and realized it was Christa, pouring champagne into glasses. She filled two nearly to the top and handed one to me, but not Daphne, while she and Gerry settled into the sofas to chat.

I didn't ask, but I gave Daphne a strange look as I held the glass in my hand.

Daphne was quiet, taking my measurements, a few photos, and then sat down with me to discuss likes and dislikes, fabrics, patterns and buttons. It was my field...sort of.

The woman was sweet natured and soft spoken, and something led me to believe that maybe she wasn't usually like that, or hadn't always been. I recognized something dampened in her spirit, maybe even broken, and when I saw her pull in an uneven breath, I couldn't help myself. I reached across the small space between us to squeeze her hand, and she looked up at me with eyes full of suffering.

That was a look I knew well.

"It's more than the divorce, isn't it?" I whispered so the other two women wouldn't hear us and she nodded slowly, her eyes drifting shut, but not before a tear slid down her cheek.

"I let myself fall in love with a man who's heart wasn't ready for what I had to offer, apparently," she said, and I raised my glass in solidarity, both eyebrows rising.

"Daphne, I think we're going to be great friends."

Daphne's hands flew over her paper, sketching quick outlines as she talked me through what she saw for two dresses tailored to my body type.

I swallowed hard as her visions came to life with pencil and paper. This was going to be expensive, I thought, and though I could handle a little setback, I wasn't used to paying for custom clothing.

"You have no idea how good this is for her," Christa sang. "She's just been moping around. Her work with Jonas's foundation keeps her busy, but she needs more. She needs..." Christa's eyes went all crafty and scheming. "I just realized, darling, you're around the same age."

"Mom," Daphne laughed, and it was a delightfully low, musical sound. "You don't need to make friends *for* me. If Natalie's hard up for an emotional basket case, now she knows where I live."

That made me grin, because I knew a thing or two about emotional basket cases.

Guilty, party of one.

Daphne disappeared down the hallway and I stood dumbly near the table we'd been hovering over, now littered with her measuring tape, various pencils and a pile of heavy white papers.

"This one for the launch party," she called, and I looked up to see her carrying a heavy roll of rose-colored fabric down the hallway. She dropped it onto the table and the sound echoed through the hollow cardboard tube down the center.

I fingered the fabric while she disappeared again. It was a heavy, matte silk and I made a mental note to check the condition of my shapewear. This fabric would hide less than nothing.

"This one for the gala."

There was a second hollow thump, and I looked up to see a thick silver satin.

"Don't worry." She grinned and I realized I was smoothing my hands self-consciously across my stomach. "I've got tricks–you'll look incredible. Trust me, if I can hide this..." She scooped a hand over her small tummy and I cocked an eyebrow, but she didn't elaborate, sitting again, adding notes to her drawings as I looked uselessly over her shoulder.

"Daphne," Christa called from the other side of the room. "You'd best take the girl into Mobile and get her set up with some proper underwear for those creations of yours."

I didn't know what "proper underwear" meant, but I could guess the stuff was expensive.

I sighed, remembering I would also need shoes–and could I talk Daphne into lingerie shopping with me? I needed another woman's honest but kind opinion.

"What are you wearing to the gala?" I asked Thomas later that night, when he walked through my kitchen door to find me chopping lettuce in leggings and a loose, raggedy sweatshirt. The top kept slipping down my shoulder as I worked, and he leaned in behind me to run his hands down my butt and back up, squeezing gently. I could feel him grinning against my shoulder and he kissed it softly, nuzzling into my neck.

I liked this version of Thomas: warm, playful, sensual, always finding a way to put his hands on me. I wanted to keep *this* guy around all the time.

"That's the easiest part of my job," he said into my hair. "I just wear a tux–usually the same one–to all the things. But if it's more casual I just wear a suit and a button-down, since I can always lose the jacket."

This was so unfair. I blew out a puff of air and set down the knife, leaning back as his arms went around my middle.

He didn't know it, but every moment of every day, I was comparing my reception in the gossip rags to the praises heaped upon Lydia. I was mentally preparing myself for the cruel things I knew would be said, and I tried to tell myself I wouldn't care, even though I knew it was a lie.

We'd spent several weeks discovering one another in a way that was decidedly more than friendly and our routine seemed to include Thomas coming to my house each evening for dinner. He usually stayed the night, frustratingly never taking it beyond holding me as we slept.

Sometimes I tried testing his resolve, crawling on top of him to kiss him silly. And though I came close to begging a couple times, he always took as much as he could handle before rolling me over, pinning my hands over my head and pleading with me to stop testing him. It was hard enough for him to wait, he said, and I wondered why we were waiting and how much longer that would be.

In the mornings I cooked breakfast and we ate together, then he drove away to go about his business. It was already oddly domestic and comfortable, and I could tell the routine was comforting to him. I wondered if he'd ever had that before and doubted he had, from what he'd told me.

It did occur to me, once or twice, that it was perhaps a little odd we weren't spending any time at his place, but he seemed more relaxed at mine, like it was easier to breathe.

When Thomas walked through the door that night, he pulled his sweaty shirt over his head and grinned at me. He knew exactly what he did to me and he loved it, watching me lick my lips as he walked to the laundry room to finish stripping.

"I had the strangest thing happen today." I announced my arrival, sliding my fingers over the warm skin of his back as he stripped down to his underwear.

I never got tired of watching him unveil the hard washboard of his stomach, the deep muscular ridge that rode his hips like spaghetti straps, or the solid muscles of his very fine butt–another part I hadn't seen with my own eyes just yet.

He stood there nearly naked, dropping his clothes into the wash machine, and for a second I couldn't think at all. I lost my train of thought and stood openly staring at him while he fished through my laundry to add to his load, added soap and selected a cycle.

"You make domestic chores so hot," I breathed when he finally turned around to look at me, and he grinned wickedly.

"I aim to please, Ms. James. Point me to my next chore so I can earn a gold star."

"You *are* the gold star," I grumbled, suddenly feeling dumpy by comparison.

He put his hands on my hips as he simultaneously lifted and spun, depositing me on the marble laundry counter he'd installed along the wall the week before. "Then you earned *me*?" he teased. "I like it." He grinned with his whole heart, kissing along the expanse of skin my shirt revealed.

By the time his mouth made it to mine, I forgot all about what I'd been meaning to tell him.

• • • •

THE WEEK BEFORE WE left for California was a wreck of commitments.

Thomas had been spending more and more time each day, holed up in his home office, working on something he refused to talk about.

I spent most of the week at Christa's place, in one capacity or another, as I began a design for two of her adjoining bedrooms, to create a nursery with adjoining work/sleep space.

It seemed that besides divorcing a congressman, Daphne was staying with her parents while she tried to get her life back on track.

Add to that a late-in-life pregnancy that I gathered was *not* the doing of the man she was divorcing, and I could understand why she was feeling a little lost.

Looking at Daphne, now that I knew, I could just begin to see it, and I commented on how impressive it was that someone so petite and curvy could hide something like that so well, and for so long.

"That's what happens when you stop eating," Daphne said sadly, and I bit my lip. She rarely smiled, and I knew from Christa that she'd had a hard time of it with morning sickness, but she was well past that point. That led me to believe Daphne was nursing a shattered heart.

The woman was a genius with pins, cleverly placed darts and a sewing machine, and on the days I wasn't poring over catalogs and placing orders, taking measurements or haggling with suppliers, I was in her workspace, being pinned into the dresses.

She ran a hand over my stomach as she smoothed and pinned and she half-smiled up at me, pins sticking out of one side of her mouth. "Impressive," she said. "You've been working hard."

I *had* been working hard. For weeks, when Thomas left in the morning, I devoted several solid hours to intensely focused writing and editing before rushing off to the small box of a gym in town. There I tested the stuff I was made of, logging half an hour on the treadmill every day before I moved to weights and resistance bands, sit-ups, push-ups and squats. It was punishing, and by the time I arrived home I'd throw together something to eat, then spend the rest of the day either working on my own projects or with Christa, working on design plans.

"Have you seen what I'm up against?" I asked, regretting it the instant the words left my mouth, and Daphne fixed me with a curious stare.

The desk wasn't far, but it was at an awkward angle, and I leaned and twisted slowly, so as not to pop any of the pins while I retrieved my phone from the large desktop. I typed in my search parameters and held a full-screen photo of Lydia in Daphne's face.

"Pfffft." She blew her breath out so hard, pins scattered across the floor. "Skinny, miserable woman. She doesn't have anything on you."

"Are we seeing the same thing?" I fussed, flipping the phone around to see the picture again.

"Mmhmm." Daphne was tucking pins back in between her lips. "Those are fake." She reached up and tapped the screen with a short fingernail.

I couldn't decide whether she meant Lydia's hair or her breasts, but I was guessing the latter.

"And her face is so full of filler and neurotoxin, it's a miracle she can smile at all. That stuff's probably completely eaten whatever brain she *did* have–oh, her teeth are fake too. All veneers."

I looked down at Daphne, carefully pinning up the hem of the dress, stopping with each pin to take a measurement.

"But she's beautiful," I protested, still flabbergasted by the woman's presence that shone through her pictures.

"If you spend enough money you can look like that too. It's all been paid for, believe me," Daphne said, her voice agreeable. "And that's where the pretty stops. It's hiding rot. There's nothing about that woman that's genuine: Not her teeth, her hair, the color of her skin, her boobs...did you know she's had her *earlobes* done? Her nose? Those pretty blue eyes of hers aren't real, either."

I gasped.

"Yep. Contacts. Oh–and she had a fat transfer surgery done last year, to take fat out of her butt and put it under her eyes. I'd say that makes her a buttface." She snorted at the same time I did.

"How do you know all this?" I asked, a little alarmed.

"Lydia's my cousin," she said nonchalantly. "I know *all* about her." Her voice dripped with disdain. "She was the *poorer relation* until she hooked up with Thomas, the poor guy. Suckered him right in...didn't know what he was signing up for until it was way too late, bless his heart."

Well, here was an interesting new development.

"Really," I said, in a tone that indicated it was not a question, but still trying not to give away that I was surprised.

"Lydia's mom was from here: my daddy's oldest sister. Disgraced the family, according to what Mama tells me.

"I've never met her. She moved out to Washington before Lydia was born and I don't think she's been back since." She whipped out a needle and thread to stitch something carefully.

So this hadn't been the middle of nowhere, not really. This hadn't been some random, backwater choice for him. Whether or not he'd told Lydia why they were moving to the south, the fact she had some sort of family base there must have factored into his decision.

I didn't say anything more, letting Daphne concentrate.

When she slipped the dress from my shoulders and I shrugged back into my old clothes, I felt like I'd come away from the Masters' home with a dirty little secret, and it was one that gave me more confidence.

• • • •

DAPHNE WAS A MIRACLE worker. She called me over the day before we were to leave, to have me try on the gowns one last time, and they were perfect. I had never looked better, which I credited entirely to her wizardry, despite all my own blood, sweat, tears and squats.

I carefully packed the gowns away so Thomas wouldn't see them and the night before we were to leave, I put my bag at the bottom of the stairs, near the door and ready to go.

Daphne had agreed to an underwear shopping trip, helping me find sexy, smoothing pieces to wear under each dress.

Then I'd dragged her toward the racier pieces with a red face and a nervous smile and she lit up, quickly selecting several things for me to try on and seriously evaluating each piece for maximum effect. She'd done a little stitching on a couple of the pieces, to reinforce areas she thought might receive extra strain, too, to save me from myself.

The sheer black lace bra and panty set embroidered with tiny red rosebuds was my favorite.

Daphne's eyes had bugged out of her head when I scooped the curtain aside, and she let out a low whistle. "Natalie, that man is not going to know what to *do* with you. You are a hurricane! That set was *made* for you. You'd better get the one in pink, too." The grin on her face was huge and I was delighted by her reaction. It felt good to be praised by another woman–encouraged–as I'd not had a lot of that in my life.

I took to bringing small things for Daphne and the baby each time I visited.

I dropped by to just sit and chat with her when I could. She was so open and sweet and encouraging that I teased Thomas one night that I might have to start dating Daphne, due to the fact she was such an ego boost. He had growled in the back of his throat and pushed me back on the sofa, stretching out over me and telling me between kisses that I. Was. His. And he didn't share. It made me sigh with delight and I pushed my fingers into his hair to pull him closer.

With this man there was no such thing as *enough*.

• • • •

THOMAS COULD TELL I was nervous, fidgeting though I was trying to be calm. I had wiped down the kitchen countertops three times, double-checked that I'd packed my phone charging cord, and I kept peeking back into my travel bag to make sure there wasn't anything I'd forgotten.

I'd made triple-sure to check the expiration on my IUD the week before.

"It's ok," he called from the sofa, where he was reading something on my tablet. "If you forget anything we can always pick it up there. They do have stores in California, you know."

His smile told me he was teasing, but I felt tense and worried.

"I like this," he murmured, leaning into my ear, his fingers in my hair as I zipped my bag for what must have been the seventh time.

I'd driven into Mobile earlier that day for a hair appointment with Christa's stylist. That was all I'd told Thomas.

What I didn't tell him was that I'd also gotten a pedicure, a manicure, and a full exfoliation and wax, just in case, and a baby's bottom had nothing on me.

"This is nice, too." He smoothed a hand over my stomach, which had flattened out and was starting to show signs of definition. "You using paint cans for kettlebells when I leave in the morning?"

I squirmed uncomfortably. I wasn't used to compliments or, as of the past few years, even feeling attractive. "I don't want to be an embarrassment," I said quietly, not sure he'd heard me until he took my chin in my hand, forcing me to look up.

"You could wear a ratty old t-shirt and leggings and you'd still be the most beautiful woman in the room."

I snorted and rolled my eyes. "Why didn't you tell me that before I went through the torture of having dresses made?"

His eyebrows wiggled a little and he reached up to tuck my hair over my ear. "Because if having your armor makes you feel more beautiful and confident, then why not? I'm just saying you don't need it. You're already all I can see."

I relaxed into his chest, my eyes a little watery. "Whatever, sweet talker." I pinched his nipple through his shirt and he made a startled noise before his eyes lit up.

"Oh, we're playing that way tonight?"

He left all the lights on–something that usually drove me insane–but I didn't care at all when he threw me over his shoulder and carried me up the stairs to kiss me silly.

THIRTY-EIGHT

Thomas

I'd spent the last few weeks with my nose to the grindstone during what the world called working hours.

Each morning I drove from Natalie's house to my own, my stomach soothed by her food and my lips warmed with her kisses.

I was so damn happy, I was scared to death. I didn't dare admit it out loud, for fear fate would overhear and swoop in to steal more from me.

Each morning I was at my bank of monitors by eight, reading code, troubleshooting, consulting with the really early risers I had out on the west coast.

By noon we were conducting daily conference calls by video, reviewing changes and sharing screen shots, discussing options and generally just pushing *that much harder* to get the project done in time.

In the end, I was not the one to save the day, for the first time in as long as I could remember. Instead, it was a nineteen-year-old kid, a sophomore from Minnesota who'd won a full ride to Stanford on account of the biomedical project he completed during a high school internship with a large hospital system. In fact, I extended the promise of future employment to him the instant he joined the team.

I had been looking for a challenge for a while, and this project had the potential to launch my company into the Medical Informatics realm, a place where I felt I could do some serious good for once.

It was four days before Natalie and I left for California when we finally instituted the last fix and suddenly the app ran seamlessly with the main system.

Holy shit, we did it.

Thank God, because the launch was in a week and I'd been scared half to death we'd have to cancel it. I had a lot riding on this: a lot of time, a lot of money, and a lot of hope.

There was my team to think of, too. Every one of them was a student, with three professors who oversaw the project from a grading standpoint, and this project stood to make careers for the thirteen dedicated people who'd lost sleep over it with me.

I had already personally guaranteed each of them employment upon the completion of their degrees, if they so chose to come work for me. I expected Harrison to fight me on it, just because fighting was the only thing he did well, but getting around him wouldn't be all that hard.

That night I put Raven's litterbox and her bag of food in my truck and took her with me to Natalie's place.

The best part of my day, besides waking up with Natalie curled around me, was stepping through the door at night and pulling her into my arms while she stood in the kitchen.

I set Raven down as I stepped through the front door and she took off for the kitchen. I heard a tiny, hoarse meow and then Natalie cooed, "Aw, baby! Where'd you come from, sweet little girl? Did your daddy bring you home with him?"

Something in my chest flip-flopped when I heard that.

By the time I got to the kitchen, seconds behind Raven, Natalie had the little cat scooped up in her arms and cradled against her chest. She was rubbing the cat's ear with one hand, her head leaning close and Raven was obliging her with a rattling purr.

"I feel bad leaving her at home by herself every night," I explained, disappearing to tuck the litter box and the bag of cat food into the laundry room.

"She can stay here as long as she wants." Natalie was grinning down at her. "She's safer in the house anyway–no indoor-outdoor cat business for her here–and Gerry can keep an eye on her while we're gone."

She was *way* ahead of me.

She fidgeted most of the evening, wiping down the countertops again and again. She checked all the houseplants, the window locks, and I think she looked inside her packed bag at least nine times. It was exhausting to watch and when she got feisty with me, I scooped her up and carried her upstairs.

I protested that I needed a shower so I didn't stink her out of the bed and when I emerged from the bathroom, I found her stretched out on the bed with a book in her hands, the cat in her lap.

I shook my head in astonishment at how quickly Raven had taken to her. The cat would have clawed Lydia's eyes out rather than sit in her lap, but it was obvious she was willingly draped over Natalie, her small paws occasionally kneading the blanket.

Natalie looked up with a small smile, folding the book over her thumb. "I like this," she said softly, and I couldn't help but drift over to kiss her and scratch Raven's chin.

"Should I make the obviously dirty comment right now?" She grinned up at me as the cat rumbled happily.

"What?" I looked at her innocently, lifting the cat off her lap to set on my pillow, moving quickly to cover her body with mine. "Does it have something to do with neglect? Or are you telling me that you'll purr for me, too?"

"Oooh, both," she giggled, tossing her book on the nightstand and reaching a hand quickly between us. She was faster than me this time, flattening her palm against the erection I swore I'd maintained for months, and I jerked back quickly.

Her eyes filled immediately with hurt and I had to draw a deep, calming breath. "This is going to sound insane," I said quietly, "but you are my reward. A reward for hard work and suffering and self-denial that I can't have yet, not completely. I have to be sure every last piece is in place before I can do you justice. Before I can lose myself—and with you that will be *so easy*."

I tipped my forehead to hers and took a deep breath through my nose, my eyes drifting shut as I breathed in the smell of her warm skin.

I wanted nothing more than to lose myself in her.

To lean into her mouth and join my body with hers and forget every care and worry, every hurt and fear.

It scared me more than I could put into words, that I could trust her so much when I trusted no one.

"Your project," she whispered against my lips, and I nodded slowly without opening my eyes. It had consumed me for so long and she'd been such a welcome distraction from the frustrations of...everything.

"Lydia and Ahmad, too," she whispered then, and my eyes flew open. "Don't think I didn't know. I knew you were stepping things up with the lawyers. Just tell me it wasn't because I made you feel guilty."

I lowered myself down to my elbows, pinning her down to her pillow as I leaned into her neck. I found her jumping pulse and kissed the spot gently. "No," I whispered against her skin. "I just want you all to myself and I want to be able to give you the same. I don't want things hanging over us and what I can resolve quickly, I will."

She sighed gently against my shoulder and brought her arms up to wrap around me. "Then I hope we have some resolution by the time we get to California, because if you can resist the lingerie I bought, I'll know you aren't human."

I pushed myself back up and looked down at her with no little heat.

She bought lingerie.

She has plans.

There was a throbbing in my pants and I sucked in my breath when she reached between us again, running her palm down and back up, her eyes wicked. And I let her, my teeth set, my shoulders straining. Another minute and I would be shaking, her light caress felt so good.

"Stop teasing me," I finally begged, rolling quickly away and Raven jumped off my pillow before I collapsed into it, breathing hard.

"But I'm your reward," she giggled, leaning over me and pressing her breasts to my chest as she trailed tiny kisses down my neck, bunching my shirt as she went.

I wanted to give in. Every nerve ending was on fire and the painful throbbing in my pants warned me she was toeing the very last line. The one before I snapped and went all caveman on her.

She stopped suddenly, lifting herself up and leaning over me. "And you are *mine*," she whispered, kissing the skin just beneath my ear.

Something broke. I don't know what it was; it was something that wasn't supposed to happen. But I couldn't stop the tear that slipped out of my eye and ran down my cheek. One stupid damn tear. Where the fuck had that come from?

I tried to wipe it away quickly, before she saw it, but she was faster than me. She pinned my hand to the bed and leaned down to the bottom of the trail, kissing her way gently up the wet path until her lips pressed against my eyelid.

"I'll stop now," she whispered against my ear, her breath warm and wet. "Because you've asked me to, and I would do anything for you, because I love you."

That was it.

I crushed her to my chest so quickly, I heard the sharp exhalation of breath leaving her lungs.

She knew immediately what it was and she shoved her arms underneath me, holding me just as tightly as I held her, her face against my chest.

I just wanted to press her into me until she was me and I was her and there was no more separation.

No more loneliness or aching or sadness.

Just two souls joined in one body, complete and whole and safe.

We fell asleep that way, all the lights on, pressed together like we could fuse our bodies and spirits.

When I woke, hours later, to turn off the lights and cover her with a blanket before gathering her back into my arms, I found the cat curled up beside us, purring contentedly.

As usual, Raven was way ahead of me, too.

THIRTY-NINE

Natalie

I'd set up a full week of pre-scheduled posts before we left, along with a few extras, just in case the jet lag was really bad.

If I was being completely honest with myself, jet lag didn't figure into the picture at all. I pictured long nights filled with champagne and kissing, then ripping Thomas's clothes off his body with my teeth. That was the real plan.

I was thankful I'd chosen some smart outfits for my trip, with Daphne's help, and my white silk boatneck blouse and tailored grey pants were an accidental match to the look Thomas had going, with his grey dress pants and crisp white button-down. We looked like we were meeting for a business lunch rather than boarding a plane.

"I have meetings this evening," he explained when I raised an eyebrow as he came up behind me.

I slipped pearl drop earrings with thin gold French wires through my ears and he caught my wrist, kissing the inside before fastening a simple gold bracelet around it and shushing my protests as he tightened it with a small screwdriver.

"You can't!" I exclaimed, catching sight of the box on the counter. "This is too expensive, Thomas!"

He grinned lazily down at me as he set down the tool and slipped his hands into my hair at the sides of my face. "Not enough," he said firmly.

It made my eyes water and I tried to protest, but he shushed me with his mouth on mine.

It did cross my mind, only with a vague discomfort as he kissed me senseless, that it might be a sign of his possession.

• • • •

I'D NEVER FLOWN FIRST class before and Thomas had shaken his head at me in amusement when I tried to raise a fuss. I had to agree it made the trip infinitely more comfortable, and when we landed at LAX it was still early afternoon.

Thomas easily took my hand, leading me through the airport to a shuttle in order to pick up our rental car.

The attendant at the desk knew Thomas by name, which made my eyes narrow. Clearly he traveled for business a great deal, and obviously he always used this car rental company, but I didn't like the way she smiled and simpered and shoved her breasts toward him as she sped us through the rental process.

"You look like you want to bite someone," he whispered in my ear as the woman turned to fetch a key fob from a set of drawers behind her. I growled in response, my eyes narrowed dangerously, and I saw a hint of amusement cross his beautiful features. I knew he wasn't used to a woman acting territorial over him and it was obvious he liked it.

The sleek black AMG lit up when he clicked the fob and when my eyes swiveled quickly to him, he looked a little embarrassed. "It's the Stealth," he explained, like I had the first clue what that was. "I thought it might be fun to drive up the coast in style. My usual rentals are probably pretty boring. I don't get very...I guess the word is splashy."

I glanced at him out of the side of my eye as he put our bags in the back.

"I used to have one–a Stealth," he said casually as he opened my door for me and waited until I was in to close it.

Rounding the car to ease into the driver's seat, he felt me working hard not to ask the question, and he sat back in the seat for a moment, chewing on his lip. "I'm like most guys," he said finally. "I like cars. I had two houses in California, one in Vancouver, a condo in Miami Beach, a co-op in New York, and before Lydia got pregnant we were trying to buy a home in Italy. I had cars for each: In California, my houses had six-stall garages and I managed to fill every stall. But when Lydia left, I sold them all...everything."

Wasn't the Sonoma house his? The one he always referred to as being Maren's place?

"Were you afraid she'd turn your possessions into a court battle?" I asked, a nagging fear in my gut that Ahmad was about to do the very same.

He nodded shortly. "Yeah. After she and Harrison split she waged a pretty hard campaign to win me back, but she'd already done something I couldn't forgive." He paused for a moment, gripping the steering wheel hard, and I watched his Adam's apple bob as he swallowed. "That was the closest to hate I've ever felt for another person."

I didn't ask what it was he couldn't forgive, since I was pretty sure I already knew. Instead, I reached across the console to put my hand on his arm, tugging at it gently, and he let go of the steering wheel to let me kiss his knuckles.

"I think she's still waging that campaign," I said softly, and understanding flashed in his eyes.

"She's why you've been so nervous about this trip. Please, Natalie...you have to know she doesn't even come close to comparing to you."

I was surprised this was the first time the thought had occurred to him.

"She's gorgeous, Thomas. The reporters vomiting her praises don't care about her personality, her integrity or her intelligence. You are one of the most eligible bachelors out there, as far as most women–and the media–are concerned, even if you're not technically back on the market. Comparisons will be drawn between your beautiful, regal, commanding wife, and..." I looked around the car for a second before folding my hands in my lap. "You know...me."

He snorted sharply. "Lydia's been dragging her feet so long and hard, I'm not sure I'll ever regain *that* title. I'll age out of it before I'm free of her. But you..." He leaned over the console to kiss me long and hard. "If I'd known you were out there, I'd have been smart enough to wait so I could have chosen you instead. I'd have spent my whole life loving you, Natalie. I would have married *you* and made beautiful babies with you and come home to you every night." His eyes misted over a little. "But maybe I needed to experience all of that with the wrong person first, because without all of that I wouldn't have found you." He shuddered a little. "I had to be taught what I was missing."

I loved it when he let himself be that sweet and I sighed contentedly, kissing him so he couldn't see the happy tears that had gathered in my eyes.

He flipped the car into reverse and backed out of the parking space, punching the gas a little more than was necessary to propel us out of the lot, and I saw the boyish glee light up his face.

"Go on." I patted his thigh. "Open her up and have some fun."

• • • •

"LOOK AT THAT." HE POINTED through his window as we streaked up the coastal highway, where the sunlight glinted off the ocean. It shimmered and sparkled and I grinned at him when he turned to look at me. He wanted to share things with me, I knew: experiences; beautiful things.

"My meetings are in Santa Barbara, so we'll stop there for the night, but tomorrow we can head up to San Simeon to see the elephant seals and the estate if you'd like."

I wondered what else he had planned for me as we pulled into the Four Seasons Resort, and Thomas tossed his fob to the valet. He took my arm, smiling down at me as he hoisted our bags onto his other arm. "Are you sure the airline didn't forget some of your luggage?"

I let him lead the way to reception.

"You saw what I brought." I was surprised this was the first time it had occurred to him I was a light packer. "Aside from my dresses, all I really needed were a few workout outfits and some comfortable, respectable things. You know, the basics."

He looked confused. "What about pajamas?" he asked as the attendant wordlessly took his card and began clacking at the keys.

I shook my head slowly, an evil grin spreading across my face. "Nope, you're just going to have to wait and see."

The young man behind the counter blushed a violent shade of red and Thomas reached down to pinch my butt, well beyond the attendant's view.

His cheeks had flushed as well, his breathing faster and I wondered if he'd thought about what we'd be like together. He'd been so busy lately, I wasn't sure he'd had the time to fantasize, often kissing me goodnight and falling asleep seconds later. Maybe it had been for the best, I thought, because if he'd truly wanted to "save me for later," lying awake with insomnia only inches away from me would have definitely led to...things.

"There are things to do while you're stuck waiting on me," he said as he opened the door to a gracious bungalow. "There's a pool, a spa, a gym–you could walk across to the beach. The grounds are beautiful too, if you want to walk around." He paused like he was reconsidering something. "I thought about booking you a massage...but the only hands I want on you are mine. I don't intend to share."

He was still talking, while I was trying to ignore what this must have cost. I was dazed.

"What is it?" He had set down the bags and moved to shut the door behind me as I gaped at the space.

"It's...this is..." Words were not my strong suit at the moment. "Thomas, I would have been perfectly happy in a Best Western...a Super Eight...some little seaside mom-and-pop hotel somewhere. This is completely insane."

"I wanted you to be comfortable," he said, looking anything but comfortable himself. "And I wanted to do something a little nice, since you never ask for anything."

"I would never ask you for this. Not for anything. You've already done so much for me." I took a step closer and placed a hand over his heart as I smiled up at him. "*You* are the only thing I've wanted. Can I ask for that now?"

There was a strange look on his face, one I thought might be a little sad, or maybe hopeful. I couldn't quite tell.

"How are you real?" he whispered, crushing me against his chest and burying his face in my hair. He spoke into it, his voice rasping in a way that I knew meant he was tightly controlling an emotion. His words were muffled then, and I couldn't make them out, but he didn't repeat himself.

He was quiet then for a long moment, holding me tight. Then he cleared his throat. "Unless you prefer to go out for dinner, I'd like to have it brought in tonight. We can eat in the courtyard. I'm going to need you all to myself after this round of meetings." He shivered.

I knew in that instant what he wasn't telling me: Tonight's meetings weren't exactly business meetings.

"Okay," I agreed, pulling back just a little and lifting my hands to hold his face. I would never tire of just looking at him and I smoothed his dark eyebrows, then brought his face down to mine for a kiss. He lingered there, never deepening the connection, just letting our lips rest against one another's, as he held me close. He seemed to be drawing strength from my touch.

Finally, reluctantly, he pulled away. "I should get going." He glanced down at his watch. "I won't be far. If you need me, I have my phone."

"Go settle the score," I said softly, leaning up to him again and kissing him slowly, licking into the deep heat of his mouth with slow strokes until I felt his breathing change. Then I brought him back down, finally breaking the seal of our lips. "I'll be waiting for you when you get back." The words were loaded with promise.

"We can pick up where we left off?" He grinned, his eyes hopeful.

"Oh no, no, we're going to start *all* over," I teased, undoing the top button of his shirt and he leaned over to nip at my earlobe.

My heart was racing. I'd been dying for ages to do more than make out like teenagers every night.

"Before dinner?" He tried to sound horrified.

"After, too. Better have an energy drink and a protein bar at your meeting." I wiggled my eyebrows, which probably made me look insane.

He released me, the smile on his face genuine and sweet, even though he was shaking his head. He kept looking up at me, a smile stealing back across his face as he unzipped his bag and pulled out a jacket and tie.

My mouth went dry as I watched him deftly knot and straighten the tie, then slip into his jacket. He smoothed his hair, tucking it behind his ears, and I couldn't help but think that later I would unwrap him like the gift he was.

"Keep that on," I instructed, pointing to the jacket. "When you come back I'm taking it off with my teeth."

"Why, Ms. James," he teased as he moved toward the door. "If I'd known what suits did to you, I'd have worn one to shingle your roof."

I reached across the space to swat at him. "I'd have been up that ladder in a flash, waylaying you behind the chimney." I grinned and he chuckled, kissing me gently before closing the door.

The space was quiet when he left–expensively so. I moved through each of the rooms, appreciating the attention to detail and I pulled a small sketchbook from my bag to take down some design notations.

I had no idea how long his meetings would run, but as it had only just gone four, I drifted outdoors to walk around, losing myself in the lush gardens. The air was cool, only warm in the sunshine, and after a time I went back inside to run a hot bath in the impressive master suite.

What I shouldn't have done, but did anyway, was take my phone with me to the bathtub. There I scrolled through correspondences I needed to return, comments I needed to respond to, my calendar, and the analytics for the fitness watch I'd been wearing lately.

There was an email from Jeanine and I clicked on it nervously, reading quickly that Ahmad had been served and had recently filed a response.

As she'd expected, he accused me of withholding financial support and flatly stated that our marriage had disintegrated because I had taken a lover, who had estranged me from my husband's affections and as a result, estranged him from *our* money.

Liar.

It made me snort. It was nothing I hadn't expected, but I was seething with anger even as I tried to soak away stress in the deliciously scented bath, and I quickly composed a response. I was concise and brief, knowing she was charging me for her blocks of time.

Attaching the report compiled by the private investigator I'd hired, and the review completed by Thomas's lawyers, I sent the email with an angry growl. What Ahmad was trying to pull, I wasn't entirely certain, but if he wanted to fight dirty he was in for some real fun.

I had an army behind me, thanks to Thomas.

When there was a chime on my phone, I looked down to see a notification dinner had arrived, so I pulled myself from the bath and slipped into a cozy bathrobe, winding a towel around my hair as I walked through the rooms to open the front door.

Dinner *was* there, set up on the dining table in the courtyard with silver covers and small burners beneath, to keep things warm. There wasn't a soul in sight and I glanced around in amazement at the soft lights illuminating the private outdoor space, dusk just beginning to dim the sky.

If Thomas had been looking for a romantic environment, he'd certainly found it.

Suddenly, I felt woefully unprepared. The butterflies in my stomach kicked up a riot, battering their wings against my insides until I felt sick with anticipation. I'd been trying to keep myself from thinking of it all day, and failing miserably. The way he'd been touching me all day was something...more. Filled with his own anticipation.

Then he'd whisked me away to Eden, so his seduction game was already pretty on point. But I hadn't tried to seduce someone in...I couldn't even count back that far. Over fifteen years?

Digging through my bag, I pulled out the sheer black set with the red rosebuds. I was going to lead with my favorite, suddenly nervous he might not like what he saw.

Then I unzipped his bag and pulled out one of his dress shirts, fairly certain he wouldn't mind.

Smoothing on a thick lotion, some lip gloss and mascara, I dried my hair into a glossy sheet before slipping into the delicate set.

I chewed on my lip the entire time I dressed, spinning out scenarios in my head that left me breathless with want and terrified of my own need for him.

I fastened a few buttons on the shirt as I critically surveyed myself in the mirror, hoping the overall effect was pleasing.

I had no idea when to expect him back and I let myself out into the courtyard to sit in comfortable seclusion. It was entirely dark now, the space lit by low lights, a proliferation of tiny bulbs hidden throughout the area.

A glass of wine might help soothe my nerves, I decided, pouring some into one of the goblets and taking a careful sip.

Stretching my legs out to rest on one of the other chairs, I leaned my head back to gaze up at the network of lights in the overhanging trees and I let myself daydream, shutting out thoughts of deadlines, Ahmad, court dates, and that I needed to take the Subaru in for service.

Instead, I dreamed about his soft lips and strong hands, the beautiful muscles I knew I would uncover and the soft sounds of want he made in the back of his throat when we kissed.

Warm fingers curled around the back of my neck and my eyes flew open to find Thomas looking down at me, his hand slipping beneath the shirt to trace my collarbone."I could get used to this," he said, pulling the shirt aside to reveal a lacy strap.

There was a light in his eyes and I stood slowly, turning to face him and unbuttoning the rest of the shirt. His breath hitched hard when he took in the scraps of lace and immediately he cleared his throat, his eyes dilating with what I hoped was lust.

I watched his expression grow heated with zero shame. We'd been in close enough proximity for weeks, in barely controlled situations rubbing up against one another.

His fitted pants confirmed he was loaded for bear. As in, I might not be able to walk tomorrow, and I wanted to clap my hands and bounce like a fangirl, giddy with anticipation.

"I thought I might be able to help take your mind off things," I offered, and I watched the worry slip away, softening the lines in his forehead and pulling his mouth into a lazy smile. The expression was sweet, but I could see in his eyes that he'd been barely controlling himself for too long and it was in danger of slipping, so I pushed up on my toes to press soft kisses to his jaw.

There was no hurry, even though my heart hammered and the blood rushed in my ears and my body screamed at me to get the show on the road.

"What did I ever do without you?" he murmured into my hair as he swept an arm under my thighs and lifted me effortlessly to carry me into the bungalow.

"Let's not find out," I whispered back, giggling when I felt his heart beating violently against my shoulder.

Admirably, we made it all the way to the master bedroom, where I helped him out of his jacket and shirt before kissing my way down his chest.

He brought me back up, seeming uncertain for a brief moment and I let him pull me close and kissed him until both of us were panting for breath.

I looked up at him as I unclasped his belt buckle. There was insecurity all over his face and I shook my head at him slowly, smiling up.

He was so nervous.

He swallowed hard as I unzipped his pants and slid them from his hips, and the soft fabric of his boxer briefs strained to contain him as I kissed my way around the band slowly, waiting to feel his body soften in surrender.

When it didn't, I stood and snapped off the lights, the light from the tiny hanging lanterns outside the window casting a soft glow in the room. It provided just enough light to see him and I eased his shirt from my shoulders.

A rough sound came from his throat as he took in the sheer lace that barely covered me and he dropped to the bed to pull me into his lap, his lips and fingers trailing down my neck, touching me reverently.

When my fingers splayed across his chest again, he grabbed my wrist and placed a wet kiss in the center of my palm, then the inside of my wrist; the inside of my elbow; the curve of my neck.

I reached for both of his hands, bringing them up to cover my breasts and he happily ran fingertips over the tiny rosebuds that ran like Braille over the flimsy cups of the bra. Then he dipped his head, the tip of his tongue running up slowly until he closed his mouth over a tight nipple, sucking and licking at me through the lace that I suddenly wanted to shred.

Slipping down the straps, he peeled one cup down and closed his mouth over my bare skin and I was putty.

Here was the passionate lover I'd expected.

I sighed contentedly, waiting for him as he nipped and licked, moving at a leisurely pace, gauging my responses.

I leaned back just a little, teasing him by retreating and coaxing with sighs, waiting for the animal I knew he kept locked in a cage. He had reined in his emotions when he'd left the bungalow earlier and I wanted him to free them again; wanted to watch him lose control.

His mouth trailed up my neck to find my lips and his arm wrapped around me as he stroked my tongue with his own, a shuddering sigh escaping him as I ran a finger over his underwear, down his hard length.

"Natalie," he whispered against my mouth. "I want to make this good for you but I'm so out of practice." He tipped his forehead down to mine. "I'm going to need your help. Tell me what to do."

I tried to reach between us, to trail my hands down his abdomen, to wrap my fingers around the pulsing erection that was pressed against my belly.

"No," he hissed before I could brush him with my fingertips. "You first. That's just as much for me. I need to taste your skin; hear the sounds you make when I drive you crazy. I need *you*."

He lifted me quickly and spread me out on the bed, crawling over me and settling between my knees to kiss his way down my throat, across my clavicle, down my breasts and stomach, my hip and back up my inner thighs.

I might burst into flames.

He nipped gently at the skin of my right thigh and I squeaked, my thighs already quaking with need. Then he breathed gently against the lace of my underwear, his fingers lightly tracing the rosebuds that ran in a trail down the front panel.

"Natalie," he breathed gently, the flat of his tongue pressing against the lace as he licked me in a long, slow, upward motion and I just about shot off the bed. I made a sound that was almost despairing and he eased the underwear down gently, over my hips, down my legs, and I heard the soft plop when they hit the floor.

He was back between my thighs, pushing his shoulders up against them so that my body opened to him and when his mouth closed over me I shivered, reaching down to clutch at his shoulders while his hair tickled the softest parts of my body.

It was exquisite.

It was earth-shattering.

It was something Ahmad had refused to do.

His pace grew more urgent and when he gently slipped a finger inside me, his tongue stroking in time, I lost my mind.

The world spun as I moaned for him, clutching at his powerful shoulders and running my hands through his hair, already dangerously close to coming undone.

He tugged gently and my body stiffened as I shrieked something long and loud that might have been his name, but maybe not. And I swear I saw stars and rainbows, and maybe even angels, and I collapsed limply into the bed as he kissed the sensitive skin of my thighs.

"That was so much better than my fantasies," he whispered, and I could hear the desire, thick and aching, when he said it.

He kissed and teased until he heard me sigh, then his mouth was on me again, his fingers working deep inside to find some magical place I hadn't known existed, and I called for him with a low, drawn out wail as a second, even more intense orgasm slammed through me.

I could feel the slight tremors running through his body and I knew what they meant: the tension, the wait, the desire was almost too much for him to control any longer.

Summoning a deep breath and pulling myself out of a spectacular haze, I pulled him up the length of my body and pushed him gently onto his back.

I peeled his underwear from him and eased him into a sitting position on the bed, slipping over the edge so my knees were on the floor.

Holy hell, that might not fit...

He still seemed uncomfortable and I lowered my face into his inner thigh, nibbling my way up. It made him chuckle and I felt him relax just a little more.

"That tickles," he whispered, and he chuckled again when I moved my head, dragging soft strands across his skin.

He was breathing hard when my tongue darted out to lick up the underside. His entire body was tight with need–I could feel it–and when I lifted onto my knees to take him into my mouth a rough, pained sound burst from him.

I didn't let it stop me, taking him deep in slow glides, circling what I knew to be a sensitive spot each time I came back up.

I felt him shift, one arm going behind him to brace himself, the other hand fisted tightly in my hair. He was battling with himself and the need to let go, to churn his hips into me as I drew my cheeks in to create suction.

"*Natalie.*" His voice was rough and desperate and I rolled him gently in my palm as I worked him with my tongue, feeling him draw up hard, tight, coiled like a spring as I administered the sweetest kind of torture with my mouth.

He unwound his hand from my hair, his fingers reaching for mine as his other arm gave out and he fell onto the bed.

His grip was tight, almost punishing, and I squeezed back as I pushed up on my knees to keep him from slipping out of my mouth. I swirled my tongue again, feeling his breath catch, and I hollowed out my cheeks, pulling upward again with a firm suction that was rewarded with another deep groan from him.

He wasn't letting go and I couldn't understand it. I was *good* at this–very good, from what Ahmad had always said. This had been one of his favorite things to do–probably because he liked to see me on my knees.

I let him slowly slip from my lips, kissing my way up the delicious wall of his abdomen until I rested on his chest. "What am I doing wrong?" I whispered, looking up slowly.

He opened his arms and I crawled the rest of the way up his body to straddle him. It would take nothing to get me off, I thought, already shaking like a junkie as he reached between us.

I couldn't help but moan when his fingers found me and he positioned me carefully, his eyes lighting up as I lifted myself to ride him.

"This is what I needed," he whispered finally, fitting himself to me and watching my face as he lifted his hips. I whimpered and it made him groan, his hands lifting to my hips to help me as I worked to fit our bodies together.

He took his time, careful not to push me too hard as I took him, and my head lolled back at the feeling of him inside of me.

Finally.

He flattened me against him suddenly and rolled, completely changing the angle, withdrawing almost completely before sliding slowly back into me.

I could hardly control myself, wrapping my thighs tightly around his hips and raking him with my nails as I clawed toward what his body promised me.

He'd driven me out of my mind again in only seconds.

He was slow and purposeful, lifting himself until our bodies were nearly separated, then swiveling his hips as he drove back into me and it was enough to make me come unhinged. I moaned and pushed against him, swallowing the grunts that came from the back of his throat as he pushed into me, retreated, then drove back in with a deep groan.

"Thomas..." It left my lips on a breath and my body went rigid as I called out something completely incoherent.

I felt his body stiffen as I went over the edge, and he shivered as his muscles jerked. Then he collapsed onto his arms, bracing himself over me, his lips immediately on my forehead, in my hair.

"Baby," he whispered softly, kissing my neck as I blinked the stars from my vision. "Next time I'll go easier. I'll be better to you."

"You just made me come *three* times, Thomas. You really think you can do better?"

He chuckled and rolled to pull me into his arms, and I snuggled into him as he drew lazy circles on my back with his fingertips.

Waking to find him cleaning me gently with a warm cloth, I giggled. "I hope dinner's not burnt."

"It'll keep for a few more minutes," he said, tossing the cloth aside and leaning down to kiss me, one hand sliding up my thigh to hook my leg over his hip.

"I don't even care if it does," I moaned into his mouth when I felt him against my thigh, hot and hard. "Just don't stop."

• • • •

THERE WAS A PROBLEM.

It was late and the twinkling lights outside the master bedroom window had long gone out.

We'd finally risen and trailed out to the courtyard, both wrapped in hotel bathrobes.

We'd eaten a delicious dinner, talking and laughing and touching.

It was beautiful and peaceful, and I was sure there were fairies living in the beautiful old trees, smiling down on us, sprinkling us with their magical light.

We'd drifted back inside to shower and ready ourselves for bed, and Thomas worshiped my body with soft words and lips as we made love again in the big bed. It was slower, tender, filled with soft sighs and unhurried touches.

Then he fell asleep in my arms, his hair spread across my chest as I held him close and prayed for more moments that were just like this: quiet, peaceful, just the two of us hidden away from the world. I could feel him at peace, the expression on his sleeping face one of contentment.

I had told him I loved him, then I'd shown him with my mouth and hands and body.

The problem was that I wanted him again, even as he slept deeply, his chest rising and falling with rhythmic breaths. His arms were wrapped around me again and when I stirred they tightened, as if he needed our skin touching at all times.

I had fallen desperately in love with him, with no way to hold him. We were on his turf now, a place he was familiar and comfortable with, and if my mother's suspicion, voiced in her last text to me, was right, he had every intention of returning.

Possibly without me.

Probably without me.

Why would I even begin to think he'd want me with him when he moved back to the Golden State? Even if I wasn't his small-town secret, and he swore I wasn't, there was very little keeping him in Alabama and even less keeping him with me.

"It was what she used as a bargaining tool, every time she wanted something." His voice was low on my skin and it startled me. I didn't say anything, letting my fingers drift slowly up and down the smooth skin of his strong, wide back. "She kind of ruined it for me. It's hard for me to imagine you wanting to...put your mouth on me without some kind of...payment." He coughed a little.

Effing Lydia.

I wanted to find that bitch and claw her beautiful eyes out. She'd even managed to taint our first experience together.

"It's not payment for anything," I said quietly, unsure of how to soothe or convince him.

I wiggled a finger into his ribs until he chuckled.

"I did it because I wanted to. Because I want *you.* I wanted you to understand that I can't keep my hands–or my mouth–or really any other part–off of you. I want you *all* the time."

"I wish that could last," he sighed, his voice full of an emotion I couldn't understand.

"Why wouldn't it?" I asked, a weird ache blooming in my heart.

Maybe we had an expiration date.

"Is it so hard to believe you could be wanted and loved, or that I could be crazy over you?"

Wow, those words were hard to say, opening me wide to rejection.

"I'm sorry." He sighed heavily, rolling to the side to prop his head up on one hand. "It's just been a while...and, you know, some bad experiences. We didn't have sex like regular people, because we didn't even sleep in the same bed, and before long she stopped coming to my bed at all. She told me if I wanted sex, I'd have to be happy with the occasional blow job. It was always when it was convenient for her and always when she wanted something. It was a transaction." His voice trailed off and my heart clenched jealously when I thought of all the years he could have been mine.

"Yuck." My stomach turned. "That's slutty."

"I guess I made the unconscious association that if she needed payment for it, I must be revolting." He sighed again and I pressed my fingers to his chest, as if I could seal the cracks and breaks with my fingertips.

"If it makes you feel any better, I'm still kind of in shock that *you* did that...without complaining."

"Did what?" He raised up on one elbow and propped his hand to look at me in the near darkness.

"Um...you know." I squirmed uncomfortably. My mother's voice rang through my head: *Good girls do not talk about sex and you are a good girl, Natalie.*

Ahmad had been very controlling in bed and once we were married, there were rules. Talking was a distraction. I wasn't allowed to direct or to ask for what I wanted.

That Thomas would solicit my input, that he would be selfless, that he might want to talk about it, was all very new.

"Ahmad...he refused to...ah...tend to the lady garden. He said it was degrading and I couldn't expect him to lower himself to that station. He was being pretty literal." Shame flooded my cheeks with heat.

"Wait a minute." He sat up completely, twisting his body so that my shoulders were caged between his big hands. "You were married to him for almost fourteen years and he *never*?"

I shook my head slowly. "Not even while we were dating."

"Fuck that," he growled, lowering himself quickly to kiss me slow and deep. "You were made to be worshiped, Natalie. He was the luckiest man on the face of the earth and he couldn't be bothered with making sure you were happy?" He was incredulous. "Please tell me you were satisfied in other ways."

My whole face had turned red by now, though I doubted he could see it in the near-darkness of the room. "Sometimes, but I think it was usually by accident. I mean, I didn't complain, because maybe I didn't know enough to complain. I thought we were adventurous enough, and it was good sometimes..."

"By accident." His voice was low and angry. It was sweet that he was getting so bent out of shape over it when he'd been in a similar boat.

"I figured out how to handle things for myself when it was necessary." I squirmed, admitting what was an ugly truth.

"Baby, it will never be necessary again. I promise you that." And he lowered his lips to my neck to kiss his way back down my body, loving me with his mouth until the powerful waves of pleasure rolled through me again and tears leaked from my eyes. Then I pulled him close and wrapped my legs around him as he moved slowly with me.

He waited for me, measuring my breaths, adjusting his pace, and when I threw my head back against the pillows he buried his face in my neck, my name on his lips.

"I want this forever," he sighed into my neck, neither of us in any particular hurry to separate, and I let my fingertips flutter over his collarbone, his lips, his cheekbones, his eyes, finally sifting through his hair, and he hummed contentedly as I rubbed gentle fingertips into his scalp.

We rolled slowly, face to face, and I slid my knee between his.

He kissed me, winding our fingers together and pressing them to his chest.

When his breathing grew deep once again, and when I was sure he was fast asleep, I twisted so that his big body was wrapped around mine.

The softest breeze began to blow as I followed him into sleep, listening to the fairies whisper jealously in the trees just outside the bedroom window.

• • • •

WHEN THOMAS'S PHONE dinged, announcing breakfast had arrived, we straggled out into the early morning light to find dinner had been cleared away and fresh fruit, pancakes, berries, coffee and orange juice waited for us.

There was even champagne chilling in a bucket, should we care to turn the orange juice into mimosas.

"I don't know if I can handle that," I said with a churning stomach as Thomas popped the cork.

Even running on no sleep, he was the most beautiful thing I had ever seen.

"This gorgeous sex kitten I know likes to mix drinks for me in the morning. Calls them 'Hair of the Dog,'" he teased, his eyes crinkling a little as he poured a generous glug into a glass filled with orange juice and passed it to me.

"Gorgeous sex kitten?" I ran a hand through my wild hair. "You mean that mess the cat dragged in." I was giving him a look and I knew it, and he quickly poured some for himself before tapping his glass to mine.

"Yeah, a real handful in bed, that one. Thank God the cat dragged her in." His grin was stretching wider. "How often do you get everything you want, right?"

"Did you get everything you wanted?" I asked seriously, sipping carefully.

"Baby, I knew you were what I wanted that first day, when you brought me a beer." His expression was very serious despite his teasing tone.

"You were pissed that I tried to force alcohol on you." I gestured toward the drink in his hand. "Clearly I am a bad influence. *And,* according to you, my tits were out.'" I rolled my eyes at him and he started dishing food onto my plate.

"You know I had to come back after that," he said innocently, setting down a lid to run one hand up my thigh and under the loose cover-up I'd thrown on. "If I'd had any idea then..."

I watched a shiver ripple through him, but he didn't finish his sentence. I hated his half-spoken thoughts, because they made my mind run rampant, but I knew asking him to elaborate was fruitless.

We ate a full breakfast and I tanked up on coffee, realizing the jet lag I was feeling was due to the fact it was five in the morning at home and if our bodies were still on that clock, we'd been up until two.

"You can catch a little more sleep in the car," he said gently, trailing his thumb down my jaw, and I was surprised by the tenderness in his expression. The grumpy, closed off man who'd frustrated me for months was vanishing before my eyes, being replaced by someone who was tender and caring.

This made him even easier to love, I thought with a pang of discomfort. When he left I would be heartbroken, and I swallowed past the lump in my throat as I tried to push the terrible thought away.

I nodded, pushing up from my chair and moving toward the bungalow.

"Natalie, thank you."

I stopped in my tracks, turning to face him.

"This." He pointed an index finger toward the trees, and I thought his expression was soft and sweet. "Every moment of this, with you, has been beautiful. I feel like I can escape everything when I'm with you, because you'll...keep me safe." He rested his other hand over his heart, but I wasn't sure he knew he did it.

I swallowed hard.

It wasn't a normal thing to say to someone.

"I'd like to make a lot more of these memories," I croaked.

He nodded slowly, opening his arms to me and I hurried back to him, to be wrapped up in the place I felt safe and cherished.

Nothing could touch me here.

Not Lydia.

Not Ahmad.

I sighed, breathing in the scent of his warm skin, and I told myself that if all I had was now, it had to be enough.

FORTY

Thomas

Driving the AMG wasn't exactly a hateful chore, and though I was tired, I enjoyed my time behind the wheel of a car I'd missed. Of course, there was something else I'd much rather do, but at some point we did have to put on clothes–which was a shame because Natalie, completely naked, was glorious.

She slept fitfully beside me, her hair dropping forward to cover part of her face. She was so fucking beautiful, I could hardly stand the moments I couldn't have my hands on her. So I drove with one hand, streaking along familiar roadways as I kept the other hand on her leg. I needed to be touching her in some small way all the time. She was a lifeline; a reassurance; warm and comforting and *mine*, never questioning my neediness.

Every time my fingers sought her in some small way, the corners of her lips turned up and she'd lean over to kiss my cheek or bring my palm to her lips, then place it over her heart.

I loved everything about this: I was allowed to touch her. She didn't flinch or shut down or resign herself to my caresses, and I needed to touch her *a lot*. She was *with* me, her beautiful blue eyes always fastened on my own, telling me the things neither of us could put into words. It made my heart want to slam out of my chest with joy and gratitude, because I hadn't known contentment like this existed.

When she woke, the windows were open and the sound of the surf and angry grunts rolled into the car. She blinked slowly, the bright daylight throwing a halo around her golden head and I couldn't help the smile that stretched across my face when she leaned back into her seat and stretched like a cat.

"Babe," she whispered softly, a smile on her lips as well.

That was me!

"How long have we been here? Did I really make you drive all that way by yourself? I meant to stay awake and keep you entertained with some witty conversation."

Yawn.

I leaned over the console, her expression soft and sweet as I pressed a kiss to her warm lips. "You needed the sleep, and now we're here. Besides," I wiggled my eyebrows at her, "you need to rest up for tonight."

I knew that made me an animal, but I couldn't get enough of her, and from what she'd shown me in the past day, she couldn't get enough of me either. It was exhilarating.

She rolled her eyes at me, but not before I saw the joy in them. "You must be exhausted."

"The best kind of exhausted." I reached for her hand, kissing it before leaning deeper into my seat.

I was used to jet lag.

I was used to whirlwind trips and short turnarounds, days spent traveling and nights spent working.

I could handle a few days running on adrenaline and caffeine fumes.

It took her a minute, but eventually she forced herself from the car and rounded it to pull me from the seat. I let her, rising and stretching my arms over my head. It pulled my shirt up and I heard "Oh my gawd," somewhere nearby. It made me instantly uncomfortable.

Had I been recognized?

Three teenage girls drifted past, their eyes wide, and I watched something happen to Natalie.

The only word I could think of was *feral.*

She leaned up to kiss me, fisting her hand in my hair and pulling me down to her. It was hot and possessive and a little rough, and I really liked it. I leaned gratefully into her lips, hearing a disappointed whimper from the group just as my arms circled her waist.

I'd felt a tiny tremor run through her the night before, one I'd hoped was jealousy, when I'd spoken of my wife.

Realistically, I'd told her very little about Lydia. She knew a few details, but I hadn't thought it the time or the place to explain the true depths of loneliness that had pervaded my marriage.

How unwanted I had been for years.

Yet the attention of any other woman had been unwelcome and suspect, and without me voicing it, Natalie seemed to understand.

"Gross." One of the girls made a gagging noise as she ambled past on her baby giraffe legs. "Get a room."

It made me smile against Natalie's lips and I pulled her tighter.

"I like you jealous," I finally whispered against her mouth, and I looked down to see an evil grin.

"How do you know I'm jealous? Maybe I just wanted to kiss you, just then. I waited for so long that now I can't get enough."

"Mmm." I felt my lips curving against her neck as I pressed her against me. "As long as you're kissing me, I'm not complaining. I'll take more, please, whenever you feel the need, because I'll *never* get enough."

We drifted to the fence and she leaned into me, the backdrop of surf and elephant seal grunts an unusual combination. I could feel the steady beat of my heart against her back and I rested my cheek on the top of her head. I couldn't say I knew what these moments were, but they quieted the deep need in my heart and I drank them in, praying she would never let go.

I was hyper-aware of our surroundings, of her touch, of the sun warming us. There was something in my brain working overtime to steal my happiness. It cataloged every precious moment and told me not to believe it, fearful she would come to her senses.

We stopped at the overlook and I pulled her into my side as we watched males battle for dominance between long breaks for rest. We stood there for a long time, watching one after another heave his girth out of the water and inch up the beach, stopping to rest every few feet with an irritated grunt. I laughed each time one of them collapsed onto the sand as if he couldn't go on.

"It's coming up on mating season," I whispered into her ear. "These guys are staking a claim."

"*I'm* staking a claim," she grumbled with a slow smile, curling her fingers into my chest, and I placed my hand over hers, holding it to my heart as we watched the vicious smack of one five-thousand-pound behemoth into another.

"You make me happy, Natalie. It's completely terrifying."

The words came out of nowhere and she froze, I felt it. She lifted her face slowly, and I knew my eyes were all shiny.

She looked completely freaked out, which caused a fist to squeeze my heart. This was everything I wanted, and everything I feared losing now that I'd found it.

She had no response, wrapping her arms around my chest and squeezing like a baby boa constrictor and I could feel something hot and wet soaking through my shirt as I breathed a prayer: *Let me be enough. Let me make her happy.*

FORTY-ONE

Natalie

It was amazing what billions, a recognizable name, and a known heart for charitable donations could do.

Thomas's arrival at the gate of the Hearst Estate was met with instant access and he parked the car in a private lot, leading me quickly up the mansion steps as I gaped in awe.

He planned this.

"A design professional can't be here and not see this," he said gently, noting that I was reeling as I took in the palm trees, the incredible gardens, the landscape rolling down toward the sea.

"I've always wanted to see it." My voice was tight with excitement. There was no way he could know how much this meant to me.

Ahmad and I, as a rule, had not taken vacations due to being something he considered an unnecessary expense. In fact, we'd barely taken a honeymoon. There were so many places I wanted to go and things I wanted to see and I'd nearly resigned myself to the fact that the clock was ticking down.

"Good morning!" There was a bright greeting over my left shoulder and I turned quickly to find an eager, smiling young woman extending her hand. "My name is Edith and I'll be your guide for the private tour."

Private. Freaking. Tour. Squee!

I looked up my shoulder at Thomas, who glanced down at me as if this were completely normal, his lips quickly touching my temple before he extended his hand to Edith. "Thomas," he said confidently. "And this is my sweet Natalie."

I choked and tried to disguise it as a cough. I'd never been introduced in such a way to anyone.

Does this mean I'm his girlfriend?

If Edith thought it was a funny way to introduce someone, she had the grace not to admit it, and Thomas folded me into him as Edith led us from one glorious, gracious space to the next.

It was early afternoon when we stumbled down the steps, into the Roman pool, and my eyes lit up. "Holy crap," I breathed as I took in the blue-tiled opulence. "This is incredible." Next to the library, I had already decided this was my favorite space on the property. I'd loved the artwork, the incredible craftsmanship, the glazed tiles, the collections of which I'd never seen the like, and would never again. But this...all azure blue tile and gold...my heart stopped.

"The lady apparently appreciates ostentatious design," Thomas chuckled, and Edith smiled benignly, spouting facts I knew I'd never remember because the warmth of Thomas's nearness was overriding any of the circuits in my brain typically associated with memory.

"You didn't have to do this," I protested as he tucked me gently back into the car and he beamed down at me, probably relieved I'd finally stopped asking questions.

We'd spent hours in the mansion and he'd patiently waited as I gaped and oohed and aahed, asking an absolute multitude of questions that Edith patiently answered. She was shockingly knowledgeable and she was thrilled I was so interested. And yes, we totally exchanged contact information, because I couldn't wait to pick her brain some more.

"I wanted to do this because I knew you'd love it. I want to show you beautiful things."

"Mr. Atholton," I teased, reaching out the window to snag his shirtsleeve as he began to move around the car. "Are you afraid I'll leave you if you don't entertain me? Lavish me with expensive gifts and trips and exotic experiences?"

He froze instantaneously, panic flashing across his face.

That was exactly it.

I threw off my seatbelt and shoved the door open, springing out and wrapping my arms immediately around the solid wall of his chest.

Sometimes he was such a lost little boy.

"Thomas." I pressed my lips into the soft cotton of his shirt. "You are enough. *Just you.* I don't need entertainment or fancy trips or expensive hotels or flashy cars or *things*. You are already *everything* I want: That sad, angry man who apologized to me for a dropped pie.

"The one who needed me to drive him home because he knew he could trust me. *You*. I want the good and the bad."

I wondered immediately if I could ever really get through to him.

He shivered and I wrapped my arms tighter.

"You are all I want," I repeated. "All that I need and everything I've spent dark nights begging God to send. I will never ask for more because you are already *more*."

I felt him crumple into me, crushing me against the side of the car, the cadence of his breaths alarming.

"I'm not her," slipped from my lips without me realizing the words had left me. "I love you, Thomas. I've known I loved you since that day I dropped that stupid pie on the walkway. And I'm sorry you don't trust me yet, but I will *never* do the things she did. I don't love you for what you can give me or do for me." I kissed his chest again. "I just want *you*. Please believe me when I say it. Tell me what I can do to prove it."

The parking lot was filled nearly to capacity, and people drifted quietly by as Thomas's shoulders heaved silently. He held me in a deathly tight grip, his face buried in my hair. It hurt, but not as much as my heart hurt as I held him close.

I wasn't the only person struggling with being enough.

• • • •

HIS GRIP ON THE WHEEL was sure as we pulled into the St. Regis in San Francisco, and he tossed the fob to the valet again as he helped me from the car.

"The benefit starts at eight," he whispered in my ear as we approached the reception desk, and I noticed a woman waiting quietly beside the counter. "Go on...Daphne helped me book all kinds of fun stuff for you. When you're done, someone will bring you up to the room. Hair and makeup will be waiting."

"Who are you?" I asked dazedly, letting him relinquish me to the woman waiting at the counter.

He grinned at me as I let her lead me away, and I spent the next several hours in a daze of bliss–no lie, I think I fell asleep for most of it.

I decided that was for the best, as I had plans for him later and maybe, I thought sleepily, that was why he'd booked me the mini reprieve.

The masseur woke me with an espresso, a particularly strong one, and encouraged me to hurry, as it was almost seven.

I stumbled into the room to find two strangers waiting, smiles on their faces.

How the hell had he arranged all of this?

"Bellisima Natalie," the man intoned graciously and I took his proffered fingertips before rushing to the closet, only to realize my dresses had already been hung and pressed.

"Raul," the man intoned graciously as I moved toward the chair set up near the bathroom, and he inclined his head toward the woman. "Petra is makeup and I am hair."

The two of them had me put together quickly, and I glanced around in a daze as they packed their gear and moved quickly from the room. Raul kissed his fingers, his eyes crinkling slightly as he and Petra closed the door behind them, and I hurried toward the closet to pour myself into the lovely underpinnings Daphne had recommended, then the silver dress.

"I want to see all of that in reverse at the end of the night."

Thomas was standing just inside the doorway, his tongue sweeping over his lower lip and he caught his lip between his teeth with a suggestive raise of his eyebrows.

He looked completely edible in his sharp tux.

How long had he been there?

His hair was slicked back and his posture relaxed and easy as he leaned casually against the wall, waiting for me to finish.

"Zip me up?" I asked, and he moved toward me with the grace of a panther. It made a little thrill run through me, watching how his eyes heated. If I could do this to him *getting dressed*, what could I do to him later when I slowly undressed?

He slipped a hand into the back of my dress, to brush the bottom of my spine with soft fingertips and he leaned into me, one hand on each of my hips as he bent down to kiss the nape of my neck.

I was instantly on fire. "Maybe," I suggested, "we could just stay in and you can see all of that in reverse right now."

He smiled lazily against my neck, his tongue slipping out to taste my skin. "As tempting a proposition as I find that, this really is something important. I've been asked to speak this evening, so I should probably show up. But when we can escape, you'd better believe I'm taking you up on your offer–possibly in the car, if you're game."

Thomas stroked my back absently like one would pet a cat, the dip of the dress ending dangerously close to my backside.

"I'm going to be the envy of every man there. You look like an angel. The one *I* get to take home." He wiggled his eyebrows, and it was easy to see his thoughts were sinful.

It filled me with warmth when he said it. For years I'd attended events with Ahmad as his plus-one, but compliments had been rare and only when he was in a good mood or I'd done something he found particularly pleasing, which was almost never. For years my goal had been to outdo myself, to really wow him, and more often than not I was disappointed by his lack of response.

Why had I tried so hard for someone who couldn't give two shits?

We had been a steady fixture in the local society pages: the tall, handsome lawyer and his in-demand designer wife. There were dozens of pictures of us, smiling as brightly as it could be conveyed in black-and-white, but in every last photo taken the past few years our smiles were entirely fake.

"One more thing," Thomas said quietly as I grabbed the beaded clutch I'd pre-packed. He took my left wrist, the one with the gold bracelet, pressing a soft kiss to my pulse point before sliding the tiny screwdriver from his pocket. "This is perfect for everyday, but tonight is special."

I felt my eyebrows draw together as he loosened the tiny screws and crossed the room to slip the bracelet into my makeup bag.

"Daphne was good enough to consult with me on a number of things," he explained, bringing a black velvet case from behind his back. He pulled the top back gently and my expression went from confused to stupid.

"What have you done?" My hand was already over my mouth. The two French gold wire cuffs were exquisite, the delicate wire woven through tiny freshwater pearls.

"To match your earrings," he said gently, and I wondered if the delicate wires with singular pearls were a mistake.

I should have chosen diamonds. Lydia would have. She wouldn't have gotten any of this wrong.

"I'm going to embarrass you." My face twisted and I fought it hard. I'd never worn such expensive mascara in my life. "I'm going to get something wrong. I'm wearing the wrong things and I'm short and I'm going to look fat in all the pictures and...she wouldn't have gotten any of this wrong. I'm not going to be good enough for you!" I looked up in a panic, terrified. It had all just come running out of my mouth.

Shit. Smooth, Natalie.

He wasn't at all ruffled. He smiled down at me, slipping a cuff over each wrist and brushing my collarbone with his knuckle, then running his thumb under my jaw.

"You are perfect," he breathed. "Every one of them will know that *I* am taking you home and I will be cursed under every breath.

"Every curve, every inch, every sigh..." His eyes glazed over for a second. "Natalie, you are *mine*."

I melted as he leaned down to brush my lips, because who wouldn't? When he wanted to, this guy really could say the right things. He wasn't half bad with words when he actually used them.

Thomas handed me carefully into the black Town Car before rounding it to take his seat next to me. The driver stood uselessly by, waiting to open and close doors, but Thomas didn't give him a chance.

"How very low profile of you, Mr. Atholton," I giggled into his ear as he fastened his seatbelt and without him telling me, I knew the nondescript car would blend into a sea of others: exactly what he wanted. He seemed uncomfortable calling attention to himself despite the fact he seemed to like calling attention to me.

The thought niggled uncomfortably again that perhaps I was a possession.

The driver eased the car into traffic and I reached for Thomas's hand, feeling the tension his body telegraphed even before our fingers linked.

Pulling his hand toward me, I rested it over my heart. "Right here, baby," I murmured even as he stared out the window. "I will be your safe place. Look for me when you need me, because you don't have to do this all on your own."

He turned briefly, his eyes catching mine. He didn't say anything, but I felt his hand squeeze mine a little tighter and he leaned over to kiss my temple.

"Thomas." My voice was low as the car pulled into the lineup dropping us at the Diablo Country Club. I summoned all my courage before drawing his hand toward my mouth, kissing the back. "You are an incredible man. Your little boy loved you so much..."

I couldn't finish, my throat congesting immediately as I thought of Aden and his sweet little face: the child I would never have and the one Thomas could no longer have.

"Natalie..." His voice was gentle as the car slowed, parked and the driver exited to open our doors. "Stay close, baby. I'll need your strength to hold me up."

• • • •

PEOPLE WERE SWIRLING as we entered the space, some on the dance floor and some socializing, and I knew my eyes were wide. To me this was all new and slightly terrifying. I was used to big cities and big crowds, but they were not in the obscenely moneyed circles Thomas was used to moving through.

These people had Monopoly-level money.

Stupid money.

Swim-in-the-money-bin money.

"Atholton!" A voice boomed and I flinched. These people were going to take him away from me, if they hadn't already.

Thomas was absorbed into a crowd almost as quickly as we arrived and though his fingers were twined through my own, we lost contact quickly. His adoring public clawed and ripped at him, the women grasping at him with their talons while the men clapped him on the back and pawed at him.

I watched as he was passed from one person to the next: worshiping, fawning, cooing over him with a fervor I was fairly certain was disingenuous. I could see it on his face: he didn't believe their adoration either, his eyes constantly flicking back to me to gauge my nearness.

Then something like panic flashed across his face and I felt a wave of chills rush across my skin. My body registered an evil presence even before my eyes could complete a scan of the room.

"I'm impressed." The deep, rich voice was so close to my ear that it tickled and I turned slowly, taking the time to put distance between our bodies so I wouldn't smack into him, because I needed that distance.

I was being hunted.

"Where has he been hiding you?"

Warm fingers curled intimately around my hip, biting into my skin.

The man's face was severely handsome, all sharply sculpted cheekbones and full lips, his eyes the clear blue of the Aegean. His blond hair was thick and streaked with a white gold I knew meant he enjoyed outdoor pursuits, unless perhaps he was just pursuing a really accomplished colorist. (That seemed equally likely.)

I knew I was staring, my brain firing rapidly, but none of the communications seemed to reach any of my muscles as he reached for my hand. He wrapped it into his own free hand, bringing the back to his lips with a wolfish grin.

It was when his lips touched my skin that my nerve endings successfully fired the message off to my brain and I jerked my hand back from him like I'd been burned.

My hip hurt. I was going to have bruises from the violent squeeze of his fingers.

"Harrison."

His smile grew wider. "You have me at a disadvantage, beautiful: You know my name, but I don't know yours."

"I'm forming the impression you're rarely at a disadvantage," I shot back, realizing I was rubbing the back of my hand like I could erase what had happened, and I hoped desperately Thomas hadn't seen his lips touch my skin.

"Surely he knew better than to leave you unattended." His mouth curved with amusement. "Such a lovely woman–these jackals will feast on you if you don't know how to handle them, and you, my dear, are clearly uninitiated."

"They'll feast on me anyway," I answered with far more bravado than I felt.

You're the biggest jackal here, anyway.

"I'm fresh meat in what's a well-established circle. Don't think I haven't been preparing myself for the frenzy."

There was the sound of a shutter dropping nearby and I knew it was a photo of Harrison and me, something to be splashed around the next morning.

He'd certainly know my name by then.

His expression changed almost imperceptibly and I turned to see Lydia, resplendent in a deep green gown, attaching herself to Thomas's arm. He jerked away from her quickly and though I knew he tried to control the angry gesture, it was written all over his face: disgust, irritation, revulsion.

"They're quite the pair, aren't they?" Harrison looked amused, scooping two glasses of champagne off a tray that was floating past, handing one to me.

"They *were* quite the pair," I corrected, taking a fortifying chug.

"Hmm." It wasn't a sound I could interpret as agreement or disagreement. "Well, Lydia always gets what she wants."

"Not this time, she doesn't." It came out brittle, and though he lifted his glass to his lips, I saw the wicked little smile before he could hide it.

"I do believe you'll keep our boy thoroughly entertained in the interim," he said, and my eyebrows shot up.

There would be no interim, thank you very much.

The last thing I would allow was for Lydia to break him down and sink her claws in again. He was still so fragile that, if I was honest with myself, I wondered if he could withstand her perseverance. It didn't have to mean he wanted her, but that she was familiar. The history they shared was long and complicated and she would use every tool she had to wind the line that dragged him back to her. She'd been managing that for three decades already.

"I'm not that easily influenced." I worked hard to smile, handing my empty glass to him. I had a tendency to chug when I was nervous. "Don't think I don't know what you're trying to do."

I thought of Thomas's wedding band, still sitting on the windowsill in my kitchen.

He accepted my glass graciously and inclined his head as if I should continue.

"If you'll excuse me," I dipped my head politely, "it appears I need to rescue Thomas from two predators this evening. As for Lydia, it appears she finally realized which one was the alpha male." My eyes hardened and he wasn't so obtuse as to miss my meaning. He returned my nod, lips thinning just slightly.

Lydia had snagged two glasses of champagne and was trying to force one on Thomas as I covered the distance between us.

I'd thought my absence would leave him to network, to move easily through the crowd unencumbered by an extra introduction or explanation, but instead the hawk had swooped in on her prey.

Slipping between them, I tucked into Thomas's side and took the proffered glass from her hand.

"Lydia." My voice was hardly warm and welcoming. "How lovely to finally meet you."

I hoped it was clear I'd rather have a cervical biopsy without local anesthesia.

Her face went momentarily blank and I watched her cold blue eyes process the new information as they moved quickly from my face, down my body, then back up.

She stood a little straighter, her posture haughty.

I felt Thomas relax against me and I wondered how many times she'd ambushed him in the past, knowing he would be alone and largely defenseless in a room filled with people. He had seen to it that the acrimony stayed out of the papers, and while cameras clicked she could run her hands all over him because, scandal aside, she *was* technically still his wife.

The thought made me shudder.

"Lydia." Thomas's voice was calm and confident and she grimaced as his hand settled with familiarity, low on my waist. I tried not to flinch, my hip sore from Harrison's fingers. "This is my sweet Natalie."

He couldn't keep the feeling out of his voice; I heard the way his tongue curved around my name, like an intimate caress.

"Thomas!" She slapped his chest with an open palm, and without meaning to, I bared my teeth. "You didn't have to hire a date when you could have asked me!" Her smile was acidic when she turned it to me.

"I wanted someone with personality, warmth and class." His voice was low, the barb taking her by surprise. "This beautiful woman is everything I thought I didn't deserve." He looked down at me adoringly and my heart stuttered in my chest. I was eating up the public declarations of his affection.

"Don't tell me you haven't noticed." His voice was teasing. "The photographers can't get enough of her; I think you've finally been bested."

"I'm astonished!" Lydia's voice was loud and brittle, drawing the attention of several people. "He's never even mentioned you! Natalie, right?"

"I've heard plenty about you, but I wouldn't expect him to discuss his private life with his ex-wife," I responded, taking a careful sip of my champagne while I let her unpack that sentence.

"Wife," she jumped in quickly, the look on her face one of triumph.

"Perhaps in a legal sense, but only because you're not very good at taking a hint." I gave her the same treatment, slowly and pointedly looking her over from head to foot and back again as I raised Thomas's ringless hand to my lips, making sure she saw his bare finger. "It's not for much longer, anyway. The courts have to be getting tired of you by now."

If looks could kill, I'd have been incinerated, cremated on the spot, as Lydia's bright eyes burned like lasers. I didn't doubt she'd have thrown her champagne in my face had the room been less crowded, but this was a charitable event and chances were good she was the publicist for someone here.

My eyes scanned the room, searching for familiar faces. There were actors, singers, dancers, well-known authors...and then I spotted him: Kyle Andrews, the man with the face that had launched an empire of action movies. He was only twenty-eight, but he carried himself with assurance. He had the build of a linebacker and the grace of a ballerina, which was unsettling, but the camera ate it up.

Lydia's eyes followed mine and I *knew* the instant her eyes rested on the man's sculpted chest.

"How long have you been swimming in the kiddie pool?" I asked, and Thomas choked beside me. I handed him my champagne for a sip, and Lydia's face paled as I gestured swiftly toward Kyle.

She huffed audibly. "I have professional integrity," she snapped, and I chuckled.

"That's a fancy way of avoiding a denial. But good for you, because it doesn't seem like you have a great deal of *personal* integrity. Something had to win out, and it may as well have been a paycheck."

Thomas was looking down at me with a surprised expression and I knew it was because I wasn't ever mean.

"Thomas!" Lydia's voice was whiny. "Why are you letting her talk to me like this?" Then she leaned closer, so close I could smell the champagne on her breath. "He'll get tired of you and whatever magic you think you have between those stubby little legs of yours. He'll come back to me when he's done with you."

"Not a chance in hell," Thomas muttered, his voice low, but not so low she couldn't hear it. "I'd cut off my dick first–not that you've ever actually wanted it."

I couldn't help the snort that rocketed out of my sinuses and erupted like an enormous fart, startling Kyle himself, who was at least twenty feet away. His head swiveled toward us and I watched a grin creep across his face. "Babe!" he exclaimed, extricating himself from the crowd that had gathered around him.

It was enough for me, and I smiled victoriously at Lydia as Thomas's movements indicated he was done. "Goodnight, Lydia," he said firmly, biting off the end of her name like it tasted bad, and we melted into the throng of people just as Kyle reached Lydia's side, his giant paw going around her waist.

Integrity, indeed.

"Publicist, my ass," I snarked as I watched Kyle envelope Lydia like a lymphocyte. "How dirty is it that she's ok with sloppy seconds, saying she'll pick you up after me? Eew."

Thomas didn't respond and he was tense; I could feel it in the way his fingers were digging into my already aching hip, and I wiggled a little, trying to get him to loosen his grip. His fingers were pressing into the bruises I knew Harrison had left.

"Ow," I finally said softly, and he let go, his eyes scanning the room as he patted me absently.

"I need to go talk to the director," he said, and I wondered if he'd been searching the room for her. "I'm giving the first talk, during dinner, and it should run about fifteen minutes. I think you'll be able to manage without me for that long." He made a meowing sound and grinned before pulling me close, kissing me possessively before he moved across the room.

I watched the fine view for as long as I could.

There was a soft gong sound and a general movement toward the dining area, so I followed along, somewhat less sure of myself, my eyes flicking over one seating card after another.

Others swept past me, doing much of the same, and when I found the cards for Thomas and myself, quite near the front, Harrison was leering at me from across the table.

What kind of idiot would seat Thomas and Harrison at the same table?

Just maybe he'd switched his place card when no one was looking.

"We meet again." He lifted his champagne glass in my direction, and my eyes darted away as I looked around frantically for Thomas.

"I'd say I'm sorry you're stuck with me, but I'm never disappointed to be stuck with a beautiful woman."

The jackal was back: the one I'd tried to put in his place only twenty minutes earlier.

He lifted a finger and a waiter bustled over to refill his glass, rounding the table quickly to fill all the glasses as people began to take their seats.

What was that now, his fifth glass? Sixth?

As people settled and began to sip their drinks, the room filled with the pleasant hum of small talk and Harrison rose from his seat to carefully round the table. He was sure on his feet and of his social standing, clapping one man's back as he passed, and I realized with a sickening feeling in the pit of my stomach that he was headed back in my direction.

He wouldn't.

He wouldn't be so bold.

Not again.

He dropped easily into Thomas's seat, a wide smile stretching across his handsome face. "You're even lovelier up close," he oozed, and I wondered if the man had goldfish brain. Had he already forgotten my very pointed insult? "I can see why Thomas is so taken with you."

"Can you?" I asked archly, my face hot as my temper flared. "I didn't realize that part was showing."

He laughed easily, and I reached for my ice water. "I like a woman with a bit of spirit. I'll bet the old boy doesn't know what to do with you."

I set my glass back down firmly and turned my upper body entirely toward the man sitting way too close to me. "The old boy knows *exactly* what to do with me," I whispered, so as not to shock the elderly gentleman to Harrison's left. "And he can do it for *hours*."

Harrison coughed, choking on a sip of his champagne, and he covered his surprise with a smooth laugh. "Yes, I can imagine you would be quite demanding."

"Too much for you, I can assure you of that." My nostrils flared as I delivered my barb and I turned back toward my place setting, feeling Thomas's eyes on me suddenly. He was seated on the platform, waiting to be introduced, his implaccable mask in place. But I knew he'd seen Harrison and he'd witnessed our exchange, though I doubted he'd heard it.

Beneath that smooth expression and his glittering dark eyes, fury was boiling.

When Harrison turned to his left to engage a woman in polite banter, I pretended to drop my napkin and as I reached down, scooted my chair with my butt, several inches to my right, and when I popped up, Thomas looked amused.

The director of the foundation introduced Thomas with praise and adoration, pointing out that Mr. Atholton was a generous donor. In addition, she reminded everyone, Thomas had been personally touched by Down syndrome. He had known the hardships and the challenges, and the room fell completely silent as the unspoken information traveled in covert looks, with lightning speed from one table to the next: *You remember that terrible story, the one where his kid was killed in a crash?*

That Lydia could show her face was astonishing to me, and Harrison leaned over to murmur in my ear: "Has he told you how he covered it up for her? Had the records sealed."

My expression must have been horrified, because his terrible smile was back, and I quickly swiveled my eyes to Thomas, who was taking the platform as he shook the director's hand.

As photos of Aden rolled slowly past on the screen behind him, I swallowed hard to dislodge the lump in my throat.

Why had he protected her?

Thomas's voice was clear and certain as he spoke about his son, his face softening and taking on a glow I knew was love.

He looked directly at me as he spoke, looking away only briefly, bringing his gaze back as he told me more about his son in that twenty minutes than he'd told me in months.

I watched Harrison through lowered lashes as Thomas told sweet stories about Aden, his expression etched with love and terrible loss.

Not once did Harrison look up at the screen to see the pictures of Aden. He sat with ramrod posture, his eyes traveling the room or resting on me while Thomas spoke about *his* son.

The waitstaff moved on silent feet, slipping dishes into place in front of each of us. And though the food smelled incredible and I was starving, I was so riveted by Thomas's passion, his warmth, the love and regret and pain flowing from him, that I could hardly eat.

This wasn't the closed off man of months before. He came alive when he remembered Aden.

By the time he finished, there wasn't a dry eye in the room. Women were practically pulling out their husbands' checkbooks then and there, to write checks with zeros trailing like ducklings.

As the director took the podium again, discreetly wiping at her eyes, Thomas moved down the steps and stalked toward the table with smoothly controlled movements. He was sex in a suit, all bunched muscle and sinew, and I could see his gaze focused on Harrison, his body coiled and ready to strike even though his elegant suit hid the tension.

Harrison hadn't been paying attention, far too busy charming the woman to his left, and when Thomas's large hand came down on his shoulder, he startled a little.

Anyone observing could see how Thomas's fingers dug in with punishing strength.

Only I knew how gentle those strong, muscled hands could be, and I felt a flutter in a very inappropriate place.

"It seems you're in my seat." Thomas's voice was steely and Harrison looked up quickly, startled but not cowed.

"Your fault for leaving such a beautiful woman to fend for herself," Harrison sniveled, snatching my hand off the table and drawing my wrist to his mouth to press his lips to the soft inner part. It made me shudder as I yanked my hand away, and I watched the same shudder ripple through Thomas.

That was his place to kiss.

"Stay away from her. You don't get to take anything else." Thomas's voice was low and filled with the promise of violence, and Harrison looked gleeful. He held up his hands in mock surrender before pushing up from the table, giving his regrets to the woman fawning over him and moving to the other side.

A waiter smoothly delivered Thomas's plate and as he picked up his utensils, I scooted my chair back, much further to the left than it had originally been placed, so I could lean into his side.

I was beginning to understand that I was like a flower that had been left untended for too long, struggling and wilting. Now that I'd been placed in the sun, warmed by affection and watered with tenderness, little shoots of hope were starting to break out.

I was greedy for his attention.

Starved for it.

He needed to touch me, but I needed his touch too, and I soaked up his desire for me each time he put his fingers on my skin.

"Your talk was beautiful," I breathed into his ear, my hand squeezing his inner thigh as he calmly cut his filet mignon and delivered a neat bite to his mouth. "Did I mention how deeply I'm falling in love with you?"

I heard him swallow hard, and he took a long draw of his water before setting his utensils on his plate, quickly turning me to take my face in his hands and kissing me hard.

I melted into him, remembering not to make the show pornographic for our tablemates, though barely, and I slipped a hand into his jacket to rest over his pounding heart.

This man could hide so much behind such an inscrutable expression.

A light applause broke out as he leaned back into his seat to resume eating, and my cheeks flushed quickly, Harrison's nasty smirk the only thing I could see.

He was fucking jealous.

I knew it in that instant, feeling something I thought might be hatred oozing toward us from across the table.

The woman to Thomas's left was still trying to catch Harrison's eye, completely oblivious to the silent pissing match taking place. She fluttered and flirted, leaning over her plate to repeatedly call questions and observations to him as her oblivious octogenarian husband worked his way through the confection that had been brought out for dessert.

When the woman rose from the table and moved sinuously away, I watched Harrison's eyes follow her lazily. He struck me as the sort who wouldn't waste an attractive woman in a building filled with hiding places, and only a moment later he brought his thick cloth napkin to rest on the table. "If you'll excuse me," he offered in a soothing tone, "I realize I've not yet bid on any of the items in the silent auction." He moved away in the same direction and I rolled my eyes.

"What a tramp," I muttered under my breath to Thomas, and he looked absently down his left shoulder, to take in the empty seat next to him.

"You think old Winston can get it up anymore?" he asked quietly, a wicked grin spreading across his face as he finished the last of his dessert.

I glanced over him, at the old man who was happily tucking into a second helping, and I shook my head slowly. That was hardly a thought I wanted to entertain. I wanted my food to stay put, and it wasn't going to do that if my very active imagination conjured up wrinkly old man junk.

"She's not really his wife, you know." Thomas leaned closer to my ear. "He keeps a few younger women...mostly they're for company. Dates to the symphony and dinner out. It's not exactly a secret they're well compensated for their trouble, and I'm fairly certain other duties are...infrequent, since most nights he's probably in bed by eight, and his wife sleeps right across the hall."

I leaned back in my chair, realizing several pairs of eyes were watching us intently as we whispered intimately back and forth.

"I was talking about Harrison," I said, reaching for my water glass and downing it quickly. It earned me a sharp laugh and he leaned over to kiss my bare shoulder.

"That has never been a question. Women have been chasing him since we were children. Things come easily to him, women especially."

Since we were children.

The phrase hit me hard and I turned wide eyes to him, a vision filling my head of them as young boys. Harrison would be the beautiful, perfect golden child, of course. And Thomas...I knew he came from blue collar roots and I wondered for a second what had brought the two of them together.

I could see him in my mind's eye, small and skinny, his hair just a little too long to be cool.

The waiter was leaning over me to ask if he could take my plate and I waved a hand dismissively. I'd been too uncomfortable in the unfamiliar setting to eat much, despite my ravenous appetite, aware of how eyes were skimming over my body and drawing comparisons.

I would be found wanting when compared to Lydia, of that I was certain, and though I'd tried not to let it bother me, I'd watched men's admiring glances caress her all night long as she moved from one person to another. The way they looked at her reminded me of the way my beautiful socialite mother was watched when she moved through a room.

Eventually we drifted toward the auction tables together, viewing the offerings for the silent auction, and I saw Thomas's face go hard when he read one of the cards. I glanced over it quickly, noting the auction was for a week's stay at a luxurious villa in Sonoma. There was a heated pool, a hot tub, a tennis court, a personal gym and a small staff on the gracious, gated property boasting eight bedrooms, nine full baths and a six-stall garage.

I watched him motion over an attendant, and with a quick gesture the card, the sheet and any associated information disappeared.

Thomas jotted down a few quick bids on various packages, then raised an eyebrow at me. I nodded, ready to escape the stuffy room filled with too many fake people.

They laughed disingenuously at one another's stories.

They gossipped behind manicured fingers stacked with expensive jewels.

They sized up each new couple, comparing themselves in terms of weight, beauty, partner, and financial success.

It was a game I didn't even want to begin playing.

When Thomas handed me into the car, I could breathe again and I quickly rolled down the window to let the cool evening air blow across my hot face.

I wanted to ask him about covering things up for Lydia, but I was pretty sure the answer was long and complicated, and certainly something I wouldn't like at all.

He was silent in his seat and I looked over to see him with an arm resting against the window, fingers across his mouth as he brooded, a furrow between his brows. He looked so alone, like he carried the weight of the world on his shoulders, and I leaned across the space to brush my fingers across his cheek. It made him lean into my touch and I knew something was hurting him, but it was something he wasn't ready to share.

The driver rounded the car to open my door and as he helped me out, Thomas drew up alongside me to take my arm and lead me through the hotel lobby.

He was quiet in the elevator and down the long hallway leading to our room. He closed the door behind me, his fingers loosening his tie and the top button of his shirt before he pulled the jacket off his shoulders.

I stood, mesmerized, hoping he was distracted enough to perform a full strip. There was something about watching this man's powerful body being revealed a little at a time that made my heart all fluttery. It made me feel like a teenager again, almost giddy, and when he stripped off his shirt and threw it aside, I moved quietly toward him to place my palms on his bare chest.

I'd been waiting to touch him all evening, waiting for the moment when he would be *only* mine again, and I rested my cheek over his heart.

I wanted his hands on me.

His arms went around me slowly and I felt the weight of his worries pressing down on me. It made me look up at him quickly and I was surprised by the deeply sad expression on his face. "I'll lose you too," he said softly, bringing the backs of his fingers up to brush across my cheek. "I lose everything I love the most."

It was as close as he'd come yet to telling me that he loved me.

Slipping my dress down very carefully, I stepped out of it and draped it over the back of a nearby chair before stepping out of my heels. I was tiny again, much smaller than him, and I quickly pulled the pins from my hair before stepping near him again.

While he'd watched me dress, he'd done so with unmistakable heat in his eyes. But now that I was undressing in front of him, all I saw was sorrow, and I was willing to do anything to take that look away.

Helping him out of his pants, then releasing the last hooks on my corset, I turned off the lights in the room and led him to the very large bed.

I could feel exhaustion and defeat rolling off him in unsettling waves, and I tucked him in like a mother would a small child, smoothing his hair back off his face and kissing his forehead before crawling in beside him.

He needed distraction and escape, of that much I was certain, and I'd had a much different end to our evening in mind. So I tugged at his wrists until he allowed me to catch both of his hands up over his head, pressing gently into them with my own weight as I leaned down to feather kisses along his face.

He opened to me slowly, gratefully, with a soft groan in the back of his throat.

"These stay here," I whispered, pressing against his wrists for emphasis before kissing my way down his chest. "I want to take your mind off things..."

He didn't fight me, but I felt him fighting himself as he struggled to relax and allow me to take the lead.

The sounds he made were pained, and more than once I stopped, moving back up his body, to his mouth, to touch his lips gently and ask if he was okay.

Each time he assured me he was, but I could taste tears when I kissed his face, and when he tensed, his hands in my hair, his hips moving to fill my mouth, the sound that came from him might have been a sob.

Shit, I think I just broke him.

He took a deep, shaking breath and pulled me up to him, reaching down between my legs, but I stopped him. I pressed him back into the pillows, kissing the heartbeat that hammered in his neck.

"My love," I breathed just beneath his ear, kissing the soft lobe. "That was for both of us. Your day has been long and difficult and you need to sleep."

"No," he protested, his voice gravelly. "That isn't fair to you. I want you, too. I always want you..."

"*This* is what I wanted," I said, kissing him gently. "I assure you I found every moment of that incredibly satisfying."

"But you didn't..."

"I wasn't trying to. I don't expect payment or reciprocation or *anything*. You're hurting and I wanted to make it stop, even if it was only for a few seconds."

He pulled me into his arms and I felt him fighting with himself again, trying not to let the feelings leak out.

So he squeezed me close.

Hard.

Until I could hardly breathe and I wiggled until he let me go.

I gathered him up in my arms instead, bringing his large torso to rest on my own, his head on my chest, and I stroked his hair while I told him the story of a silly girl who'd fallen in love with a deeply troubled man. The man was grumpy and angry and rude, generous and giving, yet mean-spirited even on the best of days.

I felt his shoulders shake with a small chuckle as I told him of the night Gerry and I ferried meal after meal into the crotchety man's home while Mrs. O'Shaughnessy kept watch from her second-floor window.

By the time I'd reached the part where Noah had come to help with the wiring, I felt his body relax, and his breaths began to grow more even.

So while he slept, I skipped to the end.

I told him how much my heart ached for him, to help him be whole and happy, and I would give anything to make that happen.

It was too soon. We'd known one another less than six months, yet my heart beat painfully against my ribs any time I thought of losing him.

There were so many ways to lose something that wasn't yours, I thought with a hitch in my chest.

He'd already voiced his fear of losing me.

If he truly thought I'd walk away, I thought with some apprehension, perhaps he was already looking for the reason.

• • • •

I WOKE EARLY AGAIN, which was becoming a pattern I didn't appreciate.

A nagging worry had eaten at me all night, finding me in dreams as I slept lightly, fitfully, my body wrapped around Thomas's.

There were a lot of things he wasn't telling me, but whatever it was that had him concerned he would lose me, it was something big.

And if I knew anything about him, he would let it drive a wedge between us, because he didn't know any other way.

Slipping from the bed, I dressed quickly in leggings and a zip-up sports bra, pulling my hair back into a ponytail and carrying socks and shoes out of the room with me.

Letting myself into the hotel gym, I nodded to the man already on the elliptical and another on one of the treadmills.

I shoved in my earbuds and pulled up some music with a strong beat while I lifted a few weights, moving quickly to push-ups, sit-ups, and a couple Pilates moves to stretch everything out.

Then, while Mr. Elliptical moved to the weights, I punched a few buttons on the free treadmill and hit an angry stride quickly.

I had a lot to fuel my footsteps: *Fuck Lydia and her perfect body.*

Screw Harrison and his smarmy attitude.

All of these people who are just coming out to people watch and feed on the crumbs, trying to ingratiate themselves with Thomas just to tear him down behind his back...

As I ran, I analyzed my reaction to the hangers-on.

Why was I so fiercely protective of Thomas?

An unwelcome thought rushed to the forefront of my mind, a memory of a time I'd needed protection but it never came.

The summer I turned fourteen, I discovered I had a weird power over men. Something about the changing shape of my body seemed to drive them out of their minds, and though I didn't understand this new power, I relished it. I wielded it poorly though, delighted to come into my own after living in the shadow of my beautiful, desirable mother for years. Finally, men were looking at *me*, though they were looking at me in a way I knew wasn't quite the same way they looked at her.

The looks they gave her were admiring and worshipful, like she was something beautiful and holy in a filthy place.

The looks they gave me were hot and roving, and more times than I could count I'd watched a man unconsciously lick his lips as he stared at my chest or watched me walk past.

That, I'd decided quickly, meant I had some kind of value, and when my mother caught me making out with the much older neighbor boy in the garage she'd laughingly sent him home, but she lit into me.

I was a tramp.

A whore.

A slut.

Only bad girls did things like that with boys they hardly knew; boys who were only too glad to catch the crumbs I threw their way.

Didn't I know any better?

Didn't I see my value, and that I was throwing myself away on trash?

No, I hadn't known any better, because she'd never taught me. I'd just assumed I would never be what she was: beautiful, graceful, sophisticated and well-spoken, and when she'd yelled at me for throwing myself away on the neighbor boy I knew she was just as shocked as I was to find that I was finally maturing into something she might have considered redeemable. The realization had hurt, as I understood quickly that my value to my mother was similar to my value to men: a marriageable currency in her opinion, but one rooted in sexual desirability, nonetheless.

The sweat was pouring off me and I looked quickly at my phone to see I'd been pounding at the treadmill belt for nearly forty minutes. It was enough, I thought, slowing my pace to a fast walk and catching a small movement in the mirror.

The man at the weight bench sat watching my ass as I ran, a glazed expression on his face that I recognized all too well. I was so used to it, I shouldn't have let the disgust flood my body, but I did, pulling the emergency brake to stop the treadmill.

"Show's over," I said angrily, yanking the earbuds from my ears and stomping out of the gym. What was supposed to be a vent for my anger had just fueled more.

Thomas was sitting at the desk, typing something furiously into his laptop when the door swung closed behind me. He was showered and dressed for the day, looking clean and crisp and perfectly delectable as his fingers flew over the keyboard, a slight crease between his eyes.

I stood watching him, awed by the contrast between Polished, Urbane Thomas and Sweaty Contractor Thomas–both were insanely hot–and it took a moment for him to realize I was in the room with him.

"You were at the gym." He smiled and I nodded, taking a long chug from my water bottle.

Then his eyes narrowed. "And you wore...that..."

"Oh, please." I rolled my eyes. "Don't go all hot and jealous on me. Everything important is covered and strapped down and nothing is see-through."

"Natalie." His voice wasn't accusatory, and I kicked off my shoes, looking up to catch his expression. "I pity the poor idiots who were in there at the same time, because you look delicious. Like a hot little treat...but you're *my* treat." He was grinning, rising from his seat and moving toward me with barely disguised purpose, and I held up my hands in defense.

His pants already looked pretty uncomfortable.

"I'm disgusting. Let me shower."

I squealed as he wrapped me up into his arms, his face in my sweaty hair as he breathed me in.

I was sweating all over his shirt, I thought, horrified.

"Not disgusting, baby. I love the way you smell." He leaned back, catching my chin with his hand and holding me still as he looked down into my eyes. "I was the envy of every man at that club last night. Every photo of the event, this morning, somehow includes you. Us. How..." He was brushing my lips with his thumb. "How did you find me, woman? How did you draw me out and make me feel something other than misery?"

It was a rare moment for him: an admission of his deeper feelings with soft, tender words. He was letting me see inside his heart, and that was everything I wanted. He ran so deep, and it was still so easy for him to shut me out.

I wished at that moment I could admit to some grand, romantic master plan. But I didn't know what to tell him, so I let him lower his mouth to mine and kiss me silly while I wound my hands into the thick strands of his silky hair.

When he lifted his head I was breathless and dazed, and I stumbled back a little when he released me. "Forget the treadmill," I panted, fanning my face with my hands. "You're all the workout I need."

He raised one eyebrow at me with a matching quirk of his lip. "Go get your shower before I shred that tiny scrap you call a top with my teeth. Then I'll show you a workout."

"Um..." I entertained a delightful vision. "Yes, please."

Snapping off the shower and stepping out, the smell of good, fresh coffee wafted into the bathroom.

Barely before I'd wound my hair into a towel, I was through the door in search of the nectar.

Thomas snapped his laptop shut again as I sauntered through the room, naked but for the towel around my head as I hurried toward the trays filled with platters and pitchers, all sitting on the coffee table near the sofas.

It was no secret that I liked to eat.

He sat back in his chair, one arm draped over the back as he watched me pour a cup and roll my eyes with delight as the caffeine hit my system.

"Natalie." His voice was sharp and concerned. "What are those marks?"

My eyes followed his, resting on my hip, and I remembered Harrison's punishing grip from the night before.

"What?" I asked, a little unnerved by the way he was looking at me.

Maybe it was too soon to walk around naked so comfortably.

"I have bruises...someone handled me too roughly."

He shook his head, an angry look on his face. "That better not have been me..." Anger flashed like a depth charge in his eyes as he made the connection. "This means I have things to say to Harrison." His nostrils flared momentarily before he seemed to distract himself.

"There's a launch party tonight, at Stanford, and we'll spend the night at the Guest House. After that, I'm whisking you away for the next few days. No appointments, no meetings, no work, no stress; you're all mine. And I'd be delighted if you'd walk around naked the entire time."

I unwound the towel from my head and threw it at him. "You're such a boy."

A lifetime in my own skin hadn't really taught me how to be completely comfortable in it yet, especially when a man was watching or commenting on it. But I liked the way this one looked at me, something soft and sweet in his expression. He wanted in my pants, but he also seemed to want into my heart.

There was a wicked gleam in his eye when I looked up again, away from the piles of toast I'd just uncovered beneath one of the silver covers.

He had gained ground quickly, silently, his arms coming up to drag me to him and I squealed, the platter lid clattering back into place.

"We'll have time for breakfast in a minute," he said into the curve of my neck, and his hands kneaded into the flesh of my backside as I felt a familiar stirring begin in the pit of my belly. "But first, there's something I've wanted to attend to since I watched you dressing last night. I wanted to get on my knees right there, while you fastened your corset..."

His hands drifted to my hips and I watched him catch his lower lip in his teeth as he looked down at my body.

I'd been exfoliated and moisturized to within an inch of my life the day before, the technician scrubbing until I saw stars, and not in a good way.

He hovered over me, kissing my neck, his hair fanning around us to tickle my skin in the wake of his mouth.

It made me sigh, the way his lips trailed down my skin, and he moved his fingers from my breast to let his mouth find me with wet, hot suction.

It made my eyes fly open as he drew deeply, and my body began twisting and churning of its own volition.

Holy crap, he found that switch and he just turned it all the way ON.

He sank to his knees as he licked and teased his way down my belly, his fingertips the lightest touch as he stroked my hips, my belly, the backs of my thighs.

I was quivering already, near tears, and he was still nowhere near to touching me where I wanted.

"Payback," he whispered, sucking the soft skin of my inner thighs before he pressed my thighs gently to widen my stance. Then he pulled his hair back from his face and slipped an arm around me, pressing me to him as his mouth closed over me.

I couldn't control the broken sound that came from my mouth, and within seconds he had me at a fever pitch, slipping fingers deep inside to find the place that drove me out of my mind. No one had ever looked for it before–I'd thought it was a myth until this week.

I screamed something, my hips frantically churning into his mouth and fingers as my vision went black and my body went limp.

He held me up, both hands holding my butt, and I leaned into his shoulders with my hands.

When I opened my eyes the fire in his was so bright, I caught my breath.

"You're so responsive," he whispered. "I barely touched you."

I think the sound that came out of me was a whimper. "I can't help it. You're all hot and broody and commanding, and when you get me naked I just...apparently come instantly."

A brilliant smile stretched across his face, like I'd given him the greatest gift, and I wanted him the same way: relaxed and sated and smiling, so I quickly slipped the buttons from their holes on his shirt.

He stood and willingly shrugged it off, his hand moving quickly between us, and I heard the swift clink of his belt buckle.

I helped to push his pants down over his hips, and before he could drag me down to the rug I slipped behind him, running soft fingertips over his shoulders before I pushed up to kiss them. It made him sigh heavily, a contented sound, and I dragged both thumbs gently down the outside of his spine, following with my tongue and lips until I reached the beautiful dimples on his pelvis. I kissed each gently, feeling the muscles in his abdomen jump as my fingers brushed his belly.

His butt was too perfect to be ignored, and I dropped to my knees behind him, kissing each firm cheek before gently sinking my teeth into the right side in a playful nip. It made him chuckle, and my fingers drifted lower to find him more than ready for me.

Before I could spin him, he was on his knees too, and turned to face me, his eyes full of lust and need, and I let him scoot me back so that I was beneath him. I wrapped my legs tightly around him, urging him, my hands moving quickly along his back as I looked up into his face and he quickly lined up our bodies, pushing slowly into me with a drawn out growl.

His eyes burned down into mine and I brought his face to mine to kiss him, my hands holding his jaw, letting the moan from my throat travel through his mouth and into his body.

I could feel him tensing already, and when he buried his face in my neck and shuddered, I closed my eyes and followed him over, squeezing him so tightly I was sure we'd never be able to separate our bodies.

He scooped an arm under me to roll me with him, bringing us both to rest on our sides as he held my face in his other hand, his thumb moving across my cheek.

The thoughts were boiling in his brain, but his mouth, the valve he needed to vent the thoughts from before his brain exploded, was set in a determined line.

I was getting the feeling he hadn't meant to let himself go like that, to lose himself in me for those too-brief, sweet moments.

I leaned across the short distance to kiss him, because I wanted more.

More of this.

More of us.

More of him.

We'd shared only a few such sweet moments, but often those were before we fell into an exhausted slumber, tangled in one another's arms and legs.

This didn't happen during daylight hours, and thus the need to talk, to discuss, to say the sweet things I felt, wasn't something that had come up.

But it was an issue now, and I feared he would shut down before my eyes, closing me out immediately after I'd let him in.

He let me hold him for moments longer, our legs tangled together, and I chuckled when I realized he was still wearing his watch and his underwear were tangled around one ankle.

"That's one way to keep from being completely naked," I said, trying to break the odd silence between us, nudging his foot with my toes.

His eyes softened a little, and he ran a hand through my hair.

"You make me impatient," he said finally. "Like the gift that's been waiting under the tree for weeks and weeks, and it's been killing me, because I have a pretty good idea what it is...and finally someone says I can open it."

"You must be a real terror at Christmas," I smiled at him, and his lip quirked up a little.

"Maybe as a kid I was. I haven't...done Christmas in a while."

This was going to require further investigation, a great deal, but now was not the time. From the look on his face, I could tell sharing time was over. He was unwinding his arms slowly, helping me sit up before collecting the fabric shrapnel scattered all around us.

We ate breakfast in silence, me sitting on the towel on the floor, largely incapable of moving just yet. My limbs were still little more than limp noodles.

After packing up and checking out of the hotel, we did a little sightseeing in the city I'd not been to since I was a child. We rode a trolley and walked through Chinatown, had lunch on Fisherman's Wharf and took a private boat tour of the harbor.

Even while we ate, I didn't let go of his hand, and he didn't try to make me.

The drive to Stanford was short and as we drove I watched even more of Carefree Thomas slip away.

As the miles flew by, his shoulders tensed again and I noticed the worry lines and tension in his face. I wanted to say something, to help somehow, but I still feared a total shutdown.

Though Gerry had confided I could get through to him like no one else, I wasn't sure I believed it. His walls were so high, they were damn near impossible to scale and if he did let me in, it never seemed to be for long. It was like being with two different people and I never knew from one moment to the next which one I was sitting next to.

Checking into the Guest House, he carried both of our bags in and quickly began hanging things in the closet. He still wasn't talking, which wasn't entirely unusual for him, but it nagged at me because I was on the outside again.

He dressed in the bathroom after his shower, while I dressed in the bedroom, slipping into the lovely dress Daphne had molded to my body. She had suggested I put up only half my hair and I quickly pinned it with the aid of a mirror, refreshing my makeup and applying a little more shadow before touching a perfume to my neck and wrists.

I was still barefoot when he came out of the bathroom and as usual, seeing him took my breath away. Seeing him dressed up absolutely stopped my heart and I staggered back a little as my eyes greedily drank him in. "You are sex on a stick," I breathed, unable to keep my thoughts to myself.

Turning to slip my feet into heels, I felt the warmth of his body behind me and I leaned gratefully back into him as he nuzzled into my neck, his arms wrapping around my stomach. He'd been distant since this morning and this felt like an apology and a plea for understanding. It was enough for the moment, and I reached up to wrap an arm around his neck, scared by what I felt radiating from him. It was that unspoken thing. Something that felt an awful lot like fear.

He stood looking at me in the mirror before retrieving something from his pocket and carefully threaded a stunning gold and onyx earring through each of my earlobes. Then he kissed my shoulder, his fingers held up to shush my protest.

Leading me wordlessly downstairs, he handed me into a car, sliding into the seat next to me with an unreadable expression on his face.

I didn't like this. At least I knew what to do with Grumpy Thomas. This one was new, the one *always* wearing the impenetrable mask. I had no idea how to help or soothe. His fears were his own again, something he wouldn't share with me.

The reception space was filled nearly to capacity and I recognized several faces from the gala of the prior night.

There were faces I didn't recognize as well, people who carried themselves with pride or haughtiness. Some were clearly well established, while others were hangers-on.

The rest were younger, a large number of them obviously students, sipping nervously from the first glasses of champagne they'd probably had in months.

"What is this for?" I asked nervously, tucking my hand into his as photographers started to crowd us. I'd seen the photos from the night before and I knew exactly what they were after: salacious photos of me kissing Thomas, the expression on my face one of rapture and total abandonment.

I'd been his "mysterious partner" for all of three hours before it was uncovered I was a designer from Boston, in the midst of a nasty divorce.

Couldn't wait for Farida to see that one.

Of course, that also kicked the hornet's nest of speculation when it came to Lydia.

"I approached the school about partnering to write and launch a medical informatics program with an app. It's for the caregivers of people with Down syndrome, to make medical records more accessible and portable. The basics remain in the patient's phone, or the caregiver's, not just in one medical system's database. That way there's no need to request records be sent electronically, or physically taken from one medical professional to the next, since that often takes too much time. There's a main program that contains the details, but the app catalogs all the recent and most important information."

I knew my eyes were wide with surprise and I knew he was only telling me this to prepare me for questions, should any press get up in my face.

"While the caregiver can access info at a glance, the detailed records are cloud-based. The program is openly accessible across healthcare networks. It's not purchased by or licensed to particular providers, like you'd expect of most record management systems. It's been tricky, making sure we were totally HIPAA-compliant, and guaranteeing the security and safety of each person's records has been a nightmare."

I pulled him down to me, kissing him gently with no regard for the photographers in our faces. "You are a good man," I said softly. "What a gift. The struggles you've experienced will help so many others."

His expression tightened but he held me close, my hand pressed to his heart. I knew he was wishing all the photographers a violent death at that moment, a few journalists hollering over one another to get his attention. But while he was in the circle of my arms, he could shut them out. I could be his safe place, even if I couldn't keep them out forever.

The event space was on the smaller side, crawling with students and photographers, journalists both in training and professional, and a few big names that even I recognized.

The event had been publicized in some capacity by the university and there was a brief blurb of the blandest acknowledgement on the Titan Tech page.

But what I really expected, as I looked around the room, were the heads of major medical institutions: Johns Hopkins.

Loma Linda.

Kaiser Permanente.

The clinic and research center and NICU groups from Baltimore.

And for the most part, I wasn't disappointed as CEO's began to introduce themselves to Thomas, practically licking his shoes in an embarrassing display of gratitude. He was giving this program to the world, and the benefits were far-reaching.

A server drifted past with a tray of martinis and I snatched one quickly, offering Thomas a sip that he declined.

He was tense and I could feel it.

Was it that he feared a negative response?

No, I knew that in my gut: He was waiting for something bad.

And on cue, it arrived.

"Uncle Thomas!" A small voice rang out, crystal clear over the hum of the crowd and I watched him pale, his handsome features suddenly going flat with fear.

"Aria." His voice broke. He was instantly on his knees, wrapping up the little blonde dynamo who'd thrown herself around his legs.

"What are you doing here?" he asked gently, and the little girl pointed across the room to where Harrison stood engaged in languid conversation with an older brunette woman. His eyes were hot, avidly watching us as his lips curved up triumphantly, even while Thomas pulled Aria into his arms, his eyes drifting shut as she threw her arms around his neck and he squeezed her tight.

He looked up at me briefly, his expression panicked, and I didn't know what to do. Why was he afraid of her?

Looking at his face, taking in his anguished expression, I knew that his heart was breaking as he held her close and he caught a sharp breath, leaning heavily into me as the little girl nestled into the side of his neck.

"Mr. Harrison brought me–uh, I mean Daddy," she said matter-of-factly, lifting a small hand to point in the direction I'd been dreading.

"Did he, now." Thomas's voice was tight and I could feel the sharp edge of emotion he was trying to disguise.

"He said it would make you happy to see me since it's been such a long time." She dropped a sweet kiss on his cheek and he pulled her close again, squeezing his eyes tightly shut, his nostrils flaring.

"I remember the last time you came to visit," she said proudly, and it took everything I had to keep my face neutral. "You and Mama were there. We had a tea party with my nan, and then we played dollies."

The princess sheets. Fuck.

I knew in that instant, my heart catching in a frantic beat as I leaned into Thomas, trying to hold him up.

How many shoes could be thrown at this man?

"I haven't seen you in a long time," he said, his face pressed into her tiny shoulder and I knew she wouldn't hear the tears in his voice. "But I think about you always. I've missed you, Ari."

"I miss you a lot. But Mr. Harrison–Daddy–" she corrected herself again with obvious frustration, "says you've been really busy with work and that's why you can't come visit."

"He's right, peanut," Thomas said, his voice soft, and I looked up to see that he'd pulled back from her small face, looking earnestly into her bright blue eyes. "I've been working on something to help people like Aden, to make things easier. Do you remember him?"

She shrugged her little shoulders and giggled, and my heart seized as he leaned to set her small feet on the floor. It was obvious it hurt him to let her go and she wrapped her arms tightly around his neck before he could straighten, smacking his cheek with her tiny lips. "You can come play at my house. I got new dollies since last time."

He blanched.

"When you're all done with the big people."

He leaned his forehead against hers, his lips tight, his eyes drinking in her beautiful golden features. "You're more important than the big people, Aria. You know that, right?"

"I know, Uncle Thomas." She giggled softly, her little hands holding his cheeks even as he crumbled. "You come see me. I'll tell Nan and she'll make a tea party."

He released her slowly and as she ran across the room toward Harrison, he swayed into me.

"Give us a minute," I barked at the reporter trying to edge in next to him, my eyes snapping with fury. "He's not feeling well."

I pulled him up, against my shoulders, bracing him as I whispered in his ear. "If you can handle the presentation, move it up. Do it now. I have something to do, but I'll be right back–I won't even leave the room.

"Fifteen minutes, baby. That's all you need to get through, and I'll be with you the whole time."

His eyes were huge and unfocused, filled with tears that threatened to spill, and I held his face in my hands.

"Thomas."

His eyes focused slightly and I quickly ran my thumbs beneath his eyes to sweep away the moisture. "Go on. Wow the press that's here for the app. Go give your accomplishment to the world, because you're still the better man. He's not taking *that* from you, either."

He took a deep breath and leaned against me. "Natalie, please..." His voice died immediately and I squeezed him quickly, pressing my lips to his temple. I'd promised to be his safe place and I was going to do that, damn it.

He moved toward the front of the room, a small stage containing a large whiteboard and several chairs.

As he moved in one direction, I moved in the other, drawing some of the reporters with me. They were eager to see what I was up to and followed me toward Harrison, whose eyes tracked me and he shrank back like I might burn him. It made me slightly gleeful, realizing at last that I might make him uncomfortable, leading the media toward him in what might be an unwelcome display.

While the photographers went bananas, I stood with Aria and Harrison. I held her on my hip and asked her about her pets, her favorite color, and just how long it had been since she'd last seen Uncle Thomas.

I desperately wanted to correct her terminology, knowing it had been pressed into her tiny brain when she'd been too young to understand differently, brainwashed by an indifferent father who was interested in possession but not involvement.

Harrison went rigid beside me and I smiled sweetly up at him, leaning closer to whisper so only he could hear it. "I know what you've done." I smiled so the photographers would think the conversation was friendly. "You're a coward and a cheat who would use his own children as pawns. I feel sorry for you." Carefully, I handed Aria back to him, smoothing her hair gently. "Mostly I feel sorry for her, because you'll always sell her short." I leaned into his ear so Aria couldn't hear my words. "You've worked hard to twist it, but you're not her father in the ways that matter."

Harrison let out a rush of breath that was either shock or consternation.

The gall of me.

Click. Another shutter dropped.

I'm pretty sure Aria was the only one smiling in that picture.

Across the room, Thomas's voice was finally strong and steady and sure. He'd run through a brief demonstration of the main program he'd written and demonstrated how the app fed information into it, maintaining key data points for a new caregiver's quick references.

Then he handed the Q&A portion to one of the students I understood he considered the star of the show.

He worked hard to hide it, but I thought he looked wrecked. I could see his eyes searching the room frantically, resting finally on me.

It hurt a little to realize he was looking for Aria, but only because now I knew *why*.

The hurt I felt was for him.

Why didn't he tell me?

Why didn't he say something?

There were so many opportunities.

People pressed him endlessly, peppering him with questions and heaping praises as he tried to cross the room.

His facial expressions were forced as he shook hands and posed for pictures and I moved to stand near him, to tuck into his side and hold him up. This was one of his greatest moments and Harrison, again, had stolen his joy.

He leaned against me as I finally pulled him toward the space I knew held the car I'd ordered only moments before. He was silent and tense, a slight tremor running through him. He had used every last ounce of resolve to get through the evening and I tucked him gently into the car, folding into him even before closing my door.

The car slowed outside the Guest House and I thanked the driver, pulling Thomas gently from the back seat and leading him into the building. The lobby was quiet, the other guests having long since departed or gone to bed, despite the relatively early hour.

He was unresponsive, flat, his expressions gone and his eyes glazed. I started to worry this meant I should dig through his baggage for medication, and I led him carefully toward our room.

"Baby." The word still felt strange on my tongue as I knelt to help him out of his shoes. "Tell me what I can do to help."

No response.

Maybe I should call Gerry.

The small room was quiet and he stood unmoving, so I guided his hands to the zipper of my dress, unwinding my hair as he pulled it down.

What did he need most right now? I tried to decide as I heard the teeth of the zipper.

I wanted him to snap him out of it.

To stop his hurting.

But at the moment, I had no idea how to do it.

Taking his hand, forgoing all my bedtime rituals, I led him carefully across the room, toward the bed I was fairly certain would fit both of us. "Come on, baby," I coaxed gently.

He seemed almost catatonic.

"It's time for you to sleep."

It had only just gone ten and it was a miracle I'd gotten him away from the party portion of the launch so easily. We'd left amidst drinks and a light dinner, and I'd made the excuse at least thirty times that he wasn't feeling terribly well.

Though I felt slightly guilty for taking him away from his adoring public, I told myself this was a result of him being blindsided, which was not untrue. All it took was the slightest knock to shatter him all over again.

He collapsed quickly into the soft pile of linens, and as I set my lovely dress aside, I slipped into the bed next to him.

He was soft and warm and his arms pulled me against him, though I had no struggle to put up.

I was quiet, breathing him in, my head on his chest. His deep breaths were measured and painful, and I wondered if he was too broken to cry.

"You lost Aden's twin, too," I whispered, the realization finally in words I could manage. It made sense now: all of the trips to California, only some of them for business while he battled the courts for the girl who wasn't really his child.

"Yes. Lydia took her when she left me, but I was going to visit her as often as possible. She was spared the crash, only because Lydia left her with someone that night...because she had planned the end." His voice sounded like it had been dragged over glass shards. "When Aden..." He took a deep, gasping breath and I lifted my hand to his neck. "Harrison filed for guardianship after the accident, but it was just a formality. That way he had the courts on his side, so he could demand his remaining living child be returned to him. That way I didn't stand a chance: I lost them both."

His heart was thundering beneath my ear and I lifted my face to press a kiss into his hair, pulling myself up to lean against the headboard so I could pull him into my arms. He let me, his huge upper body dwarfing me as I cradled his head against my chest.

"He was suddenly interested in being a parent?" I asked, pretty sure my curiosity wasn't helpful.

"He wanted to rub salt in the wound." Thomas's voice was bitter and broken. "Lydia never admitted it, but Harrison eventually did. He told me he'd let her know she was on her own when the tests confirmed one baby would suffer developmentally, and he refused to provide any form of support. Otherwise, I think she might have left me for him much earlier. But I had no idea at the time, and it was easier for both of them to let me think the babies were mine.

"It was fine to let me raise them, because the inconvenience wasn't his. But then Aden was gone...and he took Aria. I mean, her mother was in court-ordered rehab. I had no legal claim and no parental rights. I was *blindsided*, though the truth had been right in front of me the whole time.

"The worst part is that he's not even there." His voice caught. "She's being raised by a live-in nanny. It's someone who's paid to care for her physical well being, and that's where it ends."

I thought of Thomas, moving his small family from their mansions in California to the old house deep in Alabama. It had been a severe downgrade as far as any of them were concerned, putting them way under the radar. They were running from what Thomas thought was the worst threat: losing Lydia to Harrison, yet her infidelity was only the beginning of the end.

He was quiet in my arms and I let a few tears slide down my cheeks as I thought of him in that house...after. Initially he had a wife and children, a cat, to come home to every day.

Squeals of glee from Aden.

Eskimo kisses from Aria.

Though his heart must have ached for Lydia, his babies surely filled it back up.

But then...nothing.

The wife he'd tried almost too hard to keep was gone.

He had one baby in the ground and the other two thousand miles away, being raised by the man who'd established himself as his mortal enemy.

Aria was too young to remember that "Uncle Thomas" had been "Daddy" for the first several years of her life, and seeing her tonight had split him wide open.

My chest ached as I thought of all the lonely, empty nights he'd spent in that house, surrounded by the ghosts that tore at his heart.

"That arrogant son of a bitch," I seethed quietly. "For him to behave the way he has, and to be so sure of himself...the next time I see him, I want to punch his stupid teeth in." I gave it another moment's thought, sure I could do better. "I hope he gets leprosy and his dick falls off."

I was working myself into a lather. I was *pissed* as I thought of how hard Harrison had worked to cause pain.

Thomas snorted, a small laugh making his stomach contract. "It would be to the advantage of all womankind." He smiled up at me gratefully. "You're cute when you're mad."

"I'm cute all the time." I let myself be distracted for a moment. "I can't believe he had the nerve to flirt with me at the gala. He was only doing it to get under your skin!"

Thomas's soft hair tickled my chest as he shook his head slowly. "He's not an idiot, Natalie. He knows and appreciates a beautiful woman when he sees one, and I doubt he even knew you were attached to me at first. His attraction to you had nothing to do with me."

"Yeah, whatever...I still hope his dick falls off. And I'm just going to tell you right now that I see him for what he is. He's a smarmy, pompous, self-centered piece of garbage who doesn't give a crap about anyone else. What kind of stupid woman would fall for that?"

He puffed out a small breath and I hooked a finger under his chin to raise his face so I could see his eyes in the dim light of the room. "I suppose you'd be surprised," he whispered.

"She's an idiot," I whispered back, running my thumb down his cheek. "How could anyone who has you be so stupid as to walk away?" I was baffled, briefly considering how much it would hurt to lose him. "To be married to *you*...to be raising children with you...and to leave. I just don't understand." I was shaking my head, aware there was a tremor in my voice. This felt vulnerable and scary. I loved this man more than was good for me, and I wanted to tear apart the people who had hurt him.

He sat up straight and pulled me into his arms, his face in my hair and he took deep, slow breaths. "Your heart sees people and what they need," he said quietly into my hair. "You saw me right away, but I couldn't handle letting you in. It was too scary."

I had no idea what that meant, but I wasn't about to ask. I could feel him starting to relax, which was what I wanted.

Until he could shake off the awful sadness that had tried to swallow him whole, I wouldn't be able to sleep.

He pulled me down into the pillows with him, wrapping himself around me like he needed to protect me from something. I could feel a desperate fear radiating from him and I whispered softly to him in the dark. "My heart just loves you. It wants you to be happy again."

He squeezed me tighter, and as the rhythm of his heartbeat and his breath soothed me to sleep, he whispered back: "I'm so afraid of being happy. Losing again would hurt too much."

• • • •

DISTANT THOMAS WAS back with an exponent.

We'd eaten a quiet breakfast before putting our bags in the car, and though he held my hand tightly as he drove, he stared straight ahead at the road as he chewed on his lower lip.

He was silent through San Francisco and over the Golden Gate, slipping sunglasses over his eyes as the sun finally broke through the clouds and lit up the sky. It hid more of him from me and I sighed disappointedly, sinking back into my seat.

It was still only mid-morning when he flipped the blinker, turning into a wide driveway flanked by vineyards. It seemed an odd time for a wine tasting, but I decided to roll with it, watching as the vines whipped past my window, then receding as the drive neared tall gates.

Thomas pulled his phone from the center console and tapped a button, and the gates glided open. They opened into a gracious courtyard with an enormous water fountain, a sprawling Spanish style villa some distance beyond the fountain.

Hold on, this place looks familiar.

The door opened silently and a well-dressed, silver-haired man nodded stiffly to Thomas before reaching into the car to take our bags. He nodded to me then and turned to carry the bags into the house without a word.

"That's Jensen," Thomas said quietly as he took my hand and led me into the house behind the man.

I stopped dead in my tracks as we stepped into the house, overwhelmed by the terra cotta floors, the old wooden beams, the simple white plaster walls, the Moorish arches and the polished ebony staircase I could see stretching toward a second floor.

Gauzy curtains hung on substantial brass curtain rods, the huge glass and wood pocket doors pushed back into the walls of the house to afford fresh breeze and warmth from the outdoors.

A short woman with a neat grey bob and smiling blue eyes stood in the kitchen, her movements quick and efficient as she stirred and chopped. She too nodded to Thomas, then to me, and he smiled slowly in response. "This," his voice was quiet again, "is Mrs. Jensen."

He let me pull him from room to room as I drank in the architecture, the finishes, the simple and gracious decor. Everything in the home screamed understated luxury, elegance and relaxation. I could feel it working its magic on him, the tension seeming to melt from his shoulders, his breaths growing deeper and calmer.

The master bedroom was upstairs, at the far end of the house, a veritable refuge with heavy wooden doors and soft linen bedding and curtains, the huge windows overlooking the vast and soothing expanse of vineyard behind the house.

"This is heaven," I breathed, trailing my hand along the bathroom's marble vanity and eyeing the huge soaking tub that also afforded a view of the vineyard. It made him smile a little as he leaned against the doorframe, watching my wide-eyed wonder as I admired the solid glass shower enclosure.

"It is now," he said quietly, and it made me smile at him.

To have him all to myself for the next few days...I turned the taps on the bathtub and started languidly removing my clothes, watching the way his gaze heated and narrowed.

It was new to me, this feeling of power and control. I'd lost so much confidence during the long years of my marriage, and to rediscover myself through Thomas's eyes had been a gift.

He was quiet as we soaked in the warm water and thick, scented bath foam, his arms wrapped around me as I leaned back onto his chest.

I thought back to the day we met, chuckling to myself. Had someone told me, months ago, that the angry man stripping shingles off my roof was a brilliant entrepreneur, an attentive lover with a deeply wounded soul, someone thoughtful and caring...well, I'd have laughed hysterically at all of those things.

"What?" His lips were against the back of my head. "Did I tickle you?" He wiggled a little and something unmistakable pressed up against my backside.

"No, I was just thinking...if someone had told me last summer that my hot, reclusive, grumpy contractor was going to be the opposite of *everything* I expected...well, except the hot part..." I chuckled again. "I don't think I'd have survived the laughing fit."

"Hot, reclusive and grumpy, huh?"

"Crotchety," I teased. "But to be fair," I leaned my head back against his shoulder to kiss his jaw, "I don't know how you were keeping it together." I linked our fingers together in the foamy water.

"I wasn't," he answered flatly. "Sleeping for three or four hours a night in a toddler's bed and surviving on frozen and microwavable meals isn't exactly the definition of keeping it together."

It worried me a little, the incredible sadness he still carried on his shoulders. He had lost so much: his company, his wife, his children...the thought of what he must have been like months and years earlier was terrifying.

We dressed for dinner, the sweet smell of a hardy honeysuckle drifting through the windows, and when we trailed down the ebony staircase there was a cheerful fire burning in the living room fireplace.

"Dinner's ready on the terrace," he said, taking my hand and I marveled at the silent efficiency exhibited by Jensen and his wife. Everything was in place, perfect, two ice-cold martinis awaiting us on a small bar cart, yet I'd not heard a single noise or seen a flurry of movement.

These two were veritable church mice.

There was an outdoor fireplace as well, crackling and snapping, flanked by soft sofas draped with warm blankets. An arbor stretched above them, stars beginning to twinkle through the few gaps not closed over by the lovely vining bougainvillea.

We ate and drank and I remarked at someone's ability to mix a wicked martini, suspecting it was Jensen himself.

When we'd finished, we carried our dishes through the house and into the quiet kitchen, warm lights glowing and illuminating our way from beneath the cabinetry. There Thomas rinsed, and I placed the dishes in the large dishwasher before we drifted back out to sit near the fireplace and enjoy the quiet sounds of the vineyard after dark. We wrapped up in one of the huge, fluffy blankets and I settled into his side as his arms went around me.

"I can feel your brain churning," he said with a heavy sigh, and I knew I was preventing him from relaxing.

"Just lining things up," I said, and I felt him shift a little. "I recognize this house from the silent auction. You seemed upset when you saw the listing and they took everything down right away...did you win the highest bid or something?"

He drew a deep, slow breath. "Not exactly. I was upset to see it listed, yes, but it was a simple mistake. The staff at the event were misinformed. The house was used several times in the past for charitable purposes: a long weekend here or there for the appropriate price. Since it wasn't lived in full-time when it was first transferred, it was put to good use."

"But now?" I asked, sensing an undercurrent of very uncomfortable details.

"Now it's my house," he said, as if that was that. And though that answered almost none of my questions, pointing out only that *this* was *the Sonoma house*, the man sitting next to me was not about to answer them.

I tried to let it go, knowing the events of the past few days, on top of jetlag, had been a tremendous drain on him.

His body responded to me in the way it always did, but we didn't make love that night. There was something raw and emotional about him that worried me and when we crawled into the huge white bed, I pulled him close. Cradling him to myself, I hummed into his hair as my fingers trailed softly up and down his back, because his need for touch eclipsed my own.

The breeze blowing through the windows was cool, fluttering the soft curtains and whispering across the bed linens. But he was wrapped up, warm and safe in my arms.

His breaths finally became soft and deep and as he slept, I prayed and made desperate promises.

It has to be over now, right? That has to be all.

I would give anything to save him.

How much more could one man suffer?

I had a terrible feeling I was about to find out.

• • • •

MRS. JENSEN WAS A STEALTH ninja.

We were down early the next morning to find breakfast already waiting in the sunroom, the morning air just a little too cool for dining al fresco. So we ate in the gracious, glass-paneled room, the sunlight filtering through the leaves of the lemon and fiddle leaf fig trees planted in large pots around the room.

"Remember that solarium I was talking about?" I grinned at Thomas while I buttered a biscuit and he looked up quickly, distracted and tense. "This will do."

He nodded, but he didn't smile back.

"Hey." I set down my knife and reached across the small space to pull the phone from his hand. He'd been agitatedly scrolling through it since we sat down. "You said no work and I'm honoring that, but I'm wondering what's going on with you. I'm capable of amusing myself if you need some time to wrap something up, but it helps to know what's expected of me."

"I'm sorry." He looked down into his coffee and my gaze followed his as I realized he hadn't eaten anything yet from his plate. "I just have a lot on my mind."

I'd heard that before, I thought, taking a large bite of the biscuit and washing it down with coffee.

It made me nervous when he shut me out like this.

He drank four cups of coffee, but aside from some scrambled eggs and bacon, his plate was sadly neglected. It made me want to crawl into his lap and feed him like a small child, and it drove me crazy to think of him slipping back into the place he'd been when I'd first met him.

After breakfast he disappeared into the home's large office space, on the ground level, shutting the door firmly. I could hear his muffled voice if I stood near the door, but the heavy wood kept the words from being crisp and clear. All I could discern was irritation, sometimes fury, and I finally stopped snooping when I thought I heard defeat.

I raised my hand to lay upon the door, scrubbing the other across my eyes.

I don't know how to reach you. Tell me what to do.

He was in there for hours and though I further explored the house and discovered a small, wood-paneled library with two deep leather chairs in front of a fireplace, I couldn't sit still. I selected a book from one of the shelves, my senses delighted by the smell of the book, the sensuous feel of the leather in my hands, the buttery softness of the deep seat against the backs of my bare legs. But the instant my body went still, my mind started jumping all over the place again.

Grabbing the sunglasses from my bag upstairs, I let myself out of the house by crossing the terrace where we'd dined the night before. The sun had finally warmed the stone, the earth, the vines, and I stepped quickly off the path of pavers to wander into the vineyard that stretched far longer than I wanted to walk.

That line of trees, that was where I was headed. I needed to take myself away from the heavy air in the house, and one way to do that was to see what was beyond the next rolling hill.

The grapes had clearly been harvested recently, many of the leaves still left on the vines, and if I strained my eyes I could see several workers making their way through the long rows.

The grove of trees was at a much greater distance than I'd thought and as I neared them, I turned to look back at the house. The sprawling beast was smaller than my hand and I held my palm out in front of me, moving it back and forth as I opened one eye and closed the other, then reversed it, playing with perspective.

There was a small dot moving down the row of vines, moving without pausing, and I wondered if it was Thomas coming after me.

Looking down at my phone, I noted it was well past time for lunch, and my stomach rumbled in agreement.

No service.

Well crap, there was no way to tell him where I'd gone.

The long line of old, gnarled oaks stretched out in front of me and I stepped into their welcome shade, my skin hot and sticky from the heat of the midday sun. It was slightly cooler here, a dappled shade, and I was surprised to find the stand of trees was far more dense than I'd thought. These guys had been here for a while.

In fact, it seemed I'd reached the end of the vineyard, for trees stretched quite a distance in front of me.

Surprised to see tire tracks in the soft dirt, my eyes followed them down to what might have been an access road of sorts.

I wondered if this was where the vineyard workers parked their vehicles during the heat of the day.

There was a low chuckle to my left and fear squeezed my heart as I spun quickly.

"I'm surprised he let you out of his sight. I know I wouldn't be so foolish."

The man was dressed in a loose linen shirt and dark jeans, his expensive sunglasses obscuring only a small part of his handsome face.

Harrison.

Pushing my own sunglasses back into my hair, I knew my expression was wary. "What the hell are you doing here?"

He laughed again, stretching his arm out in a sweeping motion. "This used to be my place. I still come here to visit the family from time to time."

What the hell was he talking about?

I couldn't help myself. I knew I was looking at him like he was completely insane.

"Oh, Natalie...you're usually such a quick one," he clucked, shaking his head slowly back and forth. "He doesn't tell you much, does he?"

Why did I get the feeling he was about to remedy that very thing?

He moved toward me with the languid grace of a prowling jungle cat, and every muscle in my body clenched instinctively.

"I only bite if a woman asks me to." He smiled, his canines making me think otherwise as he tucked my arm into his in a fluid motion. I recoiled at the contact and he chuckled again. He obviously took a perverse pleasure in making me uncomfortable.

"Women typically don't respond to me with such aversion. I like you; you're a challenge." But he didn't look over. He was already walking, rather forcibly pulling me along with him. "I knew the instant I saw you, you were going to be different."

Was that an insult?

"You don't come from money, not exactly," Harrison observed casually as he looked down his shoulder at me. I had adopted a stiff, stilted pace. My feet were carrying me in a direction opposite from the one I wanted to go. "You don't understand the etiquette of our circle; you lack the polish."

Ouch.

He held up his free hand in a placatory gesture. "I find that fascinating, and I imagine he does as well. You're an outlier. You don't play our games. You're reasonably successful in your own right, but you don't seem to be driven by status or wealth, which I find genuinely intriguing. Is it possible there are any women left who are truly like that?"

I had a nasty retort at the ready and I swallowed it whole when I saw the look on his face, because he didn't look like the same man. Something had happened in his expression: something had collapsed, becoming vulnerable and sad.

Maybe this is a trick.

He stopped walking and I turned my head slowly, following his gaze. There was a small clearing in the trees and my brain was working hard to recognize the tall marble slabs jutting up at perfect ninety-degree angles from the ground.

Harrison released my arm and I dream-walked toward the markers, some of them clearly much older than the rest.

"This was my family's private cemetery for the past several generations," he said finally, in a tone that was almost reverent. "My family," he snorted a little when he said the word, "has many houses, but this was always my favorite.

"When my parents passed, I lived here for several years. But then I deeded this house to my beautiful wife as a wedding gift. I would *never* have thought she'd take it from me to leave to her brother." He snorted in disgust.

My brain was spinning as I read the names and dates on the stones, and I squatted down in front of the row of short markers, my knees threatening to give out when I saw the names: Micah, Abigail, Emma, Aden. That one pulled me up short, the most recent burial, but the one who'd lived the longest.

"Who was your wife?" I asked, my fingers brushing gently across Aden's name, the four letters that could break the beautiful man in the big house on the other side of the vineyard.

It didn't seem as if he'd heard and he walked past me, toward the taller row of headstones that stood several paces behind. He crouched down as well, leaning his head against one of the slabs and his whisper was broken: "Maren." He drew in a deep breath. "I'm lost without her. She took everything that was good."

I stayed where I was for a long moment, terrified by his grief but more frightened that it made me pity him. He was easier to hate–to despise, for the pain he'd caused Thomas, and I wanted to feel vindicated in watching him suffer.

But I couldn't.

His hand obscured part of the name on the stone and as I pushed to my feet and moved closer, the soft disturbance of the dirt seemed to shake him from his daze and his fingers slipped.

Maren Marie Atholton-Powell, 34. Beloved wife.

There was an etching of an angel at the top of the stone, the markings making it clear she was ascending to heaven.

"Oh, fuck." I clapped my hands over my mouth, but it was too late, and Harrison's lips twisted sardonically as he twisted to look up at me.

There was the asshole I recognized.

"I've been saying that for a while," he said, pushing himself up from his knees to stand beside me, his hand reaching out to caress the top of the stone in an intimate gesture.

I stepped away from him quickly, skirting the smaller headstones and hurrying toward the edge of the trees again.

"Aren't you curious?" he called after me, and I hated myself for stopping.

Run.

Just go find Thomas.

This guy's insane.

"My dear, devoted, beautiful wife...I loved her my whole life, you know. It took me forever to convince her to marry me, and not *one* of her brothers thought I was good enough." His voice was bitter. "It was Emma who finally took her: placental abruption.

"My wife insisted she was fine, that it was just some cramping...I rushed her to the hospital when she passed out, but it was too late. The baby she almost carried to term was the one to do her in."

There was an evil sound, something like a laugh, and I couldn't help but look back, horrified.

He was losing it.

"I'm cursed, Natalie. Didn't Thomas tell you?

"I was raised by parents who couldn't spare a moment for their only child, so I grew up with the Atholtons. I envied them for their closeness. But even on the inside, I was never a part of them.

"And then I married one, a woman who couldn't possibly love me the way I loved her. She didn't love me enough to stay alive. And of all the five children I've tried to bring into this world, only two lived past their birth."

I hardly thought a placental abruption could be held against Maren, but I didn't say so.

I was watching Harrison's expression twist as he chewed through unpleasant memories.

"Thomas is not the only man to have suffered loss...Yes, after Maren, I made some mistakes." He lifted his head, ripping off his sunglasses with one angry hand, and his eyes were glassy. "I shouldn't have let Lydia come to me like that, but I was angry with him. He had everything and I had nothing. He had a beautiful wife and a wildly successful business, and I was just the buy-in partner. None of the intellectual rights were mine. Nothing was *mine.*" He swung viciously at a nearby tree trunk.

"So I gave Lydia what he couldn't: children. And that imbecile was so desperate to make things work with her, he overlooked the obvious and *raised my kids* without question."

Remembering the dot moving through the vineyard, I searched the edge of the trees for a human form, but there was nothing and no one. I had the distinct feeling I might need someone to rescue me.

"It takes an incredibly strong man to accept his wife's indiscretions and raise someone else's children, especially once he knows," I said, my voice shaking a little. "He was willing to love and care for them, knowing Aden would need a lifetime of care, even when you refused all involvement."

"I had my reasons." He shrugged, all traces of emotion now gone from his face as he reached my side again. "But now...I have contested my wife's will for years and lost. She left her favorite home, the one we were happiest in, to her brother. Do you think she was trying to hurt me? I think so, sometimes." His lips curled up in a derisive sneer. "Since I no longer own the walls that contain some of my happiest memories, I will take something else. I will take something from him and put it where he can't find it."

Shrinking away from him a little, my eyes flicked back and forth from the grave stones to his face.

"See? I knew you were quick." His grin was sickening. "He *must* have told you about the ruling, Natalie: I'm taking my family with me."

• • • •

I DON'T KNOW HOW I made it back to the house. I was briefly aware of breaking into a dead run, doing everything I could to put distance between that sick man and myself, tearing down the rows of vines without anyone in pursuit.

It was his weird, broken laughter that followed me, chasing me with cold fingers.

By the time I reached the paved walkway nearing the house, I was gassed. My arms were windmilling, sweat running in wide rivulets down my skin, my hair crazy from being snagged by vines as I ran unsteadily.

My foot caught on the last step as I rushed up the terrace and I sprawled with a painful, heavy thud, my knees and elbows taking most of the blow to cushion what was a graceless faceplant.

My sunglasses shattered on the stones.

"Miss Natalie!" The voice was urgent, from somewhere inside the house, and I was dazed when I felt someone roll me over and scoop me up.

It was Jensen, tall and wiry but impressively strong as he carried me effortlessly into the cool living room and placed me gently on a sofa.

"What is it? What happened?" Thomas's voice sounded more panicked than I'd ever heard it, echoing through the house as his quick footsteps drew closer. He threw himself down beside me, his eyes wild. "Natalie, tell me what happened." His fingers brushed my face and came away covered with blood.

I couldn't speak, the words all clogged up and thick in my throat and instead big, fat tears welled up in my eyes and spilled down my cheeks.

"Here you are, sweet girl."

It was Mrs. Jensen, wiping the dirt, sweat and tears from my face with a cool cloth. Then, folding it over, she set to work wiping the blood from my knees, my elbows, my palms.

"She was runnin', sir." It was an unfamiliar voice, and I realized it was Jensen, his tone low and confidential. "Out the vineyard at quite a tear–caught th'last step on her way up the terrace, I'm afraid."

Mrs. Jensen fluffed a pillow and indicated I should lie back before she disappeared into the kitchen with the promise of something cold to drink. It was her husband who shushed her and told her he would mix "The very thing, lass," moving quickly after her.

"How long have you known?" I finally managed, my voice raspy, and his face paled immediately. "Your last appeal...that week you refused to eat and you were trying to murder that tree...it was for this? For Maren and Aden?"

He nodded, his Adam's apple dragging painfully in his throat, and I sat up carefully. "Come here." I opened my arms and though he was only a foot away, he moved in slow motion.

Jensen slipped back into the room on silent feet, leaving two tall glasses on an end table, just within my line of sight. Then, just as silently, he disappeared again.

I caught his eye in silent thanks as he went and he nodded shortly. I knew he understood: Thomas was not a man who liked to share emotional moments. Something told me Jensen wasn't either.

I didn't tell him about Harrison being in the vineyard. I didn't say anything at all, simply holding him against my chest and waiting for him to relax against me.

Both of my knees began to bleed again.

"This is why we're here," I said finally, a sickening understanding washing over me.

Why hadn't he told me?

Warned me.

Prepared me.

"He's digging them up–moving them." My voice caught in my throat, and I shivered so hard it rattled his teeth. "You're here to say goodbye."

There was a choking sound from the middle of our bodies and I couldn't be sure whether it had come from me or from him.

"Friday." His voice was tight, muffled against my neck. "The order gives him permission as of Friday. He'll be here at dawn, if I know him."

There was only one way to fix this, but I was in a bloodied state and hardly up to the task. Instead, I held him like a small child, soothing him with soft words and gentle touches until the fight left him and exhaustion swam up to meet him. Then I led him up the stairs and tucked him into the huge bed, where I held him carefully until he stopped fighting and fell asleep.

He had been running on fumes for days.

It was growing late, but I wasn't at all hungry. Instead, I hurried downstairs to find Mrs. Jensen putting up the kitchen for the night. I apologized for the full dinner I knew she'd had to put in the huge refrigerator and she smiled gently, understandingly.

This was a couple of few words.

An idea had come to me and I quickly conferred with her to decide whether it was feasible. Then I thanked them both for such quiet, helpful service and I let myself into the dark, humid sunroom and fished the phone from my pocket. At least in the house I had a signal.

Dialing Gerry's number, I prayed that she would pick up–and that she could help me.

FORTY-TWO

Thomas

Waking the next morning was like a slow swim up from a deep, dark place, lungs burning as I tried to stretch toward the light. I gasped a little when my eyes flew open and I relaxed when I realized where I was, but then I remembered why I was there and wanted to sink back down into sleep and forgetfulness.

Natalie was wound up tightly around me, one arm tucked tightly over my ribs, her leg thrown over mine.

No wonder I couldn't breathe.

I couldn't help but smile down at her, her face peaceful in sleep.

My little barnacle. Clinging to me ferociously, not even willing to give up in her sleep. She was trying so hard to save me from myself and the darkness I always readily welcomed in, simply because it was so familiar.

My memories of the previous afternoon were rather fuzzy and I realized I had Natalie and the Jensens to thank for a quiet evening, each allowing me to sleep rather than spend the time counting down the hours, wallowing in exhausted depression and possibly being even more self-destructive.

There was the softest sound outside the door and I moved Natalie slowly, carefully, so as not to wake her. I was surprised to feel quite rested, and I dropped a quick kiss into her hair before moving across the room.

There was a large breakfast tray waiting on the floor outside the door, and I said yet another prayer of thanks for Mrs. Jensen: quiet, efficient, fastidious, and a passionate pastry chef. The tray boasted a selection of croissants, fruit tarts, Danishes, toast, fruit and coffee. She'd left a note on the tray, indicating there were savory selections in the kitchen, but this would see us through until we felt fit to venture downstairs.

Natalie stirred as I slid the tray onto the bedside table and crawled over her to wake her properly. She'd seen to it that I was cared for the night before and all the nights previously. That meant we had been on very good behavior each of the three nights we'd already spent here. Now I would see to it she was cared for, worshiped the way she deserved, gently, considering her scraped up knees and elbows.

But if I was being completely honest with myself, it was because I was selfish.

I needed her.

I needed her closeness: something I couldn't accept from others, and something she gave me so freely.

I gazed down at her for moments longer, feeling a little guilty that I wanted to wake her in order to get inside her. I wanted to blame it on years of deprivation and the newness of our own physical relationship. She was intoxicating and I couldn't get enough.

I hadn't been fair to her when I'd invited her on this trip with me. My reasons had been one hundred percent selfish. She would be a buffer, shielding me from the unpleasantness I usually faced on my own. And finally, I would let myself have her. I would consume her: worship her with body and hands, lips and tongue. And being so distracted, perhaps I wouldn't fall apart.

Her body would be my balm.

I would find strength in the circle of her arms.

There were soft fingertips on my cheek and I looked down to find her eyes open, a soft smile on her face as she trailed her fingers across my jaw and up into my hair.

She sat up quickly and downed the glass of water at her bedside, then held her arms out to me.

How did she know?

I went to her willingly and quickly she helped me forget.

She looked disappointed when I sat up. The quiet, tender moments after were when I was able to be most open with her, offering explanations and telling her things I usually kept to myself. I knew those were the moments she loved, when I let her in and explained to her why I was the way I was. We hadn't had many of those moments yet, and today I couldn't do that.

There were no words for what was going to happen, or how I was going to get through it, and I couldn't be certain I wouldn't lash out at her: find a way to hurt her because I couldn't keep the anger to myself.

Pushing up from the bed, I walked into the bathroom and turned on the shower, because I was restless and jumpy again.

I needed to distract myself with something else, or I'd keep Natalie in my bed all day long. I liked the idea, but she was so small, I was afraid of becoming overzealous and hurting her. She hadn't initiated anything rough, only playful, and this thing seemed too young to test those boundaries in a situation where my emotions were highly volatile.

It was something Lydia had joked about with disdain when we were younger, that I kept a beast in a cage and never let it out. I had no idea what I would do if I did, and she'd made me feel ashamed that I had a dark, needy, angry side that grasped and clawed and bit when I was pushed too far.

I didn't hear Natalie slip into the shower behind me, but when her arms wrapped around my ribs and her lips pressed into the center of my back, I let out the breath I hadn't realized I was holding.

It was amazing how her touch could calm me and drive me batshit crazy in the very same moment.

"I'm not going to push you," she said, her voice vibrating against my skin.

Of course, that meant it was exactly what she was going to do.

"But it would be a really good idea to talk about it."

Leaning forward and bracing both my arms against the shower tiles, I let the water run down my head and back, cascading off my face. I wanted it to block out sound, so I had a reason not to respond. But Natalie had learned me. She was patient.

She rubbed soap together in her hands and smoothed it across my back, taking her time to wash, rinse and then kiss my skin.

She washed all the way down to my feet, then turned me to wash my front. There was a wicked gleam in her eye and I was reminded of how many times I'd fantasized about her in the shower.

She was here now.

She pulled me out of the stream just slightly, so it ran down my back, and she rubbed soap on my chest, bending carefully as her hands smoothed down the outside of my thighs. My dick jumped in response.

I wondered for a brief second whether the acoustics of the shower would advertise our morning activities to the Jensens, but then I decided I really didn't care.

She wrapped her warm fingers around me and looked up, her big blue eyes staring into my own as she pushed to her feet.

I loved her touch, reveled in it, and it had taken nothing to get me hard.

She moaned softly when I leaned down to kiss her, and when I couldn't take it any longer I pulled away from her quickly, moving to lift her into my arms.

By carefully hooking my arms beneath her knees, I could create a seat for her, and I pushed her back up against the cold tile as her arms flew to my shoulders. She gasped when she hit it, her eyes going wide.

"You couldn't handle it, then?" she teased, a small smile playing on her lips.

I didn't have any words. I was too busy trying to figure out how I was going to get inside of her without the use of my hands, and she reached carefully between us to help me.

I waited for her touch, looking down between us to see her trailing her fingers slowly over herself, and the way she looked at me made my heart skip a beat.

"I have ways to make you talk," she whispered, letting her head fall back as I lowered her just a little, trying desperately to line up our bodies.

She saw my desperation and how close to the edge I was, and she reached down to guide me. I could barely control myself, sinking carefully into her as she caught her breath, pitching forward to throw her arms around my neck.

A desperate groan left her and she sank her teeth into my shoulder. I hissed at the pain and she licked the marks softly, teasingly.

The little vixen wants to play.

She came with a long, low moan and I drank in the sight, her head pressed to the wall, her eyes closed, her mouth dropping open.

Then she wrapped her legs tighter and pushed up on my shoulders, helping me as I chased my own release. Watching hers had been almost enough to do me in and seconds later I felt my eyes rolling back in my head as she caught my mouth, nipping at my lip before pressing soft, open-mouthed kisses against my lips.

I didn't want to put her down right away, but the way she was looking at me was like she was staring into my soul. It was disconcerting and when I looked away, she took my jaw in her hand and brought my face back to hers.

"*Our* problems to deal with," she said softly, kissing me again.

"*Our* sadness.

"*Our* situation to get through–together. Stop trying to keep the unpleasant things from me, because they won't drive me away. You can't keep me at an arm's length forever."

Her voice was gentle, but she was frustrated, and she had every right to be.

Slowly, I separated our bodies and lowered her feet to the shower floor. I let her pull me close and she pressed kisses to my chest.

I wanted to relax into her.

I wanted to let her chase away the fear and sadness; the darkness that had consumed me for so long.

I was afraid of how weak it made me, and eventually I knew she would see it. Then she would find someone better; stronger; more in control of his life and everything in it.

Then I would lose her, because that was what I did: I lost things no matter how tightly I tried to hold on.

• • • •

TRUE TO HER WORD, MRS. Jensen had a great spread downstairs.

Though Natalie and I had coffee and pastries upstairs, we came down to hash browns, scrambled eggs, bacon, bagels with cream cheese and smoked salmon.

There was enough food to feed five or six people, I thought, and Natalie seemed to brighten considerably when she saw the piles of food. Her expression became expectant for the first time.

My phone rang only a few bites in and I excused myself from the table. It was one of my lawyers and I knew the discussion would be unpleasant, as it always was, so I excused myself to the main floor office.

Natalie slipped in ten minutes later, my plate in her hand. She set it on the desk in front of me and kissed the top of my head before turning to leave. She paused then, before opening the door, and the wicked grin was back. She could see from my expression that I was in no mood to play and I angrily bit off a piece of turkey bacon, listening to my lawyer yammer on in my ear as she flattened herself against the door, slipping her shirt slowly over her head.

She was going to play anyway.

She was glorious in the early morning light, all creamy smooth skin.

Ken had to repeat something I hadn't caught the first time, because Natalie was busy distracting me by running her hands up her sides and over her breasts. She squeezed, giving me a heavy-lidded look. She bit her lower lip and slid her hands back down her sides then, slipping her soft pants and underwear from her hips and sashaying toward me, completely naked.

She was fucking gorgeous.

"Ken." My voice was unnatural and I was cutting off words in weird places.

He was still talking, while Natalie sauntered in front of me and pushed my plate aside, hoisting her bare ass up onto my desk and catching a lip between her teeth, staring at me expectantly, her fingers tapping against my collarbone.

"I'm going to have to call you back; something important has come up."

Her grin was triumphant as I threw the phone across the room and surged forward.

She fell back on my desk, giggling, wrapping one leg carefully around my hips to draw me closer.

"Something *very* important has indeed come up," she teased, rocking her hips up to nudge against the desperate situation happening in my pants.

"I know what you're doing," I growled, and she didn't look at all penitent. "You're trying to distract me with lots of sex. I don't know that I have the stamina for you, woman."

She widened her eyes, the picture of innocence, just before she reached for me and palmed me through my pants.

"It doesn't seem I've been particularly effective in distracting you to this point," she said breathily, and her hips wriggled just a little on the desk. "But if at first you don't succeed..."

I sincerely hoped Ken had hung up, because twenty seconds later the rhythmic sounds of something unmistakable filled the room. Natalie left no room for doubt, the way she sighed my name and begged me for things like faster and deeper and harder, and she came with a wild cry that pushed me over the edge.

"Holy shit," I breathed as she slowly unwound her legs from my hips. "That's a hell of a way to get my mind off things."

She leaned back on her palms, her legs dangling off the edge of my desk, and something squeezed like a vice in my chest. She was so beautiful, flushed and naked and sweating, and I could read her expression plainly: She was doing this to save me from myself, because she loved me.

I leaned into her and held her close, because I couldn't convince myself I deserved her.

FORTY-THREE

Natalie

Thomas was losing a little more control every time I initiated any form of intimacy.

It wasn't that I wanted to break him, but I wanted to break *through* to him. He wouldn't let out the grief, the rage, and I was terrified it was going to shut him down and eat him up. Already it had stolen precious moments from us in just the past few days, and I began to fear that it was his pet: He would nurse it and water it and feed it until it ate us both alive.

I slipped back into my shirt and the loose pants I'd been wearing when I came into his office.

He was retrieving his phone, then reached into a desk drawer to pull out tissues to clean the surface.

I smirked at him over my shoulder.

There was a light knocking sound drifting down the hall when I opened the door, and I quickly shut the office door behind me. I had called for reinforcements and, with any luck, the cavalry had just arrived.

Opening the front door, I was engulfed by a mountain of human flesh, squeezing me until I slapped him hard, twice, on his shoulder, and he released me.

"That an official tap, Nat?" Noah grinned down at me, the smile on his face warm, but deep worry swam in his rich brown eyes.

Noah stepped through the door and Gerry trailed behind him, giving me a quick squeeze and a wink.

Behind her was another woman, one with only a faint resemblance to Thomas or Noah, as her eyes were the same rich golden brown but her hair was almost platinum. She was shockingly gorgeous, and I stared dumbly, even as she caught me and looked amused.

"Natalie." Her voice was low and raspy, like she was working on a case of laryngitis. "I've heard a lot about you." She folded me into her arms, so tall she could easily tuck me under her chin. "I'm the other trouble maker: the baby sister, Finn." Something bumped me and I looked down to realize she was pregnant.

Noah shut the door and I led all of them quietly to the kitchen, where breakfast still sat out in warming dishes and their eyes lit up.

"Someone is an angel," Noah whispered loudly. "Finn and me had to wait forever at LAX for Gerry's flight, and I ate some kind of overpriced crap that's already run right through me." He grabbed a plate and immediately began heaping it full.

When the three of them were seated, I crossed the room to fetch the coffee carafe and bring it to the table. There was a slight hitch in my step–I may have overdone things, because I should not have been this sore.

Noah was the first to notice and I could see it in the bemused way his eyebrow raised.

Gerry was looking at me funny too and I looked down quickly, feeling the flames of embarrassment lick at my cheeks because I probably smelled like sex.

"Finn?" Thomas's voice was sharp as he rounded the corner and saw his sister standing at the island, heaping food onto her plate. "What's the matter? Where's Griffin? Is he ok?" He looked panicked and she slowly set down her plate, crossing to him and wrapping her arms around him in a tight hug.

"We're fine, Thom, he's home with Mateo," she soothed in that husky voice of hers, and I saw him heave a huge sigh of relief just before he looked up and realized Noah and Gerry were sitting at his table. Confusion clouded his brow, drawing it together in a slight wrinkle, and Finn let one of her arms drop to his waist. "This time we're here for you."

Noah had pushed to his feet and was chewing as he crossed the room, throwing giant arms around Thomas and slapping his back hard. "Yeah, old fart. Nat said you could maybe use a little help getting through this...uh, thing...that's been causing you a lot of stress. So we gathered the troops we could on short notice and here we are."

Thomas stood there speechless, looking from one to the other, his eyes suddenly dangerously full of what Noah would blame on allergies.

Then finally, his eyes sought me out and he swallowed so hard, I expected him to break down.

I wanted to go to him, to close the small distance between us, but I hesitated. I'd called in the people he needed most, because I wasn't sure I was part of that small circle yet. Most days it seemed like I was still standing on the outside, waiting to be let into his heart.

He didn't say anything, but his hand lifted slightly toward me, palm open, and I went to him. He'd been holding me only fifteen minutes earlier in a much different capacity, but when I nestled into his chest he dropped his face into my hair and began to tremble.

Suddenly we were surrounded by arms, being pressed in upon by three other bodies as all of us worked to hold him together. We let him fall apart, pressing close to catch the pieces, and when he finally heaved a deep breath and looked up from my hair, all of us had red eyes and wet trails down our cheeks.

"The load is easier when you let other people help you carry it," Finn whispered, smearing mascara across her face when she wiped an eye. "You're the big brother, but we're your people. If you need something, you have to tell us. You can't always be there for us but then handle all this crap by yourself." She landed an open-handed slap on the back of his head, and he winced.

This family really liked to beat the shit out of each other.

Everyone slowly unwound themselves, and Noah and Gerry headed back toward the table to resume eating.

Finn took her plate from the counter and joined them.

"Hey Thom," Noah called, and Thomas lifted his cheek from my hair. "You might wanna go a little easier on Nat; you're gonna break your favorite toy."

There was a snort from across the table–I thought it might be Gerry–and when I finally turned to look at them, Finn was grinning too.

I shot Noah an evil glare and he held up both hands. "Metaphorically speaking, baby girl," he said before cramming a toast triangle into his mouth. He could pack it away like nobody's business.

Thomas snagged more bacon and poured another cup of coffee before moving toward the table and sitting next to Noah. I followed him with my coffee, and when I tried to sit beside him he snaked an arm around my waist and pulled me into his lap.

Gerry caught my eye as he did, and hers crinkled just a little with the smile she tried to hide.

It was much easier to distract him, now that I had three helpers. One method of distraction, however, was completely off the table–or desk–until later that evening, and while Noah dragged Thomas out to the hot tub, I drifted upstairs to clean up.

There was a sharp snap of linens, and I peered around the door to find Mrs. Jensen changing the sheets on our bed. It made my cheeks flame and I quickly offered, "Oh, I can do that!" but she didn't turn around. In fact, I repeated myself as I walked up behind her, but she didn't seem to hear me.

Putting a hand gently on her shoulder, I expected her to startle, but she turned slowly, with a patient smile, and pulled an earbud from her ear. "I'm so sorry, dear. Did you need something? I was just listening to a lovely meditation while I went about some household chores."

Oh have mercy, Mrs. Jensen had been wearing earbuds to drown out our sex noises. I had no words, and as I stuttered some nonsensical sounds and twisted my hands, she waited patiently. I gestured toward the bed, trying to mime that I could handle changing the sheets and she smiled benevolently.

"Sweetheart, it's nothing to be ashamed of, because I can manage. Right now we're all doing what we can to get through this." She fixed me with a pointed look. "If you weren't here right now..." She got a faraway look in her eye and she swallowed hard. "My husband has been saying for the past two years that he doesn't know how there's not another grave out there." She pointed vaguely. "I don't know how one person can be put through so much. And yet, here *you* are, making him smile, giving him something to care about...don't you worry about the things that come naturally."

Did she just wiggle her eyebrows at me?

"You just keep after him."

What the hell did that mean? I knew my expression was dumbfounded and she quickly rolled the pile of dirty sheets into a neat ball, smoothing an imaginary wrinkle on the bed she'd just made.

"Oh!" She was already all the way out the door, and she popped her head back in. "I put some nice salts out by the bath for you; I thought you might be a bit sore." She smiled and disappeared again, and I covered my eyes in mortification.

Nooooo. Please be referring to the face plant on the terrace.

I *was* sore, but not from tripping up the steps. I winced a little as I stretched out, achy in places that hadn't been used in years, and I hadn't a single complaint.

Gerry and Finn were sitting on the terrace, under the arbor, when I made my way outside. It wasn't yet noon, but Gerry held a large glass of white wine and was comfortably reclining on one of the sofas. It was warm in the sunshine and I settled at the end of her sofa, drawing my feet up to tuck behind my butt so I didn't flash Finn.

"Noah really likes you," Finn commented, holding up her glass of tea as if she was offering me a sip, and I shook my head.

"He just likes getting some sass back," I said, a small smile on my face, and I heard Gerry snort at the end of the sofa.

"He gets a lot of that at home." Finn laughed a soft, musical laugh.

"Eve has been so good for him...no one gets that lucky." Then she went mute, bringing her glass to her lips and I turned my head toward Gerry, looking for some kind of explanation that wouldn't be forthcoming.

Voices drifted from where the terrace wrapped around the side of the house, and Noah's favorite monkey butt insult drifted over on the breeze.

I chuckled a little.

"Thank you both for coming," I said softly. "I don't know what to expect...I wasn't sure I'd be enough to get him through it."

Finn stood slowly, walking over to the table in the shade of the arbor and pouring wine into a fresh glass, which she handed to me.

"That you were thinking that far ahead, for his sake, says something that I think all of us appreciate," she said gently, and her dark eyes were kind. "Thomas's personal life has been a real shit show for a long time now, and we all hated his stupid wife." She clapped a hand over her mouth, her eyes traveling quickly to Gerry, who nodded at her.

"That woman is poison," she continued, drawing up like she wanted to strike, spitting ugly words with a beautiful voice. "She tried to keep all of us away from him, to keep him all to herself.

"I've never met such a selfish, needy, miserable person. I have no idea what he thought he saw in her."

"You've known her since childhood?" I asked, and she nodded slowly. "Since she was a teenager and I was a kid. I'm much younger than Thomas, and yeah, she was an awful bitch all the way back then, too." There was a nasty expression on her pretty face.

"Some people hurt with fists, like my Da, but Lydia was way too sneaky for that. She hurt with words and actions and horrible behavior. He never knew where he stood. He was always on edge with her; always trying to please her." She paused and huffed out a breath. "To be good enough for her, as he put it, and she always made him feel like he wasn't."

I swallowed hard, feeling not for the first time that our lives had run at an odd parallel as far as our marriages were concerned. While it helped me understand him a little, I had been the one to leave, and he had not.

Gerry spoke in a low voice when she told us what she knew of Harrison's plans. Thomas had been far more forthcoming with her when it came to details, and Finn and I paled as Gerry detailed Harrison's deranged cruelty.

Finn swallowed hard when Gerry told me how close Thomas had been to Maren. They weren't the Irish twins he and Noah were, but their bond had been strong.

As Gerry remembered it, they were each one half of a whole soul, and may as well have been twins: Maren could start a thought that Thomas could finish. They could conduct whole conversations with looks and just a few hand gestures, and that level of closeness lasted their whole lives.

It stood to reason that both Harrison and Lydia were insanely jealous of Thomas's bond with his sister, and both did everything in their power to undermine, corrupt, pollute, and weaken.

I suspected it was because Harrison wanted Maren all to himself, and Lydia couldn't stand to share anything with another person.

I sat quietly, listening to stories about Maren, the sister they'd lost a little more than six years earlier.

Finn had only been in her early twenties at the time, but remembered clearly that Thomas's devastation had been just as deep as Harrison's, if not more so.

Gerry sighed, pushing up from the sofa to refill her glass. "All that wife of his did was take," she said bitterly, and it was the first time I'd heard her voice in a tone that was anything other than pleasant.

"He has needed what you could give him for so long...but he's a stubborn son of a bitch."

That made Finn smile.

"He was not about to choose happiness, not for anything." Gerry looked irritated.

"And then came along a little ray of blonde sunshine." Finn was grinning at me, her teeth the same straight white row as Thomas's and Noah's.

"Thank God, too–he was spiraling." Then she looked to Gerry. "What is wrong with us? All six of us have made some seriously shit decisions when it came to partners. Are we just actively seeking out people who will abuse and break us? Did Da fuck all of us up that badly?"

Gerry sat quietly, contemplating the liquid in her glass. "Most of us get into relationships to fill a need we think we've identified within ourselves, but we seek an external component to solve an internal problem. It's natural to think that an acquisition will make you happy, when the truth is that fixing yourself and learning to be content is the real key. It's a lot more work, too." She leaned back.

"In addition to being the world's best stepmom, Gerry also provided all of us kids with therapy coming up on two decades now." Finn's lips were twisted into a weird smile.

Gerry shot her daggers. "Let's just broadcast that I'm old then."

"Hey!" Finn was laughing, but it was cautiously. "I didn't say you're old–Da is older, and we know he doesn't have it half as together.

"Besides, lady, you're still hot."

Gerry smiled weakly and ran a hand through her crisp bob. Hers was razor-sharp, whereas Mrs. Jensen's was a bit more matronly.

"At this age, one settles for presentable."

There was a splash and a whoop on the other side of the house, and Finn rolled her eyes. "As I'm sure you've figured out, Noah is the perpetual toddler of the family.

"Thomas is the firstborn boy, so he's responsible and serious.

"The middle brothers, Aaron and Asher...well, Aaron is a little bit of a mess, but Asher has it mostly together. I think–I hope."

"Biblical names," I commented out of nowhere. "All the boys in your family have Biblical names."

Finn snorted. "Along with the Catholic birthrights of crippling guilt and fears of inadequacy. Mom didn't stray too far with mine, either: Seraphina is Hebrew. The only one she really went wild with was Maren."

Noah rounded the corner, giggling like a little girl, with Thomas in hot pursuit. He threw himself down on the sofa next to Gerry, his towel doing little to handle the fact he was fresh out of the hot tub, and Gerry's pant leg started to soak up water.

"Base!" he crowed, slapping a huge hand on Gerry's knee, and Finn and I burst into a fit of laughter.

"See?" Finn asked, and Thomas shook his head at Noah in disbelief, wrapping his own towel tighter.

It was mid-afternoon by the time we all drifted inside. Mrs. Jensen had left a number of covered platters out on the large island and we all built enormous sandwiches, settling in front of the huge, roaring fire I suspected Jensen built while we were otherwise amused.

The breeze blowing through the house could be cool, and the snapping fire was comfortable in the late November air.

Thomas pulled me into his side as we sat, finally depositing his plate on the low coffee table, his fingers absently stroking up and down my bare arm. It was soothing, yet distracting, and I knew it was because he was lost in thought. He had dropped out of the lively conversation, only occasionally flicking his eyes upward in recognition of the fact anyone else was in the room at all.

I had been silently counting the number of empty glasses he left on the table, on the counter, in the kitchen sink.

They hadn't been glasses of water.

As the rays of the sun grew longer and longer, more drinks mysteriously appeared on the credenza against the wall, and Noah commented on the incredible stealth of the drink-mixing fairy that seemed to live in Thomas's house.

Mrs. Jensen compiled a series of woodfired pizzas for our dinner and while everyone else nibbled, I slipped into the kitchen to try to help her with cleanup. She smiled warmly at me and gathered me into a gentle hug before telling me to go socialize. I suspected she was such a hidden part of this home's functions that it was rare anyone sought her out to thank her.

"I didn't want to interrupt you, dear," she finally said as she pulled back and smoothed my hair the way a mother would. "But your phone has been ringing all afternoon–I just thought you should know. I should imagine that means it's something rather important."

Thanking her, I slipped up the stairs to let myself into the bedroom. I'd left my phone on the nightstand, plugged in to charge with the ringer at full volume.

Holy crap, twenty-seven missed calls since eleven this morning. What the hell? I flipped over to the texting program, to see whether I could find an abbreviated version of the emergency.

There were thirteen texts, three of them from my mother, and I read those first. Then I read them again, sinking down onto the bed.

11:03 Natalie dear, you need to get in touch with Farida. There's been an accident and as you are legally Ahmad's spouse, there are certain decisions to make.

1:47 Natalie, please call your mother-in-law to make arrangements. I don't know why she can't get in touch with you, but there's nothing I can do from Omaha.

3:19 Natalie. Call me.

I dialed my mother's number with shaking fingers and put her on speaker.

"Natalie! Thank God." My mother sounded more relieved than if she'd just been awarded an obscene settlement. "Farida has been calling me incessantly, trying to find you. Your husband was injured and that man was taken into custody and it's...bad." She paused and I looked up to see Thomas in the doorway watching me, his eyes dark and flat, unreadable. He was swaying slightly against the doorframe.

"Did Farida give you details?"

"I don't know much more than that, except that she's unable to make any lasting medical decisions for him, as you're still legally his wife and hold power of attorney."

I thought I saw Thomas wince out of the corner of my eye, and he moved unsteadily toward the bed, where I sat.

Pulling up a browser tab on my phone, I Googled Ahmad and found a short article with a mugshot of Sonny.

Thomas moved toward me quickly when I dropped the phone on the floor.

"Mom..." My voice was shaky. "I should go call Farida. Thanks for telling me."

Thomas picked the phone up from the floor and skimmed the article, absolutely no expression registering on his face. That scared me.

"I'll have to go sign paperwork and make arrangements," I said weakly, and his lips flattened. He handed me the phone and sank down next to me, but he still hadn't said anything. It was eerily quiet in the room.

Instead of waiting for him to speak, I dialed Farida, the last person I wanted to talk to. I'd almost have rathered Ahmad himself.

"Natalie." Her voice was cold and clipped when she answered, and rather than apologize for taking so long to call her back, all I could say in response was, "Yes."

She cleared her throat, which was probably all the emotion she'd shown in the past several days, and in the background I heard the steady whir and beep of monitors and a respirator.

"The doctors have concluded a number of tests," she said finally, and I wondered if she'd had to wait so long to speak because she needed to tamp down an emotion. Something I knew I should be feeling. I should be horrified and sad, maybe heartbroken. But all I could feel was disbelief.

She cleared her throat again. "You will need to make a final decision," she said, and I thought I heard a tremor in her voice.

"Farida," I said, my own voice a little shaky. "Do you know what happened? I saw an article, but there wasn't much..."

Thomas had completely shut down already. He wasn't touching me. He wasn't even moving. He sat stiffly beside me, hands in his lap, looking down at his feet.

He smelled like he'd bathed in booze.

"It was an argument with a man..." She answered finally, and I could hear the distaste in her voice.

She had to know.

"This man barged into the apartment to argue with my son over money. He was...it was clear they knew one another. He wanted my son to conclude his legal business with you in order to..." She choked a little. "He wanted more than my son would give him, because he was greedy, and now my son is being kept alive with a machine while that man sits in a cell at Rikers. And I am..." Her voice finally broke.

"I need to make arrangements, Natalie, in accordance with his wishes. It should have been done within twenty-four hours, yet it has been nearly two days. You know he must be washed and buried, as there is no hope he will be returned to us."

I could feel all the color leaving my face as Thomas turned his head to look at me.

I had to travel to New York to sign the papers that would end Ahmad's existence.

I had to assist Farida with funeral arrangements.

I thought back to what I knew of Islamic burial customs.

I have to wash Ahmad's body three times.

Bile rose to my throat as I thought of what it meant. Farida would want her son buried at home–her home–the land of his birth–and there was no way in hell I was ever getting on another plane to Saudi Arabia, especially not to help my cheating husband's family save face.

"I can't be there tomorrow," I told her finally and the line was quiet but for the whirring machinery.

"There's another family emergency I'm tending to. The earliest I can get to you is Saturday."

Thomas stood finally and crossed to the window to look out over the darkened vineyard.

I'd have given anything in that moment to know what he was thinking, every muscle in his back and arms completely rigid.

"Text me your airport information," she said icily, and I knew just how angry she was. "I will have Halim book your ticket and you will come straight to the hospital."

"Probably Napa," I said wearily, and I could hear the gears whirring and grinding in her head. She knew damn well I didn't have any family in California.

"I see." Her voice was clipped. "He will send you the information once it is booked."

Then, without any sort of sign-off, the phone went dead.

• • • •

THOMAS DISAPPEARED for a few moments, slipping out of the room without looking at me. He was back only moments later, shutting the large bedroom doors and loudly throwing the lock. It startled me, and my head jerked up at the sound.

He had another drink in his hand and he looked pissed.

I was quickly learning that I didn't like Thomas when he drank, because he was living up to the mean rage monster he'd warned me he became.

I stood as he stalked toward me, unsure of what had come over him. He didn't just look intense, he looked like he was hunting me. It made my stomach flip with discomfort in a way that was alarmingly close to fear. I had seen a similar look on Ahmad's face in the past, and though he'd generally not been a violent man, there were a few times it had not gone well for me.

He stopped inches from me, his chest heaving from the exertion of deep breaths that came from either running up the stairs or...maybe fear? I couldn't tell.

He was having a hard time focusing on my face, and the nagging memory of how he said he behaved when he'd had too much to drink raised goosebumps on my arms.

"You said you wouldn't leave."

He slammed his drink down on the nightstand and some sloshed over the sides.

His voice was low, filled with hurt and accusation, and my eyes widened, my mouth dropping open. Because I...what? He'd heard the entirety of the conversation. How could he think I was leaving him?

"Baby." I stepped closer, lifting a hand to his cheek and he flinched like I'd burned him when the backs of my fingers skimmed his face. "I'm not leaving you. I'm here tomorrow, with you. I won't fly out until Saturday, and I'll be back as soon as I can."

"No. I need you *all* the time, Natalie, not just some of it. You don't belong to him anymore, you're *mine.*" His voice was fierce.

What was happening?

"Thomas, I have responsibilities as well, and though I have *chosen* to be yours, I belong to no one but myself. Don't try to make decisions for me, because it will not end well. You know this." It came out gently, even though I hadn't meant to say the words out loud. I wanted to be sensitive to his pain, not remind him of mine. But if we were being completely honest with ourselves, I'd just identified a very large flaw in our relationship: I was too available to him.

I went to him when he needed me.

I welcomed him in: into my home, my routines, my life and my body.

He, on the other hand, was getting as much of me as he wanted and when he'd had his fill, he could leave. Somehow I'd made him a bigger part of my life than I was of his and suddenly the disparity was laid bare and something in my throat closed up, hurting, the pain radiating into my chest.

He lunged suddenly, his teeth gnashing at my throat and I gasped when he caught the soft skin under my ear in a nip, drawing it into his lips and sucking.

He's let it out.

A delicious shiver ran through me, half-anticipation and half-fear. I was afraid of the beast he could become when he was angry and drunk.

This man was not my thoughtful, tender lover.

This man was angry and hurt, and he seemed to think I was causing those emotions.

I snapped back at him, sinking my teeth into his left pectoral and he grunted at the contact. "Shit, Natalie. What the hell?" His eyes focused for just a second.

"You want to play rough?" I challenged. "You want to hurt someone else because *you* can't get your shit together? You want to see how much I can take, maybe make me cry so you can feel like a big man? Go for it. See if it makes you feel better. But don't you dare punish me for *her*."

He stood staring at me for a moment, chewing on his lip until I was afraid he'd draw blood.

I said a prayer that everyone was asleep, with earplugs, because shit was about to go down, and it was going to be *loud*.

He didn't move, so I did it for him. I lowered my body and lurched forward, knocking him off balance and he stumbled back until he slammed into the wall.

"Do it," I goaded him. "You can take someone little like me. Tie me up, so you can claw and fight and fuck, but it won't make you feel better. I won't give you what you're looking for, because I won't let you break me. You need that apology from *her*, not me."

I was tired of being quiet and submissive, used and tossed aside.

That got his attention. He swiveled us quickly, before I could even register what he was doing, pinning my wrists over my head with one big hand and leaning into me until I was flattened against the wall, hardly able to breathe.

"You said you wouldn't leave; that you weren't like her," he breathed softly into my hair and I struggled to free both hands until he let them go, and I punched sharp fists into his ribs.

He grunted and stumbled back and I knocked him easily onto his ass, climbing into his lap.

"Is this like her?" I taunted angrily, pushing him back as I stripped the shirt from his body. "Did she ever want you like I do, Thomas? Did she ever come to *you*?"

He looked up at me, his eyes lazy and unfocused and hurt.

"I'm not fucking leaving you," I ground out through bared teeth. "I'm meeting a personal obligation and coming back to you. I'm defying all their religious customs to stay with you while you need me."

Angry tears were starting to well in my eyes, and I hated that I let him see me so weak.

"How can I possibly give you more than I already have?"

He didn't soften for that, but he spun me quickly, bringing us both down hard on the fluffy rug that ran under the bed.

"I can't let you go back to another man," he whispered, nudging his nose into my neck, making soft, desperate sounds as his fingers worked to tear the dress from my body.

I felt his intake of breath when he tossed the dress aside, taking in my lacy underwear and bra.

There was something hard and angry and fierce in his eyes as he looked down at me, and it was an expression I didn't recognize. I refused to believe that I did that to him, but I swallowed nervously anyway, because I didn't like this version of him.

We were so fucked up, I thought as he skimmed the lace from my body. We'd been together in the most complete way for less than a week, and he was going to allow his anger to push me away.

There was no tender preamble; no slow, sweet seduction or wet, sucking kisses. He threw my underwear aside and pressed immediately between my thighs, biting the soft inner skin as he worked his way up.

"You're *mine*," he hissed into my skin, and the score of his teeth was a pain so close to pleasure, I couldn't do more than whimper.

Where was the switch, the one that took me from furious to panting in just seconds? I needed to find it and permanently disable it.

He suctioned his mouth to me and I was floating. My body was betraying me. I heard a low, pained wail that I thought might have come from me, and he shoved his wide shoulders forward to push my thighs up, opening me to him in a way that made me wish the lights weren't on.

He was determined, incessant in his pressure and when I came, it was with a sob. I twisted my head to the side, trying not to let him see my face. The tears were streaming down my cheeks, the emotions, the feelings completely overwhelming and he paused, pushing up on his hands to stare down at me.

"You said you wouldn't leave," he whispered again, and another terrible sound escaped my lips. "But you're running to the bedside of the man you've been with for fourteen years. What am I supposed to think will happen?"

How was he even coherent right now?

"Should I *stay* in New York, Thomas? Are you trying to push me away? Is that what you want, so you can say you told me so?"

He hooked his forearms under my knees, bringing them up toward my ribcage as he moved up my body, sinking into me quickly and I winced at the intensity of the angle. He was going to punish me and I didn't deserve it, the hot anger that boiled off his skin. He was staring down at me without really seeing me, his expression glazed, his teeth grinding together. "You. Are. *Mine.*" He grunted angrily, holding himself up on one powerful arm while his other hand allowed my leg to drop, gripping my jaw and turning my face back to his, holding me there.

"You're not making me want to be yours right now," I whispered back, my throat burning. His weight was so much that I could hardly catch a breath. "You're marking me like I'm your territory."

"You *are*."

Fury and heartbreak warred in my chest, because with that statement he was just like my husband.

I was a thing.

A possession.

Something he wanted to lock up and hide away and keep all to himself.

I let him move against me, his muscles flexing and rippling powerfully, and though I wanted to appreciate the view, I couldn't. I jerked my face from his hand and turned to the side, tears continuing to run down my cheeks as he grunted against my neck. "I won't let you go back to him, Natalie, because you won't come back to *me*. You're mine. I need you, but you won't come back." His voice broke.

He was right. Just now, he'd lost me. He hadn't been paying attention at all. All the times I'd tried to show him he was the center of my world, that I loved him, that I was loyal and devoted...he'd been somewhere in his head, waiting for someone to let him down.

It turned out that person was me.

"You're hurting me." I winced, the friction from the rug beneath me beginning to burn.

That wasn't what I meant, though.

My chest ached as my heart broke, the ache spreading through my body like seeping blood.

"Turn your head." His voice was commanding. "I want your mouth, Natalie. Kiss me."

I shook my head slowly, crying harder, my shoulder slamming rhythmically into one of the feet of the bed. If he kissed me now I would lose all the little splinters of my heart that were shearing off with every violent thrust, my body betraying me as it moved against my will to meet his.

What hurt most was that I still wanted him, knowing there was a violently angry man living inside of him.

He came with an angry roar, a string of hair-raising curses falling from his lips as he dropped his full weight on me. He brought his fist down hard into the floor and I felt the sound reverberate through the wood. My heart shattered with it, and when he quickly separated our bodies and walked into the bathroom, I curled into a ball on the rug.

I'd had enough disconnected, soulless sex in my life to know what it was. It felt like he was taking out his anger on me before throwing me away.

I loved this man more than anything, but I knew now with absolute certainty that he was too fucked up to love me back.

FORTY-FOUR

Thomas

Natalie didn't join me in the shower the next morning. She stayed in the bed, turned away from me, and she waited to get up until I dressed and left the room.

I'd been struck by a wave of remorse the instant I walked away from her the night before, a cold rush of complete sobriety and clarity.

What had I just done?

I cleaned up quickly, my thinking suddenly remarkably clear, and I moved back into the room to lift her small body from the floor and tuck her into the bed.

I cleaned her gently, penitently, with a warm cloth before pressing a kiss between her thighs and I felt her whole body contract with a wince as she tried to shrink away from me.

I crawled in beside her and pulled her into my arms. She'd resisted slightly, keeping her back to me, and an apology was right behind my lips, but I didn't have all the words I needed. There were no words for what I'd done, disconnecting my heart and mind as I'd hurt her with my words and body. It hadn't been my intent, but I'd lost my shit on her, the last person who deserved it.

I kissed her shoulder gently, smoothing her hair as she heaved a shuddering sigh and she let me hold her for a few moments before pulling away. I'd been too rough with her, and without warning, and I suspected what I'd broken was something I couldn't see.

She curled into a ball, sobbing silently until the bed shook and silent tears of shame ran down my cheeks. I was a sonofabitch, because I was mostly crying for myself. I was ashamed, miserable, penitent and terrified.

Congratulations, asshole. Now you've made it a sure thing.

I didn't sleep at all and I'm pretty sure she didn't either, because when she finally came downstairs for breakfast her eyes were red, her lips swollen, and there were purple crescents beneath each beautiful blue eye.

"You fucker," Noah breathed into my ear the instant he saw her. There was a dark bruise below her ear and another on her shoulder where her sweater kept slipping down. She didn't even try to hide it.

He was sitting beside me, shoveling pancakes and coffee into his pie hole. "You're blood and I love you more than myself, but if *you* did that to that gorgeous woman, I swear to God I'll..." He stopped talking, dropping his fork as his hand clenched into a fist, and the clattering noise made Natalie jump. It intensified the pounding in my head and I put both hands over my eyes.

"I'll do it if he won't," Finn whisper-shouted across the table. "You need help, Thomas, and you can pay for my therapy while you're at it." She looked over at Noah, who looked confused, shaking her head. "Stupid, where *were* you last night? Of course he did that. Those are sex marks on her. He kept all of us up with his angry fuck noises." She made a face like she might throw up.

Noah's eyes got big.

Gerry didn't say anything. Her gaze was sympathetic, concerned, and something else I didn't like: sad. I couldn't look away, wishing she and I shared the language I'd had with Maren. I needed to communicate things without words, because words were deeply inadequate for what was happening.

I couldn't eat, knowing what was to come, and as the sun crept into the house we all rose from the table.

Mrs. Jensen made an appearance, touching all of our shoulders lightly as she collected our dishes and gestured we should head out toward the terrace. She slipped a glass of something into my hand and I drank it carefully, fearful it would make a reappearance, but it seemed to settle my stomach and take the edge off what promised to be a violent headache.

Jensen had a golf cart outside, a six-seater that was ready to go, pointed in the general direction of the vineyard. We climbed on quickly and he started it up, waiting patiently, and it took me a moment to realize Natalie wasn't there. My eyes swept a semi-circle and panic started to beat with frantic wings inside my chest.

Finn's expression was weirdly smug. "Yeah, Thom," she whispered from behind me. "That's what happens when the lion bites his tamer." She raised an eyebrow. I could feel it even without seeing it: judgment. I deserved it.

"You're rabid, bro." It was Noah, leaning forward to punch me hard in the shoulder blade, and he mouthed "Rawr," dropping his fingers into a clawing motion over my shoulder. Clearly Finn had filled him in.

My first reaction was anger and I looked over my shoulder at him. "Jealous?" I asked him, my voice low.

"Maybe a little." He grinned sheepishly. "Angry sexy time can be pretty hot. Sometimes I like to push Eve's buttons just so she'll..."

"Disgusting," Finn cut in. "I should have offered the poor girl a heating pad." She pointed an accusatory finger at me. "*You* need to say you're sorry, Tiger. She was fucking *crying*–yeah, I heard that part, too."

I sat waiting for it, the words bouncing around in my head while it tried to catalog them. But Finn had something else for me.

"I've had my fair share of rough sex," she whispered, and her eyes were fierce.

Now there was something I didn't want to think about.

"Riding her that hard has to be consensual, Thom. You probably knocked out some of her teeth with your stupid dick. But you and I both know that's not what upset her."

Noah snorted at the visual, while Gerry and Jensen pretended they weren't overhearing anything.

I should have been embarrassed we'd been overheard, especially considering the guest rooms were on the opposite wing of the house. But my brain fixated on one detail: She had been crying while I took from her what she willingly gave to me. She hadn't fought me or tried to stop me, but she'd been upset. Had I noticed that? Had I been so blinded by my own rage and booze and need that I'd ignored her responses? I'd known she was angry with me, but had I been so lost inside my own head that I'd given myself the green light to hurt her?

And now Finn was pissed at me–furious was my guess, her gaze unflinching and arctic. She could pull a hairy eyeball like no one else I knew.

I couldn't catch my breath, my head spinning as I looked around, trying to find her.

"I'll meet you there, Mr. Jensen."

Suddenly she was there, her voice soft. Her small body was covered with a fuzzy sweater thing and some tight black leggings. They skimmed the curves I'd touched with my fingertips and worshiped with my mouth, and a sharp stab of fear told me I'd never taste her skin again. The thought made me sick with fear and a desperate sort of longing.

"I'd much prefer to walk."

"Aye, lassie. I'll take them and come back fer ya, case ya change yer mind." He nodded, and I caught the look that passed between them.

Shit, shit, shit. Had it been so loud that it woke the Jensens, too?

I jumped out of my seat and moved to the very back row, which was open. It gave me the room to pat the seat next to me as Jensen rolled slowly past her, and when she shook her head at me, I stretched a hand out in a wordless plea: *I'm an asshole, but I need you more than I've ever needed anything. Please forgive me.*

She stood with her arms crossed, watching us with an expression that made my chest hurt as we zipped away from her, and something terrible started to ache as the distance between our bodies increased.

What had I done? I'd told a woman who struggled with being *enough* that she wasn't meeting my expectations.

It struck me that our shared fear was enough to be our undoing.

I had no idea what to do next or how to fix this, but I was pretty sure this was the worst I'd ever fucked up.

• • • •

I DON'T KNOW HOW, BUT we beat Harrison's crew by a solid ten minutes. It gave all of us time to walk the headstones, and I kissed Maren's and Aden's before squatting at the edge of the clearing.

Natalie still hadn't arrived and, looking over my shoulder, I couldn't see her shape moving down the rows of vines. It left me unsettled, a great, sucking feeling in my chest like my heart couldn't be depended upon to beat without her.

What was she doing to me?

A low rumble shook the earth and I swallowed hard as two huge pickup trucks brought in workers with shovels, followed by an enormous, rumbling backhoe and, finally, Harrison's dusty white luxury SUV.

Douchebag.

"That's right, boys," he called, directing the backhoe into position and firing off a volley of commands in really poor Spanish to the men carrying shovels.

My blood pressure was ratcheting up exponentially and though Thomas and Finn moved in to flank me, my gaze was still behind us, on the vineyard, waiting for the golf cart to zip up one of the rows with Natalie in one of the seats.

When had she become my air?

The minutes crawled by and the backhoe took giant bites out of the earth, the workers moving in to sift through the rest with their shovels.

I couldn't breathe, watching with a sick feeling in the pit of my stomach as the first tiny coffin was hoisted to the surface by one team of workers. The other team worked behind them, removing the larger, heavier headstones from the older graves.

"Don't mix them up!" Harrison screamed, adamant each be labeled accordingly and carefully strapped down to the first flatbed that had backed slowly down the dirt drive, waiting for its cargo. And though I had thought I'd lose my shit watching, I found I was watching Harrison with interest, because he was losing *his* shit. He directed vigorously and cursed vociferously, hands flying with outraged gestures as he tried to bridge a language barrier while in a very emotional state.

Small arms went around my ribcage and a face pressed into my back and I drew the first deep, clear breath I'd been able to take all morning. My head dropped to my chest, the ache intensifying.

She came for me, even after what I did.

Harrison's eye was caught by Natalie's movement and I watched his face set, his jaw clamping down hard as her hands moved over my chest, her palms wrapping upward, with one curling over my shoulder and the other across my ribs. She was restraining me as much as she was holding me together, and as another coffin came out of the earth, she squeezed harder, her lips warm between my shoulderblades through the thin cotton of my shirt.

I don't deserve it, but she loves me.

It hit me like a thunderbolt: She'd done nothing but show me how much she loved me and I hadn't earned any of it. She had given it freely, but all I'd done was take.

It took two flatbeds to remove twelve coffins and all twelve headstones, all members of Harrison's immediate or extended family.

He smirked gleefully at me as the giant machine backfilled the holes, the workers tamping it down with feet and shovels.

Where there had been a graveyard, now there was only sifted earth.

Noah and Finn stood beside me, Finn holding my hand and tucked into Noah's side, while Gerry stood on my other side, holding my other hand, Natalie wrapped tightly around my back.

I was surrounded by love, whereas Harrison was surrounded by emptiness and death, and with a final look of triumph he got into his car and drove away, taking it all with him.

We watched them go and I heaved a deep, shuddering breath. It was something that had plagued my nightmares for the past year, and now it was over.

In my nightmares I'd been alone, on my knees, sobbing as the last thing I loved was taken from me. But here I was, held up by the living.

I had been the one to insist on suffering in solitude, but they hadn't let me.

Noah hadn't allowed it.

Finn wouldn't have dreamed of it.

Gerry considered it unprofessional.

Natalie refused to let me.

It was Natalie who hiccupped first, in what sounded like a small sob, and all four of us turned as one to wrap ourselves around her. She folded into my arms while the other three gathered around us, holding us tight, and I pressed her to my chest. She was crying for me, taking it all into her tender heart.

Maybe, the thought occurred, I'd spent so long grieving that I'd already been through the worst of it.

There was nothing left to pour out.

I was empty, waiting to be filled up again with something better, and I said a quick prayer that I could convince her to be that something better.

I had to fix what I'd broken between us.

Jensen waited for us patiently at the treeline and as he caught sight of Natalie's crumpled face, he shot me a murderous look.

Because she's so easy to love, the thought occurred to me with a flash. I thought of the brief exchanges she'd had with Mrs. Jensen, the ones she thought I hadn't noticed when she sweetly thanked her for things, or offered her assistance.

The looks she'd exchanged with Jensen himself when they'd gone from caring for her to caring for me.

The way Finn was already jumping in to protect her–Gerry, too.

And fuck me, I thought with a sickening feeling in my gut, but I was pretty sure Noah was completely in love with her.

After arriving back at the house, Natalie was distant again. She folded back into herself, quiet and withdrawn. No questions, whatsoever. That scared me more than anything else and I spent the meal, then the afternoon, trying to draw her back out, but to no avail.

She was locked down tight.

Lunch was somber and quiet, and Jensen mixed something for each of us that may have actually been used as a chemical weapon during the First World War: noxious, but highly effective. Also, it had delightfully tranquilizing effects, and everyone collapsed into comfortable chairs after lunch.

Considering my behavior the night before, I decided to forego the liquid fortifications and opted instead for a glass of the tea Finn was drinking. She told me it would do wonderful things for the strength of my uterus and I made a face at her.

Originally, Natalie and I were flying back on the following Wednesday, having extended our trip in order to spend more time in

Sonoma, but as I got ready for bed, Natalie quickly packed and I knew she was keeping her word to her mother-in-law.

That was something I was learning about her: she was honorable. She would fly to New York tomorrow, without me, because she was doing what was right and what was expected of her, even though it was going to drive me out of my mind.

I slipped from the room to make two brief phone calls, one to my pilot and one to the man I kept on payroll in New York.

Following her into the bathroom, I tried to pull her close, sneaking up behind her and wrapping my hands around her hips as she brushed her teeth. She flinched, shrugged off my hands and took her makeup bag to drop into the larger bag she'd already packed and left by the bedroom door.

I almost resorted to begging when I crawled into bed and she scooted to the far side, facing away from me. I could feel her misery and for once, I thought, the tables might have been turned.

I hated it.

I wanted *her* back, warm and soft, snuggled up into my side even if she wouldn't let me touch her beyond that.

Instead, I crept up behind her until she huffed and pushed a pillow between our bodies.

The silent rebuke stung, but I deserved it.

When I woke in the morning, after a night of fitful, uncomfortable sleep with her in my bed but not my arms, I found all three bracelets and the earrings I'd given her resting on my nightstand.

I could feel it in the air of the room: She wasn't coming back.

FORTY-FIVE

Natalie

Noah was already in the kitchen when I hurried quietly downstairs the next morning. He was like a seal sitting at the island, clapping and barking as Mrs. Jensen tossed more eggs, more sausages, more potatoes, on the plate in front of him. The amount he could eat was truly astonishing, but I could tell Mrs. Jensen loved it.

Everyone loved Noah, because they couldn't help it, and Mrs. J. was no exception. Even she was not immune to the charms of such an overgrown child.

She passed me coffee with a sympathetic look, folding me up into her arms without a word. But I was all cried out, my head aching, my face swollen, my eyes puffy, and Noah stopped mid-chew when he caught sight of my face. He patted the seat next to him and when Mrs. Jensen released me, I moved with aching limbs to take the seat he'd pulled close.

Wrapping an arm around me, Noah tucked me against his side and squeezed with one giant bear paw. He didn't say anything, just held on, and I rested my head against his enormous shoulder, heaving a deep sigh. It was easy to be close to him, because his heart was pure and gentle.

Setting down his fork carefully, Noah reached his other arm around my front and I felt him fumbling with something. His left arm came back down and he slid his watch onto the countertop, placing his hand wrist-up on the island. I could see a long white scar running across the inside of his wrist, with two tiny birds tattooed over it.

"My girls," he said softly, clenching the fingers on that hand and I reached out to trace the small marks.

"Thom was there for me when I had no one," he said quietly, and the solemn tone of his voice scared me a little, because Noah was not serious. Not ever. It was his most endearing and his most maddening trait. But suddenly I suspected he ran deep, broken and scarred on the inside while he made the rest of the world laugh.

“He stayed with me when I was so fucked up, I was no good to anyone. He made me get help and he paid for it.” He cleared his throat and I thought he wiped his eyes with his shirtsleeve, but I hadn’t moved my head from his shoulder.

“I give him shit, Nat, cuz no one else will–keeps him even. I’ve always tried to be there for him, even when he shut me out the same way I did when I needed help. Because he made sure I had help. He hasn’t done that for himself, and he won’t let us. He’s all kinds ‘a fucked up and you don’t just snap outta that kinda space in your head. He’s still figurin’ it out, and it makes him do dumb shit.”

“Did he tell you why I have to go?” I asked quietly, my voice thick, and his stubble caught in my hair when he nodded.

“Yeah, you’re doin’ the right thing. And I’m not makin’ excuses for his sorry ass, because he’s jealous and hurt for no good reason. In a weird way he’s afraid that if you leave, you’re gone for good. Like maybe you’ll come to your senses–decide not to pull the plug and go back to your brain dead husband or somethin’. I think he feels like he’s not enough to make you stay.”

I snapped up, my eyes wide, and Noah quickly held up his hands in a gesture of peace. “Hey, sorry–dumb thing to say about the husband. But Thom’s head isn’t workin’ right, right now. It hasn’t been since he met you–well, a long time before that, but in a different way, ‘cuz like I said, he ain’t never gotten the help he needed.” He shifted uncomfortably, and I knew we were getting into scary territory for him.

“He started callin’ me again the week Gerry told ‘im he needed to replace your roof, and at first he didn’t tell me why. He hadn’t even tried to talk to me for a real long time–totally shut me out. But he was bein’ weird...and after a while he started asking me all these stupid questions about women and what they like and...well, then I knew.” He grinned a huge grin. “My Angel thought it was stupid-funny, probably ‘cuz I don’t know shit about women, and she helped me with ideas.”

“Ideas?”

“Yeah, nice stuff he could do for you to make up for being such an asshole.”

I had a suspicion this Eve person was to thank for my new kitchen, the windows in my bedroom, and quite probably the newly installed air conditioning.

Mrs. Jensen remained silent, stirring and scraping, rinsing and chopping. I couldn't tell whether she had her earbuds in, but she was being so good at minding her own business that it seemed likely.

"Make 'im come to you," Noah said quietly, and I swallowed hot coffee a little too fast, wincing. "All the other times he messed up, you were good about makin' him come to you, and he needed that, to figure out he was being a dick. He didn't have anyone tellin' 'im he was being a jackass. People don't push him 'cuz of who he is. This time he's gotta realize he's gonna lose somethin' only 'cuz he pushed it away. 'Cuz you give and give and he takes and takes...you kept lettin' 'im hurt you." He had the most serious look on his face I'd ever seen.

"What if I don't want him to come to me anymore? He pretty much told me that what I'm doing isn't enough," I said, a deep sadness making my shoulders hunch forward.

"He don't mean that." Noah's eyes went wide. "He can't. I see the way he looks at you, Nat, like you're the only woman on this green earth. It's gross." He smiled a little.

I smacked his shoulder with the back of my hand.

"What if he *doesn't* come to me?" I asked quietly, my eyes downcast. It was a real possibility and it scared me half to death. "He thinks I'm leaving him, so why would he chase me?"

He hadn't even offered to come with me, and it was something I didn't think I should have to ask him to do.

"Cuz you got somethin' he needs," he answered simply, shoveling in an enormous forkful of food, and I blew out a loud puff of air.

"Nah, not that. Well, maybe that too." He chuckled and dropped his fork on his plate. "His heart, Nat. You got his heart. It's probably all broken and stuff, but you're pretty good at fixin' things. Not your fault he's shit at tellin' you that kinda stuff."

He picked his fork back up and started shoveling more food into his mouth. "That's all I got, baby girl. I can't talk about the mushy stuff or I'm gonna hafta hand over my man card or somethin'." He shivered.

The tiniest smile was perking up the corners of Mrs. Jensen's mouth.

I finished my coffee and held up my hand to Mrs. J., who gestured toward an empty plate. There was no way I could eat, not with the way my stomach was tied up in knots.

Jensen stood in the doorway, waiting patiently and he moved quickly behind his wife, dropping a kiss into her hair. It was the first time I'd seen any affection between the two of them. In fact, it was possible it was the first time I'd even seen them in the same room together. Then he whispered something to her in a brogue so thick, I couldn't have understood it if he'd written it down. Whatever it was, it made her smile and nudge him gently in the ribs.

"No rush, Miss Natalie," he said gently, "but yer flight's at nine, an' it be goin' on seven. Take us about half an hour t'get t'the airport."

I kissed Noah's cheek and he blushed a furious shade of red as I moved around the counter to do the same to Mrs. J. She patted my cheek when I did. "I'll see you soon, dear, and don't you worry. These things have a way of working themselves out."

"Aye," Jensen agreed. "The boy's a dafty arse, but he'll come 'round."

I had no idea what that meant, but I was surprised Jensen had voiced such a strong opinion, and with so many words, and Noah grinned and chuckled when he said it.

Jensen drove in silence, his eyes occasionally flicking toward the rear view mirror to check on me. It seemed like there was something he wanted to say, but he didn't know how to say it, so I braced an elbow on the window and watched the lovely countryside roll past. I was done pushing people to talk.

"He been in touch with the family," he said finally, reaching over his shoulder to hand me a scrap of paper. "Chartered ye a flight so the family don't need to handle it. Car be waitin' when ye land."

I nodded, surprised by the thoughtfulness and the expense. It felt like another apology.

I reviewed the details carefully. It would be a long day of flying, and returning information had me back in the air two days later.

I shook my head. While I appreciated the thoughtfulness, the highhanded presumption irritated me: once again, he seemed to think I would go to him after he'd pushed me away. He had learned nothing.

An agent was waiting to take me through security procedures and Jensen handed off my bag while my flight information was verified and my ID checked. He squeezed my shoulder then, one side of his mouth drawing up in a grimace I supposed was meant to be a smile. "We'll be seein' ye soon then, lass."

Before I could thank him or even form a response, he was gone.

The pilot and flight attendant introduced themselves and I was offered a beverage, a snack, a blanket, a Dramamine, and some reading materials all in the same breath. Both of them, I noticed, seemed inordinately nervous and I assured them both that I'd take some water, but all I really wanted to do was sleep.

I'd hardly slept at all the past two nights and weariness covered my body like a blanket left to soak in water, weighing down my limbs and suffocating my thoughts. It was beyond exhaustion. I was so emotionally oversaturated, to touch me would have wrung tears from my pores.

The attendant mixed something for me that she called a "sleep aid," with a wink, and I wondered if she'd crushed up a Xanax in vodka, which seemed pretty unorthodox.

Immediately I understood this was very much not a charter. This was Thomas's plane, with his personal pilot and flight attendant, anxious to make a good impression after receiving terse instructions from their grumpy boss.

I wasn't at all surprised he had a personal plane, especially once I considered how often he traveled. Nor was I surprised he hadn't told me, or initially flown us to California on it, as he was still weirdly cagey about anything pertaining to the number of zeroes associated with his name. I understood his hesitation, his unwillingness to share information with me given his past, but it hurt anyway.

Once it was safe to leave my seat, I took my phone from my bag and let myself into the small bedroom at the back of the plane. I crashed face down onto the silky blue blanket, toeing off my shoes as I checked my phone with one eye.

What had I expected? *Nothing.* But I'd hoped. It was just after nine and I knew Thomas was awake, probably already downstairs in his office, having loaded up on Mrs. Jensen's breakfast goodies. But still...no missed calls.

No messages.

No texts.

I'm sorry.

I miss you.

I should have gone with you.

I'll meet you there.

I threw the phone under a pillow and rolled slowly, wrapping myself in the blanket as I went. Sleep was going to be a welcome way to forget.

• • • •

AFTER SLEEPING THE entirety of the flight–probably not the most auspicious first private flight ever–I awoke groggy and grumpy. According to the flight attendant, we would be landing in twenty minutes, so I needed to be in my seat and buckled as soon as possible. That left me all of five minutes to use the bathroom and change into something that would level Farida's lofty fashion playing ground.

I quickly put on the grey pants and white shell I'd worn to travel in previously, because even Farida couldn't find fault with something this simple.

For a second, I regretted leaving the jewelry on Thomas's nightstand, as Farida was always sporting something amazing. I'd never been big on jewelry, but it would have been nice to invite the questions for once, and to shock her with a little sophistication. She'd made it perfectly clear, more than once, that I was operating at a deficit in that area, and most others.

As we descended I quickly applied a little makeup and tried to fix my hair. I'd be coming off a runway, all right, but Farida would be the one looking like a supermodel.

A flash from my phone caught my attention and I looked down to see a text notification from Thomas: *Let me know you're safe.*

I didn't even bother to open it, not wanting to give him the satisfaction of a read receipt. Instead, I looked up at the flight attendant, who was strapping herself into her seat as we prepared to land. She smiled at me brightly. Expectantly.

"At some point today," I said and my voice felt strange, "would you mind letting Mr. Atholton know that we arrived safely? I'm afraid my schedule won't permit."

That was obviously a lie, as I'd have plenty of time in the car.

Her smile faltered just a little. She looked uncertain and a little confused, maybe scared. "Uh, yes...certainly, Miss James. I will see to it he's made aware."

I nodded my thanks and gave her a tight smile. Thomas was going to have to try a hell of a lot harder than that to reopen the lines of communication.

Maybe he could start by getting his ass on a plane.

• • • •

IT WAS FAROUK WHO MET me at the information desk: Ahmad's younger, less successful and extraordinarily envious brother. He, too, was well acquainted with being *less.*

He was the one who envied Ahmad's law degree, though he couldn't be bothered to finish his undergrad.

The one who admired our lovely home in Beacon Hill, but still lived at home with Farida.

The one who'd seconded Farida's opinion that I was beneath Ahmad and unsuitable as a wife, then propositioned me the night before my wedding: *Brothers should share.*

Farouk didn't have Ahmad's tall grace or beauty. Instead, he was his father's son, of average height with a stocky build and receding hairline, his nose just a little too flat to be handsome.

I shivered a little when his coal-black eyes flicked over me and his lips turned up with the slightest sneer.

"Natalie," he greeted me smoothly in what was the most shocking thing about him: a deep, rich, seductive voice. "You are radiant. My brother has been a fool to practice such neglect."

His fingers stroked the sleeve of the kitten-soft cashmere sweater I'd found waiting for me in the car. The deep grey-blue brought out my eyes, which I could tell he was appreciating.

Farouk was a pig and a lout, but that didn't mean he wasn't a charmer.

Ahmad had used a bitter expression for him for years, to the effect that pointing Farouk's dick in one direction was the way in which he would go, only to be constantly misled by it. He'd been ashamed by his brother's wandering eye, but now I knew it was only because Farouk wasn't discrete, whereas Ahmad would have rathered die than be indiscrete.

Funny how that one had washed out.

I bit back my retort about great sex giving a girl that certain glow, but I was sure it wouldn't be appreciated. Like Farida and my mother, if there was anything the Sayad men did not joke about, it was sex and money. I was operating within very familiar parameters.

Without asking my permission, he tucked my arm firmly beneath his and hustled us toward the elevators. The thought of being trapped in a small box with him was enough to cause anxiety to squeeze my throat, and I breathed a sigh of relief when the elevator stopped at the fourth floor. I silenced my phone and dropped it into my bag as Farouk led me from the elevators and down the hall.

A few of the nurses at the station looked up as we passed and I wondered how many of them he'd already tried to charm. It was a sure thing none of them knew–and would never know–he was married.

"You've arrived."

Farida's voice was at its typical level of warmth, which was to say the room was glacial. I chose not to respond, finally pulling myself from Farouk's grasp and crossing the room to lightly touch Farida's shoulders.

Kiss, kiss.

I stepped back as she surveyed me critically.

I noted that despite her bedside vigil, not a hair was out of place and though her abaya was draped neatly across a nearby chair, her simple pants and shell were flawless. Not a wrinkle. As usual, she was irreproachable.

There was a snore from the corner and I turned quickly, surprised to see Halim slumped in a chair pulled up next to the bed. He was out cold, the loose, jowly skin on his face threatening to stage a landslide as his chin tipped toward his chest.

The monitors beeped and the respirator made whooshing, sucking noises as I stood assessing the situation. I felt my eyes well a little and Farida softened immediately. "This has been shocking for all of us," she said, her voice low, as gracious as I'd ever heard it. "I can imagine it has been for you as well."

What was I supposed to say to my mother-in-law?

I'm sorry your son was sleeping with a man and not me?

I'm sorry the light of your life disappointed you at the end?

For the first time since we'd met, I was pretty sure I was the more desirable choice. But there was nothing to say–nothing nice anyway, and I moved closer to the bed.

Ahmad looked as though he was sleeping peacefully, his face beautiful in repose. Someone had been shaving him and aside from the bandage wrapped around his head, he looked like he might open his eyes and sit up. Only the monitors and respirator told a different story.

Halim's eyes slow-blinked open and took me in critically. "It's about time the wife arrived," he said, clearing his throat, and I drew myself up a little straighter.

Here it comes.

Pushing himself to his feet, he leaned over the bed toward me, getting a finger right up in my face.

"What kind of woman is across the country with another man while her husband lies in a hospital bed?"

Halim had scared me for years. He was only a few inches taller than me, but he was broad and fat. His girth was hardly sufficient to contain the temper that burst out every chance it got.

For all those wives, he seemed sexually frustrated.

I smoothed my fingers down Ahmad's arm just because I knew it would drive Halim nuts. He found public displays of affection distasteful, which wasn't really a surprise. Somewhere deep inside, I suspected he harbored Wahhabist beliefs.

"This man has not been my *husband* for nearly four years," I said in a voice far stronger than I felt, and I watched his forehead wrinkle up in confusion, then the light of understanding dawned in his eyes. It was clearly something he found distasteful.

"I was not unfaithful to him," I said more quietly. "I do not require his permission to divorce. He has humiliated me and defiled our marriage. He broke our vows when he started keeping a man in my place."

Halim shuddered and I heard Farida draw in a sharp breath. She was a lot like my mother, I thought, uncomfortable the instant anyone started to talk about money or sex. But in this case the topic was far heavier.

Ahmad's family would certainly have been more receptive to the idea of him keeping another woman.

Keeping other women was something this family found familiar. Halim was a wealthy man and could afford to indulge his tastes for variety: nice cars, big houses, racing horses, and other women seemed to take his fancy often enough.

Farida's rank in her household was that of third wife, of which Halim kept four. This was something I knew only because Ahmad and Farouk were the only sons in the household, and therefore had been doted upon by all the wives, and were still, like they were kings.

The rest of Halim's issuance were female, a troublesome and expensive lot to marry off with hefty dowries to fanatical, weak-chinned men.

My mother-in-law was the most beautiful of Halim's wives and therefore public-facing. When required, she attended events with him. She was gracious and charitable, running a mini public relations campaign to keep up the good name of his house. The other three wives worked in the background, helping her when they weren't bickering, but clearly jealous of her preferred status.

Farouk looked considerably less smarmy when he crossed the room to stand near me. He sighed heavily, looking down at his brother. "He was a hard man to love," he said quietly and I felt my eyebrows raise. "He was not warm or kind, but people were drawn to him."

I nodded in agreement. "He's beautiful; people couldn't help themselves. And he's so smart..."

I was having a hard time putting Ahmad's life in a past tense, though I knew that was appropriate. It made me terribly, deeply sad for him. He had been a poor husband, but he hadn't intentionally been a bad person. His life was dictated by his sense of honor and compunction, and I knew without a doubt that hiding his true desires from the world had been eating away at his soul.

I had been there to witness most of the battle.

"The doctors say there is no hope." Farouk leaned heavily against the rail of the bed. "There were two bullets, and there is nothing left to save." The corners of his mouth pulled down and Farida turned quickly so we couldn't see her face, her shoulders beginning to shake.

"Why did this happen?" I asked, feeling perilously close to tears myself. Everyone in the room understood I would have to be the one to sign the order, letting Ahmad slip away without the aid of the machines that were keeping him alive.

"There was an argument over money," he sighed heavily. "I know only what Umi has told me." His eyes moved to his mother. "The man had a key to the apartment and he burst in while they were having dinner. He was angry that my brother banished him to the home in Boston while our parents visited. He was angry to be kept a secret, and that my brother would not increase his allowance. He wanted more financial freedom. It meant removing the wife from the picture so that he could claim her portion of the marital assets."

"That I was divorcing Ahmad wasn't enough?" I asked, and Halim looked at me sharply.

"Divorce would have taken assets *away* from him when they were divided," Farouk said slowly and I gripped the bed rail tightly, sliding down into a squat.

Oh, there's more.

"This man somehow knew your wills remained unchanged. Yours left all your worldly wealth to your husband and they argued in front of my mother because Ahmad refused to have you...disposed of." He looked incredibly uncomfortable and I glanced up quickly, wondering if the look I saw on Halim's face meant he would have preferred that as well.

"His assets were substantial," Farida said quietly from where she sat against the opposite wall.

"*Your* assets are substantial," Farouk said as he looked at me, correcting his mother. "There will be no question, as his will was never revised."

Farida's face crumpled a little and I wondered whether it was jealousy or anger. I was fairly certain she didn't feel I should be compensated for the marriage I was trying to leave.

"It will *not* be contested." Farouk was looking meaningfully at his mother.

Since when had he become my ally?

"This woman has endured enough at the hands of your son and my brother. She has protected our family name for long enough, Umi, and he has hidden much from her unfairly."

Farouk helped me up and into a chair. I knew I looked dazed, and I was. I had no idea what Ahmad's investment accounts held or how much was in the shared account he'd taken over.

There would be debts to settle and I would have to meet with insurance people.

Deeds would have to be revised to read my name only, and then there was the question of whether I kept the homes or sold them.

Did I want to move back to Boston?

"I suspect this makes things much easier for you, Natalie." Farida's voice was bitter.

I thought about it for a moment.

"No," I finally said, pushing out of the chair and crossing the room to sit next to her. I took her hand and she flinched, as if I were a leper. "This is just a different kind of disaster. He and I will no longer fight, but this will not save any work. Farida, you cannot think I wished for this to happen."

The four of us sat quietly for a time and Farida's hand finally relaxed in my own. It would be the last meaningful contact I would have with this woman, I knew. It was a relief, yet I would not have wished the circumstances upon anyone, even her.

A nurse appeared and when Farouk nodded at her, she produced a pile of paperwork.

I read carefully before signing, though Ahmad had been very clear when we'd drawn up our wills. He did not wish to be kept on machines if anything were to happen, and I had expressed the same sentiment and had filed a similar directive. There was no question in my mind that I was doing the right thing, though it filled me with guilt, and I swiped a hand at my eyes as I signed the orders.

I couldn't stay to watch it happen.

I couldn't watch Farida fall apart as they chanted the Shahada and the Dua. Instead, I kissed Ahmad's cheek and squeezed his hand, stepping out into the hallway when Farida began to cry. She didn't need me there. None of them did.

Two men wearing keffiyehs stood with me, hands folded as they waited. I knew they'd been summoned by Farouk, who had undoubtedly taken over burial preparations. These men would remove Ahmad's body, taking him to a traditional Islamic funeral home, where the last rites would be administered in accordance with their tradition. Then his body would be shipped immediately to Saudi Arabia for burial.

"You have respected his wishes, so I will respect yours."

I startled at Farouk's low voice and I looked up to find he had stepped from the room. I knew I was staring at him with great big stupid cow eyes, and he smiled ever so slightly.

"You are not familiar with our customs and you are no longer familiar with your husband's body. This would be strange and uncomfortable for you, but that you came–despite my mother..." he rolled his eyes exaggeratedly and I couldn't help but smile back. "You have done your duty and a great service to your husband. I thank you for this and I will perform the rites for him."

I was still staring dumbly and he placed a hand on my forearm and leaned into my ear. "You are sure I cannot convince you to become my second wife?" He leaned back, an evil grin on his face, and I laughed weakly.

"I am not serious," he said, the smile slipping quickly. "You are a flower that would wither in the desert and something so lovely must be cared for and protected. I hope there is a good man in your life to do that for you now. One who will honor you as my brother did not." His voice trailed off and he looked a little hopeful, but I didn't know whether it was for me or for him.

"After all, my wife would hate you." The grin was back. "You are far too golden and lovely."

He was right. Fatima had a quick wit and sparkling eyes, but she was dark and hairy, quickly running to fat. She'd hated me instantly, possibly only because I'd married Ahmad, the beautiful, successful, more desirable son.

Farouk slipped back into the room and the men followed him. It took them only moments and while they conducted their business, I waited in the hallway.

What I was waiting for, I didn't know. I hadn't been able to think five minutes ahead all day long and it was getting late. I was weak with hunger, unsure where I would spend the night.

Farida followed closely after the men as they wheeled Ahmad's body out of the room. She brushed past me without a glance, followed shortly by Halim. The fat little man trailed after his much taller, graceful wife like a puppy and I smiled to myself as I thought about who really wore the pants in that relationship.

Thankfully, we had already said our goodbyes.

Farouk was the last to leave the room and the burden of being the only remaining son seemed heavy on his shoulders. He looked suddenly older and worn, the teasing smile gone and he rubbed a hand over sad, weary eyes before squeezing my shoulder.

I nodded at him. "Mashallah, brother. I will pray for your peace."

His eyes widened a little when I called him brother and his smile was soft. "Mashallah, kind sister." He squeezed my shoulder again and hurried down the hallway.

I watched him go, sorting my thoughts as I dug into my bag to retrieve my phone. Then I too walked down the hallway, to the elevators, and took one to the lobby.

• • • •

THERE WAS A MAN STANDING in the lobby in a full suit, looking down at his phone. He looked up as I walked past, on my way to the door to hail a cab.

"Miss James?" He looked hopeful. I wondered how many women he'd asked that question before getting it right.

"Yes." I answered with some hesitation, for obvious reasons.

His face relaxed into an expression of relief. "Mr. Atholton has sent me to collect you. I will drive you to your accomodations for the evening."

"Uh..." My brain spun. "I appreciate that, but I'm not sure that's a good idea." This was not the man who had driven me to the hospital.

"Ma'am, I am not attempting to argue with you. However, I do not question Mr. Atholton's directives and if you don't mind, it will make things much easier for me if you will permit me to do my job."

The look I gave him was probably one of surprise, and I followed him silently from the building. He directed me to wait at the front and he hurried away, pulling up moments later in a Town Car.

Settling me into the seat, he closed the door behind me and tucked my small suitcase into the trunk.

I dropped my handbag onto the seat and began fishing around for my phone again. There was another voicemail from my mother, a series of voicemails from curious reporters, one from Ahmad's lawyer and one from Thomas. I pulled his up immediately, sinking into the creaking leather. I was angry with him, but his voice was soothing to me.

I need you here.

"Baby, I need to hear from you. Passing along a message through Caroline was not what I wanted. I expected *your* voice. I need to know you're ok after whatever you've had to do today. And after...the stupid things I've done, even though I don't expect your forgiveness."

He sounded pissed, not contrite.

"Andre will drive you to the Plaza, where a room has been reserved for you. He will provide you with a credit card for your expenses–*all* expenses–and I expect you will feed yourself sufficiently."

Who was this guy, coming off all Mr. Grey? I was trying to decide whether it was hot or just made me really, really mad.

Not only was he being presumptuous, but there still hadn't been a real word of apology.

"Natalie." His voice was low, and I thought it sounded like suffering. "I need you. Please help me figure out how to do this."

There was no goodbye, and I sat staring at the face of my phone for a moment, distracted only when Andre passed a heavy black card over his shoulder.

"The room is already taken care of, ma'am. Mr. Atholton insisted you be provided with this in order to handle any other expenses."

I took the card hesitantly. "Thank you," I said, tucking it into my bag with no intention of using it.

"Andre, can I ask how long you've worked for Thomas?"

He glanced at me in the rear view mirror before answering and I thought his expression was somewhat cautious.

"Mr. Atholton has kept me on staff for the past eight years to handle incidentals."

Oh have mercy, I was an incidental.

"He has a lot of those, then?" My voice was positively acidic.

"Ah, I didn't mean it that way." He was looking at me again in the mirror, contrite. "It's not bad stuff. It's just that sometimes he has to be in two places at once and he can't, so I help out. I'm sure otherwise he'd have been here, with you..." He finished somewhat lamely.

"Well, he *should* be here with me. But he's not. So you're his eyes, then? You'll see to it I'm safely delivered places, then you'll report back to him?"

He swallowed uncomfortably. Clearly he didn't appreciate being called a glorified babysitter.

A car honked and tried to edge in front of us. Andre muttered something, waving the driver in with a disgusted look on his face.

"I make sure things are taken care of the way he's requested."

Now I was curious. "And how did he request you *take care of* me?"

He shoved one hand through thick black hair. "Ma'am, I'd feel more comfortable if you took up this discussion with him. I'm not here to be argumentative and I make it my practice not to guess his intentions. I simply follow instructions."

Well, I sure as shit was feeling argumentative, I thought grumpily. I was angry with Thomas, so arguing with his representative was about as good as things were going to get.

He handed me a card as he pulled up in front of the doorman. "My contact information. I expect you'll have things to see to tomorrow, and I will be available."

I thanked him, letting myself out of the car while he popped the trunk to retrieve my small suitcase. He'd have carried it in for me, but I held up a hand. "Thank you," I said shortly. "I appreciate your help; you may relay to Thomas that I was safely delivered."

Declining the assistance of the bellhop, I took the elevator to the nineteenth floor and let myself into the room. It was expensively sleek and pristine, overlooking the quiet interior courtyard.

I eyed the huge king size bed and asked my stomach whether it would get on board with the plan to just crash into it and stay until morning. It responded with a roar that food was necessary and if I got into bed there would be hell to pay.

I hadn't been in Manhattan for years. The smells and bustle of the city were unfamiliar after months spent in a sleepy little town, and it took a minute to work up the courage to venture outside the hotel rather than just order room service.

There was a great little Italian restaurant just down the street and for once, I didn't even bother with the salad. Instead, I ordered a nice red and "the biggest plate of fettuccine alfredo you can make."

The waiter looked amused.

I ate until I couldn't force another bite between my lips. Then I paid the bill with my own money and walked my very sluggish self back to the hotel. My phone buzzed halfway there, but I ignored it. The carbs had zapped my feisty mood and I worried the second glass of wine with chocolate cake had pushed tears too close to the surface again.

It wasn't that I didn't appreciate his gestures.

The flight was obscene.

The private driver was ridiculous.

My hotel bill would be the GDP of a third world country, as the attendant had confirmed I was booked for two nights but could extend my stay if necessary.

But there was one thing I'd come to understand about Thomas with absolute clarity in the last few months: When he wanted to say he was sorry, he did it with things instead of words. Words were hard for him, but things were not. Things and gestures were simple and cooperative, whereas words were difficult and painful.

I didn't have the energy to soak in the glorious tub. Instead, I put myself through a fast, perfunctory shower and climbed into the huge bed, naked. I didn't even want to look at any of the lingerie I'd taken to California.

It was getting late, so I fired off a quick email to Ahmad's attorney. His voicemail indicated he would be available the next morning at eleven to review things with me, and there were papers to sign. I could expect to spend a minimum of an hour with him, but more likely two.

I listened to Thomas's voicemail three more times before dropping my phone onto the nightstand. Then I flicked off the lamp and let my eyes drift shut.

The bed was cold and empty, with nothing to cuddle up to but the acres of white cotton. And I'd never admit it to Thomas, or to anyone else who asked, but for such an expensive night's sleep, I slept like absolute shit since he wasn't there to hold me.

FORTY-SIX

Thomas

Andre called me from the car to confirm Natalie's arrival at the hotel. I made a frustrated sound despite myself, pacing the floor of my office.

Maybe I'd been an idiot, to think it would be easy to take care of Natalie from a distance; to show her that I cared even when I couldn't be there, and that I was remorseful. I had to start somewhere, but now I had to start back at the beginning to repair the damage I'd caused with careless, selfish words thanks to too much alcohol and no filter.

Gerry had already called it a night, but Finn and Noah waited for me in the large living room, the lights out, the fire crackling. Each of them held a glass filled with something and I knew in Noah's case it wasn't water.

Our Welsh mother had seen to it booze and guilt ran through our veins.

It was our English father and his exploits who'd given us the original reason to drink.

"She's gone then." It was Noah.

He knew damn well she was gone, as he'd been with me all day, watching me pace and curse and shove my hands through my hair after talking to Caroline, then to Andre, when all I wanted was to hear Natalie's sweet voice.

"You haven't apologized." That was Finn.

Fuck me, this was a sibling tag team.

"You know," Finn said, taking a long chug from her glass, "when I pushed Magnus out–of whom we shall not speak again–it was because he'd pushed too hard once and for all. It wasn't that he sometimes flew off the handle–waaay off the handle.

"It wasn't that he wasn't charming, either. But because as time went on, I finally realized he had never been there when I needed him. Always Mateo, but never the man who was my husband."

The firelight was dim and I was having a hard time seeing Finn's expression. I had no idea what she was talking about. Magnus had always been an asshole; I couldn't imagine she'd ever been able to depend on him. But Mateo, I knew, had played a long game with her for years. I liked the guy. I actually trusted him to take care of my sister.

"You're a dumb monkey fuck, Thom. Useless as tits on a door."

Noah leaned back, stretching his long legs and Finn mirrored the action, wincing a little and rubbing her belly.

I startled a little, sinking down into the huge chair directly across from the fireplace.

Let's just get right to it, shall we?

It was Noah, running with the baton. He held up his fingers and started ticking off points. "You got a gorgeous woman with a huge heart. She's seen all your ugly–and you got plenty. She's handled you when you're sloppy. She's put up with your temper, which is impressive 'cuz when you're mad you can be a real dick. She's probably just about gone bankrupt tryna' keep you fed. She's a fuckin' angel and you know it, 'cuz *we* all do." He gestured between himself and Finn. "But here you are, tryna' push her away 'cuz *you're* not good enough. And you're right." He paused, half his face in shadow.

"You'll never be good enough, so don't wait for that to change. My angel will tell you she came back for me 'cuz she loved me, not 'cuz I deserved her. 'Cuz I'll never deserve that woman." His voice caught, having suddenly become gravelly.

"You have to let go of Lydia." Finn's voice was quiet. "You're not in love with her anymore, but you judge everyone by her, and that's both unfair and unhealthy. Natalie is nothing like her, and you already know it." She sighed deeply.

"It took me all of five minutes to see how much she loves you, you moron. Her eyes get all shiny when she looks at you." She took a sip of her drink. "It's adorable, but it's disgusting." She was grinning.

Another glass appeared on the table beside me and I looked over quickly, catching just a glimpse of Jensen as he hurried from the room. It was lemon water with ice, and it made me smile. I really was surrounded by people who cared for me, and not just because I saw to their financial wellbeing. Had these people only wanted my money, they'd not have been so honest and straightforward with me.

Finn kissed my cheek and Noah squeezed the hell out of my lungs before the two of them said they were calling it a night. That they were at least three drinks in meant they'd been waiting for me for a while.

Dragging myself up to bed, I let my arm stretch out over Natalie's pillow. In just a few short months she had become so integral to my functioning that I couldn't imagine a sunrise without her. And now...deep and dark and late at night...oh shit, I had screwed all of this up and I didn't know if I could fix it.

Grabbing my phone, I tapped out a text to Natalie. I didn't send it, because I wasn't sure I was ready to admit these things, but I had to start somewhere. I had to find a way to convince her that she was what gave me the hope to keep going.

She needed to know she was more than enough.

• • • •

ANDRE CALLED AGAIN, early the next morning, to let me know he had driven Natalie to a lawyer's office. She was meeting with a realtor after, he said, and I breathed a sigh of relief.

She'll sell the apartment; she won't move in.

"She's very tired, sir, and she seems quite down." His voice was low and confidential. "I was able to speak briefly with the brother yesterday and it seems the body is being shipped overseas for burial. I believe this turn of events leaves her very well provided for, though not without a great deal of paperwork. It's possible she's overwhelmed."

I should be there for her, like she was for me.

"She has mentioned staying a few extra days, as it seems she has additional meetings. Would you like me to handle the hotel?"

"Yes, please," I snapped a little more sharply than I'd intended. "She's stubborn and she'll try to leave and book her own hotel–don't let her do it. This way I'll know she's safe and comfortable."

I paused, a little unsettled as I considered what I was about to ask him to do. "She'll need clothes, Andre. What she brought to California will be insufficient for the cold in New York. Can you see to it?"

He assured me he could, and I swallowed my jealousy as I thought of him eyeballing my woman, trying to determine her size. But if anything, Andre was a lady's man, and I had no doubt he was up to the task.

I fired off a quick text to my pilot, asking him to withdraw flight plans for the next morning. I would keep him informed, I said, as I didn't yet know the extent of Natalie's stay.

It was my last day with Finn and Noah. Gerry had already gone home, but not without first sitting me down for an hour in what felt very much like a therapy session, even though her professional focus was typically on kids. Maybe it helped, I don't know. All I know is that I killed half a box of tissues while I tried not to cry like a girl in front of her. The woman had always known how to reduce me to a blithering idiot in only moments and for a long time I'd been living right on that edge.

The three of us drove out to the coast and spent an hour on the beach before heading into San Francisco for a late lunch. There, Finn bought a few small things for Griffin and Mateo, and Noah found a few things for his little family.

After Avery died, taking their baby with her, I'd almost lost my younger brother. Losing Noah would have left a huge hole in my life and every now and then, I manned up enough to tell him so. I could always hear him roll his eyes, the sarcasm was so loud. His response was always "'Cuz I'm a big guy, dumbass."

That night Finn sat on the edge of the hot tub with her feet in the water while Noah and I talked about plans for the future. They both tried to get me to talk about mine, but I suddenly didn't have any.

My original goal had been to get my board to reinstate me.

To move back to Sonoma.

To finalize my divorce and figure out how to get on with my life.

But something had changed in the past few months, because when I thought about the future now, there was a curvy little blonde in my mind's eye.

She was bouncing down the stairs in the Sonoma house to welcome me home from a business trip.

She was sitting at the kitchen island with her drawings and swatches, her hair piled up on top of her head while she concentrated and sketched and I poured wine for us.

She was smiling at me from the hot tub; laughing in the car with her hand trailing out the window; giving me sexy eyes as she soaked in the huge bathtub and, more importantly, she was in my bed.

Giggling.

Smiling sweetly at me.

Holding me in her arms.

Moaning my name.

"Hey." Noah was snapping his fingers in my face and I realized I'd spaced out. I shifted uncomfortably. In my mind's eye I'd been running my tongue up the inside of Natalie's thigh and I hoped the roiling bubbles hid the fact I had a wicked, very inconvenient hard-on.

"You were thinking about sexy time," Finn accused, and my face flamed an immediate red.

"Ha!" She barked a laugh. "I knew it!"

Noah was weirdly quiet.

"You owe her for like at least the next year–no reciprocation," Finn said and I choked on my drink. I knew exactly what she was insinuating.

"Better brush up on some tricks, because after what you did, it's not like she's going to be real eager to let you back into the Promised Land."

"You hurt her real bad," Noah said quietly, and I had to swallow hard.

"I know."

I wanted to let them know I was trying to make it up to her, but I was being fixed with accusing glares from the two people in my life who had never let me off the hook.

"Here," he said, slapping an open palm sharply over his heart three times. "No heating pad's gonna fix that, bro."

Finn snorted. She pushed herself up from her spot and pulled a light sweater over her shoulders. "I'm gonna let you boys talk this one out. I don't need any details about my future sister's kitty." She shuddered, then hurried into the house before I unraveled what she'd said, and when I looked back at Noah, he still wasn't smiling.

"You got some work to do before you're gonna get what you want," he said, and I shook my head at him.

"She won't talk to me, Noah. It makes me crazy. She's turned off her read receipts, so I don't even know if she's reading my texts. She won't return my calls, and I've been reduced to getting updates from Andre, because I have no idea what she's doing or where she is or if she's safe." It all rushed out in one big breath.

"Geez, bro. She's not a little kid. I mean, she managed to keep shit together for a pretty long time before she met you. In fact, I think her shit's gotten messier since she met *you*."

I wasn't a talker. I didn't talk about feelings or problems or hopes or dreams. But if there was one person who could get things out of me without trying, it was Noah. Our bond had always been strong, but after we lost Maren we got even closer. We expressed our love with insults and martial art sneak attacks, chokeholds and rib jabs, practical jokes and underhanded teasing. But no matter what I said, I knew he loved me with a loyalty I would never question.

We talked until Noah's eyes started to droop and suddenly his head snapped up. "Shit. What time is it? I was supposed to call my girl."

I looked over the edge of the hot tub, flinging water off my fingers to tap my phone. "Almost one. You call her this late, don't be surprised if she rips off your nuts when you get home."

"Nah." Noah's smile was sleepy but happy as he wrapped himself in a towel. "My angel likes to hear my voice before she goes to sleep at night. She'll get real mad if I don't call her, so she knows I'm ok."

I rolled my eyes at him and made a circling motion with my fingers, to indicate he should go on, but that he was very probably insane and definitely, one hundred percent pussy-whipped.

Putting the cover back on the hot tub, I wrapped up in a towel and checked my phone: No messages and no texts. It was making me panicky. She was shutting me out again, like she had when that stupid fake story about Lydia and me aired when she was in Boston.

There was a cryptic voicemail from one of my board members. Somehow I'd missed the call earlier that afternoon, even though I was so attuned to the ring that I was a twitchy disaster. But well, that could wait until tomorrow. Tessa would be pissed if I called her at one in the morning.

I scrolled through Natalie's social media feeds while lying in bed. She'd posted some beautiful photos several days earlier, in what I knew was a documentation of our time together. She'd slipped in one of me giving my speech at the benefit. I hadn't even noticed she'd taken it. Beneath it was a short caption: *The most beautiful man, with the most beautiful heart.* There were several heart-eye emojis after and I kept my fingers away from tapping the heart button. There were a lot of exploding ovary comments beneath it and I stopped reading in a hurry.

There were a few more recent photos, one of her hotel room in the early evening light. That was from today.

There were architectural shots, pictures of Central Park, photos of the horse-drawn carriages and a photo of a glass of wine and a huge plate of pasta.

I doubted she'd done this to console me, but it told me some of the things I needed to know since I wouldn't let myself go to her: She was safe, comfortable, and eating.

It was a start.

• • • •

LATER IN THE MORNING I drove Noah and Finn to the airport, and we stood for a long time in a three-person hug. We hadn't spent time like this together for a very long time. Finn was so much younger than Noah and myself, and we had kind of gotten to know each other better over the last few years, as I was out of the house long before she was a teenager. In fact, it was Noah's falling apart that had really brought me and Finn together in the first place.

"Fix it," she said gently, taking my face in one of her hands. "You're wrecked over this and so is she."

I nodded, swallowing hard, and Noah punched me so hard in the shoulder, I knew I'd have a bruise. He saw me wince and raised his eyebrows at me. "Be glad I didn't give it to you the same way Nat got her bruises." He giggled like a little girl while I made a face. Then, "I'll talk to Evie." His expression went completely serious. "She'll have some good ideas on how you can make it up to Nat."

I wanted to place any amount of hope in that it *could* be fixed, but I wasn't so sure. Natalie was easier on me than I was on myself, and that she'd left without saying goodbye and was refusing all contact meant I'd really stepped in it this time.

While I drove back home, I called Tessa back. Her tone was tired and frazzled and she told me I'd missed the board's emergency convening the night before, when they'd gathered at ten.

"What did he do this time?" I sighed heavily, one hand on the wheel, shoving the other one through my hair. "What do you need me to fix?"

"I don't think there's any *fixing* this one," Tessa said, and I flipped the blinker to get off the highway.

There was a lengthy pause, and I waited as patiently as I could. Tessa was thoughtful and very careful with her words and I valued her opinion, so I chewed on my lip a little, but I waited.

"This is a bit of a delicate situation..." She coughed. "I, ah...do you remember the intern we brought on at the beginning of the fall?"

"Yeah." I had to really sift through my memory for a second, to find her face. "Cute kid. Isn't she Michael's daughter?"

Cute kid? Where had that come from? The girl had waltzed into the office dressed like a thirty-year-old to cover up the obvious fact puberty had been generous.

Michael was one of the head engineers and damned good at his job. I'd worked hard to make sure he wasn't lured away from the company I still considered my first child.

"She is–both Michael's daughter, and a kid. And as you'll recall, the idea was to have her intern part-time, so she could get some real work experience under her belt to give her a leg up on her college applications when the time came. We wouldn't have considered it, but it was a professional courtesy to Michael–and, well, she was impressively intelligent and dedicated."

I remembered that well. As I recalled, she had some pretty expensive ambitions, education-wise, and despite Michael's bloated salary, his daughter's education would definitely set him back unless she landed a major scholarship.

Tessa cleared her throat uncomfortably. "It would seem that she's been getting a bit more...hands-on, rather than work-related, experience while she's been with us."

Guy Brain told me this was going nowhere good, and I pulled off the shoulder and put the car into park. The engine purred, the air conditioning blowing across my hot face.

"Harrison's secretary walked in on the two of them in his office yesterday afternoon, after hours. There was absolutely no way to misread the situation. There are concerns that this has been going on for months."

All the blood drained from my face and I let one hand drop heavily on the steering wheel. "I don't even know what to say."

I wanted to say that every time I thought Harrison had sunk to the lowest level, he managed something even more depraved. But this? This really did make everything else pale in comparison.

"We'll finalize things today, in terms of paperwork. We had Legal scrambling last night and they're drawing up new documents. Of course, Michael knows, since his daughter is distraught and claims she's in love with Harrison."

I let my head drop back onto the headrest as I groaned.

"Michael was removed from the building for safety reasons and Harrison was escorted out by security. I don't think I need to point out that he will not be back.

"Harrison has been removed from his position and the board would like to extend the offer to you, to resume the position you should never have left." There was regret in her voice. She'd been the one to try to talk me out of stepping down in the first place.

"Has anyone cut him a check for his buy-in?" I asked, my voice feeling weirdly gravelly.

"It's being done today." Tessa's voice was a little steadier. "He'll be furious about it, I'm sure, that we're not willing to pay him off to make him go away. It's a pretty cut-and-dried case of moral turpitude, and Legal is prepared to argue it if necessary. But if he wants to avoid several lawsuits, he'll go quietly rather than trying to take more of what he's been trying to plow under for years. I can't say Michael will be as generous: charges are probably being filed as we speak, since his daughter is a minor."

I was hardly dressed for a day at the office, but the situation required that no time be wasted. I needed to put a continent's distance between Harrison's name and Titan Tech.

"I'm on my way now."

FORTY-SEVEN

Natalie

Meeting with Ahmad's lawyer was exhausting. The appointment stretched to over three hours and though he'd thoughtfully brought in food for us, my stomach was already rumbling by the time I left the building. My appetite seemed to be operating just fine, though the rest of me could hardly keep up.

Andre sat at the curb in the Town Car and I sank into the seat wearily, thankful I didn't have to deal with taking cabs all over the city. This was about as "mass transit" as I was going to get.

I'd taken the T in Boston often enough to know I didn't want to take the Metro in New York, and cabs were a real crapshoot. I'd been regaled with tales of trying out for reality shows more often than I could count, and propositioned more than once. One Egyptian cab driver had proposed marriage, despite the fact he was nearly thirty years my senior.

The realtor met me at Ahmad's apartment and I was thankful to find the investigation had been rapidly concluded, since police tape really did tend to send a negative message.

I hadn't been inside the apartment since the day I'd confronted Sonny, and only a handful of times before that. I wasn't surprised to see expensive art on the walls, or top-of-the-line furniture. The beautiful Aubusson rolled out in the living room was one that had gone missing from my staging stash several years earlier, as well as the marble-topped coffee table that sat in front of the fireplace.

A tap at the door meant I didn't have much time to acquaint myself with the space and I opened the door to find a smartly dressed, polite realtor. She walked the apartment slowly and with a critical eye, giving her honest opinion about what to do with the space to get it ready to sell. But sell it would, she assured me, quickly, and it would go for a considerable sum. Real estate in New York was always a sure thing, but a two-bedroom in Chelsea was going to fund my retirement account with quite a few additional zeroes.

I realized a little sadly that I was grateful to Ahmad for being so ruthlessly organized, since his legal affairs were in proper order. Though I had a few hoops to jump through, probate court wouldn't be the nightmare for me that it was for most.

I called Jeanine as I locked up the apartment, to relay the news. She was not someone easily shocked, but I heard a loud noise and her voice apologizing from a distance. She had dropped the phone. "Laura, shut my door and hold my calls. This is going to take a moment." There was a rustling. "Natalie. Mr. Atholton's lawyers have been in touch and have relayed that the situation may have changed somewhat due to an accident?"

I barrelled through an explanation, aware that every word was costing me roughly three dollars, and for the first time ever I heard her laugh. "Ok, slow down. I can give you a few minutes off the clock. Start at the top."

She assured me the case would be dismissed, given the circumstances, unless I wished to withdraw my filing. I told her I would withdraw it and she wished me well: I would receive a final invoice for her time, of course.

There were so many calls to return. My mother had left several worried messages, Gerry had sent several texts, and the publisher who'd gotten in touch with me about a project wanted to know when I was free to meet. I returned that call quickly, as I was less than twenty minutes from their office. Could they squeeze me in while I was here?

While Andre drove me into Midtown, I returned my mother's call. It helped that I had a limited period of time to talk to her, otherwise she'd have kept me on the phone until my hair went grey. Not that Vivian was typically all that interested in chatting, but she liked gossip. All the juicy details I could give her would be employed as social currency at her next wine meeting–Bridge. I mean Bridge meeting.

I vaulted out of the car, catching sight of Andre slipping his phone from his pocket in the reflection of the glass doors. I had no doubt as to who he was calling and it irritated me a little, to feel like he was my babysitter.

The meeting with a junior editor and the publisher ran overly long, but we kicked around a few ideas and they provided me with a sample contract to have a lawyer review. Since my potential contribution was the brainchild of a junior editor (one who followed my blog), they'd come to me directly after finding I didn't have any sort of representation.

"What did you tell him?"

Andre's eyes snapped to the mirror. It was well after dark, but the car was filled with the lights of the city as he drove.

"I'm sorry?"

"I know you're informing on me. Thomas is probably nuts that I won't return his calls, but he *can* pay someone else to keep an eye on me."

His shoulders tensed almost imperceptibly and I wondered whether he found it more insulting that I'd called him a spy, or a babysitter.

"He was made aware you took several meetings today and that I would then drive you to the hotel. We didn't get so far as to what you were wearing."

It took me a minute to realize he was teasing. He had a great poker face. But then he jerked a thumb toward the floor behind him, and for the first time I noticed a very large shopping bag.

"Mr. Atholton mentioned you were packed for California and not New York," he said quickly. "I hope this helps. If I was wrong about sizes or what you prefer, it can be fixed."

My eyes narrowed as I considered that, once again, I was indebted to both men for time spent, for thoughtfulness, and for expense.

When he dropped me at the hotel I thanked him for ferrying me all over the city the last few days and informed him he was relieved of his duty. Since I planned to check out the next morning and find my own accomodations for a few days, there was no reason to keep him on the clock.

I hoisted the bag covered with expensively telltale black and white stripes. The bag of clothing probably cost as much as my house.

"Mr. Atholton won't allow that, ma'am. He has instructed that you are to stay here as long as you find necessary and I will remain available." He gestured toward the giant French Renaissance structure. "I am to accompany you until you are safely on a plane, either to California or to Alabama."

"That's completely ridiculous," I sputtered angrily, tallying up my already sizable hotel bill in my head. Carried a couple numbers. Adding several more nights would make the bill absolutely staggering.

"I'm perfectly capable of finding myself suitable, safe lodgings. He's overmanaging this and it's ridiculous."

"I don't think he knows any other way," Andre chuckled. "Miss Lydia expected to be fully catered to at all times and he considered it in his best interest to keep her happy."

I shook my head just a little and muttered a frustrated "Good night, Andre," before turning and walking into the hotel.

Somehow, this new information made everything a little less special.

This was *Lydia's* hotel.

Andre was *her* driver.

These were all things that had been done, arranged, booked and accommodated time and time again in the years before me.

I was just a new detail in an old pattern.

When I opened the door there was a vase of pillowy pink roses on the bedside table that had most certainly not been there this morning. It took me a minute to work up the courage to get near them, as if they'd bite me if I got too close. But after summoning my courage and thoroughly investigating the situation, I was disappointed to find there was no card.

Tossing my bag into a chair and kicking off my shoes, I hurried into the bathroom to fill the tub. It had been a long day. I was cold and tired and hungry and wanted nothing more than to order room service and soak the ache out of my bones. The one that spread all the way into my heart.

I almost fell asleep in the bath, but the water was starting to cool, so I pulled myself out and wrapped up in a big towel, when there was a soft knock at the door. I shrugged quickly into a robe, not bothering to check who it was before yanking open the door.

A man stood there in a hotel uniform, with a small wheeled cart. "Miss James." He nodded graciously at me and wheeled the cart into the room, the tips of his ears turning pink. I looked down to realize my robe wasn't quite as secure as I'd thought and he'd seen a good portion of the

Winnebagos. Whoa, very nearly the headlights, too. I yanked it closed and tightened the sash.

My hand shot into my handbag and I tucked a tip into his hand, holding my robe together with the other hand. I needed him to *get out now*, because there was a smell coming from beneath those silver covers that made my stomach roar like an angry beast.

With a polite nod, he was gone and I dove for the tray I knew I hadn't ordered: a Wagyu strip, farm salad, caviar service, a bottle of champagne and *two* slices of chocolate cake.

Maybe he likes my curves.

It was almost enough to make me forgive him.

Almost.

But first I needed to know this wasn't like a Lydia meal or something. And that, I thought as I took my first bite of steak, was what made me so mad: Andre's little spill made me feel like this was something routine.

I wasn't special.

Thomas wasn't creatively apologizing, he was just doing what he'd always done.

Remove one wife; insert the new model.

I ate every last bite. And yeah, I drank the whole bottle of champagne too–no sense in that going to waste. But...and I was pretty sure I'd never told Thomas...champagne made me do stupid things. It made me stalk exes online and buy useless things off QVC or Amazon in the middle of the night. It also turned me into a total hornball, and given that my judgment was already impaired, now seemed like the perfect time to call Thomas and really let him have it while I was both angry and wound up.

See? This was why I didn't drink champagne.

Putting the cart in the hallway, I hung the robe in the bathroom and brushed my teeth before stumbling toward the bed.

I tried composing a million different greetings in my head. I yelled and screamed and cursed in my head. Then I sank into the pillows, pulled up the blankets and tapped at my phone.

"Baby." The phone hadn't even rung once before he picked up, his voice low and desperate.

I kind of liked that.

The desperate part.

The face of my phone lit up with a FaceTime request, and because I was a glutton for punishment and I was just drunk enough to be goofy, I accepted it.

He was sitting in his office, the room still filled with the waning evening light. It backlit his wide shoulders and beautiful hair, and I knew right away that this had been a bad idea. Because I was supposed to stay mad at him, not miss him, but I did. Even though he was the asshole who'd just broken my heart, and very nearly my right shoulder.

He sat for a long time, just looking at me and swallowing hard. "You're so beautiful," he finally whispered, and I heard his voice crack just a little.

I couldn't figure out what he was seeing though, because I knew my cheeks were flushed from the champagne. My face had been scrubbed of makeup, so I was back to looking like a naked mole rat. And my hair was still a wet mess.

"Is that an apology or something?" I asked him, and I'm pretty sure I slurred "something."

He ducked his head, looking away from the screen for long moments. When he looked back up I noticed his eyes were red and tired, with deep shadows beneath them like he hadn't been sleeping. "I *am* sorry," he said quietly, and I watched his shoulders curl forward. He looked defeated. "I don't expect you to believe it. That was a great display of serious caveman on my part, acting like you were my possession to do with as I pleased."

"I'm pretty sure you did exactly that," I said, hardly willing to let him off the hook just because he looked so beat up.

"Thomas..."

His head jerked up when I said his name, like he knew something bad was coming.

"I get that you were in a weird headspace, and maybe you still are. But I had a legitimate, very unpleasant reason to leave, and it was the *last* thing I wanted to do. Instead of being the weak and wilting flower you seem to think I should be, I had to put on my big girl panties and take care of something no one else could. I'm going to be taking care of a lot of those things for a while and it's probably going to mean more trips to New York. It'll take time. I'll have a lot of legal obligations. You're either going to have to deal with that or cut me loose."

That hurt so much...something stabbed at my chest.

His eyes flared for just a second, with something I thought might be hope.

"I know you're a lot stronger than I give you credit for, but I've never thought you were a delicate flower. It takes a brave person to leave a broken marriage." He ran a hand across his mouth. "Sometimes I forget I don't get to make all the decisions, because I'm so used to having to handle everything. It's just become a habit on my part."

I sat up a little further and the sheet dropped away from my chest.

To his credit, he didn't say anything, but I knew what he could see when his eyes went all hot and he clenched a fist over his mouth.

"I got selfish," he said in a low voice. "I got used to having you all to myself and then something came along that threatened to take you away..."

"You pushed so hard, I walked away on my own."

He looked surprised for a second. "Natalie, I would never..." But he stopped himself, biting off the words and swallowing the last half of the sentence.

"When are you coming back?" He switched tack suddenly.

"I don't know that I am," I answered, purposely being a little vague. "But you don't need to worry about it. I'll be here for a few days to wrap up some stuff and then I can get myself home."

"Absolutely not." His lips were set in a firm line.

"Ah-ah." I held up a finger. "I'm a big girl and I make my own decisions. I will decide when I want to go home and where I want to be, and I will get myself there."

"I'd rather you were here, with me." His voice was soft and pleading. "There have been some...ah, developments...I have to see to. I'll be here for a while."

"I have some things to see to as well, and I'll be really busy–busier than you'd like, and you don't seem to like it when I'm unavailable to you. I think it's best if we just handle the things we need to handle and then we can reconvene to discuss where we're taking things...you know, from there."

His face tightened with an expression of frustration. "We're not going to discuss where we're taking things, because there is nothing to discuss. I fucked up and I won't do it again, and I'm not letting this be how I lose you."

"How do you know you ever had me?"

It was a low blow and I knew it, but I wanted to see the hurt expression on his face. I needed to know, for once, that I held that power.

"Because you've held me up and kept the pieces together when I couldn't do it myself. And I can't do it myself, Natalie."

I reached over to turn off the lamp, watching the little box that showed my screen go dark. "I could have used some help this week," I said quietly, and he dropped his eyes.

"I walked into a hospital room filled with snakes, because I was the only person who could sign the order to do what my husband wished. I pretty much pulled the plug." My voice caught on a hiccup because I realized how terrible that sounded. "Then I met with his lawyer to have things put in order. And a realtor, to sell the apartment. And this is going to upend my life for a while, so maybe we should just...you know...take a step back. You do what you need to do and I'll do what I need to do–no expectations."

"What the fuck does that mean?" He looked violently angry, his eyes flashing. "Are you trying to break up with me, Natalie?"

I didn't know what I was doing. I was exhausted, and pretty drunk, and I had like four back-to-back meetings tomorrow, and now it looked like I'd blown my chance at sleeping.

"I'll let you know when I've arrived home," I said finally, clicking the button to hang up the call so he couldn't protest. I knew he'd be furious, but there was no point in arguing with him all night.

He tried to call back four times but I silenced the phone every time, and when he finally got the hint, my phone dinged seven more times.

I cringed.

I would read those texts in the morning.

Or maybe never. I hadn't really decided yet.

• • • •

LANDING IN ALABAMA four days later, I was exhausted. Almost a week in New York had sucked the life right out of me, especially the part where my mother sent me screenshots of Farida's social media feeds. There were photos of what I could only assume was the service, along with several thinly veiled references to Ahmad's estranged wife, and none of it painted me in a very flattering light.

But Farida could get away with it, basking in the sympathy and well wishes of her social circle, because I kept my mouth shut and she lived in denial.

I had been able to remain strong the past four days. I hadn't caved and read Thomas's text messages, nor had I called him, though he'd tried to call me several times since. I knew it made him wild that I was unavailable to him.

And then, because I really needed to drive the point home that I was capable of independence, I booked a flight home on a commercial airline without telling him. (He'd figure it out when Andre confirmed I'd checked out of the hotel.)

Gerry picked me up from the airport and got out of her car to help me load the bag that had now turned into two, then pulled me into a tight Mama Bear Hug. I could feel myself deflate a little when her arms went around me and I hoped I wouldn't make a teary, snotty scene and blubber all over her nice shirt.

It wasn't until we were in the car that I realized we weren't alone and my head swiveled quickly toward the backseat to take in a tiny blonde girl with brilliant blue eyes.

"Aria!" It was out of my mouth like an expression of alarm, and I felt Gerry glance at me quickly.

"I 'member you!" The little girl exclaimed excitedly. "Uncle Thomas's friend. You were so nice to me at the party, and you were a princess!"

I couldn't see her bouncing in her seat, but I could feel it in the motion of the car.

"We're working on the 'Uncle Thomas' part," Gerry said under her breath, and I knew there were explanations to be had much later.

The drive from the airport really wasn't all that long, but the excitement must have been too much for Aria, because she was curled over her carseat, fast asleep by the time we pulled into Gerry's driveway.

She parked in front of her garage door and cracked the windows, turning off the engine and looking behind her to make sure Aria was still out before she began to speak in a low voice.

Gerry had received a phone call in the middle of the night, two nights earlier, from a frantic Lydia, babbling and almost incoherent. It had taken all of Gerry's professional skills to calm the woman and get her to explain that Harrison had fled the country in order to avoid prosecution. The underage girl he'd taken an interest in hadn't been seventeen at all, but days shy of sixteen, and the furious father wanted Harrison prosecuted to the fullest extent.

Suddenly, I knew why Thomas's stay in California had been indefinitely extended.

Reaching into the pocket of her door, Gerry withdrew a tri-folded piece of paper and handed it to me without a word. I had to read it three times before it began to sink in: Harrison was relinquishing his parental rights to a guardian to be appointed by the court.

"He dumped her on Lydia's doorstep and gave her that. He said it was up to her what she did with the girl, because if he stayed, she would be taken from him," Gerry said quietly. "It wouldn't have been long before someone figured out Lydia isn't allowed anything more than supervised visitation."

Sinking back into my seat, I tried to piece together what this meant, and the role Gerry played.

"Lydia claimed she couldn't get in touch with Thomas and she knows we've remained close, so she came to me for help. I told her I would take Aria until Thomas was home, but under two conditions."

"She signs the divorce papers and supports Thomas as court-appointed guardian," I breathed, and Gerry's face lit up.

I had guessed right.

"She's requested she be allowed occasional visitation, but I don't think Thomas's heart is nearly as cold as hers. She might have denied him, but he'll let the girl see her mother whenever Lydia wants...and I doubt that will be often, the poor little one."

My mind spun as I tried to consider how this would change life for Thomas. It would fill him up again and give him the purpose he'd been seeking, but it would also greatly change our dynamic.

Who are you kidding? You don't even know if he wants you to be involved, or if you want to stick around.

"Her name has never been changed," Gerry said quietly, as Aria stirred a little.

"According to her birth certificate, she's still an Atholton. It's a blessing, really. She was a possession–a pawn–to her father, anyway.

"If Thomas needs to in the future, he can claim Aria was abandoned by her parents, but I don't think we'll ever see that filing. Harrison isn't going to draw that much attention to himself and Lydia really can't afford to either."

She got out of the car slowly and I followed, reaching in to unclip Aria's seatbelt and hoist her against my shoulder.

"She should be in her house," I said quietly as I rounded the car, and Gerry nodded.

"She's a remarkably resilient child, but I fear she'll suffer severe attachment issues, thanks to the incredible amount of unrest at such a young age. But yet, maybe there's hope: Thomas can be stable and giving, and with more time I think she'll learn to see him as a father figure again."

Aria stirred sleepily on my shoulder and blinked brilliant blue eyes at me.

The three of us went into Gerry's house and a snack was fixed. Then, while Aria settled down to color, Gerry and I debated how to handle the housing situation.

Gerry sat next to the little girl and helped her color, asking gentle questions and waiting patiently for the answers that sometimes didn't come at all. But I had an idea, and I quickly whispered to Gerry before running across the lawn to my house.

Raven greeted me with her squeaky little meow, stretching up from where she'd been sleeping in a patch of sun near the large dining room window. I gathered her up and kissed the top of her head, then hurried to gather her things and just a few of mine.

When Gerry pulled into Thomas's driveway half an hour later, I was waiting in the house. Raven's things were back in their usual places and as the little girl wandered through the front door, I watched her expression change slowly. She looked around carefully, taking in the pictures on the walls, touching the sofa, trailing through to the kitchen with wide eyes.

I had pulled several of Aria's photos from one of the mystery boxes, to quickly swap out with several of Aden's.

"I 'member this place," she said solemnly to Gerry, who looked a little worried. "I was here a long time ago. Ooh, look–it's me!" She pointed to a picture and her forehead wrinkled just a little.

"You remember staying here with your family?" Gerry asked gently, and Aria's little face screwed up a bit more.

"Yes, Uncle Thomas and Mommy. And him, too." She pointed to a picture of Aden.

Oh boy, did Gerry have her work cut out for her.

"Would you like to stay here again?" Gerry asked. "Since it seems familiar, Natalie thought you might be more comfortable here. I can stay too, if you want."

Aria looked around, considering. "Daddy had to go away...and Mommy can't be with me by herself." She shrugged, but it was clear she didn't understand why. "I can stay here with Uncle Thomas?"

"He's not home yet," I took over from Gerry, who seemed as if she was struggling with Aria's name for Thomas. "But he will be, and Gerry and I can stay with you until he is, if that makes you feel better."

A flash of movement caught Aria's eye, and her face lit up. "Raven!" She tore down the hallway after Raven, who graciously allowed herself to be caught and managed to work up a rough purr, even though she was being manhandled by a five-year-old.

"I know this kitty, right?" Aria looked up at Gerry for confirmation and received a nod. She seemed satisfied with the answer, but Gerry shook her head as she watched her settle onto the sofa with the cat.

"I'm worried it's too much, too soon, but in this case we don't have many options beyond jumping in with both feet. It's not her fault she was dumped here."

"I'll stay with her until he's home," I said quietly. "I know you have patients to see most days, so if you want to continue sessions with her, I can bring her to you or you can come here."

Aria seemed remarkably unperturbed that I, a virtual stranger, would stay with her in what was only a somewhat-familiar house and when I considered the turmoil she'd seen in just a few short years, maybe it wasn't all that surprising. I wondered though if that was a sign of the attachment issues Gerry warned about.

• • • •

THE THREE OF US SETTLED into a comfortable rhythm.

The first night, Aria and I both slept in Thomas's big bed, since she wasn't used to the noises of the house and the next day, while she and Gerry had a session in the living room, I struggled to disassemble the bunk beds.

I stripped and washed the sheets, carried Aden's bed out to the garage, and quickly reorganized the room so that Aria would be comfortable until it could be decorated for her.

The second night, Aria slept in her own bed. She was delighted by the girly sheets and the ballet slippers hanging on the wall.

Raven had decided she was acceptable company and I looked in on her before bed, to find Raven curled up right under the blankets with the little girl.

My phone had been silent the past few days, but I'd been so busy acclimating Aria and trying to catch up after my extended absence that I hadn't had the time to worry about it. But as I climbed into Thomas's bed, I worried this meant he'd decided it was easier to quit than to try.

Maybe I wasn't worth the effort.

The next morning, Gerry took Aria for the day. They were going to have a session, go to the park or the beach, have lunch together, and maybe even do a little shopping. It left me with a little extra time on my hands and I knew just what to do with it, so I moved like a whirlwind.

Tearing back to my house, I threw gallons of paint, blankets, rugs, curtains, a pretty light fixture and a small table into the back of the Subaru.

When Aria got home, she would have a proper princess room.

I could ask forgiveness for my desecration later.

• • • •

ARIA WAS THRILLED WITH her new room and my effort seemed to solidify in her mind that I was interested in her and enjoyed being a part of her life.

It didn't surprise me to find I was falling in love with her, as unexpected as it had been, and as temporary as it would probably be. I didn't like to think ahead, to how things would end when Thomas finally got home.

We drove to a Christmas tree lot later that week and she picked out the tree that we dragged home and decorated. We put it up in the living room, strung it with white lights and gold bulbs, then made popcorn chains while watching Christmas movies. (Okay, so we ate most of the popcorn, but some of it did actually make it onto the tree.)

Lydia was able to fly in for Christmas, something that filled me with dread. Gerry and I had not explained the living situation to her, or that Thomas was still not home. (In fact, Thomas still didn't know and I wasn't about to tell him, since he hadn't called.)

Lydia had sworn to stay out of it, terrified someone would find out and she'd lose any and all access to Aria, and Gerry hadn't been trying to get in touch with him lately. She said he needed time to experience remorse and think on his transgressions, but I was living every day with my heart in my throat.

In the end, we decided it was best to have Aria meet with her mother at Gerry's house. They exchanged gifts and Lydia took pictures she promised would never see the light of social media, and by the next morning she was gone again. It gave her little time, if any, to question my role in the equation and Aria already knew better than to bring it up.

That meant I spent most of Christmas alone, in Thomas's house. I had piled up presents under the tree for Aria and she'd been incandescent with joy when she hurried down early that morning to find that Santa had indeed been able to find her in her new home.

The house was quiet and lonely after she left. I made a double White Russian, which I figured was festive enough, and sat on the sofa with quiet music on. The cat crawled up into my lap and we stayed there for hours while I stared at the tree and the twinkling lights and the packages that remained beneath the spiky branches, neatly wrapped and marked with Thomas's name.

I waited for Aria to come home and tried not to think about how much my heart hurt, because it felt like I was about to lose a beautiful dream.

FORTY-EIGHT

Thomas

I was no stranger to exhaustion, but this level was almost unprecedented. I spent three days reviewing every single piece of information with my board members. We conducted meetings with the legal team, in order to completely do away with Harrison without any legal repercussions. Then we worked on restructuring and I was appointed CFO, pulling Michael in for discussions about becoming the CTO. He was the best suited to the position, but I didn't want it to look like we were trying to buy him off, so negotiations were slow and cautious.

There was no doubt that I'd need to spend substantially more time in California, on-site, steering my company in the direction I wanted it to go. I would keep the support teams, the business analysts, the developers, testing leads and product heads. And while we moved a few people around, the only person without a job was Harrison.

Now that my biggest critic and underminer was out of the picture, I was free to establish the Medical Informatics arm I'd so long wanted to bring under the company's umbrella of offerings. We were growing and diversifying and without Harrison to sabotage all my hard work, we could move quickly.

My days were full and taxing. It was exhausting and when I fell into bed at night, I slept the sleep of the dead, waking in the morning to do it all over again. It left me with no time to ponder the loss of my closest friend and bitterest enemy.

It left me no time to worry about Natalie and how I was going to fix things between us. But in those moments just before sleep, sometimes my mind played tricks on me and I could smell her hair and feel the warmth of her body tucked against my own, and I felt the ache for her leak all the way into my bones.

It was another month before I even considered traveling back to Alabama, which meant I spent Christmas with my sister Finn and all my brothers, who congregated at her place for a couple days. It had been difficult. I had driven to Vegas the week before to check Asher's sorry ass out of the hospital and I took him straight to Finn's place.

It became immediately apparent that Asher and I were the only ones who didn't have our shit together.

Finn and Mateo had a new place and Aaron had brought a rescue dog with him for Finn's son, Griffin.

Noah brought his wife Eve and her son Jared, and I'd never seen the asshole so...happy.

Aaron brought a gorgeous woman with him and the girls pulled her into their circle right away, which meant he was stuck with her now...

Ash wouldn't talk about what was bothering him and it was Aaron who finally pulled the story out of him after breakfast on Christmas morning. That particular conversation had been a Bailey's-and-coffee kind of conversation for Asher, the only thing that seemed to loosen his tongue.

Noah knew exactly what I wanted for Christmas and he made sure to tease me endlessly, because we all knew how likely I was to get it.

I didn't even try to call Natalie, willing her to come to me first. I needed to know I could be forgiven.

Why were we both so damn stubborn?

Gerry had called me several times over the course of those weeks and each time I'd let her go to voicemail. She'd left only two messages, each telling me we needed to talk before I came home, and I avoided calling her back. She was going to give me hell for what I'd done to Natalie, and I couldn't handle one more thing right now. Gerry would break me down easily and completely, like a cardboard box left out in the rain.

My divorce lawyer had been in touch to set up a meeting. I'd been so busy, I'd already put him off three times and that afternoon I called him just after I boarded my plane. I was finally ready to nail down something in my calendar.

The pilot indicated it would be only a few moments until we were airborne, and I held up one finger as my lawyer's assistant put the call through.

"Atholton, you hot mess." His voice came through the line on a laugh. The only advantage to a divorce dragging on for years was that Ken and I had somehow become friends. It was an unlikely way to do things, but that seemed to be how I operated. "When's the last time you spoke to your wife?"

"On purpose?" I asked, and he chuckled again.

"Surely I can't be the first one to tell you she's finally signed the paperwork."

Stars exploded in my vision–was that an aneurysm?

Was that why Gerry kept calling?

"You're very nearly a free man, my friend. She has agreed to your demands as filed: no addendums and no bickering over Sonoma. You will be responsible for a reasonable alimony payment until she remarries, and she will maintain any of her own property."

I leaned heavily into the seat, a churning feeling happening in my stomach that was either overwhelming relief or crippling nausea.

What the hell just happened?

We set up an official video conference for the following afternoon and I ended the call, dropping the phone into the seat beside me and staring around dazedly.

Should I celebrate?

Should I be sad?

Should I be on my knees thanking God?

Maybe all of those things.

I'd planned to catch up on some reports during the flight. I also had a stack of resumes to review and some white papers to read, but I couldn't focus on any of them. Instead, after asking Caroline for something to put me out, I let myself into the back and crashed onto the bed. I needed just enough energy to get through a trip to Alabama, to take care of the most important thing on my To Do List: Fix It.

The flight wasn't long enough to make for a great nap, but I felt refreshed when I woke up. It was a feeling that I was pretty sure didn't come from sleep. I was lighter, unburdened–or very nearly. There were only two things left to fix on my list: Fix things with Natalie and track down Aria, since Lydia wasn't returning my calls to tell me what was going on custody-wise, with Harrison on the run. It was making me frantic.

Since I hadn't told anyone I was flying in, there was no one to meet me at the airport. I clicked on a car service app to order a car and within twenty minutes of disembarking I was flying down the darkened highway in the backseat of a Camry, Lil Nas assaulting my ears as my driver whooped and gestured and made noises that I assumed meant he was rapping along.

The driver dropped me at Natalie's house and sped away, the bass rattling in the trunk of his car and I saw a curtain flutter across the street. Chalk up another point with the neighbors.

Natalie had given me a key months earlier and when I didn't find her car in the driveway, I let myself in. The house was dark and it smelled empty, as if no one had been there in a long time. It was the smell of a heat pump and warmed dust, as if the life of the house had gone with her, and my heart seized.

Maybe she stayed in New York.

I ran across the yard at a frantic clip and hammered on Gerry's door. Her smile stretched wide when she found me standing there, probably looking homeless and definitely crazy. "Well," she said, giving me a gentle one-armed hug so she didn't spill her standard drink down my back. "It's about time the cat dragged you in. There have been a lot of changes in your life the past few weeks." She raised her eyebrows, but I wasn't sure there was any significance, since Gerry was generally just a very expressive person.

"Where's Natalie?" I shoved my hands into my pockets, trying not to let my frustration show.

Gerry stood for a minute, smiling at me. "I think you should go home, Thomas. There are some things that resolve themselves with a little patience."

"I need to find her!" I whisper-shouted, trying not to draw any more attention than my driver already had.

"All good things come to those who wait," she said gently and I finally realized she was completely sauced. She held up the drink. "I'd drive you, but as you can see I may have been compromised, as I was given a bottle of something delightful this Christmas, from your wonderful brother. So...we can call you a ride or you can walk home and think about what you need to do next."

I shook my head at her in irritation. "I know you know where she is and you're keeping it from me." I knew I was acting like a toddler.

She reached into the corner near the door and struggled with something. "Here, take my car for now. You need. To go. Home." Her voice was firm, her punctuation marks distinct. So I heaved a sigh and turned, throwing a hand over my shoulder to indicate my thanks and my frustration.

Pulling up to the house, I noticed a soft glow on the top floor, like a light had been left on somewhere. I was certain I'd turned everything off and locked the house down tight before Natalie and I had flown to California and my eyes swept the yard, looking for footprints, broken glass, busted doors...and landed on Natalie's little white Subaru in my driveway. It made my heart jump. *She was here.* If she was here, it was because she wanted to be near me. Just maybe she could forgive me.

There was a glow coming from the living room window as well and I stood on the porch for a moment, looking in at the pretty tree.

Maybe she's been here the whole time.

My house looked welcoming. It looked like a real home, filled with love and life.

I let myself in quietly, my heart hammering so hard that the blood battered against my eardrums. I hadn't talked to her in weeks and she hadn't tried to get a hold of me.

I was suddenly very aware of the ache in my chest: of how much I'd missed her and her calm, sweet presence.

Of how poorly I'd been sleeping without her there to soothe me.

I could hear her voice somewhere in the house, a gentle murmur that made my chest expand with contentment.

I didn't know what was waiting for me, but I was coming home to her.

FORTY-NINE

Natalie

I heard a noise in the doorway and looked up, Aria catching the book before it could slip from my fingers.

Thomas was leaning heavily against the door frame, as if he required it to stand. His expression was stricken as he stood staring at Aria and me. I'd been reading her favorite bedtime story to her and her little eyes had just begun to drift before the doorframe creaked loudly with Thomas's weight.

"You're home!" she squeaked, throwing back the blankets and dashing across the room to wrap herself around his legs.

Raven seemed unperturbed, blinking up at him from her spot at the foot of the bed.

"So are you." His voice sounded oddly strangled and he lifted one arm to swipe across his face while he held her tight with the other, a panicked look on his face as his eyes burned into mine.

She pulled back from his legs and held her arms out. He swooped down without hesitation, lifting her against his chest and pressing his face against hers, something fierce and joyful in his expression. Something exploded inside, either my heart or my ovaries–maybe both–and I held a hand over my stomach to calm the crazy butterflies that wanted to escape. The scene hurt, seeing what a tender man Thomas could be–no, was–as a father.

"Mommy has to come visit me here now," she said solemnly, and his eyes flicked back to mine with a thousand burning questions.

"Yes," I said, trying to keep my voice calm as I rose from the small bed and smoothed back the covers. "Lydia's been back once since bringing Aria here. She's...it's complicated, and I can tell you more later." I swallowed hard. "We've been working hard to do what's best for Aria."

Thomas's mouth dropped open in shock and I stood woodenly in the middle of the room as he looked around, realizing for the first time that it had been completely redone. The walls were a soft pink, a crystal chandelier hung from the center, the floor covered with a rug so fluffy, small dogs would have disappeared into the nap.

"I didn't suppose you would mind me making her feel at home," I said quietly. "I've been staying until you got back. And she's been doing so well here...haven't you, Ari?"

The little girl pulled back from Thomas's grasp just enough to smile at me. "Miss Gerry and Auntie Natalie are so nice to me." She looked guilty for a second. "Miss Gerry says it's ok for me to call her Auntie Natalie. Is that right?"

The grin stretched wide across my face. In less than six weeks I had fallen head over heels in love with this little girl. She was love and light and everything that was good, and I couldn't understand how she'd come from two people whose souls were such giant, sucking holes of need.

She was giving me yet another reason to love Thomas.

"I'll let you two catch up a little." I smiled gently at them both, leaning up to kiss Aria's cheek. "Don't keep her up too late though." I wagged a finger in his face. "It's already past her bedtime."

I listened to the steady cadence of their voices as I opened the dresser drawers to pack my clothes into the large bag I'd stowed in the closet. After a time I heard his voice rise and fall in a way that told me he was reading her favorite book to her again, and when he left her room he stood in the doorway for the longest time, just staring in at her.

I stood in the doorway with my bag looped over my shoulder, unsure whether I could squeeze past him. I decided to chance it, and as I passed behind he turned slowly to pull me against his chest. He was vibrating with an emotion I suspected was a hybrid of disbelief and overwhelming relief, and finally he looked down at me. "I don't know how you worked this magic...so many times I've left this house with nothing and no one, and I was sure I'd come back to more of the same."

Raven squeaked a protest at us from Aria's small bed.

"Sorry girl," Thomas whispered, his eyes flicking back to my face. "I made a mess, Natalie. Everything. I screwed it all up again and again. But here you are, in my house, watching over my baby. Am I crazy to hope I haven't lost you? Can I make you see that you're more than I ever hoped for?" He pulled me tight to his chest, a low groan of suffering rumbling from him, and I shivered at what I heard in that sound.

"We can talk later," I answered, and I felt his body tense. He looked down, realizing I was packed and ready to leave his house.

"No," he said firmly, sliding fingers beneath the luggage strap and dropping my bag to the floor. "I will tell you now that I can't do this without you. I have barely been human these past weeks. I did what I needed to do, but only because I had no other choice. I ate food without tasting it and slept in a lonely bed." He stopped, running his thumb over my cheek and I tensed, ready to pull myself from his grasp.

"I don't deserve any of what you've done for me," he whispered, dropping his forehead to mine. "But I need you, Natalie, more than I need food or water or air. You give my life meaning. You fill it with joy and laughter. You irritate the hell out of me, call me on being an asshole, and you take what you want. I love that. I love being what *you* want. I want to be that again–forever." His voice dropped low. "You've given me everything." His eyes moved toward the tiny girl already asleep in the bed, the cat curled around her.

I looked up finally, running my thumb back and forth across his full, soft lower lip and I crumbled. Tomorrow we could use all the words. Tonight I wanted sounds and touches and wordless pleas. I wanted him to show me what I meant to him in kisses and gasps.

"Tomorrow I'll tell you the whole story. We'll figure out how to handle this going forward. This is going to mean huge changes." My whisper voice was still really loud in the hallway, and I pulled him toward his room. "But right now, I think there are things you need to tell me. Show me, if that's easier."

I mostly shut Aria's door, then ours, and I turned out the light, unbuttoning his shirt by the weak light of the moon. He shivered when my fingers touched his bare skin and I drew in a deep breath through my nose when his lips touched mine. But this time he didn't rush or demand. His fingers shook as he undressed me, reverently kissing every inch of my skin. It was what I'd dreamed of countless lonely nights for the past weeks: finding my sweet lover beneath the facade of the angry, heartbroken man, and when he took my face in his hands and stared down into my eyes, I reopened my heart to him as he made me his again.

It took every ounce of willpower to keep myself quiet as he loved me with his hands, his mouth and his body, making up for lost time, for missing words, apologizing with his actions because he knew this time the words weren't quite enough. It left me weak and shaking, and when we were sated we clung to one another as my tears mixed with his sweat. The feelings were too strong to keep inside anymore, and I cried tears of relief and thankfulness as he folded me against himself.

Exhausted, we snuggled up under the blankets and fell asleep tangled together, and for a moment I felt whole.

• • • •

I WOKE UP WITH A START the next morning, unsure what had awakened me. I stretched a little, realizing the bed felt much more full than usual and I cracked my eyelids to find Thomas already awake, one giant arm tucked under his head to raise it off the pillow. He was staring down intently, his other hand tangled in my hair, and I realized Aria was tucked up tightly between the two of us, sound asleep.

He let go of my hair and reached for my hand, pressing the backs of my fingers to his lips before opening my palm over his heart. His eyes were all shiny and soft and I pulled his hand back toward me, to kiss the inside of his palm.

Then our hands rested on Aria, holding tight to the little girl who would need our love, our stability, and our patience more than anything.

I nodded at him. "Yeah..." my voice was a whisper, a smile stretching across my face. "We're gonna be the best parents she's ever had."

EPILOGUE

Natalie

Just Over Three Months Later...

"Daddy's home!" Aria shrieked, tearing into the kitchen like the tiny tornado she was. It had been warm out today, though perhaps that wasn't surprising for April in Alabama, and her fair skin was already beginning to take on the golden shade of a tan, since she loved spending time outside.

Gerry had worked miracles with Aria, thanks to intensive sessions, and just weeks before Aria had begun calling Thomas daddy all on her own. It had cracked his heart in half and he'd broken down crying later that night, after she was in bed. He still feared Harrison would reappear to take her away from him and I'd rushed into his office to retrieve the paper I couldn't believe I'd forgotten to show him, the one I'd sent a copy of to his lawyer the instant I had it in my hands: Harrison's rescission of all parental rights.

Holding the proof in his hand seemed enough to calm him and I watched an enormous psychological weight roll off his shoulders.

Today was his birthday and though I knew he'd be tired, just getting off a flight from California, there were several things that required celebration today. I had a house full of people who were going to help me do just that, and as Aria skipped through, shrieking that Daddy was home, loved ones dove to hide behind furniture and duck out of sight.

Thomas's siblings had come, along with their significant others and children. Most of them had managed to tuck themselves behind the sofa that sat near the front window, but Mateo, Finn and Griffin were under the dining table–a real feat, since Finn was due to give birth any day now.

Gerry was there, hiding in the front closet with Smitty and his flask, and the Jensens had flown in just that afternoon, arriving just moments before Thomas.

Daphne was there too, tucked behind one of the living room chairs, though how she managed to hide her heavily pregnant belly behind it, I didn't know.

"We're gonna surprise him all right, little bean," I whispered to myself, pressing my own homemade decoration into the cake just below the stand of candles that would belch flame in about thirty seconds.

"Where are my girls?" His voice sounded from the door and my stomach fluttered. Aria snorted so hard, her laugh sounded like a fart. She loved this game. "I hear something in my house," Thomas called in a sing-song voice. "It sounds very...ticklish." He started to stomp, making Fee-Fi-Fo-Fum noises.

Aria squealed from where she stood at my hip at the dining room table and I was aware of collective shallow breaths being taken in the living room as people tried to stay quiet. I flicked the lighter quickly, lighting the candles as Aria began to sing Happy Birthday in her little voice. Other voices joined in and Thomas turned to look behind him, a little panicked but mostly confused, as one face after another popped out of hiding.

"Blow it out, Daddy!" Aria hollered, calling his attention back as the thin candles began to leak and pool wax on the frosting. He took two giant steps and puffed out a huge breath, obliterating the flames just as he was tackled to the floor by Noah.

Another enormous brother piled on and Finn stood tucked into Mateo's side, watching the commotion with a look of distaste. "After all these years, they're still monkeys," she sniffed, shaking her head just as Gerry and Smitty spilled out of the front closet, giggling as Smitty hid a flask in the pocket of his baggy pants.

There was a lot of back clapping and cursing as the three men pulled Thomas to his feet and he gave a quick round of hugs, his face bright with joy, before he swung Ari up into his arms, smacking kisses all over her face. When he set her down she ran back to Griffin, and Eve's son, Jared. They had a very serious pillow fort construction to see to in the den, these teenage boys who were humoring a sweet little girl.

I'd been delighted to meet Asher and Olivia and their little girl, Ashton. The girl was a whirlwind of energy, words and dance, and Aria trailed after her like a puppy.

The only brother missing was Aaron, and it was because he was genuinely missing. He'd participated in a private rescue mission some weeks earlier and hadn't returned home. I knew Thomas had been working night and day with some of his more shadowy contacts, trying to locate him, and from the conversation I'd had with him the night before, he'd gotten in touch with the mission commander's wife. But what that meant, I wasn't yet entirely sure.

Thomas tipped me backward, dipping down for a deep kiss and the dining room filled with hoots and hollers and "Get a room, sickos!"

"You two are ridiculous," Noah grumbled as he moved closer to the counter and Eve, his gorgeous wife, squeezed his butt before she picked up the knife to begin cutting the cake. Noah was already plucking out candles and Eve's eyes went wide when she saw what I'd pressed into the cake and the accompanying icing: "Happy Birthday, Daddy. October 22nd." She looked up at me, her eyes swimming, and Noah's gaze snapped back to the frosting.

"I *told* you someone was gonna get pregnant!" He hooted. "Guess the old man's tackle isn't broken! The Atholton swimmers are strong!" The grin threatened to split his face and Thomas's head snapped up, his face going blank as he took in the surface of the cake.

Obviously, my IUD had failed and it had almost killed me to keep it quiet for so long. I'd only been successful in hiding the morning sickness because he'd been traveling so much, and I hadn't wanted to get his hopes up. I was older and chances were good that if anything went wrong, it would happen within the first trimester–but it hadn't, and I was closing in on fourteen weeks pregnant.

I could see him doing the math in his head. I watched the panic flare in his eyes, then melt into relief. Then the realization slammed into him and both hands clapped over his mouth, his eyes huge.

The kitchen echoed with excited voices and chatter as Eve cut and dished out the cake, and Thomas dropped to his knees in front of me to place his hands on my belly.

"Hey now," Asher hollered. "I'm pretty sure that's how this whole thing started, you two. Keep your shovel out of the garden, asshole. There are children present."

Thomas gave him the bird over his shoulder, leaning in to place a soft kiss over my middle and when he looked up at me his eyes were shining with tears. "You're my gift, Natalie. You've given me everything I wanted." Then he was fishing around in his pocket like his life depended on it.

"There's just one more thing I want today." He opened his palm, something shiny winking at me in the waning light of day. "I don't deserve any of this, baby, but I don't want to lose it. I can't lose you–you've given me everything. Please tell me you'll be my wife."

Someone made a hurling sound behind us and I leaned over to take Thomas's face in my hands. I didn't care who was watching, and I kissed him like I meant it, because I did with my whole heart.

In the background I could hear Noah giggling.

Aria was calling Griffin and Jared for cake while Ashton snatched a second piece.

Gerry was engaged in a lively discussion with Smitty, and I giggled into Thomas's mouth when I heard Smitty: "Miss Nat's gone need whole big new 'pliances in dat laundry room fo a baby–whoo-ee, Missuh Thomas!"

Thomas's thumbs stroked my cheeks and his smile was brilliant, only inches from my own. "I think I've found the Precious."

Thomas

Four Weeks Later...

I wanted Natalie to be my wife as soon as my divorce from Lydia was finalized, and she started planning a wedding in Sonoma immediately, since waiting months would mean a white tent and not a white dress–her words, not mine. I didn't care what she wore; I thought she was beautiful no matter what, and I watched her grow more radiant as our child grew in her belly.

All three of us put our houses on the market: Natalie, me, and Gerry. The plan was to all three relocate to Sonoma, where Gerry would take an office locally but would conduct the majority of her visits by telephone or video conference for established patients. She would live with us in our huge, comfortable home, as Grandma to Aria and Little Bean, as we'd been calling the baby.

We had flown to New York a few weeks earlier to see to legal issues, in order to conclude settling Ahmad's estate and while we were there, Natalie signed a contract with a publisher for a design book. She was collaborating with Edith to conduct some research and the publisher was really excited about the direction. They were dangling a three-book contract in front of her, which would really skyrocket her career.

I flew friends and family to Sonoma for the wedding, where we decided to be married in the grove of trees that was once a cemetery. My brothers thought it was creepy and morbid, but Natalie loved it. She said it meant the past had no power over us and we could celebrate our future in a place that held great emotional significance, because Maren and Aden had once been there and would give us their blessing.

I never knew what became of Harrison's morbid new collection. So little time passed between the exhumation and his disappearance that I doubted he'd managed to properly handle the situation. And honestly, it bothered me a little less since I didn't know. I could keep Maren and Aden tucked away safely in my heart and my memories.

We kept things small, away from the media, and I applied for the marriage license the day before the wedding, making sure to squeeze in just before the clerk's office closed.

Mrs. Jensen insisted on catering the wedding and I had help brought in so she could boss people around rather than pull some kind of Kitchen Nightmares, S.E.A.L. Style, staying up for a week to cook and bake.

Jensen was in his element, finding new ways to surreptitiously leave drinks around the house for a whole new crowd of people, since most of our guests stayed with us between the house and the spacious unit over the garage.

The morning of our wedding dawned bright and clear, the vineyard in full, beautiful leaf. It was the perfect day, our house filled with people who loved us, and Aria and I played in the swimming pool with her uncles, who were only slightly more mature than her.

Griffin and Jared joined us and Eve sat on a deck chair to supervise, commenting quietly that she'd never seen Noah so happy, surrounded by his obnoxious family. I liked her, watching how her love lit my brother up like a Christmas display.

Not to be outdone, Noah noticed my mood, which was damn near overjoyed, and he commented on how Natalie had balanced me out, filled me up and made me whole. It was an astute observation for someone with the emotional sensitivity of a rock I told him, and he nailed me in the kidney just for old time's sake.

The only sibling missing was Aaron, but at least we'd found him. I'd spoken several times to the man who'd been leading the mission when it went tits-up, and once he'd recovered from his own injuries at a military hospital in Germany, he'd flown straight back to Pakistan to collect my brother from the hospital.

Ideally Aaron would have been at the wedding, but he was in for a long recovery, and for now that had to be enough. At least now I knew he was alive and out of harm's way, and because of that I could sleep again.

Most of the guests were ferried to the grove in Jensen's golf cart, but those who wished to take the stroll set off toward the stand of trees about forty minutes before the ceremony started. It was the time my brothers hustled me out of the house, so the ladies could finish everything last minute without worrying they'd be seen.

Jensen was a genius. He had set up the chairs and a small pergola deep enough within the grove that Natalie could be brought by golf cart to the very edge of the trees, and when she appeared on Noah's arm, her smile brilliant, her veil a halo over her glorious hair, I almost had to take a knee. I forgot to breathe for a full three beats and I finally sucked in a lungfull with a panicky sound, terrified a case of Noah's allergies were about to make an appearance.

Natalie's belly had just begun to show: a soft swell beneath the fitted dress that hugged all my favorite places. Daphne had worked night and day to make her dress happen, and she sat toward the back with an infant in her arms, next to a tall, dark, tattooed man she introduced to me as Jack, her plus-one. I hadn't known she'd divorced her husband, Hunter, and I decided I'd ask Natalie later. The two of them were thick as thieves, always snorting and giggling together.

Noah's chest puffed out as he escorted Natalie down the path, her small arm under into his huge one. He was grinning at me like he'd won the lottery, or maybe he was about to really roast me. I couldn't tell.

The violinist concluded the song and Natalie stood before me, her eyes soft and shining with love.

I love this woman.

"Who gives this woman?" Asked Asher loudly.

One of Aaron's lesser known talents was officiating at weddings, but Asher had stepped in this time in his absence after a quick certification, and I could think of nothing better than to be surrounded by family on what was one of the best days of my life.

Silence.

Asher cleared his throat, looking pointedly at Noah. Although her mother Vivian sat in the audience, Natalie's father had died some years earlier and she'd asked Noah to give her away.

"Who gives this woman?"

"Oh." Noah's shoulders jerked upright. "No, not me. I think I'll keep her, in fact." He grinned down at Natalie.

"The hell you will," Eve muttered, and I chuckled to myself when she reached across the short distance to swat his ass. A collective laugh rippled through our gathering of friends and family, and once Noah had been convinced to part with what was clearly *his* favorite toy, as I would tease him later, Natalie took me as her husband.

It was something I'd never thought would happen. Something I couldn't have predicted when Gerry told me I was, under no uncertain terms, "going to reshingle that poor girl's roof." She'd been so irritatingly adorable and curious, so nosy and up in my business.

God knew I had needed every minute of her care and attention. She had been the one to fill up and seal the cracks.

She made Aria possible for me.

She was growing our future inside her body, having accepted me for all my shortcomings and bluster, my stupidity and completely clueless behavior.

Because of her I'd finally begun seeing a therapist in earnest, and I was attending frequent AA meetings.

She took my face in her hands as the minister announced I could kiss my bride, and she stared up at me with the look I so often saw on her face–the look I needed–one of longing and love and contentment.

I leaned down to touch her soft lips.

Together, we were enough.

The End

Curious about Daphne's story? Keep turning to get a sneak peek, where you'll meet Daphne & Jack!

Daphne

“In one tenth of a mile, take a right onto Sentinel Way,” my GPS system instructed and I frowned at the console.

I needed to take a left, not a right, I was pretty sure of that...but I was directionally challenged on a good day, and only marginally better when my GPS was being rude and vague, so I flipped on my blinker.

“This does not look right,” I muttered to myself as the lanes funneled my big truck toward several guard shacks.

“This is gonna be a problem.”

I took a deep breath, ready to put on the charm.

My mother had always called it “advanced flirting,” while I saw it more as a necessary social lubricant.

Rolling down my window and turning down the music, I ran a hand through my messy dark hair and pasted what I hoped was a winningly sweet smile on my face as the muscled, tattooed officer stepped from one of the booths.

“Uh, I'm in the wrong place,” I offered stupidly, flashing him my teeth and wishing I'd taken a little more time that morning with my makeup, or even to just brush my hair.

“Where are you trying to get to, dear?” He asked with a big smile, his dark aviators obscuring what might have been pretty eyes.

Ugh, I was “dear.” Just come out with it and call me a ditzy old lady already, why don't you?

“I'm trying to get home,” I squirmed. “I just dropped my daughter off at her summer job–it's the building over–” I gestured quickly to my right. “I knew I shouldn't have been listening to my GPS. It told me to turn right on Sentinel Way when I should have taken a left out of the parking lot in the first place.”

He grinned at me, flashing nice white teeth. He was alarmingly handsome, and even more alarmingly young.

Maybe twelve.

Not my bag.

"Ok," he said quickly. "So you're not at all familiar with this area yet."

I shook my head. "Nope, but now I know which right turn *not* to take tomorrow morning!"

He barked out a laugh and called out a complicated sounding set of commands to the guy in the other guard booth before pointing toward a gate arm up the lane and to my right.

"Ok dear, you're going to head over that way...just follow the path and there will be a sliding gate. You'll go through that and then there's another arm, where you'll wait. Then another officer will come talk to you and he'll show you the way out."

I thanked him profusely, wishing him a lovely day, realizing that traffic was stacking up in both lanes as everyone else waited for the officers in *both* booths to help me get myself together.

Pulling away from the guard booth and flipping my blinker, I followed instructions carefully, passing under the arm and driving through the gate.

Only fifty feet after the gate sat another arm, firmly across the road, a flashing red LED strip along the bottom and a sticker that said the gate was magnetic, activated only by a card. (Presumably one with the top-secret security clearance I clearly did not have.)

Smiling sweetly and flirting with it was clearly not going to do the trick.

Uh...now what? I sat there, window down, the late June morning sun beating in through my window as I waited for the mysterious officer. Minutes ticked by and I fiddled with the radio, sipping my iced coffee and shielding my face from the glare of the sun coming in through my open window. It was freaking hot already, for eight-thirty in the morning.

A black SUV with blue lettering, *POLICE*, pulled up the drive and parked in front of me, on the other side of the arm. The officer who got out of the vehicle was tall and broad, tattoos snaking up his big arms. He wore a baseball cap and bulletproof vest, his sidearm in a holster on his hip, his mouth set in a flat line that suggested he was displeased. Of course he was; lost old women could hardly be the highlight of his day.

"Took a wrong turn?" he barked, and I sat up a little straighter in my seat.

Mother trucker, I wasn't wearing a bra.

"Um...yes, sir. Stupid mistake: day two of my daughter's summer job and I was in the wrong line when God handed out directional sense."

He didn't even smile. Like not even a freaking crinkle.

Seriously?!

"License, ma'am." He held out a hand and I shoved a hand into the cupholder to retrieve the driver's license I'd dropped in earlier. I fished it out, knocking against the huge cup of iced coffee in my nervousness and it went flying, drenching my lap in a sticky spray of caffeinated goodness.

"Dad blast it," I muttered under my breath, stupidly close to tears of humiliation as he made a snorting sound that sounded an awful lot like he was laughing at me.

The rest of the world knew me as a fashion designer, put together and faultless, married to a rising member of the Republican party. My husband had been elected to congress the year before and we'd relocated from rural Alabama to the DC beltway for his job and for heaven's sake, I still didn't know my way around this impossible thing the locals called The DMV.

You know, the husband who had just announced he was leaving me for his congressional aide, only a few years older than our daughter, but could I please keep that to myself for the time being while details were sorted? It wasn't like he wanted to marry her (though I wasn't so sure she knew that), so for the time I played the role while I sorted through things for myself. I'd agreed readily, not wanting to disrupt our daughter Blair's life any more than it had already been, for something I had always been, was agreeable.

My own squeaky image, something my husband had capitalized on for years, was due to a few things: 1) The silence inherited oil money can buy. 2) An expensive PR team. And finally, all-important number 3) The fact I hadn't made a single misstep since I was twenty-one years old. I didn't get into trouble or do stupid things, because I was too busy working.

"Preston." The officer looked unimpressed as his eyes bored into the side of my head, trying to reconcile the mess in front of him with the symmetrical face he saw on the license. "Daphne Marie Masters-Preston." He said my name like there was a punctuation mark after each word. He was biting off each one and spitting it out.

"One and the same." I raised my hand, my cheeks burning from the humiliation and I thought I saw his lips quirk into the tiniest smile, just out of the corner of my eye.

"Daphne Preston, as in Congressman Hunter Preston's wife?"

Double flipping fudge.

"Guilty as charged," I sighed, turning my palms upward.

"I figured delicate ladies like you would have a driver," he chuckled and I had the sudden, insane urge to reach out my open window and slap him. *Misogynist pig.*

"Delicate ladies like me?" I couldn't keep the snark out of my voice as I gestured toward my outfit, which may or may not have doubled as pajamas. "Because I'm so fancy?"

I really, really wished I'd worn something cute that morning, but my alarm hadn't gone off and Blair couldn't find any clean pants to wear on her second day at work, because she could never be bothered to put away her laundry. So instead of getting dressed, I'd taken that fifteen minutes to help her find pants and pack a lunch for her. Points for trying to Mom, even though it was getting me nowhere right now.

"From what my wife tells me, you're *very* fancy."

I couldn't tell whether he was being sarcastic, but for the first time I noticed with some disappointment that there was a thick black band around his ring finger.

Pity.

"She insisted on buying one of your dresses for our wedding and holy shit, that thing was expensive. I wanted to put a downpayment on a new house; she wanted a designer dress. She won, and I should have known then. She looked like a fucking cream puff in that thing." He ran a hand over his eyes as if he needed to wipe away the memory. "She'd be so mad if she knew I'd met you."

I wasn't even going to try to unpack that one. I was trying too hard not to be mad at him for insulting something I had designed, though the wedding dresses lately were not my best work. For years I hadn't even been the one designing them—that was a collaboration with my assistant, hoping to make a name for herself when she struck out on her own.

"If you don't mind, sir," I said, trying to keep a forced tone of politeness even though my teeth were clenched. "I really need to get going. I have a video conference call with my New York office at ten and, as you can see, I am hardly prepared for the occasion."

He grinned at me, a dazzling display of pearly white teeth and it occurred to me again that he was heart-stoppingly gorgeous.

Darn smoking hot mountain of manly goodness.

"I don't know about that," he teased, handing my license back to me and letting his eyes rest just a moment too long on my chest. "This could be an interesting new trend. I suppose it has its merits."

I sighed heavily, tucking my hair behind my ear before gripping the steering wheel with the same hand.

Right now I wanted to be anywhere but *here.*

"Right, then," he said, suddenly remembering he was a professional with a job to do. "Be careful you don't 'accidentally' turn into this lot again." His emphasis was heavy and pointed, intimating I'd taken a purposeful tour through his parking lot. "This is the NSA and getting out of here again would be a much lengthier process." His eyebrows lifted with implied meaning.

I groaned inwardly, wondering if he was promising a strip search in a darkened room. For that I could almost be convinced to show up again tomorrow, even if this guy *was* a huge jerk, since Hunter hadn't been interested in what was under my pajamas in a very, very long time.

The gate lifted suddenly and he nodded at me once, the grumpy expression firmly back in place. I nodded back, putting the truck into gear and waiting as he got back into his SUV, backing into a small access spot in order to clear the way.

My ears burned the whole way home, half an hour of driving in the insane traffic that never seemed to let up, no matter the time of day. It was my own fault, too. I'd stupidly let Hunter do the house hunting when it was obvious we'd need to maintain another base closer to D.C. He'd chosen a quiet, wealthy neighborhood about an hour's drive from the city. It was beautiful and our property was spacious, the house far more than we needed but since we had family money on both sides, there was no issue with getting what we wanted. Or should I say, what he wanted, because I was happy with far less than he was.

It drove me insane that I needed a housekeeper for the eight thousand square foot monstrosity. It could have doubled as an airplane hangar.

And since we had a housekeeper, we also had a yard service, a pool service, a cook and a dog walker for the enormous Irish wolfhound Hunter had never even tried to keep under control. The one that he'd left with me when he moved to Georgetown.

Living an hour from the city was just inconvenient enough that Hunter kept a small carriage house there, closer to work, and while Congress was in session his trips into Maryland happened only occasionally, and only on the weekends at that. Lately they hadn't been happening at all. All his out-of-office hours had apparently been spoken for by someone who was barely out of diapers.

A glance in the rearview mirror told me I looked just as awful as I felt. My dark hair was in need of a touch up, a few strands of silver starting to peek out at my roots. I was well past due for a manicure, my gel polish obviously grown out to the point it looked tacky, and my makeup-free face boasted a little hyperpigmentation on my cheeks, lines beginning to settle between my eyebrows.

Of all the days to look as old as I feel.

Pulling the car into the driveway, I sighed as I stared up at the beautiful Georgian style home with its cobbled walkway and cream brick exterior, the shutters painted a Provencal blue–very cutting edge in our Old Money area. It was every inch the fresh young politician's home, at least until you opened the door and Carrick the wolfhound knocked you flat on your backside.

Carrick was the very reason we didn't have people over. Ever. He was known to bludgeon people into submission with his enthusiasm, frequently interpreted as aggression.

I had half an hour to prepare for the meeting with my New York office, so I gave my hair a quick spritz of dry shampoo, slapped a smear of foundation on my face and applied several coats of mascara to my lashes. Then I fished out the lipstick I'd use to pull double duty, applying some to my lips while I dabbed the same shade into my cheeks with my ring finger.

The last thing I needed was Emily asking if I felt well, because I appeared...what was her word?

Oh, right: Downtrodden.

Bless her heart.

With eight minutes to spare I dove into a simple white top and black pants, slipping classic diamond studs through my ears just as my computer chirped from the next room.

Friggin' Emily the early bird, probably hoping to catch me with my pants down.

I discussed fabrics, orders, staffing details and upcoming shows with my team for the next hour-and-a-half before breaking to slip into the kitchen and grab a cup of coffee.

My initial success was due to the support of my wealthy parents. I'd been talented enough to secure a full scholarship to a prestigious school in Alabama, where my senior project drew the attention of a famous New York-based designer after one of my professors shared some of my looks with her. But it was my oil barron mother and football royalty adoptive father who financed my foray into fashion, post-internship.

Interning for Candace after graduation had been difficult. Blair was only six months old when I left for New York, for a six month internship. She stayed behind with my parents while I moved into their two-bedroom apartment bordering Central Park and made my way over to the design office on Fifth Avenue every morning.

I spent every day of those six months missing my daughter and questioning my every decision.

While I felt Candace had valuable things to teach me and I made the necessary contacts, jetting all over the world to attend Fashion Weeks with her, we came from very different worlds. Her family had relocated from Germany decades earlier, when their presence had been unwelcome, and she was born and raised on the Upper East Side. She was also perpetually single–not to say she didn't put herself out there. She was also childless, and one of the most self-absorbed women I'd ever met. (That really was saying something, given the circles in which I'd grown up.)

Me? I was a mutt. My mother was second-generation Albanian, but my father was anybody's guess, since she didn't speak of him and Jonas Masters, of college and professional football fame, had adopted me as his own after marrying my mother when I was six. He was the only father I'd ever known.

They raised me in rural Alabama, with a sprinkling of world travel, often taking me to New York to see the shows; to Greece for summer vacation; to Madrid when I turned eighteen, to have my first drink in a football stadium while watching a Real Madrid game from Jonesy's box.

Daddy's fascination with European football was unusual, given he claimed to be Alabama-born and bred. More so, given that he was the head coach at the University of Alabama, now that his professional quarterbacking days were over.

As for Hunter...well, where to even begin?

Hunter and I met at the beginning of my sophomore year of college and I was immediately drawn to him. He was the antithesis of me: Tall and blonde, outgoing and handsome, whereas I was short and dark-haired, quiet and pretty–just never pretty *enough* by most standards.

It was my own stupid fault I got pregnant with Blair my senior year. I'd come down with a horrible late summer sinus infection and had visited the campus clinic for an exam and some antibiotics. It had never occured to me the antibiotics might render my birth control completely ineffective, and only six weeks later I was back home.

Hunter had cut me loose after learning I was pregnant and I'd rushed home to nurse a broken heart, made even more intense by hormonal fluctuations.

If anyone were to ask my advisor, I was home and attending classes under "special circumstances," due to a medical issue.

The plan was to complete my work from home, returning to school in the spring once the baby was born, in order to present my senior project. It was the project most of my grades hinged upon and thanks to a couple custom pieces I created for the wife of one of Daddy's famous friends, I'd gotten crazy publicity and a good grade, followed by Candace's offer of an internship in her New York office.

By the time Blair was three, I was a reasonably established figure in fashion design.

Now, my daughter nearing adulthood, I wondered why I'd ever let Hunter lure me back to Alabama. He had all but abandoned us for the second time and I couldn't help but wonder, somewhat bitterly, whether he'd chosen to leave now that he'd attained the pinnacle of his career. It was what he'd always wanted and what his family had always pushed him toward, and he no longer needed me, though he certainly still enjoyed my money.

I hadn't been the best choice for a politician's wife, but my family's deep pockets went a long way toward helping with his campaigns, as his father had spent the last several decades drinking, gambling and whoring his way through the family fortune. (That was where the PR firm had initially come into play.)

So here I was. After putting up with Hunter's crap for years, he had decided he was done with me. Again.

• • • •

"DON'T BE RIDICULOUS, Daph." Ava's sweet voice laughed in my ear. "My Commanding Officer dragged me in with him for some kind of awards ceremony that I won't pretend I understand, and I want to see my friend. You can't possibly look as bad as all that."

I may or may not have just told her I looked like a troll living under a bridge.

"Come on. I'll even come pick you up. I know this great little dive bar just outside of Annapolis Junction. We might get stabbed in the parking lot, but they serve the booziest, wickedest margarita you've ever had in your life. You won't be able to see straight until next Tuesday."

That sounded kind of enticing. Of course, I wasn't about to ask how she knew about a dive bar in a town filled with office parks, but at this point I didn't care. It was a Friday night and I didn't have to drive Blair to work in the morning.

"Fine," I huffed. "Drag your fancy butt over here to pick me up, since you seem to know where you're going. As for me, I accidentally turned into the NSA's parking lot a couple days ago and I am *not* eager to repeat that experience. Well...most of it."

Ava's laugh sounded in my ear like tinkling bells and I could see why Lincoln was so taken with her sweet, gentle personality. The woman had the patience of a saint, which was a good thing because he was a stubborn jerk who liked to push her buttons. But when push came to shove, Ava's gentle art of persuasion was insidious, like a rising tide, sweeping away Lincoln's objections.

"I have it on good authority it's the watering hole of choice for some of the sinfully attractive men in the area," she chuckled. "Just don't ask how I know."

"Blair," I hollered down the hallway. "I'm going out with Auntie Ava tonight. You ok ordering something through GrubHub for dinner? There are probably a ton of leftovers in the fridge, too."

There was a long pause before Blair answered. "Yeah Mom, no problem. Jake's coming over to pick me up anyway, and we're headed out. I'll probably be home late."

Thank God at least she was slightly more responsible than I'd been at eighteen. If she said she'd be home late, she'd be home late–but she'd at least come home.

"Pants on at all times," I called back and I heard the responding "Gah, Mooooom!" as I moved toward my bathroom.

I showered quickly, wrapping up my hair in hot rollers before stepping in and washing carefully, so as not to get my hair wet. If nothing else, I would look good for my best friend, for heaven's sake. It was truly all I had these days.

Pulling a pair of black jeans from my closet, I sighed at the state it was in. I had no excuses for the catastrophe that was happening in my walk-in. I had the money to have a professional organize it, but I'd been too busy to have it done, so most of my clothes still sat in boxes, stacked up in the closet and waiting for me to unwrap them like presents on Christmas morning.

I'd only just begun to unpack my summer things and I snatched a favorite grey t-shirt from the rack. It was soft from many washes and the faded cover of a Queen album graced the front, the V cut just low enough to showcase some of my better attributes, but not so low as to make me look like a desperate groupie.

Did I go a little heavy on the mascara? Perhaps. I'd always been told my deep grey eyes were my best feature. They confused people and invited them in for a closer look and, screw it, Hunter didn't want to look at them any longer, so an extra coat of Diorshow it was, for whomever *did* want to look at them. (Ava would approve.)

Applying a light spritz of perfume to my neck, I hurried down the stairs with a pair of strappy green heels in hand. I was short–short enough to wear heels every day so that people wouldn't call me a midget–and I was hopping on one foot to put them on as I answered the door.

"Shit, Daph!" Ava looked genuinely shocked as she surveyed me. "How is it possible your boobs look better every time I see you?!" She wagged a finger in my face. "Spill the details, woman. Fat injections? Hyaluronic acid? Come on. Give it."

I couldn't stop the grin that spread across my face. Forty was coming for me, hard and fast, and being told something was still giving gravity some sass made me feel a little better about myself. After all, it was no secret my self esteem had taken a beating lately.

Pulling my equally pint-sized friend into my arms, we squeezed until it hurt, rocking back and forth in the entryway. It had been a while since I'd last seen her, but no matter how much time had passed our greetings were always the same: joyful, effusive and genuine.

Personal research led me to believe the friendships you end up keeping are the ones you never expected to make in the first place.

"Blair!" Ava hollered up the stairs, an impressive set of pipes in a tiny body.

Blair appeared at the top of the stairs and smiled down at her honorary aunt. "Auntie Ava! Mama didn't tell me you were coming."

I just did.

She stumbled down the stairs on her colt-like legs, her long honeyed hair flying behind her. When she reached Ava she folded her willowy body in half to hug her tightly and Ava looked up as Blair released her, running her fingers through my daughter's long hair.

"Look at you." She shook her head. "I can't believe you're all grown up already. And clearly, you did not get this..." she gestured toward my daughter's tall, lithe body, "from your mother."

She turned to me then with a smile. "I'm taking your mother out for the night," she announced, shooting a look and a conspiratorial wink at Blair. "I wouldn't expect her back until quite late, so don't call the cops if you hear some fumbling around down here. I plan to get her good and hammered."

Blair giggled. "Mama never gets hammered. Don't be silly."

"A lady doesn't," I said, casting a warning glance in her direction. My southern roots ran deep and despite being of Balkan origin, my mother had whole-heartedly embraced the manners expected of a lady living in the deep south. She'd instilled them in me like a devout sister drilling Catechism into a group of bored four-year-olds.

Good girls don't curse.

Good girls don't drink.

Good girls don't sleep around.

Good girls are modest and sweet and tasteful.

"Tonight you are not a lady," Ava said with an evil grin, and I smacked her playfully.

"You were a southern girl for a minute," I reminded her, and the grin stretched wider.

"I was there too short a time to absorb the necessary nuances," she reminded me and I remembered my joy at the age of eleven, when Ava's military family had moved in across the street. "Besides, I barely lived there a year. It was enough time to appreciate some of the local color, but these days I'm a California girl through and through. Of course, your mama still thinks I'm a heathen." She tossed her expertly highlighted hair, in enviable shades of caramel and warm sunlight. She was definitely a California girl: flawless.

Blair pushed us out the door and told us to have fun and before I knew what had happened, Ava had easily driven the twenty minutes while I went into a heated diatribe over Hunter and his exploits.

She listened patiently as she parked the car on the street, pointing toward a rundown little bar I'd never noticed before. Probably because I'd never before driven into this part of town.

"How do you know these things?" I asked, inclining my head toward the building as I crawled out of the low, expensive car.

Lincoln was a collector and he made sure Natalie had a fun collection of her own. His favorite thing seemed to be spoiling the woman who rocked his world–the one he'd nearly lost when he went through an intensive asshole phase. (A real doozy, even for him.)

"Ah, you forget, my darling. My beautiful husband is a powerful man with many connections. There is nothing I cannot find out."

There was that evil grin again.

She grabbed my hand and hauled me across the street, and I narrowly missed being run over by an old pickup truck filled with landscaping workers. All of the men hollered something at us that I was fairly sure wasn't complimentary, and rather than give them the finger, I stuck out my tongue–not that they could see it anyway.

The smell of stale beer and cigarettes just about knocked me over when Natalie yanked at the door and a small bell mounted at the top slapped against the lacquered face, the noise lost in the din.

"Yuck," I said as I surveyed our somewhat dingy surroundings. "This is why I drink at home."

"Keep that up and you'll become an alcoholic," she commented, and I was pretty sure she was only half teasing. "I know from experience, that is a slippery slope."

Boy, did she.

Ava rarely drank anymore and her husband avoided it completely after nearly losing her after a drunken rage. To be a little fair to him, he'd been under enormous stress at the time, but he'd compounded the matter quickly when she packed a bag and left him.

Ava caught the attention of the bartender and I admired how she owned the room so easily. She was confident and beautiful. She could easily knock years off her age and people believed her. Men still flocked to her like cold water on a hot day.

It was hot outside and the humidity was trying to seep into the room, several small wall units struggling to keep up. And when it was this hot, there was only one thing for it: margaritas.

The drinks were so cold and slushy and good and everything in the room was starting to slow down a little as I ranted on and on about Hunter and his toddler aide to Ava, who listened quietly, nodding at the appropriate moments. She was so focused, I knew, because the bar was loud and she was practically reading my lips.

"So, I was going to interrupt you earlier," she finally did interrupt, "but you were really on a roll there." She was looking over my shoulder. "But there are a couple guys back there...and from what I can see, they are *really* hot...and one of them has been staring at you for like the last ten minutes."

I turned slowly, my courage high and my inhibitions low–thanks, tequila!

"Point," I instructed, feeling a little wobbly, and she lifted a finger to point diagonally across the room, where a group of four muscular guys in jeans and tight t-shirts stood near a pool table, each with a bottle of beer in hand. They were looking at us like deer caught in headlights as they watched Ava point them out.

"That one," she said, pointing to the tallest one. He was wearing a grey t-shirt that nearly matched my own, ink crawling up his arms.

Slamming back a huge mouthful of my frosty margarita–ow–I marched over to the group of men, ready to give them a piece of my mind for the sake of women everywhere.

As I drew nearer, the shortest one stepped forward. "Can we help you with something, ma'am?"

Oh. Oh, crap. He sounded like a cop. But no, I was not going to let this stop me–not even my healthy fear/respect for men involved in law enforcement. (After all, remember, I'd grown up in Alabama, where one does not mess with the boys in blue. Not unless one wished to spend an evening in jail on forthcoming-yet-nebulous charges.)

"I need to talk to that one about the scorch marks on my backside," I hiccuped, pointing a finger at the man in the grey t-shirt, and I was already standing so close I nearly stabbed him in the chest with my finger.

When I drank, my feistiness came out.

"I thought I recognized you," the man said, and there wasn't even a trace of a smile on his face. "I've been trying to figure it out for the last ten minutes, but now that you're so close, I'm certain. I didn't recognize you at first, without coffee all over your pajamas."

My eyes went wide and I almost sloshed the rest of my margarita on him.

This can't be happening.

The hot cop.

I was ready.

"I should have known it was you, by that miserable scowl on your face. You really would have better luck with the ladies if you looked a little friendlier, you miserable grump."

His face lit up with a huge grin and, have mercy, it was like staring directly into the sun, blinding in all its glory. Those teeth, that hair, those eyes, that face–it was all unfair.

"Being friendly is a liability in my line of work," he responded, the smile still on his face, and I had to lean one hand against the pool table to steady myself.

"It's ok," he said, noticing my lean, "I do that to the ladies sometimes. You wouldn't be the first to go weak in the knees."

You arrogant little... I swallowed hard and splashed the rest of my drink in his face. It ran down his nose and plopped in slushy little globs on his chest.

He looked amused rather than shocked and my hand itched to slap him, but I was still holding my empty glass. The other hand was employed keeping me upright.

"Does yer wife know yer out trolling fer easy ladies?" I almost slurred, a hiccup punctuating the end of my question, and his face fell. In fact, I could see the faces of the other three out of my peripheral vision, which was suddenly, weirdly razor-sharp. All three of them looked shocked, like I'd just said something I was going to regret, and I turned as quickly as the spinning room would allow me.

"What?"

The smallest guy shook his head at me quickly, his eyes flicking to the guy who was towering over me.

"Boys." Grumpy's voice was like ice, cold and unyielding. "I'd like you to meet Miss Daphne. She just happens to be Congressman Preston's wife."

Oh, no. No, no, no. I was that for now, but he wasn't supposed to out me like that. I jabbed an index finger into his firm, unyielding chest.

"Nuh-uh," I warned. "That wasn't fair."

"You just called him a man whore," one of the guys said, shaking his head disapprovingly and I recognized the handsome, friendly officer from the guard shack. "That wasn't fair either, so technically you started it."

Ok, he was kind of right.

I didn't like him anymore.

"I'm. Not. A cheater." The big guy was right in my face, and I'll be darned if he wasn't even bigger than he'd been just ten seconds ago. He held up his left hand so his wedding band was right in my eyeball, and I had to work to focus on it. There was some kind of pattern etched into it, but I couldn't make it out.

"Neither am I." I held up my left hand, shoving my wedding set toward his right eyeball. "But he left me for a congressional aide anyway."

There was a tug on my arm and I turned to see Ava, her face exaggeratedly apologetic. "I'm sooo sorry, gentlemen. When we planned on a night out, I'd thought it might last longer than twenty minutes. I'm afraid my friend here, and myself, are horrible lightweights. As you can imagine, we don't get out often."

The short one cracked a smile. "Not a problem, ladies. Jack was just talking about heading out." He elbowed the big guy, and my face flamed when I realized my hand had made its way back to the tall man's chest. It was possible I was actively feeling him up, his shirt soft but the muscles of his chest hard beneath my wandering fingertips. "I'm sure he can get you home safely."

There were a number of things I'd like to see whether this large man could conduct safely, but...ugh, of all the luck...my own personal police escort. Chances were good there would be no stop-and-frisk.

Jack shot an evil glare at Guard Shack, who smirked back at him.

"I rode here with Marston," the smaller man announced, pointing to one of the other men. "I'll follow you in your truck and then you can take me home."

Clearly he was speaking to my tormentor.

"If you'll give me a moment," Jack was looking at Ava with an apologetic expression, "it would seem I need to clean up a bit. If you ladies would be so kind as to wait..."

He didn't finish the sentence but as he moved toward what I assumed were the restrooms, I hurried over to the bar and ordered another margarita. If I had to be humiliated I was going to make sure I was good and smashed, so I didn't have to remember it in the morning.

"You are insane." The voice was low in my ear and I turned quickly, accidentally sloshing more of my arctic drink on his muscular chest. He winced and rolled his eyes, taking a small step back. "Don't you think you've had enough?"

"Not even close," I said, tipping it back and wincing as the cold shot daggers straight into my brain. "I still remember too much."

He sighed, shaking his head as he grabbed a cocktail napkin off the bar and dabbed at yet more stickiness on his shirt. "You really are something else."

Was that a good thing? I couldn't decide. With the way he was looking at me, chances seemed good it was not.

Natalie handed over the keys to her car and led the way to the parking lot. Jack followed, dragging me along by the arm, careful to temper his long steps so he didn't drag me, since I seemed to have forgotten how to walk in a straight line.

"You're kidding me, lady." His jaw dropped as he stared at the Alfa Romeo Ava had parked on the street. "A fucking Spider?"

Ava smiled sweetly at him. She had always been full of surprises and his jaw dropped when she responded, "Yup, not my favorite, but still a good one. The modified Corvette is still one of my favorites for Autocross."

"You do not." He was standing in the middle of the street, staring at her like she'd grown another head. "No way."

My friend had another admirer. I felt a bolt of jealousy zing all the way down to my toes, because I had never been the exciting one.

The one full of surprises.

The one who made men fall at her feet, begging.

"Davis," he hollered back across the street, and Officer Guard Shack turned. "You hear that? This little thing does Autocross." He pointed at Ava, and Guard Shack's jaw dropped too.

"You two are full of surprises," he chuckled, stopping short of the car.

"Hey, wait...one of you is going to have to ride in my truck with Officer Davis–this thing only fits two."

Ava's eyebrow arched and a tiny, wicked smile curved her full lips. "Silly me," she sighed. "Daph, you're up; I'll ride with Officer Davis." And before I could protest, she skipped back across the street, looking far more sober than she had just moments ago. (I was pretty sure I was being set up.)

"You're *both* trouble," Jack muttered as he held open the passenger door for me, and I dropped into the seat with far less grace than I'd have liked.

"I haven't been trouble a day in my life," I hiccupped and giggled at the same time. I truly had *never* been a troublemaker, but lately I'd considered getting into a little more of it. At this point I had nothing to lose, but he didn't look like he believed me.

Jack started up the car and tapped at the dash a few times, a frown creasing his handsome face. I hoped he didn't notice, but I was totally staring at him out of what I hoped was the corner of my eye.

"Stop looking at me like that," he barked, flipping the blinker and pulling into traffic. Somehow he'd located my home address on the GPS and he handled the car easily as we headed in the direction of the two-lane highway that would take us most of the way to my home.

I snapped my eyes to the road, which seemed blurry and indistinct. *How* had I been looking at him? I had definitely *not* been imagining running my fingers up and down what I knew were tight washboard abs and a delightfully defined chest. I shook my head to clear the visual, disgustingly aware of how pathetic I felt. It had been a long time, though I hadn't thought I was upset about that. Hunter had never been anything other than a two-minute man and in his opinion, foreplay was something one read about in romance novels and was completely unnecessary in real life. That, judging by his practices, was what lube was for.

Suffice to say, I had a purely physical and completely unfulfilling relationship with several pieces of plastic Hunter didn't know about, but he wouldn't have cared anyway.

The highway was surprisingly empty and Jack drove with one hand resting easily on the top of the steering wheel, his eyes intently focused on the road ahead. I chose to say nothing, so as not to distract him, and from the passenger side mirror I could see headlights following us at a respectable distance. Surely it was Officer Davis and Ava, undoubtedly engaged in a very lively conversation. Ava was so bubbly and engaging and freaking adorable, she could get rocks to talk.

The GPS directed us to turn left and Jack pulled carefully into the long, winding drive that led to the house. His eyes widened as it came into view, the impressive facade lit by flood lights recessed in the lawn. "This is what a congressional salary will get you, huh?" He looked impressed.

"This is what family money and a successful design career will get you," I said bitterly and immediately he clamped his lips shut. "Not that I was the one who wanted it," I said, weirdly incapable of getting myself to shut up. "I'd be happy with a cottage and a cat. Instead, I got an empty castle with a dog no one can control."

As if on cue, Carrick set up a terrible howling inside the house and Jack's eyes widened in alarm.

"Don't worry," I said. "The electric fence is set so that he can't even get out the front door. The back yard is his kingdom, much to the relief of the local delivery drivers." That was a lesson learned the hard way, when Carrick cornered a delivery woman on the front steps. I'd found her clinging to the front of the house as if she could climb the brick. She'd had no idea he'd rather lick her to death than harm her. All he wanted was a scratch behind the ears and she wasn't giving it.

She'd been dropping my packages at the end of the driveway ever since.

Headlights swept up the drive behind us and Jack threw open his door, rolling up the window and rounding the car quickly to open my door. It irritated me that I was such a lightweight, since I'd somehow managed to get tangled up in my own seatbelt during the course of the short drive, and he pulled my hands away from the belt as he leaned over me, reaching over to undo the clasp. Something winked in the light as he leaned and I reached up without thinking, hooking a finger beneath the thin gold chain and pulling it from beneath the neck of his soft t-shirt. A small charm hung from the necklace and I focused on it hard, my vision still blurrier than I'd have liked. He'd gone still over me, heat radiating from his huge body as I drunkenly tried to study the design pinched between my thumb and forefinger.

"First Brigade," I whispered with a hiccup and his hand moved up to pull the small emblem from my fingers.

"I'm impressed," he said, backing out of the small space and holding out a hand to me to help me from the car. "You've heard of it."

"Long story," I said, groaning as I tried to stand up straight. "I dated a First Brigade man for a minute after Blair was born. You guys are a mess."

His eyebrows went up almost imperceptibly, but I saw it.

"He was a fucking disaster; there was no way it would have worked."

I clapped a hand over my mouth. *Good girls did not say fuck.* "Pardon my French. I shouldn't have said that."

"Shouldn't have said what?" His eyes danced with amusement. "That some douchebag you dated twenty years ago was a fucking disaster?" He laughed and his features relaxed, his lips pulling back from even white teeth in a genuine smile and I swear my pants burst into flame.

"Good girls don't swear," I said, a little miffed, like I expected him to know my own secret inner code. "It's not ladylike."

"Mrs. Congressman Preston," he chuckled, his voice lilting and it sounded like he was teasing me. I made a face. "You really are a trip."

"Daphne." I frowned at him and turned, tripping up the front steps to my house.

"Daphne the Disaster," I muttered under my breath as I fished in my small bag for my keys and tried to fit the key to the lock. I was having trouble with my aim.

"Thank you, Officer Thompson." It was Ava behind me, her hand closing over mine to take the keys from me. Oh right, because I had a keyless entry. There was a series of confusing little beeps and the lock disengaged, so I stepped inside and turned slightly, expecting Jack to follow me inside for some insane reason.

Carrick sat just inside, weirdly silent, though his butt wiggled across the floor as he waited for me to give him the command that allowed him to assault me with fur and slobber and exuberance. It was the only command he knew, as it had taken me so long to teach him just that one that I'd given up after.

"You're welcome, ladies." Jack offered a lazy salute, seemingly unperturbed by the giant beast of a dog looming just behind me, his eyes meeting mine just before he turned and headed down the few steps.

Guard Shack had pulled the huge Silverado in behind Ava's car and had already moved to the passenger seat. I could see the glint of white teeth and knew he was grinning at one of us, or maybe all of us.

"Ms. Daphne," Jack said lazily, and my eyes snapped to him. "A pleasure once again. You're even lovelier when you're not wearing coffee." I expected a smile but he looked stern again, even though he was definitely still making fun of me. I wanted him to take me seriously and I didn't feel like that had happened yet, no thanks to my current state.

Ava hustled me into the house and shut the door behind her, fanning herself dramatically as Carrick wiggled and whimpered, irritated that I hadn't released him from his sitting position.

"Well," she drawled, a huge smile on her face, her eyes dancing and it made me groan. Ava had been *dying* to see me with someone other than Hunter for years, harping on and on about how he wasn't good enough for me and was too arrogant to accept it.

"That was an interesting turn of events," she said, putting a hand to the small of my back to propel me toward the sitting room I never used.

I let myself be pushed, my heels clacking noisily across the marble and I held up a hand to slow her, reaching down to yank off both shoes, tossing them haphazardly aside.

She shoved the heavy pocket doors aside, just as the dog trotted into the room on my heels, tired of waiting for me to give him his favorite command. He ambled over to one of the leather sofas and threw himself on it, sighing heavily as he rested his head on his paws and watched me with alternately wiggling eyebrows.

"That dog adores you," Ava remarked offhandedly as she moved toward the large lacquered cabinet at the back of the room.

Thank God someone does.

She poured a seltzer water for me, pulling the stopper out of Hunter's favorite bottle of scotch and pouring several fingers into a glass. She sniffed it carefully, then moved toward me with a glass in each hand, indicating we should sit.

We each sank into a creaky buttoned leather chair and I brought the seltzer to my lips as Ava brought the scotch to hers. She wrinkled her nose after a small sip. "He has appalling taste," she sputtered. "And not just when it comes to extramarital affairs."

I snorted. We were back to my favorite subject of late.

Setting her glass on the low side table, Ava tucked one leg under her petite frame and gazed at me seriously. "That man couldn't take his eyes off you," she said, not a hint of teasing in her voice.

"Yeah, whatever." I sighed. "Jack is married and Guard Shack isn't an option, because I don't date children."

"Guard Shack?" She laughed, covering her mouth with one hand. "You mean Officer Davis? You have to admit, he's pretty cute. But Jack..." She fanned herself. "That is one tasty man mountain."

"I'm not interested. I have enough going on without adding any of that drama." I gulped down another swallow of my drink and coughed a little when the bubbles fizzed in the back of my throat.

"You're not interested in that delicious wall of hot, brooding man? Nuh-uh. I saw you feeling him up at the bar. Nice try. Your fingers were telling a very different story, my friend."

I rolled my eyes at her, holding up my left hand and waggling my fingers until my engagement ring and wedding band clanged against one another. I'd never had them fused. "We're both *married*," I reminded her, a little irritated. My friend was not a slow study and I couldn't begin to comprehend how this was evading her notice.

"You are unhappily married, and if your husband's actions have any weight here, Biblically not at all," she said evenly, crossing her legs and leaning back in her chair. "I think we both remember that Hunter maintains a residence completely separate from your own." She gestured around the room. "For all we know, Cassandra is living *with* him in Georgetown."

I made a face. I really hated that name–had always, but now with double vehemence.

"How many times has this happened, Daph? You've been on your own for a long time."

My face crumpled and my shoulders sagged. I set the glass of seltzer on the side table and collapsed into the back of the chair, defeated. Ava had a point. This wasn't the first time Hunter had messed around on me. In fact, I knew of three affairs during the course of our marriage and I was fairly sure there were others. Why I'd put up with them, I wasn't so sure any longer.

"I'm tired," I said, and from the look on her face, I knew she understood that I meant I was tired in my soul.

"I was too," she said quietly, braving another sip of her drink. "It was why I left. Scariest and best thing I've ever done; I can't imagine my life without Lincoln, and I'd have lost him if I stayed."

She was probably right about that. Her leaving meant Lincoln took getting his shit together pretty seriously.

She sat quietly with me, letting me chew on my lip and sigh as I took a tipsy moment to consider the reality of my situation. I'd been letting this go on for years and had no one to blame but myself.

"I'm pretty sure Hunter married me to avoid child support," I said quietly, but Ava didn't look surprised. She'd seen worse. "Daddy's lawyers were closing in. And since he didn't have any reliable family money to fall back on, he charmed my mama to get back to me, knowing he could also count on my family to provide campaign contributions for the long slog to Capitol Hill. We've always protected our own." I said it bitterly, not bothering with the air quotes.

Ava nodded. She was familiar with my kindhearted, giving mother and her philanthropic ways.

"You are a beautiful woman, Daphne," Ava said softly, and I swallowed hard. I wasn't used to compliments. Besides, I hadn't felt beautiful in a very, very long time.

"If the way Jack was looking at you tonight is any indication, and I know it is, you've still got it. Hunter is not *it* for you. You're still young and gorgeous. You have life experience and you're successful and accomplished.

"You can't hold your liquor for shit," she grinned, "but you have a heart of gold and a great sense of humor. Stop wasting yourself on Congressman Asshat."

I snorted, spraying my sinuses with seltzer and coughing into the back of my hand.

Ava stood, abandoning the rest of her sub-par scotch. "I'll call you tomorrow," she said finally. "Lincoln is busy all day and I can only amuse myself for so long. I could use some company at the spa." She looked pointedly at my nails. "And you need to spend some time on yourself for once."

Hugging her goodbye, I locked the door behind her and debated setting the alarm, deciding against it since I wasn't sure Blair was home yet. We lived in what was probably one of the last completely safe neighborhoods left in America. There was zero crime in our wealthy community and we could have gone on vacation and left the door unlocked, returning to find everything in perfect order. If anyone broke into the house, they'd probably clean it.

Carrick was at my side, pressing his huge head into my thigh to get my attention. His aggressive leaning was his not-so-subtle hint he wanted his dinner and my feet made soft slapping sounds on the marble, Carrick's claws clacking alongside as I led him toward the back of the house to the laundry room and his food dish.

Climbing the stairs to the second floor, Carrick hot on my heels, I paused at the landing to remember the moment I'd fished Jack's necklace out of his shirt. Even three margaritas deep, I'd known what it meant when my fingers brushed the warm skin of his neck and he'd stilled over me. I'd felt the tension in the air, thick and unforgiving, and I'd heard him swallow hard–I knew I had, I couldn't have imagined it and I knew it wasn't a normal reaction.

I sighed, shaking my head and grasping the banister to haul myself up to my room. I was being completely ridiculous, wasn't I? I would never see the man again.

Acknowledgements

• • • •

TO EVERYONE WHO'S PATIENTLY followed along with me on this journey: friends, coworkers, family members and the new friends I am constantly meeting. Your support has been astonishing. Thank you for your grace and patience.

To my best friend, Heidi, thank you so much for laboring through these with me. You've caught improper references and plot holes more than once when my brain just happily skipped right over them! Our eyes might be getting older, but yours are still sharp!

And finally, to everyone going through challenges in life–and that's all of us: disintegrating relationships, employment problems, addiction issues and custody battles. Everyone is fighting a battle we know nothing about. Keep fighting. Keep your head up and keep being the light in your little corner.

About the Author

Erin's making good use of her degree in Journalism by making things up all day long.

Born in the Midwest, she's a fan of big trucks, strong-minded men, grocery delivery services and happy endings.

Years after obtaining a degree she didn't use, she's returned to writing the kinds of stories she's been penning since she was ten years old: stories of love lost, won, broken or regained. Her characters have seen some things and they tend to be a little older, a little broken, and just redeemable enough to get their shit together, usually after a few seriously stupid missteps.

Erin's family relocates with some frequency, thanks to her husband's career. For now she lives with her very own Alpha male and two children in the Metro D.C. area.

You can find her at erinfitzgeraldwrites.com[1], Facebook[2], and Instagram at erinfitzgeraldwrites[3]. If you prefer TikTok, you'll find her there under erinfitzgerald85.

1. https://www.erinfitzgeraldwrites.com/
2. https://www.facebook.com/ErinFitzGeraldWrites/
3. https://www.instagram.com/erinfitzgeraldwrites/

Other Works & Coming Soon

The Atholton Series

Forsaking All Others - (Seraphina & Mateo) Book One
The Battle Back Home - (Aaron & Harlowe) Book Two
All The Days After - (Noah & Eve) Book Three
The Things I Can't Say - (Asher & Olivia) Book Four

When I Had Nothing - (Thomas & Natalie) Book Five

Men of the First Brigade
Unexpected (Jack & Daphne) Book One
Unforgiven (Scott & Mia) Book Two
Unwelcome (Brandon & Giulia) Book Three
Unstoppable (Alex & Lauren) Book Four
Unrequited (Lincoln & Ava) Book Five
Undeniable (Adam & Madelyn) Book Six
Unrecognizable (Michael & Claire) Book Seven
Unconditional (Gerald & Emerson) Book Eight
Unforgettable (James & Gemma) Book Nine

Don't miss out!

Visit the website below and you can sign up to receive emails whenever Erin FitzGerald publishes a new book. There's no charge and no obligation.

https://books2read.com/r/B-A-GRJY-OZYIC

BOOKS 2 READ

Connecting independent readers to independent writers.

www.ingramcontent.com/pod-product-compliance
Lightning Source LLC
LaVergne TN
LVHW041053080826
845145LV00007B/1555

* 9 7 8 1 9 5 8 8 0 2 0 9 0 *